倍斯特出版事業有限公司
Best Publishing Ltd.

U0077423

一次就考到

雅思單字6.5⁺

MP3

倍斯特編輯部◎ 著

效率式建構雅思英單語庫

「聽」、「說」、「讀」、「寫」四項分數同步狂飆

3大單字學習法

1 運用主題記憶單字
► 以主題段落串起記憶連結，縮短學習時間，並逐步將單字轉化成為長期記憶。

2 巧用語境記憶單字
► 量身打造語境記憶單字(Vocabulary in Context)單元，提升從文本推測單字跟句子意思的能力，以既有的字彙量就能達到學習成果、超乎應考水準。

3 掌握同義詞轉換
► 題目以基礎、中階和進階的同義詞形式演變而成，理解同義詞並善加運用，大幅提升應試成績。

EDITOR 編者序

雅思 (IELTS) 是對到英國、加拿大、澳洲、紐西蘭等英語系國家留學、移民、海外就業所需英語能力作評估的語言測驗。本書的編寫即是針對雅思考試聽、說、讀、寫四大測驗類型中的「閱讀」，選定「科學與科技」的主題，精選 28 篇歷史上從古到今重要的發明家及其發明的英文文章，在漸進式閱讀小段文章後，完成英文字彙上下句情境的測驗練習 (Vocabulary in Context) 以增加印象，強化學習過程和成果，並藉由書中編列實用相關的同、反義詞，依「聯想法」延伸擴大學習範圍，增強記憶。

大量的相關字彙以及豐富的背景知識往往是閱讀的基礎及關鍵。本書測驗練習題的內容即根據雅思測驗常考的環境、科技、商業、生活、健康等各類型主題共編撰 336 個題目而成。讀者在完成測驗，瞭解自身實力後，不妨將該句視為單字例句閱讀，在提升猜測文意單字能力之餘，也有助於提升雅思常涵蓋主題的整體英文實力。如此有系統且有效率地累積、擴充字彙及知識庫，加上文章類型之廣泛閱讀，便可從容應付雅思的考試，無往不利了。

本書除了可提升雅思閱讀考試技巧之外，藉由廣泛類型短句的閱讀以及同、反義詞字彙的累積，也間接有助於增強聽、說、寫的實力。透過此訓練所養成的英文實力，不僅可幫助讀者輕鬆取得佳績，並且能夠確實提升基本的英語能力，開創新的學習契機。

孟瑞秋

EDITOR 編者序

在雅思四項技能的測驗中，尤其是聽、讀，題目都是以同義表達的方式進行轉換。換句話說，掌握同、反義字的表達等同於往高分邁向了更大一步。畢竟，看不懂題目的表達時，除了無法理解意思外，更無從根據關鍵字定位回去文章中找訊息。外加聽力測驗，訊息往往稍縱即逝。沒有具備一定的同、反義字彙量也無法在聽力測驗時，迅速理解意思。

編輯部在這次的雅思單字規劃中過濾掉許多太難不常見的字，納入了最常見的同、反義字，並整理成表格，讓考生更便利學習。此外，除了背誦同、反義詞表外，多練習書中精選的試題，藉由 vocabulary in context，養成閱讀時，不認識某單字也能推測出文意的能力。畢竟閱讀測驗中本來就不太可能每個字都認識，但是很多時候不見的每個字都要懂才能大致都了解文章內容。最後，考生也可由朗讀 CD 輔助，背誦精選的 28 個主題，強化自己寫作能力。

編輯部 敬上

CONTENTS 目次

PART 1 飲食民生

Unit 1 Coke 可口可樂

❶ 可口可樂的配方 / 016

❷ 可口可樂的成功 / 020

❸ 彭柏頓的其他成就 / 024

❹ 同反義詞表 / 028

Unit 2 Lego 樂高

❶ 樂高的源由 / 030

❷ 樂高的流行與面臨的挑戰 / 034

❸ 樂高公司 / 038

❹ 同反義詞表 / 042

Unit 3 Jeans 牛仔褲

❶ 牛仔褲的發明與流行 / 044

❷ 牛仔褲所帶來的利潤 / 048

❸ 潛在價值 / 052

❹ 同反義詞表 / 056

Unit 4 Peanut Butter 花生醬

❶ 日常飲食與製作過程 / 058

❷ 花生醬的益處和食用價值 / 062

❸ 一世紀前的想法改變人們飲食 / 066

❹ 同反義詞表 / 070

Unit 5 Ketchup 蕃茄醬

❶ 蕃茄醬的源由 / 072

❷ 天才商人 / 076

❸ 亨式公司的起落 / 080

❹ 同反義詞表 / 084

Unit 6 Disposable Diapers 紙尿布

❶ 尿布的發展 / 086

❷ 創意思維 / 090

❸ 阻力與不被認同 / 094

❹ 同反義詞表 / 098

Unit 7 Light Bulb 燈泡

❶ 燈泡的發展 / 100

❷ 燈泡的改良與碳化竹絲 / 104

❸ 愛迪生的成長過程 / 108

❹ 同反義詞表 / 112

2 PART
歷史懷舊

Unit 8 Steam Engine 蒸汽引擎

❶ 蒸汽引擎的發展 / 116

❷ 廣泛使用 / 120

❸ 各樣的改良 / 124

❹ 同反義詞表 / 128

Unit 9 **Photographic Film** 底片
- ❶ 底片的進展 / 130
- ❷ 喬治・伊士曼的攝影研究 / 134
- ❸ 社會貢獻及晚年 / 138
- ❹ 同反義詞表 / 142

Unit 10 **Paper** 紙
- ❶ 造紙技術的發明 / 144
- ❷ 紙技術傳至歐洲及蔡倫早年 / 148
- ❸ 指派入獄 / 152
- ❹ 同反義詞表 / 156

Unit 11 **Liquid Paper** 立可白
- ❶ 解雇促成發明了立可白 / 158
- ❷ 修正帶的發明及晚年 / 162
- ❸ 立可白的發明者及員工福利的創造者 / 166
- ❹ 同反義詞表 / 170

Unit 12 **Ballpoint Pen** 原子筆
- ❶ 捷爾吉的油墨配方 / 172
- ❷ 原子筆的潛力 / 176
- ❸ 勞德的生平 / 180
- ❹ 同反義詞表 / 184

Unit 13 **Pencil** 鉛筆
- ❶ 鉛筆的發明 / 186
- ❷ 石墨：皇室的象徵 / 190
- ❸ 康特：鉛筆製造商 / 194
- ❹ 同反義詞表 / 198

Unit 14 **Typewriter** 打字機
- ❶ 打字機的發明 / 200
- ❷ 打字機的價值 / 204

❸ QWERTY鍵盤的發明 / 208

❹ 同反義詞表 / 212

PART 3
現代化實用科技

Unit 15 **Telescope** 望遠鏡

❶ 望遠鏡功率的提高 / 216

❷ 其他貢獻 / 220

❸ 利普斯 / 224

❹ 同反義詞表 / 228

Unit 16 **Airplane** 飛機

❶ 飛機的發明 / 230

❷ 對飛行的熱情 / 234

❸ 兩兄弟的成長過程 / 238

❹ 同反義詞表 / 242

Unit 17 **Automobile** 汽車

❶ 汽車發展史 / 244

❷ 職涯發展 / 248

❸ 賓士的成就 / 252

❹ 同反義詞表 / 256

Unit 18 **Stethoscope** 聽診器

❶ 聽診器的沿革 / 258

❷ 醫學成就 / 262

❸ 聽診器帶來的便利性 / 266

❹ 同反義詞表 / 270

Unit 19 **Helicopter** 直升機

❶ 直升機的發展 / 272

❷ 直升機的發展與貢獻 / 276

❸ 西科斯基的生平 / 280

❹ 同反義詞表 / 284

Unit 20 **Dynamite 火藥**

❶ 火藥的沿革 / 286

❷ 諾貝爾獎 / 290

❸ 諾貝爾的生平 / 294

❹ 同反義詞表 / 298

Unit 21 **Plastics 塑膠**

❶ 塑膠的發現 / 300

❷ 利奧・貝克蘭塑膠工業之父 / 304

❸ 利奧・貝克蘭的成就 / 308

❹ 同反義詞表 / 312

Unit 22 **Barcode 條碼**

❶ 條碼的沿革 / 314

❷ 靈感來源 / 318

❸ 英年早逝 / 322

❹ 同反義詞表 / 326

PART

4

資訊與知識傳遞

Unit 23 **Google 谷歌**

❶ 谷歌傳奇 / 330

❷ 谷歌的成立 / 334

❸ 「谷歌」這個名字的由來 / 338

❹ 同反義詞表 / 342

Unit 24 **Facebook** 臉書

❶ 臉書成立初期 / 344

❷ 臉書的普及與沿革 / 348

❸ 扎克伯格的生平 / 352

❹ 同反義詞表 / 356

Unit 25 **Telephone** 電話

❶ 電話的發展 /358

❷ 貝爾的生平 / 362

❸ 從電話到劃時代的新發明 / 366

❹ 同反義詞表 / 370

Unit 26 **Online Banking** 線上銀行

❶ 銀行的演變 / 372

❷ 從顧慮到普及 / 376

❸ 創新想法激出新的銀行體系 / 380

❹ 同反義詞表 / 384

Unit 27 **Printing Press** 印刷機

❶ 機械化製程促成大規模發展 / 386

❷ 印刷術的發展促成民主化 / 390

❸ 古騰堡的貢獻 / 394

❹ 同反義詞表 / 398

Unit 28 **Television** 電視

❶ 電視的發展 / 400

❷ 電視後期發展和法恩斯沃思 / 404

❸ 法恩斯沃思的起落 / 408

❹ 同反義詞表 / 412

INSTRUCTIONS 使用說明

21 Plastics 塑膠

21-1 塑膠的發現　　MP3 61

Although different types of pollutions caused by plastic have been public issues for years, it seems hard to get rid of plastic for its relatively low production cost, versatility and imperviousness to water. From grocery bags to toys to even clothes, plastics are used in an enormous and expanding range of products.

雖然因為塑膠所造成的各種污染已是多年來的公共問題，但由於生產成本相對低廉，具通用性及抗滲水性，因此我們似乎無法擺脫這種材料。從食品塑膠袋到玩具，甚至服裝，塑膠產品的範圍不斷擴大。

It is also being widely used in the medical field and construction field. The very first plastic material was discovered by Charles Goodyear's during the discovery of vulcanization to thermoset materials derived from natural rubber in the 1800s.

它也被廣泛應用於醫療領域和建築領域。史上第一個塑膠材料是在 1800 年代由查爾斯‧固特異在天然橡膠的熱固性材料中發現的硫化物。

After that, many scientists contributed to the discovery of different types of plastics. It was not until 1907, a scientist Leo Baekeland invented "Bakelite" which was the first fully synthetic plastic. He also was the person who coined the term "Plastics".

在此之後，許多科學家促成了不同類型塑膠的發現。直到 1907 年，科學家利奧‧貝克蘭發明了酚醛塑料，這是第一個完全合成的塑膠。他也是命名「塑膠」的人。

The rapid growth in chemical technology led to the invention of many new forms of plastics, such as Polystyrene, Polyvinyl chloride, and polyethylene. Many traditional materials, such as wood, stone, leather, ceramic that we normally used in the past were replaced by plastics.

化學技術的極速成長導致許多形式的塑膠發明，例如聚苯乙烯、聚氯乙烯和聚乙烯。許多傳統材料，例如我們過去常使用的木頭、石頭、皮革和陶瓷都被塑膠取代了。

塑膠等日常生活中常見的物品為常考的閱讀考題，題目可能是有關於**塑膠的歷史**、**塑膠的製程**、**塑膠製品**等等的文章，熟悉相關主題文章可以大幅降低在應考時寫題目的陌生感，並加快自己熟悉主題的答題時間，將時間用在自己較陌生跟不擅長的主題上，並於時間內完成答題。

★ 相關應用包含其他日常生活中的物品，例如玻璃（Glass）於實際考試中也曾出現過，另外也可以在劍橋雅思 12 Test 8 Reading passage 1 The History of Glass 中看到。考生可以於相關主題文章中檢測自己對此敘述類型文章的掌握度。

★ 其他應用可以參考本書的 Unit 13 Pencil（鉛筆）和 Unit 14 Ballpoint Pen（原子筆），The History pf Pencil 於實際考試中考過。

人物類主題的文章例如傳記或發明者，在雅思閱讀考試中違常出現的考題，例如此圖片 **20-3** 講述的諾貝爾。

★ 除了 Alfred Nobel 相關應用包含，William Gilbert, Thomas Young, Robert Louis Stevenson 等人物均於實際考試中出現過，考生可以多閱讀相關主題的英文文章。

★ 其他應用包含劍橋雅思 9 中出現的 Marie Curie（居禮夫人）。

★ 考生還可以藉由書中 MP3 朗讀強化自己對英國腔的熟悉度，提升自己英文聽力和對字彙的掌握度。

20-3 諾貝爾的生平　　MP3 60

Nobel was born in Stockholm, Sweden on October 21st, 1833. His family moved to St. Petersburg in Russia in 1842. Nobel was sent to private tutoring, and he excelled in his studies, particularly in chemistry and languages. He achieved fluency in English, French, German and Russian.

諾貝爾於 1833 年 10 月 21 日出生在瑞典斯德哥爾摩。在 1842 年時，他舉家遷往俄羅斯聖彼得堡。諾貝爾被送往私塾，他擅長於學習，特別是在化學和語言。他精通英語，法語，德語和俄語。

Throughout his life, Nobel only went to school for 18 months. In 1860, Nobel started his invention of dynamite, and it was 1866 when he first invented the dynamite successfully. Nobel never let himself take any rests. He founded Nitroglycerin AB in Stockholm, Sweden in 1864.

終其一生，諾貝爾只去了學校 18 個月。1860 年，諾貝爾開始了炸藥的發明。1866 年，他第一次成功地發明了炸藥。諾貝爾從來沒有讓自己休息。他於 1864 年在瑞典斯德哥爾摩創立硝酸甘油 AB 公司。

A year later, he built the Alfred Nobel & Co. Factory in Hamburg, Germany. In 1866, he established the United States Blasting Oil Company in the U.S.

一年後，他在德國漢堡建立了阿爾弗雷德·諾貝爾公司的工廠。1866 年，他在美國成立了美國爆破石油公司。

And 4 years later, he established the Société général pour la fabrication de la dynamite in Paris, France.

4 年後，他又在法國巴黎成立了炸藥實驗室。

Nobel was proud to say he is a world citizen. He passed away in 1896. A year before that, he started the Nobel prize which is awarded yearly to people whose work helps humanity. When he died, Alfred Nobel left behind a nine-million-dollar endowment fund.

諾貝爾自豪地說，他是一個世界公民。他在 1896 年過世。在他過世前，他成立諾貝爾獎以鼓勵對人類有幫助的人們。當他過世時，諾貝爾留下了九百萬美元的捐贈基金。

1 飲食民生

2 歷史傳承

3 現代化實用科技

4 超現代超議題

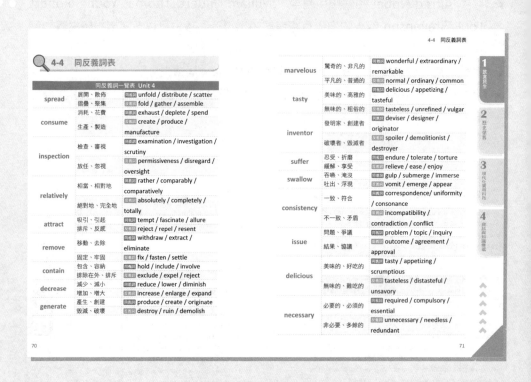

4-4 同反義詞表

同反義詞一覽表 Unit 4

spread	展開、散佈	同義詞 unfold / distribute / scatter
	摺疊、聚集	反義詞 fold / gather / assemble
consume	消耗、花費	同義詞 exhaust / deplete / spend
	生產、製造	反義詞 create / produce / manufacture
inspection	檢查、審視	同義詞 examination / investigation / scrutiny
	放任、忽視	反義詞 permissiveness / disregard / oversight
relatively	相當、相對地	同義詞 rather / comparably / comparatively
	絕對地、完全地	反義詞 absolutely / completely / totally
attract	吸引、引起	同義詞 tempt / fascinate / allure
	排斥、反感	反義詞 reject / repel / resent
remove	移動、去除	同義詞 withdraw / extract / eliminate
	固定、牢固	反義詞 fix / fasten / settle
contain	包含、容納	同義詞 hold / include / involve
	排除在外、排斥	反義詞 exclude / expel / reject
decrease	減少、減小	同義詞 reduce / lower / diminish
	增加、增大	反義詞 increase / enlarge / expand
generate	產生、創建	同義詞 produce / create / originate
	毀滅、破壞	反義詞 destroy / ruin / demolish

marvelous	驚奇的、非凡的	同義詞 wonderful / extraordinary / remarkable
	平凡的、普通的	反義詞 normal / ordinary / common
tasty	美味的、高雅的	同義詞 delicious / appetizing / tasteful
	無味的、粗俗的	反義詞 tasteless / unrefined / vulgar
inventor	發明家、創建者	同義詞 deviser / designer / originator
	破壞者、毀滅者	反義詞 spoiler / demolitionist / destroyer
suffer	忍受、折磨	同義詞 endure / tolerate / torture
	緩解、享受	反義詞 relieve / ease / enjoy
swallow	吞嚥、淹沒	同義詞 gulp / submerge / immerse
	吐出、浮現	反義詞 vomit / emerge / appear
consistency	一致、符合	同義詞 correspondence/ uniformity / consonance
	不一致、矛盾	反義詞 incompatibility / contradiction / conflict
issue	問題、爭議	同義詞 problem / topic / inquiry
	結果、協議	反義詞 outcome / agreement / approval
delicious	美味的、好吃的	同義詞 tasty / appetizing / scrumptious
	無味的、難吃的	反義詞 tasteless / distasteful / unsavory
necessary	必要的、必須的	同義詞 required / compulsory / essential
	非必要、多餘的	反義詞 unnecessary / needless / redundant

書籍中每個單元收錄了同、反義詞表，並刪除了不常見的字彙，考生能藉由這些字彙大幅提升應考水平。

★ 考題的敘述均在檢測考生對同、反義字的掌握能力，掌握一定程度的同、反義字彙在獲取高分上扮演重要的關鍵，例如聽力測驗題本的敘述僅是聽力講者另一個形式的換句話說，閱讀測驗亦同。此外考生也可以藉由這些字彙增進自己在口說和寫作時的表達能力。

書籍中每個小節後均附有Vocabulary in Context的設計，考生可以藉由題型演練增進自己閱讀能力和推測能力。

★ 英語考試尤其是閱讀測驗中，不太可能每個字我們都懂，其中還包含的專業字彙等等，但考試僅在測驗語文跟閱讀能力等，並非在檢測我們對該專業主題的了解度，Vocabulary in Context就是其中一個設計，能增進考生藉由上下文推測出某些字可能是什麼意思，面對陌生的字彙也不影響答題，大幅增加應考實力。

Vocabulary in Context

❾ The dazzling northern lights, also called "the aurora borealis," display as one of nature's greatest spectacles, and are _____ to only certain regions in Canada, Scotland, Norway, and Sweden.

Special is in the closest meaning to this word.

A. unique   C. practical
B. conceptual   D. invisible

❿ After surviving the horrible plane crash, Pamela came to realize the value of life and was _____ to social charity causes.

Changed is in the closest meaning to this word.

A. emigrated   C. improved
B. navigated   D. converted

⓫ The refined merchandise exhibited in the Trade Fair last month was _____ by Morrison Company and has received great numbers of orders since then.

Produced is in the closest meaning to this word.

A. approached   C. manufactured
B. combined   D. rejected

⓬ The rich and renowned CEO remained modest and was _____ about charitable affairs by donating millions of dollars each year.

Zealous is in the closest meaning to this word.

A. violent   C. popular
B. indifferent   D. enthusiastic

❾ 炫目的極北之光，又稱為「北極光」，展現大自然絕佳的奇觀之一，並且是加拿大、蘇格蘭、挪威及瑞典特定地區獨具的景觀。
Special 的意思最接近於這個字。
A. 獨特的   C. 實際的
B. 概念的   D. 隱形的

❿ 潘蜜拉在可怕的墜機事件倖存後，領悟到生命的可貴，並轉而致力於社會慈善工作。
Changed 的意思最接近於這個字。
A. 移民   C. 改善
B. 航行   D. 轉變

⓫ 上個月在貿易展示的優質商品是由莫里森公司所製造的，並從那時起接獲大量的訂單。
Produced 的意思最接近於這個字。
A. 接近   C. 製造
B. 結合   D. 排斥

⓬ 這位富有且著名的執行長依舊保持謙遜的態度，並且熱心於每年捐贈數百萬元贊助慈善事業。
Zealous 的意思最接近於這個字。
A. 暴力的   C. 受歡迎的
B. 冷淡的   D. 熱忱的

答案 ❾ A ❿ D ⓫ C ⓬ D

1 教員民生
2 歷史懷舊
3 現代官員科技
4 資訊網知識傳遞

PART 1

飲食民生

單元三大學習法

key 1 主題式記憶
透過主題學習將字彙累績至長期記憶，
而非片段背誦。

key 2 上下文推敲文意
閱讀時不因不熟悉的單字而影響句意理解。

key 3 熟記同反義詞
在雅思各單項中要獲取 7 分以上
需要具備同反義詞轉換的能力。

Unit 1 Coke 可口可樂

Even though the formula and the marketing strategy remain controversial, Coke for years is the number 1 sold carbonated drink in the world. It is being sold in over 200 countries and consumed in over 1.7 billion servings per day. Coke is a registered trademark of Coca-Cola company of Atlanta, Georgia.

雖然配方和營銷策略仍然存在爭議，可口可樂多年來一直是世界銷售第一的碳酸飲料。它被銷往 200 多個國家，每天的總銷售量超過 170 億份。可樂是在喬治亞州亞特蘭大市的可口可樂公司所擁有的一個註冊商標。

The name refers to the two main ingredients, kola nuts and coca leaves. These are the only 2 main ingredients that are published. The actual formula of Coke remains to be a family secret. Although some companies such as Pepsi tried to recreate the drink, still no

這個名字來自兩個主要成分，可樂果和古柯葉。這兩個主成分是唯一被公布的。可樂實際的組成內容仍然是一個家族秘密。雖然有些公司如百事

one can overcome the success of Coke.

可樂試圖拷貝這個飲料，仍然沒有人能比可樂來得成功。

John Pemberton, a pharmacist, invented Coke in 1886. His goal was to invent something that would bring him to commercial success. Pemberton created the syrup and combined it with carbonated water which was believed to be good for health back in the 19th century.

藥劑師約翰‧彭伯頓在 1886 年發明了可口可樂。他的目標是創造一個能帶來商業上成功的一項產品。彭伯頓創造了藥水並結合在 19 世紀被認為是可以帶來健康的碳酸水。

He then claimed that Coke cured many diseases, including morphine addiction, neurasthenia and headache. Later on, Frank Robinson registered the formula with the patent office.

然後，他聲稱可樂能治好許多疾病，包括嗎啡癮、神經衰弱和頭痛。後來，弗蘭克－羅賓遜在專利局為可樂成分註冊專利。

1 飲食民生

2 歷史懷舊

3 現代化實用科技

4 資訊與知識傳遞

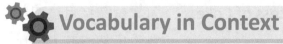

Vocabulary in Context

❶ The newly elected administration has launched an aggressive
_____ for federal counterterrorism in hopes of solidifying
national security.

Planning is in the closest meaning to this word.

A. transaction   C. strategy

B. prejudice   D. disconnection

❷ The research findings about hypnosis healing remain
inconclusive and _____; therefore, the curing method still
has a long way to go.

Debatable is in the closest meaning to this word.

A. potential   C. magnificent

B. anxious   D. controversial

❸ Animal rights groups _____ to take more drastic measures
unless the cosmetic manufactures stopped inhumane animal
tests.

Announced is in the closest meaning to this word.

A. claimed   C. surrendered

B. unraveled   D. liberated

❹ The Internet's _____ among adolescents brought about
serious academic and personality problems and has
gradually aroused social attention.

Dependence is in the closest meaning to this word.

A. governance   C. retreat

B. addiction   D. provocation

1 新上任的內閣已經推動積極的國家反恐策略，為的是希望鞏固國家安全。

Planning 的意思最接近於這個字。

A. 交易   C. 策略
B. 偏見   D. 中斷

2 有關於催眠治療的研究發現依舊是未定且有爭議的；因此，這種治療方式仍有待努力。

Debatable 的意思最接近於這個字。

A. 有潛力的   C. 壯麗的
B. 焦慮的   D. 有爭議的

3 動物權益團體宣稱，除非化妝品製造廠商停止不人道的動物實驗，否則將採取更激烈的手段，。

Announced 的意思最接近於這個字。

A. 宣稱   C. 投降
B. 闡明   D. 解放

4 青少年的網路成癮導致嚴重的課業及人格問題，並且逐漸地引發社會關切。

Dependence 的意思最接近於這個字。

A. 管理   C. 撤退
B. 上癮   D. 挑釁

答案 **1** C **2** D **3** A **4** B

飲食民生 1
歷史懷舊 2
現代化實用科技 3
資訊與知識傳遞 4

The actual success of Coke came in 1891 after Asa Griggs Candler bought the business.

可樂的實際成功是在 1891 年阿薩・格里格斯・坎德勒收購業務之後。

Candler decided to offer free drinks to people in order to raise the popularity. He also put the Coca-Cola logo on goods such as posters and calendars to increase the visibility.

坎德勒決定提供免費飲料以提高能見度。他還把可口可樂標誌的放上不同商品，如海報、月曆等，以增加能見度。

Because of his innovative marketing techniques, Coke became a national brand and became a multi billion-dollar business. It is very hard to imagine that it was once sold for only 5 cents a glass.

因為他的創新營銷技巧，可口可樂成為了國家品牌，成為一個數十億美元的生意。很難想像它曾經一杯只賣 5 美分。

Born on January 8th, 1831 in west central Georgia, John Pemberton is well-known for inventing Coca-Cola, A.K.A Coke.

於 1831 年 1 月 8 日出生於喬治亞西環的約翰・彭伯頓因發明可口可樂，又稱為可樂而聞名。

Having studied medicine and pharmacy at Reform Medical College of Georgia, Pemberton was gifted for medical chemistry. He was licensed to practice Thomsonian, which is based on botanic principles at the age of nineteen.

彭伯頓在佐治亞改革醫學院學習醫學和藥學，在醫用化學上很有天賦。他在 19 歲時便被授權實踐以植物藥學為基礎的 Thomsonian。

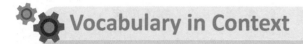 **Vocabulary in Context**

❺ Thanks to the decreased costs of 3D printers, the technology of the three-dimensional printing has recently gained _____ among different fields of industry.

Prevalence is in the closest meaning to this word.

A. richness   C. manipulation

B. popularity   D. capability

❻ The financial institution posted an advertisement to offer jobs for business school graduates with _____ consciousness and abilities.

Creative is in the closest meaning to this word.

A. rigid   C. optional

B. innovative   D. retrospective

❼ Young generations should be taught from their early childhood to practice the 3R _____ — Reduce, Reuse, and Recycle to protect and sustain the earth.

Regulations is in the closest meaning to this word.

A. Groups   C. Principles

B. Facilities   D. Restrictions

❽ Mr. Banks is a lawyer _____ in criminal laws and is dedicated to defending against criminal charges.

Professionalized is in the closest meaning to this word.

A. franchised   C. abolished

B. managed   D. specialized

❺ 幸虧有**3D**立體印刷機的降價，**3D**立體印刷科技近日在各個不同產業領域受到歡迎。

Prevalence的意思最接近於這個字。

A. 財富

B. 受歡迎

C. 操弄

D. 能力

❻ 這家經融機構刊登職缺廣告來徵求具創新意識及能力的商學院畢業生。

Creative 的意思最接近於這個字。

A. 僵化的

B. 創新的

C. 可選擇的

D. 回顧的

❼ 年輕世代應從小被教導力行**3R**原則 — 減量、重複使用，以及回收，以保護並延續地球。

Regulations的意思最接近於這個字。

A. 團體

B. 設施

C. 原則

D. 限制

❽ 班克斯先生是一名專精於刑事訴訟法的律師，並致力於刑事訴訟的辯護。

Professionalized的意思最接近於這個字。

A. 加盟

B. 設法

C. 廢除

D. 專攻

答案 **❺** B **❻** B **❼** C **❽** D

1 飲食民生

2 歷史懷舊

3 現代化實用科技

4 資訊與知識傳遞

Pemberton is not only a remarkable pharmacist and chemist, but also a smart businessman. He established a wholesale-retail drug business specialized in medical materials. He also established laboratories, which they claimed were unique because all the pharmaceutical and chemical preparations used in the arts and sciences are made in house back in 1855.

彭伯頓不僅是一個了不起的藥劑師和化學家，也是一個精明的商人。他建立了一個專攻草本的藥品批發零售企業。早在1855年，他還建立了實驗室。他們聲稱所使用於藝術及製藥的化學製劑都是獨一無二的。

The most updated and improved equipment was invested in the labs as well. The original laboratory which he opened 125 years ago is still operating today, and it is now converted into the first testing labs in Georgia operating as part of the Georgia Department of Agriculture.

實驗室中也引進最新的設備。125年前開設的原始實驗室至今仍在運轉。它現在轉換成由喬治亞州所經營的第一實驗室，為喬治亞州農業部的一部分。

In April 1865 in the Civil War, Pemberton served in the Third Georgia

在1865年4月的內戰時，彭伯頓曾在佐

Cavalry Battalion and was almost killed. He was wounded badly so like most veterans, he became addicted to morphine used to ease pain. As a pharmacist himself, he started working on painkillers that would serve as opium-free. This is actually the beginning of the invention of Coke.

治亞州第三騎兵營，且差點被打死。他受傷嚴重，所以跟其他的老兵一樣，他開始沉迷於嗎啡，以緩解疼痛。作為一名藥劑師的他，開始研發無鴉片的止痛藥。這其實就是可樂發明的開頭。

His business scale didn't end there. He also established his own brands of pharmaceuticals which he manufactured on a large scale in Philadelphia, Pennsylvania. Unfortunately, Coke did not become popular until after Pemberton passed away.

他的業務規模並沒有就此結束。他還在賓州的費城建立了自己品牌並量產的藥品。不幸的是，可口可樂並沒有在他有生之年成為流行。

Vocabulary in Context

❾ The dazzling northern lights, also called "the aurora borealis," display as one of nature's greatest spectacles, and are _____ to only certain regions in Canada, Scotland, Norway, and Sweden.

Special is in the closest meaning to this word.

A. unique   C. practical

B. conceptual   D. invisible

❿ After surviving the horrible plane crash, Pamela came to realize the value of life and was _____ to social charity causes.

Changed is in the closest meaning to this word.

A. emigrated   C. improved

B. navigated   D. converted

⓫ The refined merchandise exhibited in the Trade Fair last month was _____ by Morrison Company and has received great numbers of orders since then.

Produced is in the closest meaning to this word.

A. approached   C. manufactured

B. combined   D. rejected

⓬ The rich and renowned CEO remained modest and was _____ about charitable affairs by donating millions of dollars each year.

Zealous is in the closest meaning to this word.

A. violent C. popular

B. indifferent D. enthusiastic

❾ 炫目的極北之光，又稱為「北極光」，展現大自然絕佳的奇觀之一，並且是加拿大、蘇格蘭、挪威及瑞典特定地區獨具的景觀。

Special 的意思最接近於這個字。

A. 獨特的 C. 實際的

B. 概念的 D. 隱形的

❿ 潘蜜拉在可怕的墜機事件倖存後，領悟到生命的可貴，並轉而致力於社會慈善工作。

Changed 的意思最接近於這個字。

A. 移民 C. 改善

B. 航行 D. 轉變

⓫ 上個月在貿易展展示的優質商品是由莫里森公司所製造的，並從那時起接獲大量的訂單。

Produced 的意思最接近於這個字。

A. 接近 C. 製造

B. 結合 D. 排斥

⓬ 這位富有且著名的執行長依舊保持謙遜的態度，並且熱心於每年捐贈數百萬元贊助慈善事業。.

Zealous 的意思最接近於這個字。

A. 暴力的 C. 受歡迎的

B. 冷淡的 D. 熱忱的

 答案 ❾ A ❿ D ⓫ C ⓬ D

27

1-4　同反義詞表

同反義詞一覽表 Unit 1		
strategy	策略、計謀	同義詞 planning / tactics / manipulation
	破壞、毀滅	反義詞 wrecking / demolition / destruction
controversial	爭論的、爭議的	同義詞 debatable / arguable / contradictory
	明確的、確切的	反義詞 definite / precise / exact
claim	宣稱、要求	同義詞 announce / demand / require
	放棄、否認	反義詞 disclaim / surrender / deny
addiction	沉溺、上癮	同義詞 indulgence / dependence / habituation
	獨立、自主	反義詞 independence / freedom / self-support
combine	結合、聯合	同義詞 integrate / merge / coordinate
	分開、區分	反義詞 divide / separate / segregate
popularity	流行、大眾化	同義詞 prevalence / fashion / vogue
	不受歡迎	反義詞 unpopularity / aversion / disfavor
innovative	創新的、革新的	同義詞 creative / imaginative / inventive
	模仿的、仿效的	反義詞 imitative / mimic / reproductive

principle	原則、原理	同義詞 regulation / law / rule
	例外、異常	反義詞 exception / exclusion / anomaly
specialize	專門、專攻	同義詞 professionalize / major
	泛論、概括	反義詞 generalize / universalize
raise	舉起、促進	同義詞 lift / elevate / boost
	放下、減低	反義詞 lower / degrade / reduce
remarkable	出色的、非凡的	同義詞 outstanding / exceptional / extraordinary
	平凡的、普通的	反義詞 average / ordinary / normal
unique	獨特的、唯一的	同義詞 special / peculiar / distinctive
	一般的、平常的	反義詞 general / usual / common
convert	轉換、轉變	同義詞 transform / change / alter
	平靜、維持	反義詞 settle / preserve / maintain
manufacture	製造、生產	同義詞 produce / make / fabricate
	消耗、耗盡	反義詞 exhaust / drain / deplete
enthusiastic	熱情的、熱心的	同義詞 passionate / zealous / ardent
	冷淡的、冷漠的	反義詞 distant / unconcerned / indifferent
veteran	經驗豐富的人	同義詞 old-timer / oldster
	業餘外行的人	反義詞 amateur / layman / rookie
wound	受傷、傷害	同義詞 hurt / injure / harm
	治療、癒合	反義詞 heal / cure / restore
proud	驕傲的、自負的	同義詞 arrogant / conceited / boastful
	謙卑的、謙遜的	反義詞 humble / unpretentious / modest

1 飲食民生

2 歷史懷舊

3 現代化實用科技

4 資訊與知識傳遞

Lego 樂高

2-1　樂高的源由

It has been 50 years since the first Lego block was made. Lego company estimated that over 400 billion Lego blocks have been produced. In another word, approximately 36 billion pieces of Lego blocks are manufactured every year. There is an amazing story behind this little brick.

距離第一塊被製作出的樂高積木已經有五十年。樂高公司估計，距今已生產出超過四千億塊樂高積木。換句話說，每年樂高積木的生產量約為三百六十億塊。看似簡單的一塊小磚，其實有背後個驚人的故事。

Ole Kirk Christiansen, a carpenter from Denmark formed the toy company Lego in 1932. The name Lego came from the Danish phrase "leg godt" which means "play well". Lego originally was specialized in wooden toys only, but expanded to produce plastic toys in 1947.

奧萊‧柯克‧克里斯琴森，一位來自丹麥的木匠，在 1932 年組成了樂高玩具公司。樂高這個名字來自於丹麥語的「leg godt」，就是「玩得好」的意思。樂高原本是一家專門從事木製玩具的公司，在 1947 年開始涉獵塑膠玩具。

並在 1949 年創造出第一版的連扣磚，當時取名為「自動綁定磚塊」。在兩年後，塑膠玩具的產量佔了樂高公司產量的一半。1954 年，克里斯琴森的兒子，古德佛德，成為樂高的管理部初階經理。他就是想出了「創意性玩法」的人。

It was 1949 when Lego produced the first version of the interlocking brinks called "Automatic Binding Bricks." Two years later, plastic toys accounted for half of the Lego Company's output. In 1954, Christiansen's son, Godtfred, became the junior managing director of Lego. He was the person who came up with the creative play idea.

The Lego group then started their research and development of the brick design which is versatile and has universal locking ability. Also, they spent years finding the right material for it. Finally, on January 28th, 1958, the modern Lego brick made with ABS was patented.

樂高集團於是乎開始了積木的研究和開發，使得積木可具多功能性和鎖定能力。此外，他們花費了數年的時間來找到合適的材料。最後，在 1958 年 1 月 28 日，由 ABS 材質所製造的現代樂高積木取得了專利。

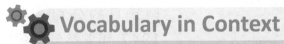 **Vocabulary in Context**

1 It is _____ that producing books in hard copy format may bring several million tons of harmful CO2 into the atmosphere, so E-books are definitely here to stay.
Calculated is in the closest meaning to this word.

A. rebelled   C. undertaken

B. estimated   D. humiliated

2 According to neuroscientists, _____ 20 percent of short-term memory can be improved by regular physical exercise, especially to the elderly.
Roughly is in the closest meaning to this word.

A. recently   C. perpetually

B. approximately   D. ironically

3 With _____ pop music superstars creating extraordinary performances, Korean pop music trend has prevailed worldwide.
Talented is in the closest meaning to this word.

A. mandatory   C. renewable

B. economical   D. versatile

4 Music, with its functions of offering soothing feelings and full relaxation, remains a _____ language for all times.
General is in the closest meaning to this word.

A. separate   C. defiant

B. constructive   D. universal

❶ 據估計，製造硬皮書籍可能將數百萬公噸有害的二氧化碳氣體帶入大氣層，所以電子書當然應該普遍推廣。

Calculated 的意思最接近於這個字。

A. 反叛   C. 從事

B. 估計   D. 羞辱

❷ 根據神經科學家的說法，將近百分之二十短暫的記憶可以經由規律的體能運動得到改善，尤其是對老年人而言。

Roughly 的意思最接近於這個字。

A. 近來   C. 永久地

B. 將近   D. 諷刺地

❸ 有著多才多藝流行音樂超級巨星創造傑出的表演，韓國流行音樂的潮流遍及全世界。

Talented 的意思最接近於這個字。

A. 命令的   C. 可更新的

B. 節約的   D. 多才多藝的

❹ 音樂，具有提供舒緩情緒及全面放鬆的功用，一直以來是一個世界性的語言。

General 的意思最接近於這個字。

A. 分隔的   C. 違抗的

B. 積極的   D. 全世界的

1 飲食民生

2 歷史懷舊

3 現代化實用科技

4 資訊與知識傳遞

答案 ❶ B ❷ B ❸ D ❹ D

Lego bricks have been popular since. Even astronauts build models with Lego bricks to see how they would react in microgravity. In 2013, the largest model was made and displayed in New York. It was a 1:1 scale model of an X-wing fighter which used over 5 million pieces of Lego bricks.

樂高積木從此流行。即使太空員都用樂高積木建立模型來測試他們在微重力時的反應。在 2013 年,最大的樂高模型被製作出來,並在紐約展示。這是一個 1:1 比例模型的 X 翼戰機,它使用了 500 多萬個樂高積木。

Lego might have created a lot of amazing facts, but the most incredible fact should be the universal system. Regardless of the variation in the design and the purpose of individual pieces over the years, each piece remains compatible with any existing pieces, even the one that was made in 1958.

樂高可能已經創造了很多驚人的事實,但最令人難以置信的事實應該是它的通用系統。無論多年來在設計的變化或各個單片的目的,每一塊仍然與任何現有積木相容,甚至與 1958 年製造的積木也同樣相容。

The founder of Lego, Ole Kirk Christiansen was born in a family of 12 in Jutland Denmark on April 7th, 1891. He was trained to be a carpenter, and he founded his own shop which sells daily use wooden tools such as ladders and ironing boards.

樂高的創始人，奧萊‧柯克‧克里斯琴森在 1891 年 4 月 7 日出生於丹麥德蘭半島的一個 12 人家庭。他被培養為一位木匠，並創辦了自己的店，在店裡販售日常使用的木製工具，如梯子、燙衣板等。

However, due to the global financial crisis, the demand had fallen sharply. In order to keep the cash flow, Christiansen needed to find a new niche. He unexpectedly had an idea, and a little incident prompted him to put duck toys into production.

然而，由於全球金融危機的影響，需求大幅下滑。為了保持資金的流動，克里斯琴森需要找到一個新的利基。他意外間有了想法，而一個小事件促使他將鴨子玩具投入生產。

1 飲食民生

2 歷史懷舊

3 現代化實用科技

4 資訊與知識傳遞

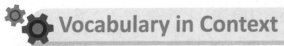

5 Some extreme-sports enthusiasts are capable of achieving difficult and challenging extreme tasks with _____ perfection.

Unbelievable is in the closest meaning to this word.

A. synthetic   C. incredible

B. luxurious   D. thorny

6 Due to wide _____ of public opinion, the political figure caught in a dilemma had a hard time getting away from the scandal.

Changes is in the closest meaning to this word.

A. variations   C. approaches

B. solitude   D. isolation

7 The company has recently renewed the computer software, and is working on tests to make sure the new system will be _____ with the existing apparatus.

Agreeable is in the closest meaning to this word.

A. sympathetic   C. compatible

B. experimental   D. interruptible

8 Martin has lived in comfort and luxury ever since he made successful _____ investments and piled up a considerable fortune.

Pecuniary is in the closest meaning to this word.

A. financial   C. superstitious

B. profound   D. awkward

❺ 有些極限運動的愛好者有能力以令人難以置信的完美方式達成艱困且具挑戰性的極限任務。

Unbelievable 的意思最接近於這個字。

A. 綜合的   C. 令人難以置信的
B. 奢華的   D. 棘手的

❻ 由於輿論的眾說紛紜，這位深陷進退兩難困境的政治人物很難從醜聞中脫身。

Changes 的意思最接近於這個字。

A. 變化   C. 方法
B. 孤獨   D. 隔離

❼ 這家公司最近更新了電腦軟體，並正在測試以確保新的系統與現有的裝置相容。

Agreeable 的意思最接近於這個字。

A. 同情的   C. 相容的
B. 實驗的   D. 可中斷的

❽ 馬汀自從金融投資成功且積聚可觀的財富後，一直過著舒適奢華的生活。

Pecuniary 的意思最接近於這個字。

A. 金融的   C. 迷信的
B. 深奧的   D. 笨拙的

答案 ❺C ❻A ❼C ❽A

The name of the company is derived from Danish origin, meaning play well. Starting with a company of 7 employees, Christiansen hired all enthusiastic carpenters who had great pleasure from creating new things.

公司的名稱是源於丹麥文，其意思是玩得好。公司一開始只有 7 名員工，克里斯琴森聘請的木匠都富有熱誠，他們從創造新事物中得到極大的樂趣。

In 1942, the only facility of Lego burned down. It was then that Christiansen decided to manufacture only toys after restoration. Two years later, Christiansen officially registered the company name "LEGO".

1942 年，樂高的唯一廠房被燒毀。就在那時，克里斯琴森決定恢復生產後只生產玩具。2 年後，克里斯琴森正式註冊公司名稱為「樂高」。

It was 1947, when the company decided to start producing plastic toys, Ole and his son Gotdfred got the first sample of the plastic self-locking building blocks.

那是 1947 年，當時該公司決定開始生產塑料玩具，奧萊和他的兒子古德佛德得到了塑料自鎖積木的第一個樣本。

Christiansen family then purchased the biggest injection-molding machine in Denmark and started the master production of different plastic toys.

Years later, on January 28th, 1958, the Lego brick we know today was patented. In the same year, Christiansen passed away from a heart attack and Godtfred took over the business.

克里斯琴森的家庭購買了丹麥最大的注塑機，開始主生產不同的塑料玩具。

幾年後，於 1958 年 1 月 28 日，我們今天所知道的樂高積木被授予了專利。同年，克里斯琴森因心臟病過世。古德佛德接手經營。

1 飲食民生

2 歷史懷舊

3 現代化實用科技

4 資訊與知識傳遞

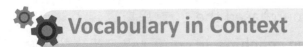

9 Most volunteers are delighted to help needy people, for they can not only learn useful skills to prepare them for work but mainly _____ great pleasure from doing it.
Obtain is in the closest meaning to this word.

A. justify   C. multiply

B. abandon   D. derive

10 It's predictable that the confrontation will persistently go on since the management and the _____ failed to reach any satisfactory agreement.
Workers is in the closest meaning to this word.

A. executives   C. employees

B. individuals   D. retailers

11 Mrs. Newman planned to move to the countryside, following her doctor's advice that the rural environment might be conducive to the _____ of her health.
Recovery is in the closest meaning to this word.

A. stimulation   C. restoration

B. contribution   D. introduction

12 Given that dust storms have been _____ in huge amounts with greater forces, scientists all over the world are working on the causes and the solutions.
Created is in the closest meaning to this word.

A. accompanied   C. summoned

B. produced　　　　D. degenerated

❾ 大多數的志工樂於幫助貧困的人，目的不僅在於學習職場技能，主要是能從中得到極大的樂趣。

Obtain 的意思最接近於這個字。

A. 辯護　　　　　　C. 成倍增加

B. 拋棄　　　　　　D. 獲得

❿ 由於管理階層和員工無法達成任何滿意的共識，雙方將會持續地抗爭是可預期的。

Workers 的意思最接近於這個字。

A. 主管　　　　　　C. 員工

B. 個人　　　　　　D. 零售商

⓫ 遵循醫生所提出關於鄉村環境有助於恢復健康的勸告，紐曼太太計畫搬到鄉下去居住。

Recovery 的意思最接近於這個字。

A. 刺激　　　　　　C. 復原

B. 貢獻　　　　　　D. 介紹

⓬ 考慮到沙塵暴以更強的威力大量地成形中，世界各地的科學家正努力於探討成因及解決之道。

Created 的意思最接近於這個字。

A. 陪伴　　　　　　C. 召喚

B. 生產　　　　　　D. 衰退

答案　❾ D　❿ C　⓫ C　⓬ B

2-4　同反義詞表

同反義詞一覽表 Unit 2		
estimate	估計、估價	同義詞 judge / calculate / evaluate
	忽視、忽略	反義詞 disregard / overlook / neglect
approximately	大概、近乎	同義詞 probably / roughly / nearly
	精確地、精準地	反義詞 precisely / exactly / accurately
versatile	多彩多藝的	同義詞 skilled / talented / capable
	缺乏才能的	反義詞 untalented / incompetent / ungifted
universal	全體的、全球的	同義詞 general / worldwide / global
	個人的、局部的	反義詞 individual / local / regional
expand	擴張、展開	同義詞 spread / broaden / enlarge
	限制、縮小	反義詞 confine / narrow / diminish
creative	有創造力的	同義詞 inventive / imaginative / innovative
	模仿的、模擬的	反義詞 imitative / mimic / simulate
incredible	難以置信的	同義詞 unbelievable / doubtful / questionable
	可信的、可靠的	反義詞 believable / credible / trustworthy
variation	變動、差異	同義詞 change / alternation / transformation
	相同、一致	反義詞 uniformity / monotony / correspondence

compatible	相容的、適合的	同義詞 agreeable / congruous / congenial
	不適合的	反義詞 unsuitable / uncongenial / incoordinate
financial	財政的、金融的	同義詞 economic / fiscal / pecuniary
	精神上的	反義詞 spiritual / mental
display	陳列、展出	同義詞 demonstrate / exhibit / illustrate
	隱蔽、隱藏	反義詞 conceal / hide / disguise
individual	個人的、個體的	同義詞 personal / separate / single
	一般的、全體的	反義詞 general / whole / entire
derive	取得、得到	同義詞 get / obtain / acquire
	失去、丟棄	反義詞 lose / forfeit / abandon
employee	員工、雇員	同義詞 personnel / worker / staff
	老闆、雇主	反義詞 boss / supervisor / employer
restoration	恢復、復原	同義詞 recovery / cure / healing
	惡化、衰退	反義詞 deterioration / degeneration / decline
produce	生產、製造	同義詞 manufacture / make / create
	消耗、耗盡	反義詞 consume / exhaust / drain
pleasure	愉快、滿足	同義詞 enjoyment / happiness / satisfaction
	不滿、生氣	反義詞 dissatisfaction / annoyance / fury
officially	官方地、正式地	同義詞 formally / regularly
	非正式地	反義詞 informally / casually

1 飲食民生

2 歷史懷舊

3 現代化實用科技

4 資訊與知識傳遞

Jeans 牛仔褲

3-1　牛仔褲的發明與流行

From homeless men to multi-billionaires, no one can ever say that they have never owned a pair of blue jeans in their lives. Even Apple founder Steve Jobs wore them with a black turtleneck shirt daily as his signature look. Jeans, originally called overalls was first designed as a practical solution to protect labors from injuries.

從流浪漢到億萬富翁，沒有人能夠說自己從未在自己的生活裡擁有過藍色牛仔褲。即使是蘋果公司創始人史蒂夫·賈伯斯日常都以穿著牛仔褲與黑色高領衫作為自己的註冊商標。牛仔褲，原名工作服原先是被設計當成一個實用的解決方案，以保護勞動者不受傷。

It was during the Gold Rush-era when jeans were invented. Levi Strauss founded Levi Strauss & Co. in 1853. In 1871, his tailor Jacob Davis invented jeans, and in 1873, the two of them patented and manufactured the first pants which is the famous Levis 501.

牛仔褲是在淘金時代期間被發明。利維·斯特勞斯在 1853 年成立了 Levi Strauss & Co. 公司。1871 年，他的裁縫師雅各·戴維斯發明了牛仔褲。在 1873 年，他們兩個申請了第一件牛仔褲的專利，這也就是著名的李維斯 501。

It was patented under No. 139,121 for revert-reinforced pants under the heading, "Improvement in Fastening Pocket-Openings." Originally designed for cowboys and miners, jeans became popular among young people in the 50s. It is no longer for protection but for fashion statements.

這樣產品的專利編號為 139121，內容是在「改善緊固口袋開口。」最初牛仔褲是設計給牛仔和礦工，但在 50 年代深受年輕人的喜愛。它不再只是保護，而是時尚的指標。

Especially musicians from punk rock, heavy metal to hip hop, no one doesn't wear jeans as one of their fashion items. In the 2010s, jeans remained a popular item, and they came in different fits, including slim, cigarette bottom, boot cut, straight, etc. You name it, and they have it.

特別是從龐克搖滾、重金屬，到嘻哈的音樂人，沒有一個人不以穿牛仔褲作為他們的時尚項目之一。在 2010 年代，牛仔褲仍然是一個受歡迎的單品，他們有不同的款式，包括超窄管、香煙腿型、喇叭褲，只要你說的出來，他們就一定有。

1 飲食民生

2 歷史懷舊

3 現代化實用科技

4 資訊與知識傳遞

Vocabulary in Context

❶ During the process of brainstorming, several _____ solutions to the thorny problem were eventually worked out.

Useful is in the closest meaning to this word.

A. practical   C. superficial

B. rectangular   D. competitive

❷ The sudden collapse of the bridge during the rush hour was the major cause of the severe _____ to the commuters and passers-by.

Damage is in the closest meaning to this word.

A. continuity   C. magnitude

B. illnesses   D. injuries

❸ Cathy had a hard time writing her thesis, for her professor requested that she should _____ her argument with more exact and innovative points of view.

Strengthen is in the closest meaning to this word.

A. reinforce   C. meditate

B. correspond   D. familiarize

❹ Luke _____ on the idea that people should protect rare and extinct animals, and he constantly sponsored campaigns of the kind.

Held is in the closest meaning to this word.

A. commenced   C. negotiated

B. fastened　　　　　D. ridiculed

❶ 腦力激盪的過程中，數種解決這個棘手問題的實用方案終於被激盪出來。

Useful 的意思最接近於這個字。

A. 實用的　　　　　C. 膚淺的

B. 矩形的　　　　　D. 競爭的

❷ 在交通尖峰期間，橋梁突然的倒塌是造成通勤族和行人嚴重傷害的主因。

Damage 的意思最接近於這個字。

A. 持續　　　　　　C. 強度

B. 疾病　　　　　　D. 傷害

❸ 凱西寫論文寫得很辛苦，因為她的教授要求她應該使用更確切且更創新的觀點來加強論證。

Strengthen 的意思最接近於這個字。

A. 加強　　　　　　C. 沉思

B. 通信　　　　　　D. 熟悉

❹ 路克堅持於人們應該保護稀有瀕臨絕種動物的想法，並且時常贊助此種類型的活動。

Held 的意思最接近於這個字。

A. 開始　　　　　　C. 協商

B. 堅持　　　　　　D. 揶揄

答案　❶ A　❷ D　❸ A　❹ B

The market for jeans is amazingly big. Statistic reviews showed that in 2005, US citizens spent over 15 billion US dollars on jeans and the number keeps going up.

牛仔褲的市場是驚人的大。統計評價顯示，2005 年，美國公民花費超過一千五百億美元在牛仔褲上，且其需求數量依然不斷上升。

North America accounts for 39% of global purchases for jeans, followed by Western Europe at 20%, Japan and Korea at 10% and the rest of the world at 31%.

北美佔全球牛仔褲購買率的 39%，其次是西歐為 20%，日本和韓國為 10%，其他國家總和為 31%。

Who would have thought that a pair of pants originally designed for work nowadays became a multi billion-dollar business!

誰曾想到，當初為工作用所設計褲子如今盡成為了數十億美元的生意！

Levi Strauss, born in Buttenheim, Germany on February 26, 1829 moved to the United States with his mother and two sisters when he was 18.

利維・斯特勞斯，於 1829 年 2 月 26 日出生於德國布滕漢姆。他與他的母親，及兩個姊姊在他 18 歲時移居到美國。

Joining his brothers Jonas and Louis who had already begun a wholesale dry goods business in New York City, Levi decided to open his dry goods wholesale business as Levi Strauss & Co. and imported fine dry goods such as clothing, bedding, combs from his brothers in New York.

後來他決定加入兩個哥哥喬納斯及路易斯的乾貨批發業務，於是在舊金山開啟了利維‧勞特勞斯公司，並從他紐約的哥哥那進口乾貨精品如衣服、床單、梳子等。

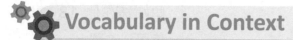

Vocabulary in Context

❺ The private art gallery, seemingly a building of small scale, had an _____ large collection of Oriental and Western paintings.

Surprisingly is in the closest meaning to this word.

A. eventually   C. inevitably

B. amazingly   D. automatically

❻ The company aimed at recruiting new staff members familiar with international trade and fluent with Japanese, since the Japanese market _____ for 40% of its revenue.

Occupied is in the closest meaning to this word.

A. prescribed   C. accounted

B. explored   D. restrained

❼ It's amazing that nowadays consumers can _____ almost anything through shopping websites on the Internet.

Buy is in the closest meaning to this word.

A. purchase   C. rehearse

B. adopt   D. coordinate

❽ Electronic products _____ from Japan have always received great welcome because they tend to be functional and durable.

Introduced is in the closest meaning to this word.

A. imported   C. appreciated

B. settled   D. vaccinated

❺ 這間私人經營的藝術畫廊，表面上似乎是座小規模的建築，卻有著驚人數量東西方畫作的收藏。

Surprisingly 的意思最接近於這個字。

A. 最終地　　　　　C. 無可避免地

B. 驚人地　　　　　D. 自動地

❻ 由於日本市場佔了公司收入的百分之四十，這家公司的目標是招募熟悉國際貿易以及精通日語的新職員。

Occupied 的意思最接近於這個字。

A. 開藥方　　　　　C. 佔…

B. 探索　　　　　　D. 限制

❼ 今日而言，消費者能夠透過網際網路的購物網站購買得到幾乎任何東西是很驚人的。

Buy 的意思最接近於這個字。

A. 購買　　　　　　C. 預演

B. 採用　　　　　　D. 協調

❽ 從日本進口的電子產品一向大受歡迎，因為他們的產品既實用又耐用。

Introduced 的意思最接近於這個字。

A. 進口　　　　　　C. 欣賞

B. 定居　　　　　　D. 接種疫苗

答案　❺ B　❻ C　❼ A　❽ A

Jacob Davids on the other hand was born in Riga, today Latvia, in 1831. During his time in Riga city, he was trained and worked as a tailor.

另一方面，雅各‧戴維斯在 1831 年出生於麗塔，也就是今天的拉脫維亞。他在麗塔市的期間被訓練作為一個裁縫師。

He emigrated from the Russian Empire to the United States when he was 23. He moved to San Francisco in 1856 and ran a tailor's shop there.

他 23 歲時從俄羅斯帝國移民到美國。他在 1856 年搬到了舊金山，並開了一間裁縫店。

In December 1870, Davis was asked by a customer to make a pair of strong working pants for her husband who was a woodcutter.

在 1870 年 12 月，一位客戶要戴維斯替她的丈夫做出一件堅固的工作褲給她的丈夫，因為她的丈夫是一位樵夫。

Davis was making these working pants in duck cotton and, as early as 1871, in denim cotton. Before long, he found he

早在 1871 年戴維斯便利用牛仔布做這些工作褲。不久，他發

could not keep up with demand.

現自己已經無法跟上需求的增長。

Realizing the potential value for his reinforced jeans concept, in 1872, he approached Levi Strauss, who was still his supplier of fabric, and asked for his financial backing in the filing of a patent application.

在瞭解他的加固牛仔褲概念的潛在價值後，1872 年時，他找了他的布料供應商利維斯，並請求他的財務協助以申請專利。

Strauss agreed, and on May 20. 1873, US Patent No. 139,121 for "Improvements in fastening pocket openings" was issued in the name of Jacob W. Davis and Levi Strauss and Company.

斯特勞斯同意了，並於 1873 年 5 月 20 日以雅各‧W‧戴維斯與利維－斯特勞斯公司的名義發佈美國專利號 139121 的「改善緊固口袋開口。」

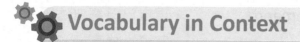

Vocabulary in Context

9 The Anderson family decided to _____ to Australia to try their luck and start a new life there.

Move is in the closest meaning to this word.

A. suspend   C. reconcile

B. qualify   D. emigrate

10 Kevin's doctor warned him of the fact that improper diet and living habits may pose _____ danger to his health.

Possible is in the closest meaning to this word.

A. appropriate   C. potential

B. discriminated   D. trustworthy

11 With the violent hurricane _____, residents were advised to take immediate precautions.

Advancing is in the closest meaning to this word.

A. vanishing   C. approaching

B. contrasting   D. renovating

12 The _____ of technology to our daily life enables us to live comfortably and joyfully.

Utilization is in the closest meaning to this word.

A. glamour   C. monotony

B. sophistication   D. application

❾ 安德森一家人決定移民到澳洲去謀求發展並試圖在那裡展開新生活。

Move 的意思最接近於這個字。

A. 懸掛　　　　　　　　C. 妥協

B. 合格　　　　　　　　D. 移民

❿ 凱文的醫生警告他不適當的飲食以及生活習慣可能對他的健康造成潛在的危險。

Possible 的意思最接近於這個字。

A. 適當的　　　　　　　C. 潛在的

B. 歧視的　　　　　　　D. 值得信賴的

⓫ 隨著猛烈颶風的逼近，居民被建議採取立即的預防措施。

Advancing 的意思最接近於這個字。

A. 消失　　　　　　　　C. 接近

B. 對照　　　　　　　　D. 整修

⓬ 把科技運用於我們的日常生活中促使我們能夠過著舒適及享受的生活。

Utilization 的意思最接近於這個字。

A. 魅力　　　　　　　　C. 單調

B. 世故　　　　　　　　D. 應用

答案　❾ D　❿ C　⓫ C　⓬ D

3-4　同反義詞表

同反義詞一覽表 Unit 3		
practical	實用的、實際的	同義詞 useful / utilitarian / pragmatic
	理論的、假設的	反義詞 theoretical / conjectural / hypothetical
injury	傷害、損傷	同義詞 harm / hurt / damage
	修理、修補	反義詞 repair / fix / mend
reinforce	加強、強化	同義詞 intensify / strengthen / fortify
	削弱、減少	反義詞 weaken / enfeeble / impair
fasten	繫緊、閂住	同義詞 secure / tie / hitch
	鬆開、解開	反義詞 loosen / slacken / undo
solution	解答、辦法	同義詞 resolution / answer / result
	疑問、問題	反義詞 question / query / inquiry
protection	保護、保存	同義詞 defense / shelter / preservation
	傷害、欺負	反義詞 hurt / bullying / humiliation
remain	仍然是、持續	同義詞 stay / persist / last
	枯萎、死去	反義詞 whither / expire / perish
amazingly	令人驚奇地	同義詞 surprisingly / fabulously / marvelously
	一般地	反義詞 normally / ordinarily / commonly
account	說明、佔...	同義詞 explain / state / occupy
	混淆、遮掩	反義詞 obscure / dim / conceal

purchase	購買、採購	同義詞 buy / shop / market
	賣出、銷售	反義詞 sell / vend / merchandise
import	進口、輸入	同義詞 inlet / introduce
	出口、輸出	反義詞 export / transport
nowadays	當今、現代	同義詞 today / now / presently
	昨日、過去	反義詞 yesterday / aforetime / past
join	連接、結合	同義詞 connect / combine / link
	分開、分離	反義詞 detach / divide / separate
emigrate	移居國外	同義詞 migrate / expatriate / move
	遷移、遷入	反義詞 immigrate / enter
potential	潛在的、可能的	同義詞 possible / likely / promising
	不可能發生的	反義詞 unlikely / implausible / impossible
approach	接近、要求	同義詞 advance / ask / offer
	疏遠、回應	反義詞 alienate / evade / respond
application	應用、申請	同義詞 use / utilization / petition
	摒棄、駁回	反義詞 discard / disallowance / rejection
realize	領悟、了解	同義詞 understand / comprehend / grasp
	曲解、困惑	反義詞 misunderstand / misconceive / confuse

1 飲食民生

2 歷史懷舊

3 現代化實用科技

4 資訊與知識傳遞

Unit 4 Peanut Butter 花生醬

4-1 日常飲食與製作過程

 MP3 10

Patented by Marcellus Gilmore Edson in 1884, peanut butter has been one of the most popular foods in the United States for over hundreds of years. According to peanutbutterlovers.com, each American eats three pounds of peanut butter every year which in total is enough to coat the floor of the Great Canyon!

由馬塞勒斯·吉爾摩·艾德森在 1884 年獲得專利後的幾百年來，花生醬一直是美國最流行的一種食品。根據 peanutbutterlovers.com 的數據，每個美國人一年要購買 3 磅的花生醬，總數來說，足以覆蓋整個大峽谷的表面！

As popular as it is, people not only use peanut butter as bread spread, but also use it in different kinds of dishes. American children love peanut butter so much that parents even spread it on vegetables such as celery or carrots to attract their kids to consume their daily vegetables.

花生醬是如此的受歡迎，以至於人們不僅用它來當麵包塗料，也將它利用在不同的菜餚。美國兒童非常喜歡花生醬，所以家長甚至把它塗在如芹菜或胡蘿蔔的蔬菜

Manufacturing peanut butter is rather simple. After inspection, peanut butter manufacturers roast the peanuts in special ovens. The third step is blanching, which removes the outer skin of the peanuts.

Finally, the peanuts will be ground to the desired smoothness, and add flavors such as salt by need. Because the step of process is relatively simple, the product today is remarkably similar to that produced a century ago.

上，以吸引他們的孩子食用他們的日常蔬菜。

花生醬的製作是相當簡單的。外觀檢查結束後，花生醬廠家會用特殊烤爐烘烤花生。第三個步驟是預煮，這個步驟會除去花生的外皮。

最後，花生將被研磨到期望的平滑度，並添加需要的香料，如鹽巴。由於製作過程相對簡單，今天的產品與一個世紀前的產品是非常類似的。

1 飲食民生

2 歷史懷舊

3 現代化實用科技

4 資訊與知識傳遞

Vocabulary in Context

❶ Irene had better watch out for those her gossip friends who may once in awhile _____ rumors about her.
Scatter is in the closest meaning to this word.

A. decorate   C. pacify

B. spread   D. experience

❷ At the present time, scientists spare no efforts to find resources of the alternative energy to substitute for the fossil fuels _____ by industry.
Exhausted is in the closest meaning to this word.

A. occurred   C. represented

B. consumed   D. prospered

❸ After most of its safety _____ failed to meet the standards, the mall was seriously penalized and had to make immediate improvement.
Examination is in the closest meaning to this word.

A. motivation   C. purification

B. inspections   D. concessions

❹ Compared with others, people tortured by depression _____ need more care and attention, for they don't easily reveal their emotional problems.
Comparatively is in the closest meaning to this word.

A. viciously   C. relatively

B. competently   D. punctually

❶ 艾琳最好要小心她那群偶爾會散播有關於她謠言的八卦朋友。

Scatter 的意思最接近於這個字。

A. 裝飾　　　　　　　C. 平和

B. 散播　　　　　　　D. 經歷

❷ 目前來説，科學家們不遺餘力地尋找替代能源的資源來取代工業所消耗的化石燃料。

Exhausted 的意思最接近於這個字。

A. 發生　　　　　　　C. 代表

B. 消耗　　　　　　　D. 繁榮

❸ 在大部分的安全檢驗無法符合標準之後，這個大賣場被嚴厲地處罰，並且必須做立即的改善。

Examination 的意思最接近於這個字。

A. 動機　　　　　　　C. 淨化

B. 檢查　　　　　　　D. 讓步

❹ 和一般人比較起來，為憂鬱症所苦的人相對地需要更多的關心和注意，因為他們不輕易地透露他們的情緒問題。

Comparatively 的意思最接近於這個字。

A. 邪惡地　　　　　　C. 相對地

B. 勝任地　　　　　　D. 準時地

 ❶ B　❷ B　❸ B　❹ C

Peanut butter is not only tasty but also great for your health. It contains multiple types of vitamins such as vitamin E and vitamin B6, which research shows can decrease the risk of heart disease, diabetes, and other chronic health conditions. Moreover, with 180 – 210 calories per serving, peanut butter also helps you lose weight.

It is because it has the enviable combination of fiber and protein that fills you up and keeps you from feeling hungry for longer. Not only tasty but also healthy, no wonder peanut butter remains one of the most popular food and keeps generating more fans over the years.

花生醬不僅味道好，也有益健康。它含有多種類型的維生素如維生素 E 和維生素 B6。研究表示可以減少心臟疾病、糖尿病和其他慢性健康狀況的風險。此外，每份 180 到 210 卡路里的熱量，花生醬還可以幫助你減肥。

這是因為它有令人羨慕的纖維和蛋白質的組合，不但填飽你，也延長你不感到飢餓的時間。不僅味道好，而且健康，難怪花生醬仍然是最受歡迎的食品之一，愛好者年年增加。

An American inventor, George Washington Carver, born in Missouri in 1860 was known for his research in crops such as peanuts, soybeans and sweet potatoes. He invented over 100 recipes from peanuts and also developed useful products including paints, gasoline and even plastic.

一位在 1860 年左右出生於密蘇里州的美國發明家喬治·華盛頓·卡爾弗因他在如花生、黃豆、番薯等作物的研究而著名。他發明了超過 100 個花生的食譜,並利用花生開發出實用的產品,包括油漆、汽油,甚至塑膠。

Because of his marvelous inventions with peanuts, he was often mistaken as the inventor of peanut butter. He might have used peanut butter in many of his recipes, but the first person to patent peanut butter in 1884 was Marcellus Gilmore Edson.

因為他利用花生所創造的巧妙發明,他經常被誤認為是花生醬的發明者。他也許在他的多項食譜內利用了花生醬,但第一個在 1884 年申請花生醬專利的是馬塞勒斯·吉爾摩·艾德森。

1 飲食民生

2 歷史懷舊

3 現代化實用科技

4 資訊與知識傳遞

Vocabulary in Context

❺ To keep healthy, one should be careful not to consume too much the food that _____ additives, such as preservatives, coloring, or artificial flavorings.

Includes is in the closest meaning to this word.

A. contains   C. huddles

B. digests   D. transforms

❻ The manager informed the factory that they might _____ or even cancel the original ordes if the goods shipped in continued to be in poor quality.

Reduce is in the closest meaning to this word.

A. resolve   C. withhold

B. approve   D. decrease

❼ To make both ends meet, Roy had no choice but to take several part-time jobs to _____ additional income.

Produce is in the closest meaning to this word.

A. despise   C. generate

B. supervise   D. overlook

❽ The magician's _____ performances attracted full attention of the audience and won him long and loud applause.

Wonderful is in the closest meaning to this word.

A. marvelous   C. reckless

B. exclusive   D. feasible

❺ 為了維持健康，人們應該小心不要吃太多含有添加物的食物，例如：防腐劑、色素，或者人工調味料。

Includes 的意思最接近於這個字。

A. 包含　　　　　　　C. 蜷縮

B. 消化　　　　　　　D. 轉變

❻ 經理通知工廠，假使進貨的商品仍舊品質不良的話，他們會減少或甚至取消原有的訂單。

Reduce 的意思最接近於這個字。

A. 下定決心　　　　　C. 阻擋

B. 贊同　　　　　　　D. 減少

❼ 為了收支均衡，羅伊不得不兼職數份兼差的工作來賺取額外的收入。

Produce 的意思最接近於這個字。

A. 鄙視　　　　　　　C. 產生

B. 監督　　　　　　　D. 忽略

❽ 魔術師奇妙的表演吸引全場觀眾的目光，並且為自己贏得許久響亮的喝采聲。

Wonderful 的意思最接近於這個字。

A. 奇妙的　　　　　　C. 粗率的

B. 獨家的　　　　　　D. 可行的

1 飲食民生

2 歷史懷舊

3 現代化實用科技

4 資訊與知識傳遞

答案　❺ A　❻ D　❼ C　❽ A

Marcellus Gilmore Edson was born on February 7th, 1849 in Montreal, Quebec, Canada. Working as a pharmacist, he often saw patients with chewing problems suffer from swallowing food. Therefore, Edson came up with the idea of peanut paste which can help people who couldn't chew well enjoy delicious food and get necessary nutrition at the same time.

馬塞勒斯·吉爾摩·艾德森於 1849 年 2 月 7 日出生於加拿大，魁北克的蒙特利爾。作為一個藥劑師，他常常會看到患者由於咀嚼問題而受吞嚥食物之苦。因此，艾德森有了花生糊的想法，它可以幫助不能咀嚼的人享受美味的食物並同時獲得必要的營養。

It might seem to be an easy thought to us now, but was a great invention back then. It was sold for six cents per pound and was very much liked by patients. He also added in sugar to change the consistency of peanut paste which became peanut candy.

這對我們來説似乎是一個簡單的想法，但在當時卻是一個偉大的發明。它當時的售價為每磅六毛錢，並非常受到患者的青睞。他還增添了糖來改變花生糊的黏稠度，便製成了花生糖。

Edson patented peanut butter and was issued with United States patent #306727(4) in 1884. This patent is based on the preparation of peanut paste which we call peanut butter these days.

艾德森申請了花生醬的專利，並在 1884 年拿到美國專利 #306727（4）。該專利的內容是關於花生糊的製作基礎，也就是我們今天所稱的花生醬。

Several other people patented similar products after Edson, including John Harvey Kellogg and George Bayle. Even peanut-butter-making machine was invented by Joseph Lambert. As simple as peanut butter is, what a smart invention Edson came up with over a century ago.

繼艾德森後尚有幾位人士申請類似的產品專利，包括約翰‧哈維‧凱洛格和喬治‧培爾。約瑟夫‧藍伯特甚至發明了花生醬製造機。如此簡單的花生醬，居然是由艾德森在一個世紀多以前想出來了。

1 飲食民生

2 歷史懷舊

3 現代化實用科技

4 資訊與知識傳遞

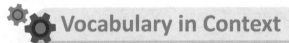 **Vocabulary in Context**

9 People who _____ from a migraine can relieve the pain effectively by all forms of relaxation, a lot of water-drinking, or keeping away from noises and bright lights.

Torture is in the closest meaning to this word.

A. guarantee   C. proceed

B. suffer   D. investigate

10 Mr. Cosby had a serious cold and coughed a lot; thus, he could hardly _____ anything because of the painful throat.

Gulp is in the closest meaning to this word.

A. fumble   C. swallow

B. console   D. nominate

11 The movie adapted from a novel was disappointing to the moviegoers because they could hardly find any _____ between the two.

Correspondence is in the closest meaning to this word.

A. insistence   C. integrity

B. metabolism   D. consistency

12 In my opinion, to settle the dispute, all you need to do is come out and clarify your stand on the controversial _____ __.

Problem is in the closest meaning to this word.

A. vacancy   C. revision

B. issue   D. diagnosis

❾ 罹患偏頭痛的人可以藉由各種放鬆的方式，喝大量的水，或遠離噪音及亮光來有效地紓緩疼痛。

Torture 的意思最接近於這個字。

A. 保證　　　　　　　C. 行進

B. 受苦　　　　　　　D. 調查

❿ 寇斯比先生由於嚴重的感冒加上咳嗽咳得厲害，以致於喉嚨疼痛而無法吞嚥任何東西。

Gulp 的意思最接近於這個字。

A. 摸索　　　　　　　C. 吞嚥

B. 安慰　　　　　　　D. 提名

⓫ 這部由小說改編的電影讓電影觀賞者感到失望，因為他們幾乎找不出兩者間情節相符之處。

Correspondence 的意思最接近於這個字。

A. 堅持　　　　　　　C. 廉潔

B. 新陳代謝　　　　　D. 一致性

⓬ 依我之見，為了解決紛爭，你所必須做的是出面並澄清你對於這個具有爭議性議題的立場。

Problem 的意思最接近於這個字。

A. 空缺　　　　　　　C. 修訂

B. 議題　　　　　　　D. 診斷

答案　❾ B　❿ C　⓫ D　⓬ B

4-4　同反義詞表

同反義詞一覽表 Unit 4		
spread	展開、散佈	同義詞 unfold / distribute / scatter
	摺疊、聚集	反義詞 fold / gather / assemble
consume	消耗、花費	同義詞 exhaust / deplete / spend
	生產、製造	反義詞 create / produce / manufacture
inspection	檢查、審視	同義詞 examination / investigation / scrutiny
	放任、忽視	反義詞 permissiveness / disregard / oversight
relatively	相當、相對地	同義詞 rather / comparably / comparatively
	絕對地、完全地	反義詞 absolutely / completely / totally
attract	吸引、引起	同義詞 tempt / fascinate / allure
	排斥、反感	反義詞 reject / repel / resent
remove	移動、去除	同義詞 withdraw / extract / eliminate
	固定、牢固	反義詞 fix / fasten / settle
contain	包含、容納	同義詞 hold / include / involve
	排除在外、排斥	反義詞 exclude / expel / reject
decrease	減少、減小	同義詞 reduce / lower / diminish
	增加、增大	反義詞 increase / enlarge / expand
generate	產生、創建	同義詞 produce / create / originate
	毀滅、破壞	反義詞 destroy / ruin / demolish

marvelous	驚奇的、非凡的	同義詞 wonderful / extraordinary / remarkable
	平凡的、普通的	反義詞 normal / ordinary / common
tasty	美味的、高雅的	同義詞 delicious / appetizing / tasteful
	無味的、粗俗的	反義詞 tasteless / unrefined / vulgar
inventor	發明家、創建者	同義詞 deviser / designer / originator
	破壞者、毀滅者	反義詞 spoiler / demolitionist / destroyer
suffer	忍受、折磨	同義詞 endure / tolerate / torture
	緩解、享受	反義詞 relieve / ease / enjoy
swallow	吞嚥、淹沒	同義詞 gulp / submerge / immerse
	吐出、浮現	反義詞 vomit / emerge / appear
consistency	一致、符合	同義詞 correspondence / uniformity / consonance
	不一致、矛盾	反義詞 incompatibility / contradiction / conflict
issue	問題、爭議	同義詞 problem / topic / inquiry
	結果、協議	反義詞 outcome / agreement / approval
delicious	美味的、好吃的	同義詞 tasty / appetizing / scrumptious
	無味的、難吃的	反義詞 tasteless / distasteful / unsavory
necessary	必要的、必須的	同義詞 required / compulsory / essential
	非必要、多餘的	反義詞 unnecessary / needless / redundant

Ketchup 蕃茄醬

 5-1 蕃茄醬的源由

Over 97% of households have a bottle of ketchup on their dinning tables in the U.S. As much as ketchup is being loved by Americans, the origins of ketchup was surprisingly not America. The name "ketchup" comes from a Chinese word which means fish sauce.

在美國，超過 **97**％的家庭會在餐桌上擺上一瓶蕃茄醬。蕃茄醬被美國人所熱愛，但令人驚訝的是蕃茄醬的起源並不是美國。「Ketchup」這個名字的由來是源自於一中國字，意指魚露。

In the late 17th and early 18th centuries, the British encountered ketchup, but it turned out to be a watery dark sauce which often added to soups, sauces and meats that was nothing like the ketchup today. It didn't even have the most important ingredient "tomato" in it.

在 17 世紀末和 18 世紀初，在英國發現了蕃茄醬，但它竟然是水狀的黑色醬汁，往往加入湯或醬汁或肉裡。和今天的蕃茄醬不同。它甚至沒有最重要的元素「蕃茄」在裡面。

The first tomato ketchup recipe was found in 1812 written by a scientist James Mease. The invention of ketchup was a huge success because the tomato growing season was short and preservation of tomato ketchups was challenging.

第一個蕃茄醬的配方是在 1812 年由科學家詹姆斯·米斯所寫的。蕃茄醬的發明是個偉大的成功，因為蕃茄生長期很短，維持蕃茄醬的新鮮是具有挑戰性的。

Some producers handled or stored the product poorly that ended up with contaminated sauce. To avoid problems like this and keep the beautiful red color, some unsafe levels of preservations such as sodium benzoate were added to the commercial ketchup, which later on were proven to be harmful to health.

一些生產商將產品的處理或貯存不當，造成了醬汁被污染的結果。為了避免這樣的問題並保持美麗的紅色，一些商業用的蕃茄醬在裡面加入了一些過量的防腐劑，如苯甲酸鈉，這後來被證明是有害健康的。

1 飲食民生

2 歷史懷舊

3 現代化實用科技

4 資訊與知識傳遞

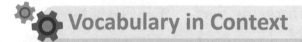 **Vocabulary in Context**

❶ After a long separation from each other since senior high, Julie had a surprising and pleasant _____ with Alex.

Meeting is in the closest meaning to this word.

A. machinery   C. reputation

B. encounter   D. assortment

❷ It is imperative that we humans put emphasis on ecological _____ and set up as many wildlife reserves as we can.

Protection is in the closest meaning to this word.

A. authority   C. tranquility

B. frustration   D. preservation

❸ As an optimistic and diligent college graduate, James is willing to explore a new working field and take up _____ tasks.

Confronting is in the closest meaning to this word.

A. challenging   C. prompt

B. stubborn   D. easy-going

❹ The world surrounding us is a seriously _____ one, and we must take precautions to cope with the global ecological crisis.

Polluted is in the closest meaning to this word.

A. released   C. contaminated

B. outdated   D. engaged

❶ 自從高中彼此分開一段長時間後，茱莉和艾力克斯有一次驚喜且愉快的邂逅。

Meeting 的意思最接近於這個字。

A. 機械　　　　　　　C. 名譽

B. 偶遇　　　　　　　D. 分類

❷ 我們人類現在急需要做的是重視生態保育並且盡可能多設置野生動物保護區。

Protection 的意思最接近於這個字。

A. 權威　　　　　　　C. 寧靜

B. 挫折　　　　　　　D. 保存

❸ 身為一名樂觀且勤奮的大學畢業生，詹姆斯很樂意去探索新的工作領域並承擔具挑戰性的任務。

Confronting 的意思最接近於這個字。

A. 挑戰的　　　　　　C. 快速的

B. 固執的　　　　　　D. 隨和的

❹ 環繞在我們周遭的是一個嚴重污染的世界，我們必須採取預防措施來對抗全球的生態危機。

Polluted 的意思最接近於這個字。

A. 釋放的　　　　　　C. 汙染的

B. 過時的　　　　　　D. 忙於…的

答案　❶ B　❷ D　❸ A　❹ C

飲食民生 **1**

歷史懷舊 **2**

現代化實用科技 **3**

資訊與知識傳遞 **4**

In 1876, Henry J. Heinz started to produce ketchup without chemicals. He developed a recipe that used ripe, red tomatoes which have more of the natural preservative. He also increased the amount of vinegar to reduce risk of spoilage.

1876 年，亨利・亨氏開始生產無化學物質的蕃茄醬。他開發了一個食譜，利用成熟並更具有自然防腐效果的紅蕃茄。他也增加醋的用量，減少腐敗變質的風險。

By producing the chemical free ketchup, Heinz had sold 5 million bottles of ketchup in 1905 which dominated the market. Having dominated the ketchup market and brought his business to success at the age of 61, Henry Heinz was a talented businessman who was born in Pittsburgh, Pennsylvania on October 11, 1844.

通過生產無化學製品的蕃茄醬，亨氏曾在 1905 年主導市場並銷售了 500 萬瓶蕃茄醬。主導蕃茄醬市場並在他 61 歲時帶來了他企業的成功，亨利・亨氏是在 1844 年 10 月 11 日出生在賓州匹茲堡的一位天才商人。

When Heinz was a child, he already found his way to sell vegetables and

當亨氏還是個孩子時，他已經找到了自

bottled horseradish at his family's garden.

己的方式，在他家的花園裡銷售蔬菜及瓶裝辣根。

Even though he was young, he already knew the key to a successful business is to create differences to produce the high quality products.

儘管他很年輕，他已經知道成功的關鍵。一個成功的企業是在於創造出差異性及生產高品質的產品。

Therefore, while he was selling prepared horseradish at his teenage years, in order to increase sales, he stood out by using clear glass containers and allowed the customers to see the quality of his products.

因此，在他銷售辣根的少年歲月時，為了增加銷量，他利用透明的玻璃容器讓客戶看到自己產品的品質。

1 飲食民生

2 歷史懷舊

3 現代化實用科技

4 資訊與知識傳遞

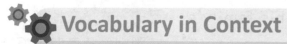

Vocabulary in Context

5 Scientists are _____ robots with multiple functions to provide services that can meet varied needs of all the users.

Producing is in the closest meaning to this word.

A. developing   C. hallmarking

B. objecting   D. perishing

6 The applicant's additional language skills and working experience definitely _____ the chance of being employed.

Add is in the closest meaning to this word.

A. abbreviate   C. occupy

B. increase   D. withstand

7 To _____ the risk of clogged arteries and heart attacks, one had better get away from trans fats, which may cause the rise of cholesterol in the blood.

Decrease is in the closest meaning to this word.

A. reduce   C. conclude

B. accumulate   D. utilize

8 Jason's bossy character and his wish to _____ over others make him the least popular person among all.

Control is in the closest meaning to this word.

A. dominate   C. prevent

B. accommodate   D. segregate

⑤ 科學家正在研發具多重功用的機器人以提供服務來滿足所有使用者各種不同的需求。

Producing 的意思最接近於這個字。

A. 發展　　　　　C. 標記

B. 反對　　　　　D. 滅亡

⑥ 這名應徵者額外的語言技能和工作經驗必定可以使他增加被僱用的機會。

Add 的意思最接近於這個字。

A. 縮寫　　　　　C. 佔據

B. 增加　　　　　D. 抵抗

⑦ 為了降低動脈堵塞及心臟病發生的風險，人們最好遠離會導致血液中膽固醇提高的反式脂肪。

Decrease 的意思最接近於這個字。

A. 減少　　　　　C. 下結論

B. 累積　　　　　D. 利用

⑧ 傑森愛指使人的個性以及總是喜歡控制別人的作風，使他成為所有人當中最不受歡迎的一個。

Control 的意思最接近於這個字。

A. 統治　　　　　C. 預防

B. 容納　　　　　D. 隔離

答案　⑤ A　⑥ B　⑦ A　⑧ A

1 飲食民生

2 歷史懷舊

3 現代化實用科技

4 資訊與知識傳遞

At the age of 25, Heinz formed his first company to sell bottled horseradish. The products were popular; however, due to the repercussions of a financial panic, the business failed. Heinz had no choice but to declare bankruptcy in 1875.

在 25 歲的時候,亨氏開了他的第一家公司,銷售桶裝辣根。該產品很受歡迎。然而,由於金融恐慌的影響,生意失敗。亨氏只好在 1875 年宣布破產。

A year later, he became the manager of F&J Heinz. By law, he was not allowed to start another business because of his financial problems, but in reality, Heinz was the owner of F&J Heinz. It was the same year that ketchup was added to the product line.

一年後,他成為了 F&J 亨氏的經理。根據法律規定,因為他的財務問題,他無法開公司,但在現實生活中,亨氏其實是 F&J 亨氏的所有者。就在同一年,番茄醬加入到該產品線。

Two years later, after his bankruptcy obligations were discharged, Heinz again changed the company name to the H.J. Heinz Company. In 1905, Heinz

2 年後,在他破產義務結束後,亨氏再次改變公司名稱為亨氏公司。1905 年,亨

became the president of the Heinz Corporation. In 1906, the Pure Food and Drug Act occurred and many food manufacturers were affected.

氏成為亨氏公司的總裁。1906 年，純食品和藥品法開跑，許多食品製造商因此被影響。

However, because of Heinz's advocacy of its passage, his sales were increasing.

但是，由於亨氏公司倡導的行銷方式促使他的銷量呈逐年上升。

Heinz passed away in 1919 and left behind a business with more than 6,500 employees and 25 factories. His products now are still being sold around the world.

亨氏去世於 1919 年，留下一個擁有超過 6500 名員工和 25 家工廠的企業。現在他的產品仍然被銷往世界各地。

Vocabulary in Context

9 Due to the continuous bad selling condition, the company _____ that a certain percentage of the staff members had to be laid off.

Announced is in the closest meaning to this word.

A. cultivated   C. declared

B. migrated   D. submitted

10 The poor financial management of Mr. Smith's enterprise was responsible for his unfortunate _____ in the end.

Failure is in the closest meaning to this word.

A. achievement   C. innocence

B. recommendation   D. bankruptcy

11 It's essential for every global villager to keep it in mind that we all should undertake the _____ to protect the environment for our future generations.

Duty is in the closest meaning to this word.

A. structure   C. hospitality

B. obligation   D. irrigation

11 Dr. Martin Luther King Jr.'s _____ of non-violence in struggling against racial discrimination and segregation won him the utmost respect from the world.

Maintenance is in the closest meaning to this word.

A. shortcoming   C. probation

B. opportunity   D. advocacy

❾ 由於不良的銷售狀況持續地發生，這家公司宣佈特定比例的職員必須被裁員。

Announced 的意思最接近於這個字。

A. 培養   C. 宣佈

B. 遷徙   D. 投降

❿ 企業不良的財政營運狀況導致史密斯先生最終不幸面臨破產。

Failure 的意思最接近於這個字。

A. 成就   C. 無辜

B. 推薦   D. 破產

⓫ 每位地球村的居民必定要謹記在心：我們都應該為後代子孫承擔起保護環境的義務。

Duty 的意思最接近於這個字。

A. 結構   C. 好客

B. 義務   D. 灌溉

⓬ 馬丁・路德・金恩博士在對抗種族歧視和隔離政策所倡導非暴力的方式為他贏得世人最崇高的敬意。

Maintenance 的意思最接近於這個字。

A. 缺點   C. 緩刑

B. 機會   D. 倡導

1 飲食民生

2 歷史懷舊

3 現代化實用科技

4 資訊與知識傳遞

答案　❾ C　❿ D　⓫ B　⓬ D

同反義詞一覽表　Unit 5		
encounter	遭遇、遇到	同義詞 confront / collide / meet
	逃避、擺脫	反義詞 flee / evade / escape
preservation	保護、保存	同義詞 protection / maintenance / conservation
	丟棄、遺棄	反義詞 rid / discard / desert
challenging	挑戰的、質疑的	同義詞 daring / confronting / questionable
	安穩的、贊同的	反義詞 safe / secure / approving
contaminate	汙染、弄髒	同義詞 pollute / defile / stain
	清潔、淨化	反義詞 clean / purify / purge
origin	起源、根源	同義詞 beginning / birth / root
	結果、結束	反義詞 result / end / conclusion
avoid	避免、躲開	同義詞 escape / evade / shun
	面對、接近	反義詞 face / confront / approach
develop	發展、進步	同義詞 produce / flourish / progress
	衰敗、衰退	反義詞 decay / fail / decline
increase	增加、增強	同義詞 add / raise / strengthen
	減少、減弱	反義詞 decrease / diminish / weaken
reduce	減少、降低	同義詞 lessen / slump / lower
	增加、增大	反義詞 increase / elevate / enlarge
dominate	支配、統治	同義詞 control / rule / govern
	隸屬、服從	反義詞 subordinate / submit / obey

ripe	成熟的、圓滑的	同義詞 developed / ready / mellow
	不成熟、無經驗	反義詞 raw / immature / inexperienced
talented	有才能、天才的	同義詞 gifted / skillful / capable
	缺乏才能的	反義詞 untalented / clumsy / incompetent
declare	宣佈、宣告	同義詞 announce / state / proclaim
	隱瞞、隱藏	反義詞 conceal / hide / cover
bankruptcy	破產、失敗	同義詞 breakdown / loss / failure
	獲利、成功	反義詞 gain / profit / success
obligation	義務、責任	同義詞 duty / compulsion / responsibility
	選擇、自願	反義詞 option / discretion / voluntariness
advocacy	提倡、擁護	同義詞 maintenance / support / upholding
	反對、對立	反義詞 opposition / disapproval / confrontation
panic	恐慌、驚慌	同義詞 fear / scare / terror
	鎮定、平靜	反義詞 calm / peace / stillness
allow	允許、同意	同義詞 consent / permit / agree
	禁止、阻礙	反義詞 prohibit / forbid / bar

1 飲食民生

2 歷史懷舊

3 現代化實用科技

4 資訊與知識傳遞

Unit 6

Disposable Diapers 紙尿布

6-1 尿布的發展

The diaper, one of the very first items that distinguished human from animals, was found being used from the Egyptians to the Romans. Though back then, people were using animal skins, leaf wraps, and other natural resources instead of the disposable diapers as we know today. The cotton "diaper like" progenitor was worn by the European and the American infants by the late 1800's.

尿布是最早區分人類與動物的項目之一。從埃及人到羅馬人都有被發現使用尿布。雖然當時人們用獸皮、樹葉和其他自然資源包裹，與我們現今所知的紙尿布有所不同。尿布的前身在 1800 年底被歐洲及美國的嬰兒所穿著。

The shape of the progenitor was similar to the modern diaper but was held in place with safety pins. Back then, people were not aware of bacteria and viruses. Therefore, diapers were reused after drying in the sun. It was not until the beginning of the 20th century that people started to use boiled water in order to reduce common rash problems.

尿布前身的形狀設計非常類似現今的尿布，但卻是使用安全別針。 那時，人們還沒有細菌和病毒的意識。因此，尿布曬乾後便再被重複使用。直到 20 世紀初，人們開始使用開水（燙

However, due to World War II, cotton became a strategic material, so the disposable absorbent pad used as a diaper was created in Sweden in 1942. In 1946, Marion Donovan, a typical housewife from the United States invented a waterproof covering for diapers, called the "Boater." The model of the disposable diaper was made from a shower curtain.

Back then, disposable diapers were only used for special occasions such as vacations because it was considered a "luxury item." Though, the quality of the disposable diaper was not that good. The total capacity of these diapers was estimated to be around 100ml, which means it was only for one-time use.

尿布），這才減少了常見的皮疹問題。

但由於第二次世界大戰，棉花成為了戰略物資，因此，拋棄式的尿布墊於 1942 年在瑞典被製作出來。1946 年，瑪麗安·唐納文，一位來自美國的典型家庭主婦發明了一種防水的尿布，她稱之為「船工」。她利用浴簾製作了紙尿布的模型。

當時，紙尿布由於是被認為是奢侈品，因此只有特殊場合，如休假，可以使用它。但是當時紙尿布的品質並不好。這些尿布的總容量估計約為100ml 以下，這意味著它只能使用一輪。

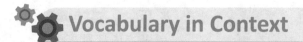

Vocabulary in Context

❶ Jeremy Lin _____ himself as a humble and prominent Asian American NBA player.

Differentiates is in the closest meaning to this word.

A. laments   C. installs

B. distinguishes   D. tolerates

❷ To reduce the impact of global warming on humans, researches and scientists all over the world are developing alternative energy _____.

Assets is in the closest meaning to this word.

A. equipment   C. prosecution

B. resources   D. assurances

❸ The reckless truck driver, talking on the cell phone while driving, wasn't _____ of the approaching car and got crashed.

Conscious is in the closest meaning to this word.

A. iconic   C. aware

B. silent   D. complacent

❹ All those present were bothered by the intruder, who both inappropriately dressed himself and rudely behaved on the solemn _____.

Circumstance is in the closest meaning to this word.

A. calamity   C. occasion

B. suburb   D. moderation

① 林書豪以身為一名謙遜且傑出的美籍亞裔NBA球員獨樹一格。

Differentiates 的意思最接近於這個字。

A. 哀嘆　　　　　　　　C. 安裝

B. 顯出特色　　　　　　D. 忍受

② 為了要減少全球暖化對人類所造成的衝擊，世界各地的研究學者和科學家正在研發替代能源。

Assets 的意思最接近於這個字。

A. 設備　　　　　　　　C. 起訴

B. 資源　　　　　　　　D. 保證

③ 這位粗心的卡車司機邊開車邊講手機，沒有意識到前來的車輛而撞車。

Conscious 的意思最接近於這個字。

A. 圖像的　　　　　　　C. 有意識的

B. 沉默的　　　　　　　D. 自滿的

④ 所有出席這個莊重場合的人皆受到這位穿著不合宜且行為粗魯的入侵者的干擾。

Circumstance 的意思最接近於這個字。

A. 災難　　　　　　　　C. 場合

B. 郊區　　　　　　　　D. 適度

答案　① B　② B　③ C　④ C

The well known disposable diaper brand "Pampers" was created by the Procter and Gamble company in 1961. The development of the new disposable diaper was a great hit, and when the baby boom started at the 70's, the world demand exceeded the production capacity.

眾所周知的紙尿布品牌「幫寶適」是由寶潔公司在 1961 年創造的。這個新紙尿布的發展大獲成功。開始於 70 年代的嬰兒潮使得全球的需求量超過生產能力。

Marion Donovan, born in a family where her father and brother were both inventors, it would be hard for her not to have the inventive spirit.

瑪麗安・唐納文，出生在一個爸爸與哥哥都是發明家的家庭中，她很難不具備創新的精神。

During World War II, as a housewife and a mother of two, Donovan used her creative mind on many things to help herself with her busy life.

在第二次世界大戰期間，作為一個家庭主婦和兩個孩子的母親，唐納文在很多事情上利用她的創意思維，以幫助自己忙碌的生活。

In order to ease her job from repetitively changing her children's cloth diapers, bed sheets and clothing, she came up with the idea of the diaper cover.

為了緩解重複更換孩子們的布尿布、床單和衣服的工作,她有了尿布罩的想法。

She used the shower curtain and successfully created a waterproof diaper cover. She also added the snap fasteners to replace the safety pins to reduce the possibility of careless injuries.

她利用浴簾,成功打造了防水尿布罩。她還添加了按扣來取代安全別針,以減少許多不小心受傷的可能性。

1 飲食民生

2 歷史懷舊

3 現代化實用科技

4 資訊與知識傳遞

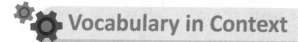

Vocabulary in Context

⑤ To fill the growing _____ for their merchandise, the workers of the factory were required to work overtime.

Need is in the closest meaning to this word.

A. discount   C. demand

B. notification   D. nomination

⑥ Though careful with the budget, with the soaring high living costs, Michael's expenses invariably _____ his income every month.

Surpassed is in the closest meaning to this word.

A. exceeded   C. conquered

B. subsidized   D. immigrated

⑦ Alexander Bell had a highly _____ mind. After making many yearsof experiments, in 1876, his "talking machine," the telephone, finally came out and changed people's lives.

Creative is in the closest meaning to this word.

A. cooperative   C. inventive

B. disastrous   D. reliable

⑧ Although Tom was the best player of the team, Coach Miller had to _____ him with another player because of his serious knee injury.

Substitute is in the closest meaning to this word.

A. predict   C. litter

B. replace   D. conflict

❺為了要應付他們商品數量逐漸增加的需求，工廠員工被要求加班。

Need 的意思最接近於這個字。

A. 打折   C. 需求

B. 通知   D. 提名

❻雖然小心翼翼地做預算，但隨著生活費用的高升，麥可每個月必定入不敷出。

Surpassed 的意思最接近於這個字。

A. 超過   C. 征服

B. 補助   D. 遷入

❼亞歷山大‧貝爾擁有高度發明的創意。經過多年實驗之後，在1876年，他那部"會講話的機器"，也就是電話，終於問世並且改變了人類的生活。

Creative 的意思最接近於這個字。

A. 合作的   C. 發明的

B. 毀滅的   D. 可靠的

❽儘管湯姆是球隊中最好的球員，由於他的膝蓋嚴重受傷，米勒教練不得不以另一名球員取代他。

Substitute 的意思最接近於這個字。

A. 預測   C. 亂丟

B. 取代   D. 衝突

1 飲食民生

2 歷史懷舊

3 現代化實用科技

4 資訊與知識傳遞

答案 ❺ C ❻ A ❼ C ❽ B

Even though her invention was brilliant, no manufacturers bought the idea. Donovan had no choice but to start the production herself.

儘管她的發明是聰穎的，沒有廠家同意她的想法。唐納文只好開始自己生產。

The product debuted at Saks Fifth Avenue in 1949. She also applied for a patent for it and received the patent in 1951.

她的產品於 1949 年首次在薩克斯第五大道（百貨公司）亮相。她同時申請了專利，並在 1951 年獲得專利。

She then started her invention of a fully disposable diaper. She had to recreate a type of paper that was not only strong and absorbent, but also conveyed water away from the baby's skin. Her creation was a great success but no one saw the demand back then.

爾後，她開始了紙尿布發明。她必須重新創造一個類型的紙張不僅強韌，吸水性強，而且還能使水遠離寶寶的皮膚的紙。她的創作是一個偉大的成功，但當時沒有人看見需求。

People thought it was superfluous and impractical. It was not until 1961 when Pampers was created did the disposable diaper become a hit item.

Throughout her extraordinary life, Donovan explored numerous ventures besides diapers. She had a total of 20 patents and also received an Architecture degree from Yale University in 1958.

人們認為這是多餘的，不切實際的。直到 1961 年，幫寶適的創建成為了紙尿布一炮走紅的原因。

在她不平凡的一生中，唐納文探索尿布以外的眾多冒險。她一共擁有 20 項專利，並於 1958 年獲得了耶魯大學的建築學學位。

1 飲食民生

2 歷史懷舊

3 現代化實用科技

4 資訊與知識傳遞

Vocabulary in Context

❾ On Christmas, every household decorates their Christmas trees and the house will be _____ with the twinkling lights, adding warmth and joy to the atmosphere.

Bright is in the closest meaning to this word.

A. confident   C. brilliant

B. stressful   D. panoramic

❿ As soon as the renowned company posted an advertisement of a position for a manager, a large number of qualified jobseekers _____ for the job.

Administered is in the closest meaning to this word.

A. applied   C. monitored

B. disobeyed   D. transferred

⓫ In different countries, all kinds of hand gestures _____ varied hints; thus, to avoid offending others, tourists had better look into them first.

Express is in the closest meaning to this word.

A. admire   C. convey

B. stimulate   D. reconfirm

⓬ It still remains a mystery that just how certain people possessing the special ability to generate electricity should have the _____ power.

Unusual is in the closest meaning to this word.

A. harmful   C. classical

B. unemployed　　　D. extraordinary

❾ 耶誕節時，每個家庭裝飾耶誕樹，房子因閃閃發亮的燈飾而明亮，增添了溫馨歡樂的氣氛。

Bright 的意思最接近於這個字。

A. 自信的　　　　　C. 明亮的

B. 有壓力的　　　　D. 全景的

❿ 這間聲譽卓越的公司一張貼徵求經理職位的廣告，大批符合資格的求職者前來申請這個工作。

Administered 的意思最接近於這個字。

A. 申請　　　　　　C. 監督

B. 反抗　　　　　　D. 移轉

⓫ 在不同的國家中，各種手勢傳達不同的暗示；因此，為了避免冒犯他人，觀光客最好事先做了解。

Express 的意思最接近於這個字。

A. 仰慕　　　　　　C. 傳達

B. 刺激　　　　　　D. 再確定

⓬ 某些擁有產生電力能力的人士究竟是如何能夠具有此特殊的本領依舊是一個謎。

Unusual 的意思最接近於這個字。

A. 傷害的　　　　　C. 經典的

B. 失業的　　　　　D. 非凡的

答案　❾ C　❿ A　⓫ C　⓬ D

6-4　同反義詞表

同反義詞一覽表 Unit 6		
distinguish	區分、辨別	同義詞 discern / separate / differentiate
	相近、一致	反義詞 resemble / conform / correspond
resource	資源、財力	同義詞 asset / possession / wealth
	貧困、缺乏	反義詞 scarcity / deficiency / shortage
aware	察覺的、知道的	同義詞 conscious / knowing / sensible
	未察覺、無知的	反義詞 unaware / unconscious / ignorant
occasion	活動、時機	同義詞 circumstance / chance / opportunity
	未必發生、困境	反義詞 improbability / adversity / dilemma
progenitor	祖先、先驅	同義詞 ancestor / ascendant / forerunner
	後裔、後代	反義詞 offspring / posterity / descendant
infant	嬰兒、幼兒	同義詞 baby / newborn / toddler
	成年人、大人	反義詞 adult / grownup
luxury	奢侈、奢華	同義詞 sumptuousness / affluence / lavishness
	貧乏、寒酸	反義詞 poorness / impoverishment / shabbiness
demand	需求、要求	同義詞 need / require / request
	提供、給予	反義詞 furnish / provide / supply

exceed	勝過、優於	同義詞 surpass / better / excel
	不足、劣於	反義詞 lack / deteriorate / worsen
inventive	發明的、創造的	同義詞 creative / imaginative / ingenious
	模仿的、模擬的	反義詞 imitative / mimic / mock
replace	取代、替代	同義詞 substitute / switch / exchange
	固定、穩定	反義詞 fix / settle / stabilize
possibility	可能性	同義詞 probability / potentiality / likelihood
	不能、無法實施	反義詞 impossibility / unlikelihood / infeasibility
careless	粗心的、草率的	同義詞 reckless / unmindful / heedless
	仔細的、小心的	反義詞 careful / thoughtful / cautious
brilliant	明亮的、聰慧的	同義詞 bright / smart / intelligent
	暗淡的、遲鈍的	反義詞 dull / foolish / stupid
apply	應用、申請	同義詞 administer / request / petition
	回答、回應	反義詞 answer / reply / respond
convey	傳達、運送	同義詞 express / communicate / deliver
	接收、得到	反義詞 accept / receive / obtain
extraordinary	特別的、非凡的	同義詞 exceptional / unusual / remarkable
	普通的、一般的	反義詞 normal / ordinary / average
impractical	不切實際的	同義詞 unfeasible / unrealistic / unworkable
	實用的、實際的	反義詞 functional / pragmatic / practical

1 飲食民生

2 歷史懷舊

3 現代化實用科技

4 資訊與知識傳遞

Unit 7 Light Bulb 燈泡

 7-1   燈泡的發展　　　　MP3 19

If you think that Thomas Edison invented the first light bulb, you are technically wrong. There were several people invented the light bulb, but Thomas Edison mostly got credited for it because he was the person who created the first practical light bulb that is available for the general public.

如果你認為愛迪生發明第一個燈泡，嚴格上來說你是錯誤的。世上有幾個人發明了電燈泡，但湯瑪斯‧愛迪生得到大部分的榮耀，因為他創造了第一個可用於一般大眾的實用電燈泡。

76 years before Thomas Edison filed the pattern application for "Improvement in Electric Lights", Humphrey Davy invented an electric battery. When he connected wires to the battery and a piece of carbon, the carbon glowed. That was the first electric light ever invented.

早在湯瑪斯‧愛迪生提出「電燈的改善」專利的 76 年之前，漢弗萊‧戴維發明了電池。當他連接了導線、電池與一塊碳，碳發光了。這是首個電燈的發明。

Though it was not ready for the general use because the light didn't last long enough, and it was too bright for practical use.

不過，由於無法長時間維持光亮，且光線太亮，所以這個發明還沒準備好被實際應用。

Years after, several other inventors tried to create light bulbs but no practical products were created. It was even made with platinum which the cost of platinum made it impractical for commercial use.

幾年後，其他幾個發明家也試圖創造燈泡，但沒有實用的產品被創作出來。有人甚至提出用鉑作為材料，但鉑金的成本無法作為商業用途。

Vocabulary in Context

❶ When writing his doctoral thesis, Frank made good use of the _____ facilities in the school library and finally got graduated with honors.

Obtainable is in the closest meaning to this word.

A. chaotic   C. religious

B. available   D. paradoxical

❷ In _____, when asking someone for help while you travel in Europe, you may speak English. However, the local people will be much pleasant if you ask in their language.

Common is in the closest meaning to this word.

A. general   C. advance

B. memory   D. circulation

❸ We are fortunate to live in an era of convenience and information. Through the far-reaching Internet, we can easily get _____ with the world.

Linked is in the closest meaning to this word.

A. connected   C. submerged

B. delayed   D. organized

❹ Online shoppers always find themselves get attracted by the dazzling _____ advertisements and increase the unnecessary spending.

Mercantile is in the closest meaning to this word.

A. vulnerable   C. commercial

B. idiomatic　　　　　　　D. reluctant

❶ 法蘭克在寫博士論文時，善用學校圖書館裡可利用的設備，並在最後以優異的成績畢業。

Obtainable 的意思最接近於這個字。

A. 混亂的　　　　　　　　C. 宗教的

B. 可利用的　　　　　　　D. 自相矛盾的

❷ 一般而言，在歐洲旅遊時，你可以使用英語向他人請求幫助。然而，假使你使用他們的語言，當地人會更樂於提供協助。

Common 的意思最接近於這個字。

A. 一般　　　　　　　　　C. 預先

B. 記憶　　　　　　　　　D. 循環

❸ 我們很幸運地生活在一個資訊便利的時代。經由無遠弗屆的網際網路，我們可以很輕易地和世界接軌。

Linked 的意思最接近於這個字。

A. 連結的　　　　　　　　C. 淹沒的

B. 延遲的　　　　　　　　D. 組織的

❹ 線上購物者發現自己經常會被炫目的商業廣告所吸引而增加不必要的消費。

Mercantile 的意思最接近於這個字。

A. 易受傷的　　　　　　　C. 商業的

B. 慣用語的　　　　　　　D. 不情願的

答案　❶ B　❷ A　❸ A　❹ C

During the next 50 years, many inventors did different prototype of light bulbs but could not produce enough lifetime to be considered an effective product.

在接下來的 50 年中,許多發明人進行了不同原型的燈泡,但還是無法創造出足夠壽命的有效產品。

Until 1874, Canadian inventors Henry Woodward and Mathew Evans built different sizes and shapes of carbon rods held between electrodes in glass cylinders filled with nitrogen. It was the basic design of a light bulb.

直到 1874 年,加拿大發明家亨利·伍德沃德和馬修·埃文斯以不同尺寸及形狀的電極放在碳棒之間並放入充入氮氣的玻璃瓶中。這完成了一個燈泡的基本設計。

Interestingly, Thomas Edison started his research into developing a practical incandescent lamp at the same period of time. In 1879, he bought the pattern from Woodward and Evans and continued to improve upon his original design.

有趣的是,湯瑪斯·愛迪生也在相同的時間開始自己研發實用的白熾燈。愛迪生在 1878 年申請了第一個專利申請「電燈的改善」。在 1879 年,他買了伍德沃德和埃文斯的專利，並不斷改善他的原始設計。

Edison and his team discovered that a carbonized bamboo filament would last over 1200 hours.

愛迪生和他的研究小組發現，碳化竹絲可以持續壽命超過 1200 小時。

In 1880, Edison's company Edison Electric Light Company manufactured light bulbs commercially. The man that acquired a record number of 1,093 patents, Thomas Edison is mostly known for the invention of the light blub.

1880 年，愛迪生的公司：愛迪生電燈公司開始生產商用燈泡。擁有 1093 項專利的人，湯馬斯·愛迪生大多是因燈泡的發明而聞名。

1 飲食民生

2 歷史懷舊

3 現代化實用科技

4 資訊與知識傳遞

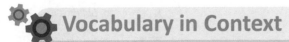

⑤ Though the Dutch painter, Vincent Van Gogh, had a miserable life all his life, he was _____ of as one of the most talented and the most influential artists in the world.
Thought is in the closest meaning to this word.

A. dismissed   C. considered

B. reflected   D. nurtured

⑥ According to medical researches, nuts are very _____ at lowering cholesterol levels and preventing heart and blood vessel diseases.
Effectual is in the closest meaning to this word.

A. redundant   C. compassionate

B. nimble   D. effective

⑦ DNA was _____ by a German scientist, Friedrich Miescher, in 1869. From the information in DNA, a lot about a human's family, health, and personality can be revealed.
Found is in the closest meaning to this word.

A. discovered   C. notified

B. preferred   D. interviewed

⑧ Pablo Picasso, probably the most important painter of the 20ᵗʰ century, _____ an enviable reputation for his outstanding artistic ability.
Obtained is in the closest meaning to this word.

A. compensated   C. acquired

B. forbade   D. subordinated

❺ 雖然荷蘭畫家，文森・梵谷，這一生命運多舛，他仍被視為全世界最具天分且最具影響力的藝術家之一。

Thought 的意思最接近於這個字。

A. 解散   C. 認為

B. 反射   D. 養育

❻ 根據醫學研究，堅果在降低膽固醇以及預防心血管疾病方面非常有效果。

Effectual 的意思最接近於這個字。

A. 多餘的   C. 同情的

B. 敏捷的   D. 有效的

❼ DNA是由德國科學家，弗雷德里希・米歇爾，在1869年所發現的。從DNA所呈現的訊息，可以充分了解一個人的家族血緣、健康狀況，以及人格特質。

Found 的意思最接近於這個字。

A. 發現   C. 通知

B. 寧願   D. 面試

❽ 巴布羅・畢卡索可說是20世紀最重要的畫家，他以他傑出的藝術才能獲得令人仰慕的聲譽。

Obtained 的意思最接近於這個字。

A. 賠償   C. 獲得

B. 禁止   D. 居次要地位

 答案 ❺ C ❻ D ❼ A ❽ C

He was mostly home schooled. During his home school years, he was working part time on the railroad between Detroit and Port Huron, Michigan, where his family then lived. His overtly enthusiasm for science once almost led to an explosion accident in the train, and he was fired.

愛迪生主要是在家裡接受教育。在他的家校歲月裡，他在密西根州的底特律和休倫港間的鐵路兼職，這時他的家人正住在那裡。因為他顯然對科學的熱衷，他有一次差點炸毀了整個車廂。他因此被解僱。

Edison was working as a telegrapher and traveled around the country during the Civil War. Edison had developed hearing problems later on, so he began to invent devices that would help make things possible despite his deafness. In 1869, he quit the telegraph and started to pursue invention full time.

愛迪生在內戰期間是一位電報員，他旅行於全國各地。愛迪生有了聽力問題以後，他便開始發明可以幫助即使是耳聾的他也可工作的設備。1869年，他放棄了電報，並開始全職於他的發明事業。

In 1878, Edison focused on inventing a safe, inexpensive electric light. He set up the Edison Electric Light Company and began research and development.

1878 年，愛迪生專注於發明一種安全，廉價的電燈。他成立了愛迪生電燈公司，並開始研究和開發。

In 1880, the company found out that carbonized bamboo can be a viable alternative for the filament, which proved to be the key to a long-lasting light bulb.

1880 年，該公司發現了炭化竹可以為長絲，這是讓長效燈泡變可能的一個關鍵。

In 1881, the light bulb became available to the public. Edison also created the world's first industrial research laboratory known as the "Wizard of Menlo Park," in New Jersey. He had become one of the most famous men in the world by the time he was in his 30s.

1881 年，燈泡開始提供給大眾。愛迪生也創造了世界上第一個被稱為新澤西「精靈門洛帕克」的工業研究實驗室。他在 30 歲時已經成為世界上最有名的人。

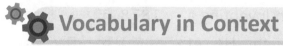 **Vocabulary in Context**

❾ With a strong _____ for childcare, Rebecca has devoted herself to teaching in a kindergarten and has done a great job.

Enthusiasm is in the closest meaning to this word.

A. complaint   C. tradition

B. passion   D. service

❿ Mark made up his mind to be a doctor and worked hard for it. No hardness could stop him from _____ his goal.

Seeking is in the closest meaning to this word.

A. regretting   C. commemorating

B. pursuing   D. integrating

⓫ This brand of laptop has been selling well for it's _____, portable, and easy to operate.

Cheap is in the closest meaning to this word.

A. ambiguous   C. dialectic

B. weighty   D. inexpensive

⓬ You can of course contact a travel agency to make travel arrangements for you; one _____ to this is that you and your family can organize your own trip.

Choice is in the closest meaning to this word.

A. recipe   C. alternative

B. seclusion   D. depreciation

❾ 蕾貝嘉對於照顧兒童有著強烈的熱忱，她一直致力於幼稚園的教學並且勝任稱職。

Enthusiasm 的意思最接近於這個字。

A. 抱怨　　　　　　C. 傳統

B. 熱情　　　　　　D. 服務

❿ 馬克下定決心並致力於成為一名醫生。沒有任何困難可以阻止他追求他的目標。

Seeking 的意思最接近於這個字。

A. 後悔　　　　　　C. 紀念

B. 追求　　　　　　D. 融合

⓫ 這個品牌的筆電銷路一向不錯，因為它價格便宜、便於攜帶，並且易於操作。

Cheap 的意思最接近於這個字。

A. 模稜兩可的　　　C. 方言的

B. 沉重的　　　　　D. 便宜的

⓬ 你當然可以接洽旅行社為你做旅遊行程的安排；此外的另一選擇是你可以和你的家人共同籌畫你們自己的行程。

Choice 的意思最接近於這個字。

A. 食譜　　　　　　C. 可供選擇的事物

B. 隱居　　　　　　D. 貶值

答案　❾ B　❿ B　⓫ D　⓬ C

右側邊欄：

1 飲食民生

2 歷史懷舊

3 現代化實用科技

4 資訊與知識傳遞

同反義詞一覽表 Unit 7		
available	可得的、可用的	同義詞 reachable / acquirable / usable
	得不到、無用的	反義詞 unavailable / unobtainable / ineffectual
general	一般的、普遍的	同義詞 common / ordinary / universal
	獨特的、特有的	反義詞 special / particular / characteristic
connect	連接、連結	同義詞 combine / link / join
	分離、隔開	反義詞 disconnect / separate / isolate
commercial	商業的、盈利的	同義詞 mercantile / profitable / lucrative
	無利益、無效的	反義詞 profitless / unrewarding / fruitless
improvement	改善、改進	同義詞 progress / advance / amelioration
	退步、衰退	反義詞 decline / degeneration / deterioration
last	持續、耐久	同義詞 continue / endure / persist
	停止、中斷	反義詞 cease / interrupt / intermit
consider	考慮、認為	同義詞 regard / think / contemplate
	不理會、忽視	反義詞 ignore / overlook / neglect
effective	有效的、生效的	同義詞 effectual / efficient / valid
	無效的、無價值	反義詞 ineffective / invalid / useless

discover	發現、找到	同義詞 find / disclose / locate
	失去、錯過	反義詞 lose / miss / slip
acquire	得到、獲得	同義詞 gain / earn / obtain
	失去、喪失	反義詞 lose / miss / deprive
basic	基本的、必需的	同義詞 essential / fundamental / primary
	複雜的、不必要	反義詞 complicated / unnecessary / needless
interestingly	有趣地、迷人地	同義詞 fascinatingly / attractively / intriguingly
	乏味地、無聊地	反義詞 boringly / tediously / monotonously
continue	繼續、持續	同義詞 last / endure / persist
	停止、中斷	反義詞 stop / cease / intermit
passion	熱情、熱忱	同義詞 zeal / enthusiasm / fervor
	冷淡、無感情	反義詞 indifference / coolness / apathy
pursue	追趕、追求	同義詞 chase / search / seek
	逃走、逃離	反義詞 escape / flee / evade
inexpensive	不貴的、便宜的	同義詞 economical / low-priced / cheap
	昂貴的、高價的	反義詞 expensive / costly / pricey
alternative	選擇、替代	同義詞 choice / option / replacement
	限制、束縛	反義詞 restraint / confinement / bondage
entire	全部的、整個的	同義詞 whole / total / full
	部分的、局部的	反義詞 partial / fractional / fragmentary

1 飲食民生

2 歷史懷舊

3 現代化實用科技

4 資訊與知識傳遞

歷史懷舊

PART 2

單元三大學習法

key 1 主題式記憶
透過主題學習將字彙累績至長期記憶，
而非片段背誦。

key 2 上下文推敲文意
閱讀時不因不熟悉的單字而影響句意理解。

key 3 熟記同反義詞
在雅思各單項中要獲取 7 分以上
需要具備同反義詞轉換的能力。

Unit 8 Steam Engine 蒸汽引擎

 8-1 蒸汽引擎的發展 MP3 22

The scene where Jack and Rose were chased by the police in the hot steamy engine room must be unforgettable for the Titanic movie fans. Titanic, a 52,310-ton boat which planned to travel from Southampton to New York actually was powered by 24 double-ended and 5 single-ended boilers feeding reciprocating steam engines.

電影鐵達尼號的粉絲一定很難忘傑克和蘿絲在炎熱潮濕的機房被警察追逐的畫面。鐵達尼號，一艘 52310 噸重，計畫由南安普敦前往紐約的船，實際上搭載了 24 個雙鍋爐和 5 個單鍋爐往復式蒸汽機。

As you can imagine how a powerful steam machine could be. A steam engine is a heat engine that performs mechanical work using steam as its working fluid. People have been using the steam machine to create power for hundreds of years. It could be as small as an iron to as powerful as the Titanic.

你可想而知蒸汽機有多麼強大的力量。蒸汽機是一個利用蒸氣啟動動能來執行工作的熱動能機器。幾百年來，人們不停使用蒸氣機來創造動力。它可以小到一個蒸氣熨斗，大到如巨大的鐵達尼號。

The first steam machine was patented by a Spanish inventor in 1606. After that, several steam machine related patents were filed but none of them were practical.

第一台蒸汽機的專利在 1606 年由一位西班牙發明家所提出。爾後，陸續有幾個相關的專利提出，但卻不實用。

Thomas Savery, in 1698, patented the first practical, atmospheric pressure steam engine of one horse power, though it was not very effective and could not work beyond a limited depth of around thirty feet.

1698 年，湯瑪士・薩弗里提了第一個實用且具有一匹馬力的氣壓蒸汽機。雖然效用不大，無法在超出約三萬英尺的深度下工作。

1 飲食民生

2 歷史懷舊

3 現代化實用科技

4 資訊與知識傳遞

Vocabulary in Context

❶ The most _____ trip for the happy couple was the trip to Europe for their 10th Wedding Anniversary.

Memorable is in the closest meaning to this word.

A. routine   C. constant

B. unforgettable   D. subsequent

❷ It's hard to _____ what life would be like if there were no waterand electricity in the world.

Fancy is in the closest meaning to this word.

A. nourish   C. imagine

B. unlock   D. dismantle

❸ Scientists have found that the music that Mozart composed and _____ has a miraculous healing and calming effect to its listeners.

Played is in the closest meaning to this word.

A. performed   C. desolated

B. exchanged   D. necessitated

❹ Dealing with _____ from all sources is no easy task; however, to gain true happiness, it's worth making the efforts.

Stress is in the closest meaning to this word.

A. ecstasy   C. pressure

B. morality   D. transport

❶ 對這對幸福的夫婦來説，最難忘的旅遊是歡慶十周年結婚紀念前往歐洲的那趟旅遊。

Memorable 的意思最接近於這個字。

A. 例行的　　　　　　C. 時常的

B. 難忘的　　　　　　D. 隨後的

❷ 很難想像世界上假使沒有水和電，生活將會是什麼樣子。

Fancy 的意思最接近於這個字。

A. 提供養分　　　　　C. 想像

B. 解開　　　　　　　D. 拆除

❸ 科學家發現莫札特所創造和演奏的樂曲對於聽眾具有奇蹟般治療和鎮定的效果。

Played 的意思最接近於這個字。

A. 演奏　　　　　　　C. 使荒涼

B. 交換　　　　　　　D. 需要

❹ 處理各種壓力不是件簡單的事；然而，為了獲得真正的快樂，努力是值得的。

Stress 的意思最接近於這個字。

A. 狂喜　　　　　　　C. 壓力

B. 道德　　　　　　　D. 運輸

答案 ❶ B　❷ C　❸ A　❹ C

It was not until 1712, when Thomas Newcomen invented the first commercial steam engine using a piston for pumping in a mine. Steam engine started to be widely used in various products. James Watt patented a steam engine that produced continuous rotary motion in 1781.

直到 1712 年，湯馬仕・紐科利用活塞的方式發明了第一個用在礦井的商業蒸汽機。 蒸汽機開始被廣泛用於各種不同的產品。詹姆斯・瓦特，在 1781 年申請了連續旋轉運動的蒸汽機專利。

Another 100 years later by 1883, steam engines were already able to be applied to vehicles and trains. Steam engines was one of the moving forces behind the Industrial Revolution.

再過 100 年後的 1883 年，蒸汽機已經能夠應用於汽車和火車。蒸汽機是工業革命背後的動力之一。

Thomas Newcomen was born in Dartmouth, Devon, England on February 24th 1664. He became an ironmonger and a Baptist lay preacher by calling.

湯馬仕・紐科於 1664 年 2 月 24 日出生在英格蘭的德文郡，達特茅斯。他成為了一個鐵匠和浸禮會通過的佈道者。

His ironmonger's business was greatly engaged with a mining business since it designed and offered tools to it.

他的鐵匠業務與開礦業節節相關，因為他幫助設計和提供工具。

Since flooding in coal and tin mines was a major and frequent problem, Newcomen decided to create a machine that could help solve the problem. He created the first practical steam engine for water pumping which he got famous for.

由於洪水對於煤炭和錫礦業造成一個重要和常見的問題，紐科決定製作一個機器來幫助解決問題。他創造了第一個實用的蒸汽機來抽水，他也因此而成名。

1 飲食民生

2 歷史懷舊

3 現代化實用科技

4 資訊與知識傳遞

Vocabulary in Context

⑤ The serial killer's bold and _____ murdering finally resulted in his being arrested and sentenced.

Ceaseless is in the closest meaning to this word.

A. worthwhile   C. tropical

B. continuous   D. contemporary

⑥ The methods of mass production and mass markets were first provided by the Industrial _____ in the 18th century, which in turn contributed to the development of international business.

Revolt is in the closest meaning to this word.

A. Fair   C. Engineering

B. Cooperation   D. Revolution

⑦ Richard was the "Workaholic" in his office because he always kept himself busy and was fully _____ in his work.

Occupied is in the closest meaning to this word.

A. engaged   C. signified

B. condensed   D. underwent

⑧ The Dinosaur Park in Canada has always been a _____ and popular tourist spot, where visitors can appreciate all kinds of dinosaur fossils.

Renowned is in the closest meaning to this word.

A. famous   C. notorious

B. delicious   D. subconscious

❺ 這名連續殺人犯大膽且持續地犯案，終究導致他被逮捕並判刑。

Ceaseless 的意思最接近於這個字。

A. 值得做的　　　　　C. 熱帶的

B. 持續的　　　　　　D. 當代的

❻ 18世紀的工業革命提供大規模生產的方式以及市場，進而促成國際商業的發展。

Revolt 的意思最接近於這個字。

A. 展覽會　　　　　　C. 工程學

B. 合作　　　　　　　D. 革命

❼ 理察是他辦公室裡的"工作狂"，因為他總是十分忙碌並且全神貫注於他的工作。

Occupied 的意思最接近於這個字。

A. 從事　　　　　　　C. 表示

B. 濃縮　　　　　　　D. 經歷

❽ 加拿大的恐龍公園一向是著名並且受歡迎的觀光景點，訪客在這裡可以欣賞到各式各樣的恐龍化石。

Renowned 的意思最接近於這個字。

A. 著名的　　　　　　C. 惡名昭彰的

B. 美味的　　　　　　D. 潛意識的

 答案　❺ B　❻ D　❼ A　❽ A

The steam engine he created was developed in 1712. He got the idea from Thomas Savery and Denis Papin who also created a steam engine called "a fire engine".

他的蒸汽機是在 1712 年被開發出來。他是從由湯瑪士·薩弗里和丹尼斯·帕潘所創造，命名為「The Fire Engine」的蒸汽機所得到的想法。

It is a kind of thermic syphon in which steam was admitted to an empty container and then condensed.

它是一種熱虹吸管，蒸氣在真空管中冷卻製造出空間。

The vacuum then sucked water from the bottom of the mine. However, this creation was not very effective and couldn't work beyond a limited depth of around thirty feet.

真空的吸管便可由礦底吸水。然而，這種創作不是很有效，無法在超出約三萬英尺的深度工作。

Newcomen inverted Savery's design and used a cylinder containing a piston based on Papin's design. It drew down the piston instead of vacuum drawing in water.

紐科倒置薩弗里的設計並使用含有帕潘設計的活塞氣缸。它在水中利用活塞來代替真空吸引。

The first successful engine was then created by Newcomen and his partner John Calley. Newcomen passed away in 1729 at the age of 65 in London. Even so, the engine he created held its place without material change for about 75 years. It also spread gradually to more areas in the UK and Europe.

紐科和他的合夥人約翰‧可雷因此創造了第一個成功的引擎。紐科去世於 1729 年倫敦，享年 65 歲。即便如此，他所創造的引擎在 75 年間都沒有重大的變化。它也逐漸蔓延到英國和歐洲的地區。

1 飲食民生

2 歷史懷舊

3 現代化實用科技

4 資訊與知識傳遞

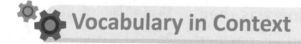

❾ Fanny studied and researched diligently and finally got ____
____ to her ideal graduate school.

Consented is in the closest meaning to this word.

A. admitted   C. perplexed

B. immigrated   D. resembled

❿ It took Philip one whole month to _____ the long novel
into one with only three chapters.

Shorten is in the closest meaning to this word.

A. wander   C. solicit

B. condense   D. forecast

⓫ Owing to the _____ resources, we must do our utmost to
come up with practical measures for sustainable
development.

Restricted is in the closest meaning to this word.

A. swift   C. marginal

B. limited   D. radioactive

⓬ _____, with the company of a new pet dog, Raymond
recovered from the depression and the guiltiness of losing
his old dog.

Progressively is in the closest meaning to this word.

A. Splendidly   C. Attractively

B. Previously   D. Gradually

❾ 芬妮十分勤勉地讀書及做研究，最終錄取並進入她理想的研究所。

Consented 的意思最接近於這個字。

A. 錄取　　　　　　　C. 困惑

B. 移民　　　　　　　D. 相似

❿ 菲力普花了整整一個月的時間把一本長篇小說濃縮成只有三個章節。

Shorten 的意思最接近於這個字。

A. 徘徊　　　　　　　C. 請求

B. 濃縮　　　　　　　D. 預測

⓫ 由於資源有限，我們必須盡最大的努力提出可供持續發展的實際措施。

Restricted 的意思最接近於這個字。

A. 迅速的　　　　　　C. 邊緣的

B. 有限的　　　　　　D. 放射性的

⓬ 逐漸地，有著新寵物狗的陪伴，雷蒙從失去原有的狗所引發的憂鬱和愧疚中恢復過來。

Progressively 的意思最接近於這個字。

A. 華麗地　　　　　　C. 吸引人地

B. 先前地　　　　　　D. 逐漸地

 答案　❾ A　❿ B　⓫ B　⓬ D

8-4 同反義詞表

同反義詞一覽表 Unit 8		
unforgettable	令人難忘的	同義詞 memorable / unfadable / indelible
	易被忘記的	反義詞 forgettable / unimpressive / unnoted
imagine	想像、猜想	同義詞 conceive / fancy / envision
	實踐、實行	反義詞 practice / execute / implement
perform	執行、演奏	同義詞 do / execute / play
	疏忽、忽視	反義詞 neglect / overlook / ignore
pressure	壓力、負擔	同義詞 burden / stress / load
	放鬆、悠閒	反義詞 relaxation / ease / leisure
related	有聯繫、相關的	同義詞 connected / associated / relevant
	無關的、不相關	反義詞 unconnected / irrelevant / unassociated
beyond	再往後、越過	同義詞 farther / past / exceedingly
	在裡面、在內部	反義詞 within / interiorly / internally
continuous	連續的、不斷的	同義詞 continual / constant / ceaseless
	中斷的、間歇的	反義詞 interrupted / intermittent / disconnected
revolution	革命、變革	同義詞 revolt / rebellion / overthrow
	繼承、接替	反義詞 inheritance / progression / succession

engage	從事、聘僱	同義詞 occupy / employ / hire
	解僱、開除	反義詞 discharge / dismiss / expel
famous	出名的、著名的	同義詞 famed / renowned / celebrated
	默默無聞的	反義詞 unknown / obscure / nameless
major	較大的、主要的	同義詞 larger / superior / main
	較小的、次要的	反義詞 minor / inferior / subordinate
frequent	頻繁的、慣常的	同義詞 recurrent / regular / habitual
	罕見的、偶見的	反義詞 infrequent / rare / occasional
admit	承認、准許	同義詞 acknowledge / confess / consent
	禁止、不許	反義詞 prohibit / forbid / exclude
condense	壓縮、濃縮	同義詞 compress / concentrate / shorten
	擴大、擴張	反義詞 expand / enlarge / lengthen
limited	有限的、受限的	同義詞 restricted / confined / restrained
	無限制、無約束	反義詞 limitless / uncontrolled / carefree
gradually	逐步地、漸漸地	同義詞 slowly / leisurely / progressively
	很快地、立即地	反義詞 rapidly / swiftly / promptly
empty	空缺的、空洞的	同義詞 vacant / hollow / void
	豐富的、充滿的	反義詞 full / substantial / affluent
bottom	底部、基部	同義詞 foundation / base / ground
	上方、表面	反義詞 top / summit / surface

1 飲食民生

2 歷史懷舊

3 現代化實用科技

4 資訊與知識傳遞

Photographic Film 底片

Before digital photography became popular in the 21st century, photographic film was the dominant form of photography for hundreds of years. Without the invention of photographic film, movies would not be invented and many historical records would be much less realistic.

在 21 世紀數位攝影開始流行前，底片是攝影數百年來的主要形式。如果沒有底片的發明，電影將不會被發明，眾多的歷史記錄也會較不真實。

The first flexible photographic roll of film was sold by George Eastman in 1885. It was a paper-based film.

第一個柔性膠卷是由喬治‧伊士曼於 1885 年售出。它是一種紙基膜。

In 1889, the first transparent plastic roll film was invented. It was made of cellulose nitrate which is chemically similar to guncotton. It was quite dangerous because it was highly flammable.

在 1889 年，第一個透明的塑料筒膜被發明出來。它是利用硝酸纖維素所製造，化學性質是類似於硝化纖維素。這其實是相

Therefore, special storage was required. The first flexible movie films measured 35-mm wide and came in long rolls on a spool. Similar roll film for the camera was also invented in the mid 1920s.

By the late 1920s, medium format roll film was created and had a paper backing which made it easy to handle in daylight.

當危險的，因為它是高度易燃的。

因此，特殊的儲存方式是必要的。第一個柔性電影底片是 35 毫米寬，排列在長卷的捲筒上。相機類似的膠卷也在 1920 年代中期被發明出來。

到了 1920 年代末期，中寬幅的底片被發明出來，它也有紙襯，使得它容易攜帶於日光下。

1 飲食民生

2 歷史懷舊

3 現代化實用科技

4 資訊與知識傳遞

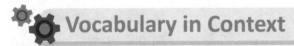

Vocabulary in Context

❶ In the action movie, the superheroes, with each of whom equipped with combating skills, finally won the victory with _____ forces.

Supreme is in the closest meaning to this word.

A. temporary   C. seasonal

B. dominant   D. fundamental

❷ Undoubtedly, it is the parents that should strictly regulate their children not to watch TV programs that are too _____ in violence.

Lifelike is in the closest meaning to this word.

A. realistic   C. conventional

B. amiable   D. luxuriant

❸ After transferring to the new company, Lucy could pleasantly work in a much more _____ and efficient way.

Adjustable is in the closest meaning to this word.

A. agricultural   C. flexible

B. uncertain   D. legitimate

❹ As a safety policy against terroism, all passengers are _____ to undergo and pass the strict security check at the airport.

Demanded is in the closest meaning to this word.

A. compiled   C. worshipped

B. required   D. overestimated

❶ 在這部動作片中，超級英雄們各個身懷絕技，最終以絕佳優勢贏得勝利。

Supreme 的意思最接近於這個字。

A. 暫時的　　　　　　　C. 季節的

B. 優勢的　　　　　　　D. 基本的

❷ 無疑地，父母親應該嚴格規範孩童不要觀看過於暴力寫實的電視節目。

Lifelike 的意思最接近於這個字。

A. 寫實的　　　　　　　C. 傳統的

B. 和藹的　　　　　　　D. 繁茂的

❸ 露西在轉任到新公司後，可以很愉快地以更加彈性而且有效率的方式工作。

Adjustable 的意思最接近於這個字。

A. 農業的　　　　　　　C. 彈性的

B. 不確定的　　　　　　D. 合法正當的

❹ 基於對抗恐怖主義的安全政策，所有的乘客被要求接受並且通過機場嚴格的安全檢查。

Demanded 的意思最接近於這個字。

A. 編纂　　　　　　　　C. 崇拜

B. 要求　　　　　　　　D. 高估

答案 ❶ B　❷ A　❸ C　❹ B

1 飲食民生

2 歷史懷舊

3 現代化實用科技

4 資訊與知識傳遞

133

Triacetate film came later and was more stable, flexible, and fireproof. This technology was widely used in the 1970s. Today, technology has produced film with T-grain emulsions. These films use light-sensitive silver halides (grains) that are T-shaped, thus rendering a much finer grain pattern. Films like this offer greater detail and higher resolution, meaning sharper images.

三醋酸纖維薄膜的膠卷後來被發明出來，它較為穩定、靈活和防火。這項技術於 1970 年代廣泛採用。今天，製造技術已經發展到 T 型顆粒乳劑。這些膜使用 T 型的光敏鹵化銀粒，使得圖像更為細緻。像這樣的底片提供了更多的細節和更高的解析度，這意味著更清晰的圖像。

George Eastman was born on July 12, 1854, in Waterville, New York. His father passed away when he was 8 and one of his sisters passed away when he was 16. Therefore, Eastman grew up very close with his mother and his other sister. As the son of the family, Eastman dropped out of school at the age of 14 to help with the family income.

喬治·伊士曼於 1854 年 7 月 12 日出生於紐約，沃特維爾。他的父親在他 8 歲時去世。他的姊姊則是在他 16 歲時去世。因此，伊士曼在成長的過程中與他的媽媽和其他姊姊的關係非常密切。作為家中的兒子，伊士曼在 14 歲時便輟學，以幫助家庭收入。

At the age of 24, Eastman started his research on how to make photography less cumbersome and easy for people to enjoy. After a couple of years of research, Eastman launched his fledgling photography company in 1880. 5 years later, he patented a roll-holder device which allowed cameras to be smaller and cheaper.

在 24 歲的時候，伊士曼開始了他對如何使攝影不太笨重，亦供人欣賞的研究。經過幾年的研究，伊士曼在 1880 年推出了他無經驗的攝影公司，並在 5 年以後，他獲得滾架裝置的專利，使相機更小、更便宜。

In 1888, he made the Kodak camera, which is the first camera designed specifically to use roll film. He also came up with the company slogan. You press the button; we do the rest." It is because the camera would be sent back to the company after the 100 exposures on the roll of film had been used up. Later Kodak would develop the pictures and send it back to the clients.

1888 年，他做了第一台柯達攝影機，這是專門使用底片的第一台相機。他還提出了公司的口號「你按下按鈕；剩下的我們來做」。這是因為相機在用完 100 張底片後，會被送回柯達公司，之後柯達便會洗出相片，並將其寄送回客戶。

Vocabulary in Context

❺ What the general public expects from the government is a __ _____ economic development that it is supposed to achieve.

Steady is in the closest meaning to this word.

A. changeable   C. stable

B. alcoholic   D. waterproof

❻ A lot of celebrities dressed up and attended the party tonight to support the charity campaign that was _____ by the association.

Started is in the closest meaning to this word.

A. amplified   C. launched

B. prolonged   D. twinkled

❼ The news reporter purchased the newest laptop computer _____ for the purpose of covering instant news.

Particularly is in the closest meaning to this word.

A. affectionately   C. gloriously

B. narrowly   D. specifically

❽ Doctors warned people against the long _____ to the burning sunlight, which might easily cause skin cancer.

Uncovering is in the closest meaning to this word.

A. reliability   C. exposure

B. dedication   D. negligence

❺一般民眾對於政府的期許是一個理當由它所達成穩定的經濟發展。

Steady 的意思最接近於這個字。

A. 易變的　　　　　C. 穩定的

B. 含酒精的　　　　D. 防水的

❻許多名流盛裝出席今晚的宴會來支持由協會所發起的慈善活動。

Started 的意思最接近於這個字。

A. 放大　　　　　C. 發起

B. 延長　　　　　D. 閃爍

❼這名新聞記者為了採訪即時新聞特地購買了最新型的筆記型電腦。

Particularly 的意思最接近於這個字。

A. 關愛地　　　　C. 輝煌地

B. 狹隘地　　　　D. 特別地

❽醫生警告人們不要長時間曝曬在熾熱的陽光下，因為這樣容易罹患皮膚癌。

Uncovering 的意思最接近於這個字。

A. 可靠　　　　　C. 曝曬

B. 奉獻　　　　　D. 輕忽

答案 C　 C　 D　 C

Eastman was not only a businessman and an inventor, but also an outstanding philanthropist. He was not stingy on sharing his fortune.

伊士曼不僅是一個商人，一個發明家，也是一位傑出的慈善家。他不吝嗇的分享他的財富。

In 1901, he donated $625,000 to Mechanics Institute which is the Rochester Institute of Technology today.

1901 年，他捐贈了 625,000 美元到力學研究所，也就是今天的羅切斯特技術學院。

He also helped the Massachusetts Institute of Technology to construct buildings on its second campus. He shared more of his fortune to establish educational and health institutions.

他還幫助美國麻省理工學院建立了其第二校舍。他分享了他更多的財富，建立教育和保健機構。

Unfortunately, in his later years, Eastman suffered from an intense pain caused by a disorder which affected his spine.

不幸的是，在伊士曼的晚年，他因為疾病造成了他脊椎的劇烈疼痛。

He was not able to stand or walk which effected greatly his daily life. He decided to commit suicide and shot himself through the heart.

He left a note which read, To my friends, my work is done-why wait?" It was March 14th, 1932.

他不能站立或行走，顯著的影響了他的生活。他決定朝他的心臟開槍自殺。

他留了張紙條，上面寫著「給我的朋友，我完成了我的工作，何需等待。」這發生於 1932 年 3 月 14 日。

1 飲食民生

2 歷史懷舊

3 現代化實用科技

4 資訊與知識傳遞

Vocabulary in Context

⑨ President Barack Obama, the first African-American president has been admired worldwide for his _____ achievements in both domestic and foreign affairs.
Prominent is in the closest meaning to this word.

A. conceited   C. short-sighted

B. identical   D. outstanding

⑩ It's amazing and puzzling how the ancient Egyptians could have had the ability to _____ the Great Pyramids of Giza.
Build is in the closest meaning to this word.

A. construct   C. predict

B. whisper   D. intervene

⑪ Oliver is at present a resident doctor in the hospital his father _____ and plans to take over his father's business in the future.
Founded is in the closest meaning to this word.

A. appealed   C. smuggled

B. established   D. broadcast

⑫ Patrick has been under _____ pressure recently as he has to make an immediate decision on whether to work in the hometown or to accept the challenging position overseas.
Forceful is in the closest meaning to this word.

A. reputable   C. intense

B. climatic   D. merciful

❾ 巴拉克・歐巴馬總統是首位非裔美籍的總統，以他在內政及外交方面傑出的成就為世人所崇拜。

Prominent 的意思最接近於這個字。

A. 自負的　　　　　　C. 短視的

B. 相同的　　　　　　D. 傑出的

❿ 人們對於古代埃及人竟然有能力建造吉薩的大金塔感到驚奇而且困惑。

Build 的意思最接近於這個字。

A. 建造　　　　　　　C. 預測

B. 耳語　　　　　　　D. 干預

⓫ 奧利佛目前在他父親所建立的醫院裡擔任住院醫師，並且計劃在未來接管父親的事業。

Founded 的意思最接近於這個字。

A. 吸引　　　　　　　C. 走私

B. 建立　　　　　　　D. 轉播

⓬ 派翠克最近身處於極大的壓力之下，因為他必須要盡快決定留在家鄉工作或是接受國外具挑戰性的職務。

Forceful 的意思最接近於這個字。

A. 聲譽好的　　　　　C. 強烈的

B. 氣候的　　　　　　D. 仁慈的

答案　 D　 A　 B　 C

同反義詞一覽表 Unit 9		
dominant	優勢的、統治的	同義詞 supreme / ruling / governing
	次等的、隸屬的	反義詞 inferior / lower / subordinate
realistic	真實的、實際的	同義詞 lifelike / truthful / practical
	不切實、夢幻的	反義詞 impractical / unrealistic / dreamy
flexible	彈性的、變通的	同義詞 adaptable / stretchable / adjustable
	僵化的、頑固的	反義詞 rigid / inflexible / stubborn
require	需要、要求	同義詞 need / demand / request
	提供、供給	反義詞 supply / furnish / provide
transparent	透明的、清晰的	同義詞 clear / obvious / evident
	不透明、晦暗的	反義詞 opaque / obscure / vague
stable	穩定的、可靠的	同義詞 steady / firm / reliable
	易變、不可靠的	反義詞 changeable / shaky / unreliable
launch	發起、開始	同義詞 start / commence / initiate
	結束、終結	反義詞 end / finish / terminate
specifically	明確地、具體地	同義詞 definitely / precisely / particularly
	一般地、普遍地	反義詞 generally / commonly / universally
exposure	暴露、揭發	同義詞 disclosure / uncovering / revelation
	隱瞞、隱藏	反義詞 concealment / veiling / hiding

sensitive	敏感的、易怒的	同義詞 perceptive / conscious / touchy
	未察覺、溫和的	反義詞 insensitive / insusceptible / gentle
income	收入、收益	同義詞 earnings / revenue / profit
	支出、消費	反義詞 expense / payment / consumption
outstanding	傑出的、重要的	同義詞 prominent / distinguished / important
	普通的、平凡的	反義詞 commonplace / usual / ordinary
construct	建造、構成	同義詞 build / create / manufacture
	毀壞、破壞	反義詞 demolish / destroy / ruin
establish	建立、創辦	同義詞 build / found / initiate
	毀壞、破壞	反義詞 break / devastate / demolish
intense	激烈的、強烈的	同義詞 drastic / extreme / forceful
	溫和的、軟弱的	反義詞 moderate / temperate / powerless
stingy	吝嗇的、小氣的	同義詞 miserly / mean / uncharitable
	慷慨的、大方的	反義詞 generous / openhanded / unselfish
fortune	好運、運氣	同義詞 luck / chance / fate
	厄運、不幸	反義詞 misfortune / tragedy / mishap
donate	捐贈、給予	同義詞 give / contribute / grant
	收到、得到	反義詞 receive / obtain / accept

10-1 造紙技術的發明

Before paper was invented, several materials such as papyrus, parchment, palm leaves and vellum were being used as written materials, but they were all expensive and limited. Paper was invented by Cai Lun, an official of the Imperial Court, in 105 A.D. in China during the Han Dynasty.

在造紙術發明前，紙莎草、羊皮紙、棕櫚葉和上等紙都被用作書面材料，但他們都價格昂貴而且供給有限。紙是在公元 105 年，在中國漢朝由一位朝廷的官員蔡倫所發明的。

He broke the bark of a mulberry tree into fibers and added in rags hemp and old fish nets which created the first piece of paper. He reported to the emperor and received great honor for his ability. Because of this invention, paper can be produced with trees at a vey low cost, which popularized the use of paper. In a few years, paper was

他打碎了桑樹的樹皮做為纖維，在裡面加入了碎布麻與舊漁網，製造了第一張紙。他向皇帝報告，並因此受到了極大的榮譽。因為這個發明，紙就可以利用樹生產低成本的紙，使

widely used in China.

紙被廣為利用 。在短短幾年內，紙被廣泛應用於中國。

Even though the Chinese invented paper in 105 A.D., invented printing technology at around 600 A.D., and printed the first newspaper by 740 A.D., this amazing technology was only spread to the eastern countries including Korea and Japan at as early as the 6th century.

儘管中國人在公元 105 年發明了紙，在公元 600 年發明了印刷技術，並在公元 740 年打印了首次的報紙，這個驚人的技術卻到第六世紀時傳播到東方國家，包括韓國和日本。

The paper making technique was brought to the western countries along the Silk Road. The technique was found at Tibet at around 650 A.D.

造紙技術因為絲綢之路被帶到了西方國家。該技術約在公元 650 年左右在西藏被發現。

1 飲食民生

2 歷史懷舊

3 現代化實用科技

4 資訊與知識傳遞

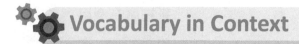

Vocabulary in Context

❶ The ancient Machu Picchu used to be a summer resort for Incan emperors and their _____ family.

Royal is in the closest meaning to this word.

A. abusive   C. imperial

B. tempting   D. contemplating

❷ All the students unwillingly _____ the cancellation of the field trip because of the approaching typhoon.

Accepted is in the closest meaning to this word.

A. deserted   C. symbolized

B. received   D. prolonged

❸ The publicity campaign did much to _____ the new product, promoting its unexpected big sale.

Advertise is in the closest meaning to this word.

A. anticipate   C. depopulate

B. retire   D. popularize

❹ Donald adopted practical and clever marketing _____ and earned great profits for his company.

Skills is in the closest meaning to this word.

A. balances   C. techniques

B. supposition   D. coincidence

❶ 馬丘比丘古城過去曾經是印加國王和他們的皇室家族避暑的地點。

Royal 的意思最接近於這個字。

A. 虐待的　　　　　　　C. 皇室的

B. 誘人的　　　　　　　D. 深思的

❷ 由於颱風即將來臨,所有的學生不情願地接受戶外教學的取消。

Accepted 的意思最接近於這個字。

A. 遺棄　　　　　　　　C. 象徵

B. 接受　　　　　　　　D. 延長

❸ 這項宣傳活動對於提升新產品的知名度有很大的幫助,促成了意想不到的大賣。

Advertise 的意思最接近於這個字。

A. 預期　　　　　　　　C. 減少人口

B. 退休　　　　　　　　D. 受歡迎

❹ 唐納採用實際而且靈活的行銷技巧為他的公司賺取大量的利潤。

Skills 的意思最接近於這個字。

A. 均衡　　　　　　　　C. 技巧

B. 猜測　　　　　　　　D. 巧合

 答案　❶ C　❷ B　❸ D　❹ C

飲食民生　1

歷史懷舊　2

現代化實用科技　3

資訊與知識傳遞　4

China used to be a closed country. For a long time, the Chinese kept the paper manufacture as a secret to ensure a monopoly.

中國曾經是一個封閉的國家。長期以來,中國一直將造紙技術保密,以確保壟斷。

However, losing in a battle at the Talas River, the Chinese prisoners revealed the paper making technique to the Arabs which helped them built the first paper industry in Baghdad in 793 A.D.

然而公元 793 年,由於在失去塔拉斯河的戰役,中國戰俘透露製作技術並幫助阿拉伯人在巴格達建立了第一個造紙行業。

Interestingly, the Arabs also kept the first technique as a secret from the European. As a result, the paper making technique did not reach Europe until hundreds of years later. Spain built the first European factory in 1150 A.D. Finally, after another 500 years, the first paper industry was built in Philadelphia in the USA. That is 1500 years after the first piece of paper was made!

有意思的是,阿拉伯人也將此技術保密。因此,造紙技術在幾百年後才傳到歐洲。西班牙在公元 1150 年時建立了第一個歐洲的造紙廠,再過 500 年後美國的費城才建立了美國的第一個造紙廠。這是從第一張紙被發明算起的 1500 年後!

Around 2000 years ago, Cai Lun was born in Guiyang during the Han Dynasty. Because of his father's accusation, Cai was brought to the palace and got castrated at the age of 12. Even so, Cai loved to study and was designated to study along with the Emperor's son.

大約 2000 多年前，蔡倫出生於漢朝的貴陽。由於他的父親犯罪，因此蔡被帶到了皇宮，在 12 歲時便被閹割。即便如此，蔡倫喜愛學習，所以被指定當作皇帝兒子的陪讀。

He was a very hard working person , so he was given several promotions under the rule of Emperor He. He was given the right to be in charge of manufacturing instruments and weapons.

他是一個很努力工作的人，因此在漢和帝的執政下被多次的升官。他被任命負責儀器及武器的製作。

1 飲食民生

2 歷史懷舊

3 現代化實用科技

4 資訊與知識傳遞

Vocabulary in Context

❺ Besides the strict enforcement of laws against drunk driving, our government should conduct public education to alert people to the dangers of drunk driving to _____ their safety.

Assure is in the closest meaning to this word.

A. ensure   C. switch

B. overload   D. undermine

❻ The candidate suffered a serious setback when the newsweekly _____ a series of disgraceful scandals about his family.

Uncovered is in the closest meaning to this word.

A. flourished   C. revealed

B. paraded   D. discouraged

❼ It was irresponsible of Miss Hope to make the serious _____ against Carl that he had stolen her cell phone before she had any positive proof.

Charge is in the closest meaning to this word.

A. occupation   C. inhabitant

B. harassment   D. accusation

❽ Since the merchandise of his company has superior quality and famous branding, Sam could easily achieve successful sales and _____.

Advancement is in the closest meaning to this word.

A. treatment　　　C. convenience

B. promotion　　　D. depiction

⑤ 除了取締酒駕法律嚴格的執行，我們的政府應該實施大眾教育使民眾警覺酒駕的危險以確保自身的安全。

Assure 的意思最接近於這個字。

A. 確保　　　C. 轉換

B. 超載　　　D. 破壞

⑥ 當新聞週刊揭露一連串有關於他的家族丟臉的醜聞時，這名候選人遭受嚴重的挫折。

Uncovered 的意思最接近於這個字。

A. 茂盛　　　C. 揭露

B. 遊行　　　D. 氣餒

⑦ 霍普老師非常不負責任，因為她在還沒有任何證據之前就嚴正地指控卡爾偷竊她的手機。

Charge 的意思最接近於這個字。

A. 職業　　　C. 居民

B. 騷擾　　　D. 指控

⑧ 由於山姆公司的商品具有優異的品質以及著名的品牌，他可以輕易地達成成功的販售及促銷。

Advancement 的意思最接近於這個字。

A. 治療　　　C. 便利

B. 促銷　　　D. 描繪

 **答案** ❺ A　❻ C　❼ D　❽ B

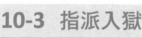

Later on, he was promoted to become a Regular Palace Attendant which is known as the staff officer now.

後來，他被晉升中常侍，即是現在的參謀。

He was in charge of everything being produced for the palace which started his thought on a papermaking process.

他負責宮中一切物品的製作。這開始了他造紙過程的想法。

Cai was given recognition for his invention of paper and named as one of the greatest inventors of China until now. As loyal as he was, Cai unfortunately was ordered to report to prison after Emperor An assumed power. Cai was rogued to frame the grandmother of Emperor An.

由於紙的發明，蔡倫受到認可且直到現在都被認為是中國最偉大的發明家之一。忠誠的他在漢安帝上位後指派入獄。原因是蔡倫被誣告陷害皇帝的祖母。

He felt greatly insulted, so before he was to report, he committed suicide by drinking poison.

他感到極大的侮辱，因此在他需要向監獄報到前，蔡倫服毒自殺。

Hundreds of years later during the Song Dynasty, a temple in honor of Cai Lun was erected in Chengdu.

幾百年後，在宋朝，紀念蔡倫的廟宇被建立在成都。

Nowadays, people in the paper business travel a long distance to pay respect.

如今，從事紙類商務的人們仍長途旅行以瞻仰蔡倫。

1 飲食民生

2 歷史懷舊

3 現代化實用科技

4 資訊與知識傳遞

153

Vocabulary in Context

9 Due to her thoughtful personality and language capability, Lydia was fully qualified as a competent flight _____.
Stewardess is in the closest meaning to this word.

A. rebel   C. attendant

B. detective   D. principal

10 Mother Teresa's lifelong devotion to the welfare of people and the advocacy of humanity won worldwide _____ and was awarded the Nobel Peace Prize in 1979.
Acknowledgement is in the closest meaning to this word.

A. trifle   C. appointment

B. permanence   D. recognition

11 It was naïve of Anna to _____ that everyone would support her proposal wholeheartedly.
Suppose is in the closest meaning to this word.

A. assume   C. renovate

B. compose   D. overwhelm

12 His making a scene of trifles in the middle of the party _____ not only himself but his family present on the scene.
Disgraced is in the closest meaning to this word.

A. amused   C. dedicated

B. insulted   D. reproached

❾ 由於她善解人意的個性及語言的能力，莉迪亞有充分的資格成為勝任的空服員。

Stewardess 的意思最接近於這個字。

A. 反叛者　　　　　　C. 服務員

B. 偵探　　　　　　　D. 校長

❿ 德蕾莎修女因一生奉獻於人類的福祉以及人道主義的倡導而贏得世人的讚譽，並且在1979年獲頒諾貝爾和平獎。

Acknowledgement 的意思最接近於這個字。

A. 瑣事　　　　　　　C. 任命

B. 永久　　　　　　　D. 讚譽

⓫ 安娜過於天真地認為每個人都會全心地支持她的提案。

Suppose 的意思最接近於這個字。

A. 假定　　　　　　　C. 整修

B. 組成　　　　　　　D. 壓倒

⓬ 他在宴會中為小事大吵大鬧，不僅侮辱自己也使得在場的家人蒙羞。

Disgraced 的意思最接近於這個字。

A. 取悅　　　　　　　C. 致力

B. 侮辱　　　　　　　D. 責備

答案　❾ C　❿ D　⓫ A　⓬ B

同反義詞一覽表 Unit 10		
imperial	帝國的、宏偉的	同義詞 royal / majestic / magnificent
	平民的、簡樸的	反義詞 civilian / simple / plain
receive	接受、得到	同義詞 accept / gain / obtain
	給予、提供	反義詞 give / present / offer
popularize	流行、傳播	同義詞 prevail / advertise / spread
	不流行、無人緣	反義詞 disfavor / unlove / dislike
technique	技巧、技術	同義詞 method / means / skill
	目的、結果	反義詞 end / aim / outcome
official	正式的、合法的	同義詞 authorized / certified / legitimate
	非正式、私人的	反義詞 officious / casual / private
honor	榮譽、敬意	同義詞 glory / renown / respect
	不名譽、羞辱	反義詞 dishonor / disgrace / shame
ensure	保證、確保	同義詞 guarantee / promise / assure
	不確定、懷疑	反義詞 question / doubt / suspect
reveal	展現、揭示	同義詞 show / display / uncover
	隱瞞、掩飾	反義詞 hide / disguise / conceal
accusation	指控、控告	同義詞 charge / indictment / impeachment
	釋放、赦免	反義詞 discharge / release / pardon

promotion	晉升、提升	同義詞 advancement / improvement / raise
	降級、降低	反義詞 degradation / demotion / reduction
battle	戰鬥、作戰	同義詞 fight / combat / contention
	投降、屈服	反義詞 surrender / submission / yield
attendant	服務員、參加者	同義詞 waiter / steward / participant
	主人、缺席者	反義詞 master / host / absentee
recognition	認出、讚譽	同義詞 identification / acknowledgement / honoring
	未察覺、否定	反義詞 unawareness / negation / denial
assume	假定、推測	同義詞 suppose / presume / infer
	證明、證實	反義詞 prove / confirm / verify
insult	羞辱、侮辱	同義詞 disgrace / humiliate / shame
	尊敬、敬重	反義詞 respect / revere / honor
loyal	忠誠的、忠心的	同義詞 faithful / trustworthy / devoted
	不忠的、背叛的	反義詞 disloyal / traitorous / betraying
frame	建造、制定	同義詞 construct / build / plan
	破壞、摧毀	反義詞 destroy / ruin / damage
erect	樹立、建立	同義詞 establish / set / build
	毀壞、破壞	反義詞 destroy / demolish / shatter

1 飲食民生

2 歷史懷舊

3 現代化實用科技

4 資訊與知識傳遞

Unit 11 Liquid Paper 立可白

 11-1 解雇促成發明了立可白 MP3 31

Back in the late 90's while computers were not as common, liquid paper could be found in every pen case and on every desk. It is actually a brand name of the Newell Rubbermaid company that sells correction products.

在九零年代，當電腦還不普及時，你幾乎可以在每一個鉛筆盒，每一張桌子上看到立可白。它實際上是 Newell Rubbermaid 公司所銷售之修正產品的品牌名稱。

It is not a surprise that liquid paper was invented by a typist. Bette Graham who used to make many mistakes while working as a typist, invented the first correction fluid in her kitchen back in 1951. Using only paints and kitchen ware, Graham made her first generation correction fluid called Mistake Out and started to sell it to her co-workers.

立可白是由一位打字員所發明的，這並不意外。貝蒂·格雷厄姆在當打字員時經常發生錯誤。因此，在 1951 年時格雷厄姆在她的廚房裡，只利用了油漆及廚具，發明了她的第一代修正液，並且將它賣給自己的同事。

Graham for sure saw the business opportunity with her invention and founded the Mistake Out Company back in 1956 while she was still working as a typist. However, she was later on fired from her job because of some silly mistakes. Just like that, she worked from her kitchen alone for 17 years. At 1961, the company name was changed to Liquid Paper and it was sold to the Gillette Corporation for $47.5 million in 1979.

格雷厄姆肯定看到了這個發明的商機,在 1956 年她還在擔任打字員時便創辦了 Mistake Out 公司。爾後,她因為一些愚蠢的原因被公司解雇。就這樣,她在廚房裡獨自工作了 17 年。在 1961 年,該公司的名稱改為立可白,並在 1979 年以 $47.5 百萬美元出售給吉列特公司。

Vocabulary in Context

❶ Little did we expect that the minor misunderstanding between the couple should have _____ caused them to break up.

Unexpectedly is in the closest meaning to this word.

A. gracefully   C. abundantly

B. luxuriously   D. dramatically

❷ It was a _____ belief in the past that after the appearance of a comet, which was regarded as an omen, great disasters and tragedies might occur.

General is in the closest meaning to this word.

A. common   C. passionate

B. solitary   D. luminous

❸ Those naughty students were insistently requested to make a(n) _____ of their misbehavior, or they might receive a severe punishment.

Alteration is in the closest meaning to this word.

A. efficiency   C. separation

B. mistakes   D. corrections

❹ People all over the world used to view the United States as a land of golden _____ and tried their luck by emigrating there.

Chance is in the closest meaning to this word.

A. warehouse   C. remedy

B. opportunity   D. derivation

1 飲食民生

2 歷史懷舊

3 現代化實用科技

4 資訊與知識傳遞

❶ 我們一點都沒料到這對情侶間小小的誤會竟然會戲劇性地導致他們分手。

Unexpectedly 的意思最接近於這個字。

A. 優雅地   C. 豐富地

B. 奢華地   D. 戲劇性地

❷ 在過去，人們普遍地相信在被視為是凶兆的彗星出現後，巨大的災難和悲劇可能會發生。

General 的意思最接近於這個字。

A. 普遍的   C. 熱情的

B. 孤單的   D. 發光的

❸ 那些頑皮的學生一再地被要求改正他們不良的行為，否則他們可能將得接受嚴厲的處分。

Alteration 的意思最接近於這個字。

A. 效率   C. 分開

B. 錯誤   D. 修正

❹ 在過去，世界各地的人們把美國視為是一個充滿絕佳機會的國度因而移民到那裏去開創契機。

Chance 的意思最接近於這個字。

A. 倉庫   C. 治療藥方

B. 機會   D. 起源

答案 ❶ D ❷ A ❸ D ❹ B

Liquid paper contains titanium dioxide, solvent naphtha, mineral spirits and also trichloroethane which later on was found to be toxic.

立可白包含二氧化鈦、溶劑石腦油、礦油精和之後被發現是有毒的三氯乙烷。

Since it affects the human body, fewer and fewer people use liquid paper. Instead of fluid, a later invention by the same company, correction tape, is getting more popular these days. What will come next? Let's wait and see.

由於它影響人類的身體，因此越來越少的人使用立可白。取代液態式的修正液，由同一家公司所發明的修正帶越來越趨於流行。接下來還會有什麼發明呢？讓我們拭目以待。

A half a million-dollar business owner, an artist, an inventor, and a single mother, Bette Graham was an independent woman with multiple successful roles in her life. Graham was born Bette Clair McMurray in Dallas, Texas in 1924.

擁有價值 50 萬美元的企業家、藝術家、發明家和一個單身母親，貝蒂·格雷厄姆是一個在生活中擁有多個成功角色的獨立女人。格雷厄姆的原名為貝蒂·克萊爾·

麥克默里，於 1924 年出生於德州的達拉斯。

She got married and had her only one child Robert Michael Nesmith in 1942. In 1946, she filed in her first divorce.

她在 1942 年結了婚，並有了她唯一的孩子羅伯特・邁克爾・奈史密斯。1946 年，她申請了第一次的離婚。

She raised her child alone and got married again to Robert Graham in 1962. Unfortunately, the marriage didn't last, and they were divorced in 1975.

她獨自扶養她的孩子，並且在 1962 年嫁給了羅伯特・格雷厄姆。不幸的是，婚姻並沒有持續多久，他們在 1975 年離婚。

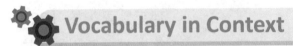

Vocabulary in Context

⑤ Carlos bought an apartment near the MRT station as he considered it _____ and time-saving for him to commute by MRT.

Handy is in the closest meaning to this word.

A. convenient   C. annoying

B. slight   D. theoretical

⑥ According to TV reports, the sending out of the _____ gas and fumes of the factory might be the cause of the serious sickness of the residents.

Poisonous is in the closest meaning to this word.

A. harmless   C. toxic

B. spacious   D. architectural

⑦ In America, young people will often move out and live an _ _____ life when they turn eighteen or go to college.

Autonomous is in the closest meaning to this word.

A. anxious   C. undermined

B. energetic   D. independent

⑧ _____, the speedy passenger ship hit on an iceberg and got crashed, resulting in heavy casualties.

Unluckily is in the closest meaning to this word.

A. Gratefully   C. Unfortunately

B. Collectively   D. Mutually

❺ 卡洛斯在捷運站附近買了一間公寓，因為他認為坐捷運通勤既方便又節省時間。

Handy 的意思最接近於這個字。

A. 便利的　　　　　　C. 煩人的

B. 輕微的　　　　　　D. 理論的

❻ 根據電視新聞報導，這座工廠排放出的有毒氣體和煙霧可能是導致居民罹患嚴重疾病的主因。

Poisonous 的意思最接近於這個字。

A. 無害的　　　　　　C. 有毒的

B. 寬敞的　　　　　　D. 建築的

❼ 在美國，當年輕人到了十八歲或是上大學的時候，他們經常會搬離家庭並且過著獨立的生活。

Autonomous 的意思最接近於這個字。

A. 焦慮的　　　　　　C. 破壞的

B. 有活力的　　　　　D. 獨立的

❽ 很不幸地，疾馳而行的客輪撞上冰山撞毀，因而導致慘重的傷亡。

Unluckily 的意思最接近於這個字。

A. 感激地　　　　　　C. 不幸地

B. 集體地　　　　　　D. 相互地

1 飲食民生

2 歷史懷舊

3 現代化實用科技

4 資訊與知識傳遞

 答案 ❺ A ❻ C ❼ D ❽ C

As an artist, Graham had a special talent in painting. Aside from being a typist, she used to paint holiday windows for banks to earn extra money. She said that she realized that with lettering, an artist never corrects by erasing, but always paints over the error.

作為一個藝術家,格雷厄姆是個繪畫天才。從事打字員外,她利用假日油漆銀行的櫥窗來賺外快。她說當時她意識到,就刻字來說,藝術家從不刪除錯誤而是利用描繪掩蓋錯誤。

That's her million-dollar idea! Graham made her first correction fluid in her kitchen and secretly she began marketing it as Mistake Out. Soon after she began her company, she changed the name yet again to Liquid Paper which became well-known by the popularity.

這可是她價值數百萬美元的主意!格雷厄姆在她的廚房裡做了她第一代的塗改液並爾後她偷偷地開始了營銷 Mistake Out。在她成立公司後不久,她再次將產品更名為廣受人知的立可白。

Graham was a brilliant woman who built her business in a unique way. She

格雷厄姆是一個以獨特的方式做生意的聰

believed in quality over profit which brought her the half a million-dollar business. She also believed that women could bring more humanistic quality to the male world of business.

明女性。她相信品質比利潤重要，這個想法帶給了她超過五十萬美元的營業利潤。她還認為，女性更可以在這個以男性為主的企業社會裡帶來更多的人文素養。

Therefore, she started an employee library and a childcare center in her new company headquarters in 1975. Her steps were followed by many international corporations these days. Bette Graham should not only be known as the inventor of Liquid Paper but should be called as the employee benefit creator.

因此在 1975 年，她在她的新公司總部開始了員工圖書館和托兒中心。她的腳步在近期內被許多跨國公司相繼跟進。貝蒂‧格雷厄姆不僅應該被稱為立可白的發明者，更應該被稱為員工福利的創造者。

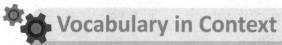

Vocabulary in Context

9 The method of trial and _____ helped Mrs. Cooper a lot in her raising the three children.

Mistake is in the closest meaning to this word.

A. error   C. refund

B. contract   D. notification

10 Owing to economic recession, Mr. Norman's company met with the dramatic plunge in _____ and finally went bankrupt.

Earnings is in the closest meaning to this word.

A. beverage   C. equality

B. profits   D. findings

11 The American singer and song writer, Bob Dylan, gained _____ prestige by winning the 2016 Nobel Prize in Literature for his achievements in creating new poetic expressions within the great American song tradition.

Global is in the closest meaning to this word.

A. obscure   C. tribal

B. functional   D. international

12 Traveling a lot can be of great _____ to young people in broadening their horizons.

Advantage is in the closest meaning to this word.

A. morale   C. benefit

B. ailment   D. regularity

❾「嘗試錯誤」的方法在庫柏太太撫育三個孩子方面有極大的幫助。

Mistake 的意思最接近於這個字。

A. 錯誤   C. 退款

B. 合約   D. 通知

❿ 由於經濟不景氣，諾曼先生的公司遭逢利潤銳減的窘境，最終宣告破產。

Earnings 的意思最接近於這個字。

A. 飲料   C. 平等

B. 利潤   D. 發現

⓫ 美國歌手兼作曲家，巴比·狄倫，由於在偉大的美國歌曲傳統中注入創新詩意表達的成就而獲頒2016年諾貝爾文學獎，並因此贏得國際盛讚。

Global 的意思最接近於這個字。

A. 模糊的   C. 部落的

B. 功能的   D. 國際的

⓬ 經常旅遊對於年輕人拓展視野具有很大的益處。

Advantage 的意思最接近於這個字。

A. 士氣   C. 利益

B. 疾病   D. 規則性

答案 ❾ A ❿ B ⓫ D ⓬ C

1 飲食民生

2 歷史懷舊

3 現代化實用科技

4 資訊與知識傳遞

11-4 同反義詞表

同反義詞一覽表 Unit 11		
dramatically	戲劇性、誇張地	同義詞 unexpectedly / exaggeratedly / suddenly
	典型地、一般地	反義詞 typically / commonly / ordinarily
common	一般的、普遍的	同義詞 normal / general / regular
	稀有的、獨特的	反義詞 unusual / rare / unique
correction	修正、改正	同義詞 alteration / modification / improvement
	錯誤、不正確	反義詞 error / mistake / incorrectness
opportunity	機會、時機	同義詞 chance / timing / occasion
	絕境、滅絕	反義詞 desperation / obsoleteness / extinction
drop	落下、掉下	同義詞 fall / plunge / descend
	攀登、上升	反義詞 climb / soar / ascend
actually	實際地、真實地	同義詞 factually / truly / authentically
	理想地、完美地	反義詞 ideally / perfectly / faultlessly
found	建立、創辦	同義詞 build / establish / create
	毀壞、破壞	反義詞 demolish / destroy / ruin
silly	愚蠢的、荒謬的	同義詞 foolish / ridiculous / absurd
	聰明的、合理的	反義詞 intelligent / wise / reasonable

convenient	方便的、合宜的	同義詞 available / handy / comfortable
	不方便、不宜的	反義詞 inconvenient / troublesome / unsuitable
toxic	有毒的、有害的	同義詞 poisonous / venomous / harmful
	無害的、有益的	反義詞 harmless / wholesome / healthful
independent	獨立的、單獨的	同義詞 autonomous / unconnected / individual
	依賴的、從屬的	反義詞 dependent / reliant / subordinate
unfortunately	不幸地、遺憾地	同義詞 unluckily / miserably / pitifully
	幸運地、適時地	反義詞 fortunately / happily / opportunely
error	錯誤、失誤	同義詞 mistake / fault / blunder
	正確、適當	反義詞 accuracy / correctness / rightness
profit	收益、利潤	同義詞 gain / benefit / earnings
	虧損、損失	反義詞 loss / deficit / shortage
international	國際的、全球的	同義詞 worldwide / cosmopolitan / global
	國家的、本國的	反義詞 national / state / domestic
benefit	利益、好處	同義詞 advantage / profit / gain
	損害、損失	反義詞 damage / cost / loss
believe	相信、認為	同義詞 trust / suppose / think
	懷疑、不相信	反義詞 doubt / suspect / distrust
follow	跟隨、追蹤	同義詞 pursue / trace / chase
	領導、指揮	反義詞 lead / precede / direct

1 飲食民生

2 歷史懷舊

3 現代化實用科技

4 資訊與知識傳遞

Ballpoint Pen 原子筆

12-1 捷爾吉的油墨配方

MP3 34

A seemingly simple concept and an easy invention, ballpoint pens were developed in the late 19th century. The first patent for a ballpoint pen was issued to John J. Load in October 1888. The idea was to design a writing instrument that would be able to write on rough surfaces such as wood which fountain pens could not.

原子筆，看似一個簡單的概念和發明，是在 19 世紀後期被開發出來的。但其實它並不如你認為的如此容易。原子筆的第一個專利是在 1888 年 10 月由約翰·勞德所取得。他一開始的想法是設計一個能在粗糙表面，如木頭，上書寫的工具。這是鋼筆做不到的。

Unfortunately, the potential was not seen and the ink technology was not reliable enough to make the ballpoint pen commercially available. The ink was either too thick or too thin which caused overflowing or clogging

不幸的是由於時機未到且油墨的技術還不夠可靠到能將原子筆市售。當時的油墨不是太濃稠就是太稀，因而造成油墨溢出或

problems.

Until 1931, a Hungarian newspaper editor Laszlo Biro was smart enough to use newspaper ink for pen since newspaper ink dried quickly and was smudge free However, news paper ink dried too fast to be held in the reservoir.

Luckily, his brother Gyorgy, a chemist, developed viscous ink formulas for the ball point pens which compatibly prevent ink from drying inside the reservoir while allowing controlled flow. The Biro brothers later on filed a new patent in 1943 with their friend Juan Jorge Meyne and started to manufacture the Birome Pens in Argentina.

阻塞的問題。

直到1931年，匈牙利報紙拉斯洛‧比羅很聰明的想到利用報紙油墨作為筆的墨水，因為報紙的印刷油墨快乾，且沒有暈染的問題。但他面臨了另一個問題。報紙的油墨乾燥過快，無法存放在筆芯中。

幸運的是，他的弟弟捷爾吉是位化學家，他發明初粘性不同的油墨配方，可放於原子筆的筆芯中，在防止乾涸的同時有能控制流量。 比羅兄弟後來與他們的朋友胡安‧豪爾赫‧美恩在1943 年時提出新的專利，並開始在阿根廷製造 Birome 原子筆。

1 飲食民生

2 歷史懷舊

3 現代化實用科技

4 資訊與知識傳遞

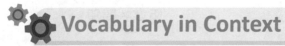

Vocabulary in Context

❶ Andrew had a natural talent for learning and playing all kinds of musical _____, and he formed a rock band of his own when entering college.

Devices is in the closest meaning to this word.

A. animation   C. substitute

B. gestures   D. instruments

❷ Due to the reddish coloring from the iron oxide on its _____, Mars is often referred to as the "Red Planet".

Exterior is in the closest meaning to this word.

A. surface   C. carpet

B. galaxy   D. maintenance

❸ The corporation planned to establish chain stores all over the world and made great efforts to look for superior and _____ store managers.

Trustworthy is in the closest meaning to this word.

A. absent-minded   C. reliable

B. sanitary   D. descriptive

❹ To achieve immortality and enjoy the afterlife, the ancient Egyptian pharaohs were mummified after their death to _____ their bodies from decaying.

Stop is in the closest meaning to this word.

A. abandon   C. celebrate

B. prevent   D. stipulate

❶ 安德魯有學習和演奏各種樂器的天份，一上大學他就組了一支他自己的搖滾樂團。

Devices 的意思最接近於這個字。

A. 動畫　　　　　　　C. 替代品

B. 手勢　　　　　　　D. 儀器

❷ 由於來自於星球表面的氧化鐵而形成紅色色澤，火星經常被稱為 "紅色星球"。

Exterior 的意思最接近於這個字。

A. 表面　　　　　　　C. 地毯

B. 銀河　　　　　　　D. 維修

❸ 這家公司計畫在全世界建立連鎖店，因而努力尋找優秀且可靠的分店經理。

Trustworthy 的意思最接近於這個字。

A. 心不在焉的　　　　C. 可信賴的

B. 衛生的　　　　　　D. 描述的

❹ 為了追求不朽以及享受來生，古埃及法老在死後被製作成木乃伊以防止遺體腐化。

Stop 的意思最接近於這個字。

A. 遺棄　　　　　　　C. 慶祝

B. 防止　　　　　　　D. 規定

答案 ❶ D ❷ A ❸ C ❹ B

1 飲食民生

2 歷史懷舊

3 現代化實用科技

4 資訊與知識傳遞

The Birome was brought to the United States in 1945 by a mechanical pencil maker, Eversharp Co. Eversharp Co. and Eberhard Faner Co. teamed up and licensed the rights to sell the Birome ballpoint pen in the US.

Birome 原子筆在 1945 年由自動鉛筆公司 Eversharp 公司聯合 Eberhard Faner 公司拿下特許權，並在美國販售 Birome 原子筆。

At the same time, an American entrepreneur Milton Reynolds saw the potential of the ballpoint pen, and therefore founded the Reynolds International Pen Company.

在同時，美國企業家米爾頓－雷諾茲看到原子筆的潛力，並因此成立了雷諾國際製筆公司。

Both companies were doing great and ballpoint pen sales went rocket high in 1946, though people were still not 100% satisfied.

兩家公司都在做得非常好。原子筆銷量在 1946 年到達高峰，雖然人們仍然不是 100%滿意。

Another famous ballpoint pen maker would be Marcel Bich. Bich was the founder of the famous pen company

另一個著名的圓珠筆製造商是馬塞爾－畢克。畢克是著名的筆

Bic we all recognize today.

公司 Bic 的創辦人。

The Bic ballpoint pen has the history since 1953.

Bic 原子筆擁有自 1953 年以來的歷史。

Unlike most inventors, whose inventions were appreciated by the society when they were alive, John Jacob Loud did not.

與大多數發明家不同的是，約翰勞德於生前的發明並未受到社會重視。

Vocabulary in Context

⑤ The factory was forced to slow down its manufacturing speed after parts of its _____ apparatus went wrong.

Machine-operated is in the closest meaning to this word.

A. artistic   C. mechanical

B. symbolic   D. therapeutic

⑥ What is great about Bill Gates is that he is not only a successful _____ but a person dedicated to his ideals of making the world better by working for charitable causes.

Businessman is in the closest meaning to this word.

A. critic   C. publisher

B. narrator   D. entrepreneur

⑦ In the class reunion, we could hardly _____ Henry, who has changed a lot in appearance over the past ten years.

Identify is in the closest meaning to this word.

A. coax   C. inspect

B. recognize   D. enlighten

⑧ It's rather a pity that man _____ little what he has but craves much for what he doesn't own.

Values is in the closest meaning to this word.

A. explains   C. tolerates

B. mingles   D. appreciates

5 這座工廠在它部份的機械設備出狀況後,被迫放慢製造的速度。

Machine-operated 的意思最接近於這個字。

A. 藝術的　　　　　　　C. 機械的

B. 象徵的　　　　　　　D. 有療效的

6 比爾蓋茲了不起的地方在於他不僅是一名成功的企業家,並且是一名致力於藉由從事慈善事業而使得這個世界更美好的理念的人。

Businessman 的意思最接近於這個字。

A. 評論家　　　　　　　C. 出版商

B. 敘事者　　　　　　　D. 企業家

7 在同學會中,我們幾乎認不出亨利了,因為他的外表在過去十年來改變很多。

Identify 的意思最接近於這個字。

A. 哄騙　　　　　　　　C. 檢查

B. 認得　　　　　　　　D. 啟蒙

8 人們不珍惜他們所擁有的反而去過度渴望他們所沒有的東西是件令人相當遺憾的事。

Values 的意思最接近於這個字。

A. 說明　　　　　　　　C. 忍受

B. 混和　　　　　　　　D. 賞識

 答案 **5** C　**6** D　**7** B　**8** D

As a very smart kid, he later graduated from Harvard College, but instead of becoming a lawyer, Loud followed his father's footsteps and became a loyal cashier at the Union National Bank. He remained at his job for over 20 years until his resignation in 1895 for health reasons. Loud obtained the first patent for the ballpoint pen in 1888.

身為一個聰明的小孩，他之後於哈佛學院畢業，追隨父親的腳步成為國家聯邦銀行一個忠實的出納員，而不是律師。勞德在 1888 年獲得的第一個原字筆的專利。

The idea was to use a tiny steel ball as the tip of the pen and make a writing instrument that can be used on leather products, which fountain pens could not.

當時的想法是利用一個小鋼球作為筆尖，使書寫工具可以用在皮革製品上。這是當時鋼筆所不能做到的。

He noted in the patent: My invention consists of an improved reservoir or fountain pen, especially useful, among other purposes, for marking on rough surfaces-such as wood, coarse wrapping-paper, and other articles

他在該專利中指出：我的發明包括一種改進的貯存器，使鋼筆有特別用途，可用於標記在粗糙表面上，如木材、粗包裝紙，

where an ordinary pen could not be used."

和其它製品。這是一般筆所做不到的。

However, the potential of the ballpoint pen went unexploited because it was too coarse for letter writing.

然而，原子筆的潛力未被開發，因為設計的過於粗糙，無法使用於書信中。

It was not until viscous ink formulas were developed did the ballpoint pen become popular, about 27 years after Loud passed away.

直到開發出油墨配方，原子筆才走紅，大約是勞德死後的27年了。

1
飲食民生

2
歷史懷舊

3
現代化實用科技

4
資訊與知識傳遞

Vocabulary in Context

9 The notorious mayor, who committed bribery and embezzlement, finally handed in his _____ and was put in jail.

Quitting is in the closest meaning to this word.

A. thesis   C. resignation

B. measurement   D. disapproval

10 To _____ a higher level of education is vital to your getting better employment and fairer salaries in the future.

Receive is in the closest meaning to this word.

A. obtain   C. inquire

B. promise   D. exaggerate

11 Talking too loudly on a cell phone may cause disturbance to people around you, _____ in a cinema.

Particularly is in the closest meaning to this word.

A. especially   C. potentially

B. consequently   D. righteously

12 To achieve the sustainability of the earth and humans, it's essential that we cherish and conserve the _____ natural ecosystems.

Undeveloped is in the closest meaning to this word.

A. doubtful   C. refundable

B. unexploited   D. communicative

❾ 因犯下賄賂及盜用公款罪行而聲名狼藉的市長最後的結局是遞交辭呈並且被關入監獄裡。

Quitting 的意思最接近於這個字。

A. 論文　　　　　　　　C. 辭職

B. 測量　　　　　　　　D. 不贊同

❿ 獲得較高學位對於日後你要取得較佳的工作及較高的薪水是很關鍵的。

Receive 的意思最接近於這個字。

A. 獲得　　　　　　　　C. 詢問

B. 允諾　　　　　　　　D. 誇大

⓫ 手機講太大聲可能會對你週遭的人造成困擾，尤其是在電影院裡的時候。

Particularly 的意思最接近於這個字。

A. 尤其　　　　　　　　C. 潛在地

B. 結果　　　　　　　　D. 正直地

⓬ 為了要達成地球和人類永續的生存，我們必須要珍惜並保護未開發的自然生態系統。

Undeveloped 的意思最接近於這個字。

A. 可疑的　　　　　　　C. 可退款的

B. 未開發的　　　　　　D. 溝通的

 C A A B

12-4 同反義詞表

同反義詞一覽表 Unit 12		
instrument	儀器、工具	同義詞 implement / device / tool
	成品、傑作	反義詞 outcome / masterwork / masterpiece
surface	表面、外面	同義詞 exterior / face / outside
	內部、裡面	反義詞 interior / core / inside
reliable	可靠的、忠誠的	同義詞 dependable / trustworthy / faithful
	不可靠、不忠的	反義詞 unreliable / disloyal / unfaithful
prevent	預防、阻止	同義詞 shield / stop / prohibit
	允許、同意	反義詞 allow / permit / consent
mechanical	機械的、技巧的	同義詞 machine-operated / technological / skillful
	勞動的、費力的	反義詞 laboring / laborious / strenuous
entrepreneur	企業家、實業家	同義詞 businessman / enterpriser / industrialist
	勞工、雇員	反義詞 laborer / worker / employee
recognize	認出、認識	同義詞 identify / know / acknowledge
	漠視、忽視	反義詞 disregard / ignore / neglect
appreciate	欣賞、感謝	同義詞 admire / value / thank
	鄙視、看不起	反義詞 depreciate / disesteem / despise
satisfied	滿意的、滿足的	同義詞 pleased / delighted / contented
	不滿的、抗議的	反義詞 unsatisfied / discontented / protesting

founder	創立者、創始人	同義詞 creator / establisher / promoter
	毀壞者、破壞者	反義詞 destructor / devastator / spoiler
alive	活著的、存在的	同義詞 living / extant / existent
	死亡的、已故的	反義詞 dead / lifeless / deceased
resignation	辭職、順從	同義詞 quitting / submission / compliance
	就職、違抗	反義詞 inauguration / resistance / disobedience
obtain	得到、獲得	同義詞 acquire / gain / receive
	給予、提供	反義詞 give / present / offer
especially	特別地、主要地	同義詞 particularly / specially / primarily
	通常地、一般地	反義詞 commonly / normally / generally
unexploited	未開發、原始的	同義詞 undeveloped / uncivilized / primitive
	文明的、先進的	反義詞 civilized / advanced / developed
useful	有用的、有益的	同義詞 helpful / practical / beneficial
	無用的、無效的	反義詞 vain / useless / ineffectual
coarse	粗糙的、粗俗的	同義詞 rough / crude / vulgar
	精巧的、精緻的	反義詞 fine / delicate / exquisite
ordinary	平常的、通常的	同義詞 usual / average / common
	非凡的、特別的	反義詞 exceptional / extraordinary / special

13-1 鉛筆的發明

Back in ancient Rome, scribes used a thin metal rod called a "stylus" to leave a readable mark on papyrus. Styluses were made of lead which we call pencil core now, whereas pencil cores now are no longer made with lead but non-toxic graphite.

早在古羅馬，文士用細金屬絲作成「手寫筆」在莎草紙上留下可讀的標誌。手寫筆是由鉛所製造，我們現在也稱之為鉛筆芯，而鉛筆芯已經不再是由鉛製成而是由無毒的石墨製成。

In 1564, a large graphite deposit in Borrowdale, England. The graphite could leave much darker mark than lead which is more suitable to be used as stylus, but the material was much softer and was hard to hold. Nicolas-Jacques Conte, a French painter, invented the modern pencil lead at the request of Lazare Nicolas Marguerite Carnot.

1564 年在英格蘭博羅發現了大型的石墨礦床。石墨可以留下比鉛更深的標記，但該物質更柔軟並且難用手握。尼古拉斯·雅克·康特，一個法國畫家，依照拉扎爾尼古拉斯·瑪格麗特卡諾的要求，發明了鉛筆。

Conte mixed powdered graphite with clay and pressed the material between two half-cylinders of wood. Thus was formed the modern pencil. Conte received a patent for the invention in 1795.

During the 19th century industrial revolution, started by Faber-Castell, Lyra and other companies, pencil industry was very active. United States used to import pencils from Europe until the war with England which cut off imports.

康特混合粉狀石墨和粘土，並在兩個半圓柱木材的材料上施壓。由此形成了現代鉛筆。孔特在 1795 年獲得了專利。

在 19 世紀的工業革命，輝柏嘉、天琴座等公司為開端，鉛筆行業非常活躍。美國使用從歐洲進口的鉛筆，直到與英國的戰爭，切斷了進口。

1 飲食民生

2 歷史懷舊

3 現代化實用科技

4 資訊與知識傳遞

Vocabulary in Context

❶ Mr. Goodman enjoyed collecting the _____ Chinese art and antiques; he even opened an antique shop for his hobby.

Old is in the closest meaning to this word.

A. optimistic   C. ancient

B. venomous   D. supernatural

❷ At the embarrassing moment, Anthony had a hard time finding _____ words to express his apology.

Proper is in the closest meaning to this word.

A. fragrant   C. proficient

B. suitable   D. antisocial

❸ In _____ days, making proper health management is essential since health is the foundation of success and happiness.

Contemporary is in the closest meaning to this word.

A. modern   C. attractive

B. justifiable   D. prehistoric

❹ As long as you make the _____, the department store counter will consent to allow a full refund of the amount paid.

Demand is in the closest meaning to this word.

A. ancestor   C. performance

B. flare   D. request

❶ 古德曼先生喜愛收集古代中國藝術品和古董；他甚至因為這項嗜好開了一家古董店。

Old 的意思最接近於這個字。

A. 樂觀的　　　　　　　C. 古代的

B. 有毒的　　　　　　　D. 超自然的

❷ 在尷尬的那一瞬間，安東尼找不出貼切的話來表達他的歉意。

Proper 的意思最接近於這個字。

A. 芳香的　　　　　　　C. 精通的

B. 適合的　　　　　　　D. 反社會的

❸ 就今日來說，由於健康是成功以及快樂的基礎，做好適當的健康管理是必要的。

Contemporary 的意思最接近於這個字。

A. 現代的　　　　　　　C. 吸引人的

B. 有理由的　　　　　　D. 史前的

❹ 只要你提出要求，百貨公司櫃台會同意給予退還全部的付款。

Demand 的意思最接近於這個字。

A. 祖先　　　　　　　　C. 表演

B. 閃光　　　　　　　　D. 要求

 答案 ❶C　❷B　❸A　❹D

In 1812, a Massachusetts cabinet maker, William Monroe, made the first wooden pencil. The American pencil industry also took off during the 19th century. Starting with the Joseph Dixon Crucible Company, many pencil factories are based on the East Coast , such as New York or New Jersey.

1812 年，麻省的一個櫥櫃製造商，威廉・莫瑞，製作了第一個木製鉛筆。美國製筆業也是在 19 世紀起飛。由約瑟夫・狄克遜公司開始，很多鉛筆工廠都開在東岸，如紐約或新澤西州。

At first, pencils were all natural, unpainted and without printing company's names. Not until 1890s, many pencil companies started to paint pencils in yellow and put their brand name on it. Why yellow? Red or blue would look nice, too." You might think. It was actually a special way to tell the consumer that the graphite came from China.

起初，鉛筆都是天然的，沒有油漆，沒有印刷公司的名稱。直到 1890 年代，許多鉛筆公司開始把鉛筆漆成黃色，並把自己的品牌名稱印上。你可能會認為「為什麼是黃色？紅色或藍色的也很好看。」。它實際上是用一種特殊的方式在告訴大家，石墨是來自中國。

It is because back in the 1800s, the best graphite in the world came from China. And the color yellow in China means royalty and respect. Only the imperial family was allowed to use the color yellow. Therefore, the American pencil companies began to paint their pencils bright yellow to show the regal feeling.

這是因為早在 1800 年時，世界上最好的石墨來自中國。而在中國，黃色意味著皇室和尊重。只有皇室允許使用的黃色。因此，美國的鉛筆公司開始將自己的鉛筆漆成明亮的黃色，以顯示帝王的感覺。

Here we will be introducing Nicolas Jacques Conte who was credited as the inventor of the modern lead pencil from France. Born in 1755, Conte was not only an inventor but also a painter, chemist, physicist, engineer and even scientist.

在這裡，我們將介紹尼古拉斯‧雅克‧康特，一位來自法國的現代鉛筆發明人。出生於 1755 年，康特不僅是一位發明家又是畫家、化學家、物理學家、工程師甚至科學家。

1 飲食民生

2 歷史懷舊

3 現代化實用科技

4 資訊與知識傳遞

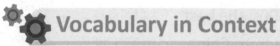 **Vocabulary in Context**

⑤ It's _____ for people to yearn for longevity and scientists who have been working on ways of lengthening mankind's life span.

Normal is in the closest meaning to this word.

A. natural   C. impulsive

B. sociable   D. legitimate

⑥ The painful bothering and torments to celebrities and the __ _____ are the endless pursuit and photographing of the paparazzi.

Nobles is in the closest meaning to this word.

A. guardians   C. royalty

B. minority   D. artists

⑦ The brutal man committed serious crimes out of impulse; __ _____, he was sentenced to life imprisonment and was deprived of his civil rights.

Consequently is in the closest meaning to this word.

A. firstly   C. previously

B. however   D. therefore

⑧ It's generally believed that during the fourth century B.C., Alexander the Great _____ the arrival of perfume in Greece.

Presented is in the closest meaning to this word.

A. wrinkled   C. radiated

B. meditated　　　　D. introduced

❺ 人們渴望長壽是很自然的，而科學家正致力於尋找延長人類壽命的方法。

Normal 的意思最接近於這個字。

A. 自然的　　　　C. 衝動的

B. 擅長交際的　　D. 合法的

❻ 名流和皇室成員痛苦的困擾及折磨在於狗仔隊永無止盡的跟蹤和拍照。

Nobles 的意思最接近於這個字。

A. 監護人　　　　C. 皇室成員

B. 少數民族　　　D. 藝術家

❼ 這個殘暴的人因衝動犯下嚴重的罪行；因此，他被判處終身監禁並且被剝奪公民權。

Consequently 的意思最接近於這個字。

A. 首先　　　　　C. 先前地

B. 然而　　　　　D. 因此

❽ 一般人相信在西元前第四世紀期間，亞歷山大大帝把香水引進至希臘。

Presented 的意思最接近於這個字。

A. 弄皺　　　　　C. 輻射

B. 沉思　　　　　D. 介紹

 答案　❺ A　❻ C　❼ D　❽ D

Very different from the invention of the pencil, Conte also has the reputation as an expert in balloon warfare which ensured his inclusion in the party of some 200 academics and scientists to accompany Napoleon on his expedition to Egypt in 1798.

與鉛筆的發明大不同的是，康特也享有氣球戰專家的美譽，並在 1789 年與 200 位學者與科學家一同陪同拿破崙遠征埃及。

Unfortunately, the event ended as a disaster. The balloon caught fire and the Egyptians received the impression that what had been demonstrated was a machine of war for setting fire to the enemy encampments.

不幸的是，活動在災難中結束。熱氣球起火，埃及人便認為這是一台為了火燒敵人營地而設計的戰爭機器。

Prior to Conte's pencil invention, the writing material had been nothing but a lump of pure graphite putting into a wooden stick.

在康特發明鉛筆之前，書寫材料一直只是將純石墨泥投入木棍之中。

Instead of using the pure English graphite, Conte found a way to mix graphite in a powdered form with clay

代替使用純英國石墨，康特發明了一種混合石墨粉末與粘土

and then baked it in a way that the lead could be produced in varying degrees of hardness.

Conte not only made the manageable writing material, but is also credited with inventing the machinery needed to make round lead which no other inventors who created for pencil creation did.

Up until today, Conte's brand name is still known as the pencil manufacture in France.

的形式，然後經過烘烤，發展出可以製造不同硬度的鉛。

康特不僅發明出容易控制的書寫材料，發明製作了圓形筆芯所需的機也歸功於他，這是其他鉛筆創造人沒做到的。

直至今日在法國，康特的品牌名稱仍然被稱為鉛筆製造商。

1 飲食民生

2 歷史懷舊

3 現代化實用科技

4 資訊與知識傳遞

Vocabulary in Context

9 The extraordinary director, Ang Lee, has won himself an international _____ for his amazingly unique ways of directing films.

Fame is in the closest meaning to this word.

A. conservation   C. reputation

B. heritage   D. program

10 Out of pity, Rick _____ the old man who seemed to have lost his way to the police station and helped him return home.

Escorted is in the closest meaning to this word.

A. distorted   C. idolized

B. accompanied   D. supervised

11 Recently, a team of scientists, teachers, and students went on an _____ to explore some of the wonders of the Amazon Rainforest.

Journey is in the closest meaning to this word.

A. expedition   C. isolation

B. orchestra   D. unemployment

12 The board of directors announced several measures to minimize the problem to a more _____ level.

Controllable is in the closest meaning to this word.

A. opposing   C. casual

B. diplomatic   D. manageable

⑨ 卓越的李安導演因其令人驚嘆獨特的導演方式而贏得國際聲譽。

Fame 的意思最接近於這個字。

A. 保存　　　　　　　C. 聲望

B. 遺產　　　　　　　D. 節目

⑩ 出自於同情，瑞克陪伴那位似乎迷路的老先生到警局並協助他返家。

Escorted 的意思最接近於這個字。

A. 扭曲　　　　　　　C. 崇拜

B. 伴隨　　　　　　　D. 監督

⑪ 最近，一支由科學家、教師，以及學生組成的隊伍進行遠征去探索亞馬遜河熱帶雨林區的一些奇景。

Journey 的意思最接近於這個字。

A. 遠征　　　　　　　C. 孤立

B. 管弦樂隊　　　　　D. 失業

⑫ 董事會宣佈數項措施來把問題降低到比較能應付的程度。

Controllable 的意思最接近於這個字。

A. 對立的　　　　　　C. 隨意的

B. 外交的　　　　　　D. 可處理的

1 飲食民生

2 歷史懷舊

3 現代化實用科技

4 資訊與知識傳遞

 答案　⑨ C　⑩ B　⑪ A　⑫ D

同反義詞一覽表　Unit 13		
ancient	古老的、陳舊的	同義詞 old / antique / obsolete
	現代的、最新的	反義詞 modern / contemporary / newest
suitable	適當的、適合的	同義詞 proper / fitting / adequate
	不合適、不相稱	反義詞 inappropriate / inadequate / unfit
modern	現代的、最新的	同義詞 contemporary / present / progressive
	過時的、守舊的	反義詞 aged / out-dated / conservative
request	要求、請求	同義詞 demand / requisition / asking
	回答、答覆	反義詞 answer / reply / response
active	主動的、活潑的	同義詞 dynamic / lively / energetic
	被動的、無生氣	反義詞 passive / inactive / spiritless
natural	自然的、天生的	同義詞 normal / genuine / original
	不自然、奇異的	反義詞 unnatural / artificial / eccentric
royalty	皇室貴族、高尚	同義詞 noble / aristocrat / loftiness
	庶民、粗俗	反義詞 commoner / vulgarity / crudeness
therefore	因此、因而	同義詞 hence / consequently / accordingly
	因為、由於	反義詞 because / as / since

introduce	介紹、引出	同義詞 present / launch / elicit
	結束、終止	反義詞 end / conclude / terminate
respect	尊敬、敬重	同義詞 regard / esteem / reverence
	侮辱、蔑視	反義詞 insult / humiliation / contempt
credit	歸功於、相信	同義詞 honor / believe / accept
	不信任、懷疑	反義詞 distrust / doubt / question
reputation	名譽、聲望	同義詞 fame / renown / prestige
	惡名、聲名狼藉	反義詞 discredit / infamy / notoriety
accompany	陪同、護衛	同義詞 companion / escort / guard
	離開、離棄	反義詞 leave / abandon / desert
expedition	遠征、探險	同義詞 journey / trek / pilgrimage
	短途旅程、遠足	反義詞 outing / excursion / hike
manageable	可管理、控制的	同義詞 administrable / governable / controllable
	難控制、難駕馭	反義詞 uncontrollable / unruly / wild
expert	專家、達人	同義詞 professional / adept / veteran
	外行、新手	反義詞 amateur / layman / rookie
warfare	鬥爭、競爭	同義詞 fight / conflict / battle
	和諧、友好	反義詞 harmony / concord / amity
disaster	災難、不幸	同義詞 adversity / misfortune / mishap
	好運、幸福	反義詞 fortune / blessing / happiness

Typewriter 打字機

14-1 打字機的發明　　　　　MP3 40

A typewriter is a writing machine that has one character on each key press.

打字機是一個寫作的機器，在每個按鍵上各有一個字母。

The machine prints characters by making ink impressions on a moveable type letterpress printing. Typewriters, like other practical products such as automobiles, telephones, and refrigerators, the invention was developed by numerous inventors. The very first record of the typewriter invention was back in 1575.

機器利用活字凸版印刷通過墨水打印字符。打字機，如同其他實用的產品，如汽車、電話和冰箱，是由眾多的發明人所開發出來的。打字機發明的第一個記錄最早在 1575 年。

In 1575, an Italian printmaker, Francesco Rampazzetto, invented the "scrittura tattile" which is a machine to impress letters on papers. Hundreds of years passed by and many different

1575 年，意大利的版畫家，弗朗西斯，發明了「scrittura tattile」，這是一台用來打字的機器。幾

types of typewriters were being developed. However, no commercially practical machine was created. It wasn't until 1829 that an American inventor William Austin Burt patented a machine called the "Typographer" which is listed as the "first typewriter".

However, the design was still not practical enough for the market since it was slower than handwriting. In 1865, Rasmus Malling-Hansen from Denmark invented the first commercially sold typewriter, called the Hansen Writing Ball. It was successfully sold in Europe. In the US, the first commercially successful typewriter was invented by Christopher Latham Sholes in 1868.

百年過去了，很多不同類型的打字機被開發出來。然而，沒有商業實用機的創建。直到 1829 年，美國發明家威廉‧奧斯汀伯特申請了一台機器的專利稱為「字體設計」，它被列為「第一台打字機」。

然而，設計仍然不夠實用，因為它比寫字要緩慢。 1865 年，來自丹麥的拉斯穆斯莫林‧漢森發明了第一台在市場上銷售的打字機，叫做漢森寫作球。它成功地在歐洲銷售。在美國，第一個商業成功的打字機是在 1868 年由克里斯托弗‧萊瑟姆‧肖爾斯所發明的。

1 飲食民生

2 歷史懷舊

3 現代化實用科技

4 資訊與知識傳遞

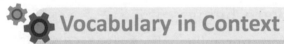

Vocabulary in Context

❶ The admirable NBA basketball players are not only _____ in their basketball skills but passionate and generous in supporting charity work.

Well-trained is in the closest meaning to this word.

A. different   C. territorial

B. antisocial   D. professional

❷ Though separated far apart, Melissa still maintained regular _____ with her best friend these years.

Letter-writing is in the closest meaning to this word.

A. landscape   C. correspondence

B. poverty   D. temptation

❸ Her elaborate presentation and smooth use of the powerpoint slides gave the _____ that she was well-prepared and organized.

Feeling is in the closest meaning to this word.

A. cultivation   C. possession

B. impression   D. reservation

❹ Due to _____ serious delays of shipment, the company decided to ask for compensation or even a full refund.

Many is in the closest meaning to this word.

A. numerous   C. scarce

B. logical   D. observant

❶令人欽佩的NBA籃球球星不僅專業於他們的籃球技巧，並且熱情慷慨地支持慈善工作。

Well-trained 的意思最接近於這個字。

A. 不同的　　　　　　　C. 領土的

B. 反社會的　　　　　　D. 專業的

❷儘管相隔遙遠，梅莉莎這些年來仍然持續地和她最要好的朋友保持定期的通信。

Letter-writing 的意思最接近於這個字。

A. 風景　　　　　　　　C. 通信

B. 貧窮　　　　　　　　D. 誘惑

❸她詳盡的報告以及流暢的簡報運用給予人們她事前準備充分並且條理分明的印象。

Feeling 的意思最接近於這個字。

A. 栽培　　　　　　　　C. 擁有

B. 印象　　　　　　　　D. 預約

❹由於多次貨物運送的嚴重延遲，這家公司決定要求索賠或甚至全額退款。

Many 的意思最接近於這個字。

A. 許多的　　　　　　　C. 稀少的

B. 合邏輯的　　　　　　D. 善於觀察的

 ❶ D　❷ C　❸ B　❹ A

Another 50 years later, the typewriter designs had reached a standard. Most typewriters followed the concept that each key was attached to a type bar with a corresponding letter molded. The platen was mounted on a carriage which moved left or right, automatically advancing the typing position horizontally after each character was typed. The paper rolled around the typewriter's platen.

For decades, the typewriter was the major tool for work. It wasn't until the early 1980s did typewriters start to be replaced by word processors and eventually personal computers. The typewriter now is considered an antique. Many companies stopped manufacturing it anymore. Therefore, if you still have one in your home, take good care of it because it might be worth a fortune in the future.

50 年後，打字機的設計已經達到了標準。大多數打字機都是以每個鍵被附加到與相應的字母模型的概念。壓板被安裝在一個左右滑動的滑架，自動推進每個字母，再輸入水平的打字位置。紙張是圍繞在打字機的滾筒上。

幾十年來，打字機是工作的主要工具。直到 1980 年代初期，打字機開始由文字處理器和個人電腦取代。打字機，現在被認為是一個古董。很多公司停止製造它了。因此，如果你仍然有一台在你家，請照顧好它，因為它可能未來會非常值錢。

Born and raised in Pennsylvania, Christopher Latham Sholes-born on February 14th, 1819, was educated to become a printer as his 3 brothers. He became an editor of the post at Madison and founded a weekly newspaper called the Southport Telegraph. Different from other newspapers, the Southport Telegraph would give free ad space to any writers or teachers who have thoughts about society.

It is because Sholes believed that people should communicate as much as possible to bring together thoughts. After the Southport Telegraph, Sholes also worked or funded several different newspapers, such as Republican papers, the Milwaukee Daily Sentinel and News and even the Federal Post.

於 1819 年 2 月 14 日出生於賓州的克里斯托弗・萊瑟姆・肖爾斯與他的三個兄弟一起被教育要成為一位打印員。他成為了麥迪遜一家新聞社的編輯，並創辦了一家週報叫做南港電訊報。與其他報紙不同的是，南港電訊報每天都給予對於社會上擁有想法的作家或教師免費的（寫作）空間。

這是因為肖爾斯認為，人們應該盡可能地匯集想法並溝通。南港電訊報後，肖爾斯還曾任職或資助了幾個不同的報紙，如共和黨報紙，密爾沃基哨兵日報和新聞，甚至聯邦日報。

1　飲食民生

2　歷史懷舊

3　現代化實用科技

4　資訊與知識傳遞

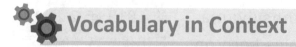

Vocabulary in Context

⑤ Ralph got fired this month because his performance failed to reach the required _____; however, he planned to start all over again.

Criteria is in the closest meaning to this word.

A. publication   C. expansion

B. standard   D. trademark

⑥ As soon as Steven got his year-end bonus, he purchased a highly functional digital camera that could adjust _____.

Spontaneously is in the closest meaning to this word.

A. constructively   C. irrelevantly

B. gradually   D. automatically

⑦ The _____ cars shown in the International Car Fair attracted lots of car fans all over the world to appreciate.

Antique is in the closest meaning to this word.

A. pointed   C. vintage

B. accurate   D. sympathetic

⑧ Owing to generation gap, modern parents find it more and more difficult to _____ with their children.

Link is in the closest meaning to this word.

A. bewilder   C. project

B. exempt   D. communicate

❺勞夫由於表現未達到要求的標準而在這個月遭到解雇;然而,他計畫全部重新開始。

Criteria 的意思最接近於這個字。

A. 出版　　　　　　　C. 擴張

B. 標準　　　　　　　D. 商標

❻史蒂芬一拿到年終獎金就去購買具有自動調節功能高度實用的數位相機。

Spontaneously 的意思最接近於這個字。

A. 建設性地　　　　　C. 無關地

B. 逐漸地　　　　　　D. 自動地

❼國際車展中陳列展示的古董車吸引許多世界各地的車迷慕名前來觀賞。

Antique 的意思最接近於這個字。

A. 尖銳的　　　　　　C. 古董的

B. 正確的　　　　　　D. 同情的

❽由於代溝,現代的父母覺得越來越難和他們的孩子溝通。

Link 的意思最接近於這個字。

A. 困惑　　　　　　　C. 投射

B. 免除　　　　　　　D. 溝通

1 飲食民生

2 歷史懷舊

3 現代化實用科技

4 資訊與知識傳遞

答案　B　D　C　D

Because of his long experience in journalism and politics, he understood the pain in long articles writing ink smudge, misunderstood due to messy hand writing, etc. were all caused by hand writing. Therefore, he invented a machine that would do the task using preset type and a treadle which we called "typewriter" now.

由於他長期在新聞和政治圈的經驗，他理解寫長篇文章所造成的手痛，油墨的沾染，或因為手寫字跡所造成的誤會。因此，他發明了一種使用預置和踏板的機器，我們稱之為「打字機」。

Of course there were many other people invented typing machines years before him, but his invention was different. Sholes' creation was to carve each single letter onto a short metal bar. The very first prototype was built in 1867. Later on, he and his partners worked on a simplified version in order to produce typewriters that were affordable for the general public. Another great invention that Sholes did which made him the "inventor of typewriter" was his keyboard design.

當然，還有許多其他人在肖爾斯之前發明了輸入設備，但與他的發明是不同的。肖爾斯的創作是雕刻每一個字母到一個短的金屬條。第一個原型是建於 1867 年。後來，他和他的夥伴，開始生產一般大眾可以負擔得起的簡易型打字機。另一個肖爾斯的偉大發明使他被認定為打字機的發明家是他的鍵盤設計。

The earliest typing machines usually arranged the letters in an alphabetical order. It is not hard for us to imagine that it would jam easily while typing. Sholes changed the order of the keys as he created prototype after prototype of his machine, trying to eliminate the most frequently occurring jams. The layout kept frequently combined letters separated mechanically, which limited the number of possible collisions between type bars.

The keyboard he created is called the Qwerty Keyboard which is what we still use today. Because of Sholes creation, it opened office careers to women. It was because of his typewriter, typewriter manufacturers started to train women as typists and offered both machine and operator as a package to clients. This was the beginning of women working in offices.

最早的打字機是按字母順序排列。我們不難想像它會很容易在打字時堵塞。肖爾斯改造了鍵盤的順序。他做了非常多的樣本，企圖消除最常堵塞的按鍵，這個排列分開了經常結合的字母，限制了按鍵之間可能的碰撞次數。

他創建的鍵盤被稱為QWERTY 鍵盤，這是我們今天仍然使用的東西。由於肖爾斯的創作，它使職業婦女進入了辦公室。因為他的打字機，使得打字機製造商開始培訓女性打字員，並提供機器和操作員作為一個整體服務給客戶。這是婦女在辦公室裡工作的開始。

1　飲食民生

2　歷史懷舊

3　現代化實用科技

4　資訊與知識傳遞

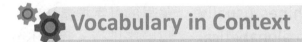

Vocabulary in Context

9 The _____ expressions the professor used made it easier for the students to comprehend the difficult theories.

Condensed is in the closest meaning to this word.

A. simplified   C. desolate

B. arbitrary   D. nominal

10 The real estate prices brought up by rich investors recently have become hardly _____, especially to young people with low income.

Buyable is in the closest meaning to this word.

A. radical   C. unified

B. affordable   D. economical

11 The police tried to find the true murderer by _____ the suspects one by one through investigation.

Excluding is in the closest meaning to this word.

A. deceiving   C. overlapping

B. standardizing   D. eliminating

12 The heavy casualties on the superhighway last weekend resulted from the serious chain _____ among seven cars, accompanied by terrifying car-burning afterward.

Smashing is in the closest meaning to this word.

A. exception   C. collision

B. participation   D. reconciliation

❾ 這位教授所使用簡化的解釋用語讓學生比較容易理解困難的理論。

Condensed 的意思最接近於這個字。

A. 簡化的　　　　　　　C. 荒涼的

B. 獨斷的　　　　　　　D. 名義上的

❿ 近日由富有的投資者所帶動提高的房地產價格超出人們所能負擔，尤其是對低薪的年輕人而言。

Buyable 的意思最接近於這個字。

A. 徹底的　　　　　　　C. 統一的

B. 負擔得起的　　　　　D. 節約的

⓫ 警方經由調查一一排除嫌疑犯試著去找出真正的兇手。

Excluding 的意思最接近於這個字。

A. 欺騙　　　　　　　　C. 重疊

B. 標準化　　　　　　　D. 排除

⓬ 上週末在高速公路上的慘重傷亡肇因於七部車嚴重的連環追撞，伴隨著後續恐怖的火燒車意外。

Smashing 的意思最接近於這個字。

A. 例外　　　　　　　　C. 碰撞

B. 參加　　　　　　　　D. 和解

答案 A B D C

右側邊欄：

1 飲食民生

2 歷史懷舊

3 現代化實用科技

4 資訊與知識傳遞

14-4 同反義詞表

同反義詞一覽表　Unit 14		
professional	職業的、專業的	同義詞 well-trained / occupational / expert
	業餘的、外行的	反義詞 amateur / dilettante / inadept
correspondence	通信、符合	同義詞 letter-writing / accordance / agreement
	不和、分歧	反義詞 discord / conflict / divergence
impression	印象、影響	同義詞 feeling / influence / impact
	模糊、不明確	反義詞 vagueness / obscurity / indefiniteness
numerous	很多的、許多的	同義詞 many / several / considerable
	很少的、不足的	反義詞 little / few / deficient
widely	寬廣地、廣泛地	同義詞 broadly / extensively / comprehensively
	狹小地、有限地	反義詞 narrowly / restrictedly / limitedly
standard	標準、規範	同義詞 criteria / rule / model
	混亂、不規律	反義詞 chaos / variation / irregularity
automatically	自動地、直覺地	同義詞 spontaneously/ voluntarily/ instinctively
	手工地、被動地	反義詞 manually / inactively / passively
vintage	經典的、古老的	同義詞 classic / ancient / antique
	時髦的、流行的	反義詞 fashionable / modern / trendy

communicate	傳達、通訊	同義詞 covey / link / correspond
	分離、脫離	反義詞 disconnect / separate / detach
reach	到達、延伸	同義詞 arrive / land / extend
	離去、啟程	反義詞 leave / depart / start
simplified	簡化的、單純的	同義詞 condensed / easy / plain
	複雜的、繁複的	反義詞 complicated / complex / elaborate
affordable	負擔(買)得起的	同義詞 buyable / purchasable / vendible
	昂貴的、高價的	反義詞 unaffordable / expensive / costly
eliminate	去除、排除	同義詞 remove / exclude / expel
	增加、加入	反義詞 add / combine / join
collision	碰撞、衝突	同義詞 smash / clash / conflict
	和諧、一致	反義詞 harmony / correspondence / consistency
misunderstand	誤會、曲解	同義詞 misapprehend / misinterpret / misread
	了解、理解	反義詞 realize / comprehend / grasp
arrange	安排、整理	同義詞 organize / categorize / sort
	擾亂、攪亂	反義詞 disturb / interrupt / confuse
frequently	頻繁地、慣常地	同義詞 recurrently / regularly / habitually
	不常地、難得地	反義詞 infrequently / seldom / rarely
separate	分離、分隔	同義詞 part / segregate / divide
	連接、結合	反義詞 link / join / combine

1 飲食民生

2 歷史懷舊

3 現代化實用科技

4 資訊與知識傳遞

3
PART

現代化實用科技

單元三大學習法

key 1 主題式記憶
透過主題學習將字彙累績至長期記憶，
而非片段背誦。

key 2 上下文推敲文意
閱讀時不因不熟悉的單字而影響句意理解。

key 3 熟記同反義詞
在雅思各單項中要獲取 7 分以上
需要具備同反義詞轉換的能力。

Unit 15 Telescope 望遠鏡

15-1 望遠鏡功率的提高

The invention of telescope has led us to the moon, the sun, the milky way, and even the galaxy.

望遠鏡的發明帶領我們到月亮、太陽、銀河系、甚至星系。

The earliest working telescope was made by Hans Lippershey from the Netherlands in 1608. The early telescope consisted of a convex objective lens and a concave eyepiece.

最早的望遠鏡是由來自荷蘭的漢斯‧利普斯在 1608 年所發明。早期的望遠鏡包括一個凸物鏡和一個凹透鏡。

It had only 3x magnification. The design was rather simple. In the following year, Galileo Galilei solved the problem of the construction of a telescope by fitting a convex lens in one extremity of a leaded tube and a concave lens in another one.

它只有 3 倍的放大倍率。設計相當簡單。在第二年，伽利略在含鉛管的一個末端配裝一個凹透鏡，並在另一端裝配凸透鏡，解決了望遠鏡的結構問題。

216

Galileo then improved the telescope and greatly increased the power of the telescope.

伽利略之後提升了望遠鏡的結構並大大提高望遠鏡的功率。

His first design magnified three diameters. The second design magnified to eight diameters and then even thirty-three diameters.

他的第一個設計放大了三個直徑。第二個設計放大了八直徑，然後是三十三直徑。

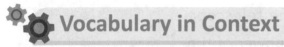 **Vocabulary in Context**

❶ The team going on the journey of exploration into the Brazilian tropical jungles _____ professors, researchers, and scientists.

Included is in the closest meaning to this word.

A. consisted of   C. worshipped

B. scattered   D. prohibited

❷ The sample was observed carefully under _____ of 1,000 times their actual size through the powerful microscope.

Enlargement is in the closest meaning to this word.

A. projection   C. destruction

B. exclusion   D. magnification

❸ According to archaeologists, the _____ of the Stonehenge in Southern England was originally to serve as an observatory and an astronomical calendar.

Building is in the closest meaning to this word.

A. disillusion   C. construction

B. prevalence   D. significance

❹ After working in the company for ten years, Joseph decided to quit the job owing to the _____ of his enduring the heavy workload.

Limitation is in the closest meaning to this word.

A. serenity   C. charity

B. extremity   D. regularity

❶ 這支前往巴西熱帶叢林考察的隊伍是由教授、研究人員,以及科學家所組成的。

Included 的意思最接近於這個字。

A. 組成　　　　　　　　C. 崇拜

B. 分散　　　　　　　　D. 禁止

❷ 這份樣本是透過放大**1000**倍於實物的高倍率顯微鏡加以仔細觀察的。

Enlargement 的意思最接近於這個字。

A. 投射　　　　　　　　C. 毀壞

B. 排除　　　　　　　　D. 放大

❸ 根據考古學家的說法,建造英國南方巨石陣原先的目的是用作天文觀測台以及天文曆法的功用。

Building 的意思最接近於這個字。

A. 幻滅　　　　　　　　C. 建造

B. 流行　　　　　　　　D. 意義

❹ 約瑟夫在這家公司工作十年後決定要辭職,因為他對於沉重工作負擔的忍耐已經到極限了。

Limitation 的意思最接近於這個字。

A. 寧靜　　　　　　　　C. 慈善

B. 極端　　　　　　　　D. 規則性

 ❶ A　❷ D　❸ C　❹ B

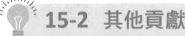

Because of this design, the satellites of Jupiter were discovered in 1610. Later on, the spots of sun, the phases of Venus were all found.

由於這種設計，木星衛星於 1610 年被發現，後來，太陽的斑點及金星的軌跡皆被發現。

Because of his telescope, Galileo was able to demonstrate the revolution of the satellites of Jupiter around the planet and gave predictions of the configuration.

由於他的望遠鏡，伽利略能夠示範操作木星的行星環繞軌跡，並預測衛星的結構。

He was also able to prove the rotation of the Sun on its axis. In 1655, Christian Huygens created the first powerful telescope of Keplerian construction.

他還能夠證明太陽的旋轉在它的軸上。1655 年，克里斯蒂安‧惠更斯創造了開普勒建設的第一個強大的望遠鏡。

Huygens discovered the brightest of Saturn's satellites -Titan- in 1655.

惠更斯並發現了最明亮的土星衛星-Titan。

Four years later, he published the "Systema Saturnium", which was the first time a given true explanation of Saturn's ring-founded on observations made with the same instrument.

4 年後，他出版了「Ｓｙｓｔｅｍａ Saturnium」，這是第一次給土星環的一個真正解釋。這也是用同一台儀器觀測到的。

1　飲食民生

2　歷史懷舊

3　現代化實用科技

4　資訊與知識傳遞

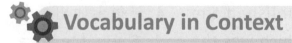# Vocabulary in Context

5 With his smooth body language, the salesman successfully _____ the operation of the kitchen appliances.

Displayed is in the closest meaning to this word.

A. cultivated   C. proclaimed

B. smuggled   D. demonstrated

6 It's odd that some people should be able to make accurate _____ about the future happening. They even claimed to have seen those incidents in person in their dreams.

Forecasts is in the closest meaning to this word.

A. expeditions   C. predictions

B. temptation   D. generation

7 The distant _____ of the Pluto at the furthest reaches of the sun has always aroused astronomers' curiosity and interests to know more about it.

Revolving is in the closest meaning to this word.

A. deposit   C. milestone

B. rotation   D. obstacle

8 Galileo was a famous Italian astronomer. He used his telescope to make _____ of the moon and the Jupiter, and then made great theories.

Watching is in the closest meaning to this word.

A. actions   C. selections

B. decisions   D. observations

❺ 這名銷售員運用流暢的肢體語言成功地示範廚房用具的操作方式。

Displayed 的意思最接近於這個字。

A. 耕作   C. 宣佈

B. 走私   D. 示範

❻ 很奇怪的是有些人竟然能夠對於未來即將發生的事做準確的預測。他們甚至宣稱在他們的夢境中親眼目睹那些事件。

Forecasts 的意思最接近於這個字。

A. 探險   C. 預測

B. 誘惑   D. 產生

❼ 冥王星在距離太陽最遙遠地方的旋轉一向引起天文學者的好奇以及興趣而想作進一步的了解。

Revolving 的意思最接近於這個字。

A. 存款   C. 里程碑

B. 旋轉   D. 障礙

❽ 伽利略是著名的義大利天文學家。他曾使用望遠鏡對月亮及木星作觀測，因而提出重要的理論。

Watching 的意思最接近於這個字。

A. 行動   C. 挑選

B. 決定   D. 觀察

1 飲食民生

2 歷史懷舊

3 現代化實用科技

4 資訊與知識傳遞

答案 ❺ D   ❻ C   ❼ B   ❽ D

Hans Lippershey, a master lens grinder and spectacle maker was born in Wesel Germany in 1570. He then got married and settled in Middelburg in the Netherlands in 1594.

身為一位鏡片研磨師和眼鏡製造商的漢斯・利普斯在 1570 年誕生於德國韋塞爾。爾後，在 1594 年定居於荷蘭米德爾堡，並在同一年結婚。

Eight years later, he immigrated in the Netherlands. Lippershey filed a patent for telescope in 1607 and this was known as the earliest written record of a refracting telescope.

8 年後移民荷蘭。利普斯在 1607 年申請了望遠鏡的專利，這被稱為是折射望遠鏡最早的文字記錄。

There are several different versions of how Lippershey came up with the invention of the telescope.

對於利普斯如何想出望遠鏡的原因有幾種不同的版本。

The most interesting one has to be the one in which Lippershey observed two kids playing with lenses and commented how they could make a far away weather-vane seem closer when

最有趣的版本是有一次利普斯觀察到兩個小孩玩耍時的對話，他們在評論如何利用鏡頭讓一個遙遠的天

looking at it through two lenses.

Lippershey's original instrument consisted of either two convex lenses for an inverted image or a convex objective and a concave eyepiece lens so it would have an upright image. Lippershey remained in Middelburg until he passed away in 1619.

氣風向標看起來似乎更接近。

利普斯的原始工具包括利用兩個凸透鏡以呈現出一個倒置的圖像，或利用凸物鏡和凹透鏡的眼鏡片以呈現出一個正面的圖像。利普斯終其一生留在米德爾，直到他在 1619 年去世。

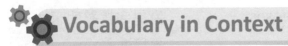 **Vocabulary in Context**

9 Though astronomers and scientists have been trying to make it real for humans to _____ to Mars, the biggest challenge lies in how to get people to and from the planet.

Move is in the closest meaning to this word.

A. express   C. provoke

B. immigrate   D. transplant

10 When asked about the political scandal, the former minister refused to _____ and walked away in haste.

Remark is in the closest meaning to this word.

A. comment   C. idolize

B. expire   D. rehearse

11 Ashley doesn't like to follow trends in her dressing. She has her unique and _____ styles, which makes her distinctive from others.

Creative is in the closest meaning to this word.

A. dedicated   C. righteous

B. original   D. potential

12 Mr. Hamilton was respected for both of his _____ character and boundless enthusiasm in helping others.

Honest is in the closest meaning to this word.

A. mobile   C. upright

B. deceptive   D. controversial

❾ 雖然天文學者及科學家一直試圖要把人類移民火星的夢想付諸實現，然而最大的挑戰在於如何讓人們在火星間來回。

Move 的意思最接近於這個字。

A. 表達　　　　　　　C. 激怒

B. 移民　　　　　　　D. 移植

❿ 當被問及政治醜聞的時候，這名前部長拒絕作評論並且倉促離去。

Remark 的意思最接近於這個字。

A. 評論　　　　　　　C. 崇拜

B. 過期　　　　　　　D. 排演

⓫ 艾旭麗在服裝穿著方面不喜歡趕流行。她有她自己獨特且原創的穿衣風格，而就是這一點使得她與眾不同。

Creative 的意思最接近於這個字。

A. 奉獻的　　　　　　C. 正直的

B. 有創意的　　　　　D. 潛在的

⓬ 漢彌頓先生以他正直的品格以及助人的高度熱忱受到大家的敬重。

Honest 的意思最接近於這個字。

A. 移動的　　　　　　C. 正直的

B. 欺騙的　　　　　　D. 有爭議的

答案　❾ B　❿ A　⓫ B　⓬ C

15-4 同反義詞表

同反義詞一覽表 Unit 15		
consist	組成、構成	同義詞 compose / include / constitute
	解構、拆毀	反義詞 deconstruct / demolish / disassemble
magnification	放大、擴大	同義詞 amplification / enlargement / expansion
	收縮、減小	反義詞 shrink / diminishment / reduction
construction	建造、建設	同義詞 building / establishment / erection
	毀壞、破壞	反義詞 destruction / demolition / wreck
extremity	盡頭、極限	同義詞 end / terminal / limitation
	起源、開端	反義詞 beginning / start / commencement
objective	目標、計畫	同義詞 target / aim / goal
	成就、成果	反義詞 achievement / accomplishment / attainment
following	接著的、其次的	同義詞 next / sequent / successive
	先前的、以前的	反義詞 former / prior / previous
solve	解決、解答	同義詞 settle / explain / answer
	提問、詢問	反義詞 question / ask / inquire
demonstrate	展示、說明	同義詞 display / show / illustrate
	隱藏、掩飾	反義詞 conceal / hide / cover

prediction	預言、預報	同義詞 forecast / foretelling / prophesy
	事實、真實	反義詞 reality / actuality / truth
rotation	旋轉、交替	同義詞 turning / revolving / substitution
	固定、一致	反義詞 settling / accordance / consistency
observation	觀察、注意	同義詞 watching / inspection / notice
	分心、轉移	反義詞 distraction / confusion / diversion
powerful	強有力、影響的	同義詞 mighty / forceful / influential
	軟弱的、無用的	反義詞 powerless / useless / ineffectual
immigrate	遷移、遷入	同義詞 migrate / enter / move
	移居、遷出	反義詞 emigrate / expatriate / leave
comment	評論、批評	同義詞 review / remark / criticize
	順從、讚賞	反義詞 comply / agree / praise
original	原始的、獨創的	同義詞 primary / initial / creative
	最後的、模仿的	反義詞 ultimate / final / imitative
upright	直立的、誠實的	同義詞 erect / honest / truthful
	不正當、虛假的	反義詞 deceitful / dishonorable / pretentious
settle	安頓、平穩	同義詞 steady / calm / pacify
	打擾、妨礙	反義詞 interrupt / distract / disturb
interesting	有趣的、迷人的	同義詞 funny / entertaining / fascinating
	無聊的、單調的	反義詞 boring / dull / monotonous

1 飲食民生

2 歷史懷舊

3 現代化實用科技

4 資訊與知識傳遞

16 Airplane 飛機

16-1 飛機的發明

MP3 46

According to the document from IATA in 2011, 2.8 billion passengers were carried by airplane, which means on average there are 690,000 passengers in the air at any given moment.

據國際航空運輸協會在 2011 年的文件指出，一年中一共有 28 億的乘客搭乘飛機，這意味著無論任何時候都有平均 69 萬位乘客在空中飛行。

Air travel is known as the safest way to travel and it shortens the distance between countries. How would the world be today without the invention of airplane? We would never know.

航空旅行號稱是最安全的旅行方式，它縮短了國與國之間的距離。如果沒有飛機的發明，今天這個世界會變如何？我們永遠不會知道。

The first airplane was invented by Orville and Wilbur Wright in 1903. Before the Wright's invention, many

在奧維爾和威爾，萊特於 1903 年發明第一架飛機以前，很多

people made numerous attempts to fly like birds. In 1799, Sir George Cayley designed the first fixed-wing aircraft. In 1874, Felix duTemple made the first attempt at powered flight by hopping off the end of a ramp in a steam-driven monoplane.

In 1894, the first controlled flight was made by Otto Lilienthal by shifting his body weight. Inspired by Lilienthal, the Wright brothers experimented with aerodynamic surfaces to control an airplane in flight and later on made the first airplane that was powered and controllable.

人嘗試了像鳥一樣的飛翔方式。 1799年，喬治・凱利爵士設計了第一架固定翼的飛機。 1874 年，菲利克斯・杜湯普跳躍過斜坡，利用蒸汽驅動單翼，第一次嘗試動力飛行。

1894 年，奧托・李林塔爾利用轉移他的體重，創造出第一架可控飛行機。由於李林塔爾的啟發，萊特兄弟實驗氣動表面來控制飛行的飛機，後來提出電動並可控制的第一架飛機。

1　飲食民生

2　歷史懷舊

3　現代化實用科技

4　資訊與知識傳遞

Vocabulary in Context

1 The tragic sinking of the British luxury liner *Titanic* in 1912 resulted in the heavy casualties of 1,500 deaths out of around 2,500 _____.

Riders is in the closest meaning to this word.

A. documents   C. passengers

B. inhabitants   D. villagers

2 The famous American jazz musician, Louis Armstrong, was not only a popular entertainer but an innovative jazz composer, who greatly _____ and influenced the young music generations.

Encouraged is in the closest meaning to this word.

A. judged   C. inspired

B. delayed   D. intensified

3 Groups of animal lovers held protests to show their disapproval of scientists and labs _____ on animals.

Testing is in the closest meaning to this word.

A. implying   C. testifying

B. opposing   D. experimenting

4 It bothered Barney a lot that his wife had been such a shopaholic that their debts were worsened to a hardly _____ level.

Manageable is in the closest meaning to this word.

A. academic   C. volcanic

B. controllable　　　　D. responsible

❶ 在1912年，英國豪華郵輪鐵達尼號的不幸沉沒導致大約2500名乘客中有1500名死亡的重大死傷。

Riders 的意思最接近於這個字。

A. 文件　　　　C. 乘客

B. 居民　　　　D. 村民

❷ 美國著名的爵士音樂家路易斯・阿姆斯壯，不僅是一名受歡迎的藝人，並　且是一名創新的爵士樂作曲家，他大大地鼓舞以及影響年輕的音樂世代。

Encouraged 的意思最接近於這個字。

A. 批判　　　　C. 鼓舞

B. 延遲　　　　D. 加強

❸ 愛護動物團體為了表明不贊成科學家及實驗室利用動物做實驗而進行抗議。

Testing 的意思最接近於這個字。

A. 暗示　　　　C. 證實

B. 反對　　　　D. 實驗

❹ 巴尼十分困擾於他的妻子是如此糟糕的購物狂以至於他們的債務已經嚴重到無法應付的程度了。

Manageable 的意思最接近於這個字。

A. 學術的　　　　C. 火山的

B. 控制的　　　　D. 負責的

  ❶ C　❷ C　❸ D　❹ B

The first aircraft soared to an altitude of 10 feet, traveled 120 feet, and landed 12 seconds after takeoff. The miracle 12 seconds led to the invention of jets which are now being used for military and commercial airlines, even space flights.

第一架飛機飆升至 10 英尺的高空，前進 120 英尺，並在起飛後 12 秒降落。這奇蹟的 12 秒引導了噴射機的發明，目前已被用於軍事和商業航空公司，甚至太空飛行。

The jet engine was developed by Frank Whittle of the United Kingdom and Hans von Ohain of Germany in late 1930s. Because jet engine can fly much faster and at higher altitudes, it made all the international flights possible these days.

噴射機是由英國的法蘭克‧惠特爾和德國的漢斯‧馮歐韓在 1930 年代後期所開發。由於噴射機能飛得更快，更高，這讓所有的國際航班成為可能。

The Wright brothers, Orville (August 19, 1871-January 30, 1948) and Wilbur (April 16, 1867-May 30, 1912), were two American brothers, born and

萊特兄弟，奧維爾（1871 年 8 月 19 日－1948 年 1 月 30 日）和威爾伯（1867

raised with 6 brothers and sisters in a small town in Ohio. Even though Orville and Wilbur were 4 years apart, they shared same interests and had very similar life experiences.

When both of them were kids in 1878, their father bought them a toy "helicopter" which was a toy version of an invention of French aeronautical pioneer Alphose Penaud. This device was the initial spark of the brother's interest in flying.

年 4 月 16 日－5 月 30 日，1912 年），是兩個美國兄弟，在俄亥俄州的一個小鎮出生。與 6 個兄弟姐妹一起長大，即使奧維爾和威爾伯相差 4 歲，他們分享相同的興趣並有著非常相似的人生經歷。

1878 年當他們倆都還是小孩時，他們的父親送了他們一個「直升機」玩具，這是法國航空先驅 Alphose Penaud 一項發明的玩具版本。該裝置正是燃起兄弟倆對飛行產生興趣的火花。

1 飲食民生

2 歷史懷舊

3 現代化實用科技

4 資訊與知識傳遞

Vocabulary in Context

⑤ With the economic recession getting worse, currency inflation has continued and the unemployment rate has _____ to 20%, which in turn triggered social problems.

Towered is in the closest meaning to this word.

A. soared   C. dwelt

B. animated   D. modified

⑥ The holy water in a small town in France is famed for creating magical curing powers and has yearly attracted lots of pilgrims and tourists all over the world to witness the _____.

Wonder is in the closest meaning to this word.

A. reform   C. portrait

B. miracle   D. civilization

⑦ The American industrialist, Henry Ford, was a _____ in auto industry, who mass produced cars affordable to average people with the assembly-line technique.

Forerunner is in the closest meaning to this word.

A. victim   C. pioneer

B. critic   D. delinquent

⑧ Nancy's _____ reaction was to accept Warner's invitation, but after careful consideration, she decided to decline it to avoid misunderstanding.

Beginning is in the closest meaning to this word.

A. initial　　　　　C. component

B. negative　　　　D. hypothetical

❺ 隨著經濟不景氣日益嚴重，目前通貨膨脹持續不斷，失業率高升
至百分之二十，進而引發社會問題。

Towered 的意思最接近於這個字。

A. 高升　　　　　C. 居住

B. 動畫　　　　　D. 修改

❻ 法國一座小鎮裡的聖水以創造神奇的治療功效而著名，每年吸引
許多世界各地的朝聖者及觀光客來見證這一個奇蹟。

Wonder 的意思最接近於這個字。

A. 改革　　　　　C. 肖像畫

B. 奇蹟　　　　　D. 文明

❼ 美國工業家亨利・福特是汽車工業的先驅，他利用生產線的技術
大量製造一般民眾負擔得起的汽車。

Forerunner 的意思最接近於這個字。

A. 受害者　　　　C. 先驅

B. 評論家　　　　D. 青少年罪犯

❽ 南西起初的反應是接受了華納的邀請，但是經過仔細考慮後決定
予以婉拒以避免誤會。

Beginning 的意思最接近於這個字。

A. 最初的　　　　C. 組成的

B. 否定的　　　　D. 假設的

 答案 ❺ A　❻ B　❼ C　❽ A

Both brothers attended high school but neither of them got a diploma. Orville started a printing business in 1889 which Wilbur later on joined.

兩兄弟都唸了高中，但都沒有拿到文憑。奧維爾在 1889 年開始了印刷業務，威爾伯則後來加入。

Three years later, the brothers opened a bicycle repair and sales shop, and in 1896 they started to manufacture their own brand.

3 年後，兄弟倆開了一家自行車修理和銷售的店。在 1896 年，他們開始生產自己的品牌。

Even though they were running the bicycle business, they still held their interests in flying. Therefore, when they found out information about the dramatic glides by Otto Lilienthal in Germany, they decided to use the endeavor to fund their interest in flight.

即使他們正在運行自行車業務，他們仍然堅持自己對飛行的興趣。因此，當他們發現了德國奧托·里鄰塔爾戲劇性的滑軌信息，他們決定用他們的努力來資助他們對飛行的興趣。

In designing their airplane, the Wrights drew upon a number of bicycle concepts such as the importance of balance and control, the strong but lightweight structures, the concerns about wind resistance and aerodynamic shape of the operator. To them, flying is just like riding a bicycle.

Together, the Wright brothers developed the first successful airplane in Kitty Hawk, North Carolina in 1903. They became national heroes. Named as the fathers of modern aviation, they developed innovative technology and inspired imaginations around the world.

在設計飛機時，萊特兄弟利用了許多自行車概念，如平衡和控制，堅固但重量輕的結構，風的阻力和操作氣動時外形的重要性等。對他們來說，飛行就像騎自行車。

兄弟倆一起在 1903 年北卡羅來納州研製了第一架飛機。他們成為了國家英雄。並被命名為現代航空之父。他們研發出創新的技術並激發了世界各地的想像力。

1 飲食民生

2 歷史懷舊

3 現代化實用科技

4 資訊與知識傳遞

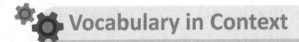

Vocabulary in Context

9 The _____ drop in temperatures these days has brought about great damage to crops and the farmed fish.
Sudden is in the closest meaning to this word.

A. charming   C. relevant

B. dramatic   D. overcrowded

10 We all should make every _____ to strengthen our environmental awareness and work out measures to cope with global warming.
Effort is in the closest meaning to this word.

A. endeavor   C. operation

B. impression   D. revenge

11 On hot summer days, children and adults alike find the _____ to eating refreshing ice cream too hard to break down.
Refusal is in the closest meaning to this word.

A. mishap   C. illusion

B. benefit   D. resistance

12 The successful writing of the magic adventures of Harry Potter by J. K. Rowling aroused the _____ of readers all over the world.
Fantasy is in the closest meaning to this word.

A. extinction   C. imagination

B. legislation   D. relaxation

❾ 近日氣溫的驟降導致農作物和養殖魚場的重大損傷。

Sudden 的意思最接近於這個字。

A. 迷人的　　　　　　C. 相關的

B. 戲劇性的　　　　　D. 過度擁擠的

❿ 我們都應該努力加強環保意識並且制定對抗全球暖化的對策。

Effort 的意思最接近於這個字。

A. 努力　　　　　　　C. 操作

B. 印象　　　　　　　D. 復仇

⓫ 在炎熱的夏日裡，小孩和大人都認為清涼冰淇淋的誘惑太難以抗拒了。

Refusal 的意思最接近於這個字。

A. 不幸　　　　　　　C. 幻覺

B. 利益　　　　　　　D. 抗拒

⓬ J. K. 羅琳成功撰寫的哈利波特魔法冒險激發全世界讀者的想像力。

Fantasy 的意思最接近於這個字。

A. 滅絕　　　　　　　C. 想像

B. 立法　　　　　　　D. 放鬆

  ❾ B　 **❿** A　⓫ D　 ⓬ C

16-4 同反義詞表

		同反義詞一覽表 Unit 16
passenger	乘客、旅客	同義詞 rider / fare / commuter
	駕駛、司機	反義詞 driver / coachman / chauffeur
inspire	激發、鼓勵	同義詞 arouse / stimulate / encourage
	沮喪、氣餒	反義詞 depress / deject / discourage
experiment	試驗、證明	同義詞 try / test / prove
	假設、假定	反義詞 suppose / assume / presume
controllable	可管理、可控制	同義詞 manageable /administrable /commandable
	難管理、難控制	反義詞 incontrollable / ungovernable / unruly
shorten	縮短、壓縮	同義詞 condense / abridge / compress
	加長、擴充	反義詞 lengthen / extend / expand
shift	變動、搬移	同義詞 change / alter / move
	固定、安頓	反義詞 fix / stabilize / settle
soar	高飛、猛增	同義詞 hover / ascend / tower
	下降、暴跌	反義詞 drop / descend / slump
miracle	奇蹟、非凡事蹟	同義詞 marvel / wonder / prodigy
	一般、常態	反義詞 normal / ordinary / routine
pioneer	先驅、開拓者	同義詞 forerunner / settler / leader
	追隨者、部屬	反義詞 follower / successor / subordinate
initial	開始的、最初的	同義詞 beginning / primary / original
	最後的、最終的	反義詞 last / final / conclusive

possible	可能的、合理的	同義詞 likely / probable / reasonable
	不可能、未必的	反義詞 impossible / unlikely / improbable
dramatic	戲劇的、誇張的	同義詞 theatrical / sudden / exaggerative
	平淡的、一般的	反義詞 prosaic / gradual / ordinary
endeavor	努力、苦幹	同義詞 effort / striving / struggle
	怠惰、懶散	反義詞 idleness / laziness / indolence
resistance	抵抗、反對	同義詞 refusal / disapproval / opposition
	順從、服從	反義詞 compliance / submission / obedience
imagination	想像、創造力	同義詞 fantasy / illusion / creativeness
	現實、事實	反義詞 reality / factuality / actuality
attend	參加、專注	同義詞 participate / join / concentrate
	忽視、分心	反義詞 neglect / ignore / distract
concern	關心、涉及	同義詞 regard / consideration / involvement
	冷漠、不關心	反義詞 unconcern / indifference / inattention
balance	平衡、權衡	同義詞 stableness / steadiness / equality
	失衡、不公平	反義詞 imbalance / inequality / unfairness

1 飲食民生

2 歷史懷舊

3 現代化實用科技

4 資訊與知識傳遞

Automobile 汽車

💡 17-1 汽車發展史

There were many people who made a great contribution to the invention of different types of automobiles. But it was only when Karl Benz built the first petrol automobile that vehicles become practical and went into actual production.

許多人都曾對發明不同類型的汽車有偉大的貢獻,但直到卡爾‧賓士製造了第一台汽油汽車,汽車才真正能被有效利用,走進實際生產。

The first gasoline-powered automobile built by Karl Benz contained an internal combustion engine. He built it in 1885 in Mannheim and was granted a patent for his automobile in 1886. Two years later, he began the first production of automobiles. In 1889, Gottlied Daimler and Wilhelm Maybach also designed a vehicle from scratch in Stuttgart.

卡爾‧賓士製作了第一個汽油動力汽車內所用的內燃機。他於 1885 年製作,並在 1886 年於曼海姆取得第一台汽車的專利。2 年後他開始了第一輛汽車的生產。1889 年,古特蘭‧戴姆勒和威廉‧邁巴赫也在斯圖加特開始了汽車的設計。

In 1895, a British engineer, Frederick William Lanchester built the first four-wheeled petrol driven automobile and also patented the disc brake. Between 1895 and 1898, the first electric starter was installed on the Benz Velo.

1895 年，一名英國工程師，腓特烈·威廉在曼徹斯特製造了第一台四輪驅動的汽油汽車，並申請了盤式制動器的專利。在 1895 年和 1898 年間，賓士在車內安裝了首款的電動起動器。

By the 1930s, most of the mechanical technology used in today's automobiles had been invented. But due to the Great Depression, the number of auto manufacturers declined sharply. Many companies consolidated and matured. After that, the automobile market was booming for decades until the 1970s.

到了 1930 年代，今天汽車內使用的大部分機械技術已被發明出來。但由於經濟大蕭條，汽車製造業的數量急劇下降。許多公司合併且趨於成熟。在此之後，汽車市場蓬勃發展了幾十年直到 70 年代。

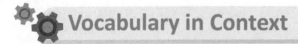 **Vocabulary in Context**

❶ Albert Einstein, the 1921 Nobel Prize winner in physics, made great _____ to the world by his Theory of Relativity, which changed mankind's understanding of science.

Service is in the closest meaning to this word.

A. explanations   C. contributions

B. breakthrough   D. steadiness

❷ The entire country is going through an economic _____ and is filled with an atmosphere of uncertainty and anxiety.

Recession is in the closest meaning to this word.

A. famine   C. observance

B. depression   D. assertion

❸ Though Mr. Cook's health had notably _____, he remained optimistic and lighthearted for fear that his family might be sad.

Weakened is in the closest meaning to this word.

A. declined   C. kidnapped

B. survived   D. economized

❹ The extraordinary new Hollywood actress _____ her position as the most promising future star by her excellent performing skills and high popularity with movie fans.

Secured is in the closest meaning to this word.

A. ruined   C. gossiped

B. portrayed   D. consolidated

❶ 艾伯特‧愛因斯坦是**1921**年諾貝爾物理學獎得主,他以改變人類對科學了解的相對論對世界做出極大的貢獻。

Service 的意思最接近於這個字。

A. 解釋   C. 貢獻

B. 突破   D. 穩定

❷ 這整個國家正經歷經濟蕭條的情境,並充塞著不確定和焦慮的氛圍。

Recession 的意思最接近於這個字。

A. 饑荒   C. 遵守

B. 不景氣   D. 聲稱

❸ 雖然庫克先生的健康狀況明顯惡化,但他依然保持樂觀輕鬆的態度,以免他的家人悲傷。

Weakened 的意思最接近於這個字。

A. 衰退   C. 綁架

B. 倖存   D. 節省

❹ 卓越不凡的好萊塢新興女星以她精湛的演技以及超高的人氣鞏固最有前途明日巨星的地位。

Secured 的意思最接近於這個字。

A. 毀壞   C. 閒聊

B. 描繪   D. 鞏固

1 飲食民生

2 歷史懷舊

3 現代化實用科技

4 資訊與知識傳遞

 答案 ❶ C   ❷ B   ❸ A   ❹ D

The 1970s were turbulent years for automakers. Starting from the 1973 oil crisis, stricter automobile emissions control and safety requirements, the market was no longer dominated by the US makers. Japan became the world's leader of car production for a while.

Until 2009, China took over the leading position and became the world's leading car manufacturer with production greater than all other countries. Most of the time, when people hear the name Karl Benz, they automatically associate the term with the luxury car brand. But not everyone knows that the world's first practical gasoline powered vehicle was actually invented by him.

70 年代是汽車製造商的動盪年代。從 1973 年的石油危機到更嚴格的汽車排放控制和安全的要求，市場不再由美國製造商主導地位。有段時間日本成為世界汽車生產的龍頭。

直到 2009 年，中國接手領先地位，並成為全球領先的汽車製造商，生產量超過所有其他國家。大多數時候，當人們聽到賓士這個名字，他們通常會自動與豪華汽車品牌連接。但並不是每個人都知道，世界上第一台實用的汽油動力車實際上就是由他發明的。

Karl Friedrich Benz was born in Muhlburg, Germany on November 25th, 1844. Because of his mother's persistence, Benz attended the local Grammar School in Harlsruhe and was a prodigious student. Benz was very smart.

卡爾・弗里德里希・賓士於 1844 年 11 月 25 日誕生於德國的穆伯格。由於他母親的堅持，賓士參加了邗蘇赫當地的文法學校，且是一個驚人的學生。賓士非常的聰明。

At the age of 15, he already followed his father's steps toward locomotive engineering, and passed the entrance exam for mechanical engineering at the University of Karlsruhe. After graduation, Benz did some professional training in several different companies, but he didn't feel like he fit in any of them.

在 15 歲的時候，他已經跟隨父親的腳步走向汽車工程，並通過卡爾斯魯厄大學機械工程的入學考試。他畢業於 1864 年。在 19 歲畢業後，賓士在幾個不同的公司做了一些專業的訓練，但他並不覺得自己適合任何一份工作。

1 飲食民生

2 歷史懷舊

3 現代化實用科技

4 資訊與知識傳遞

Vocabulary in Context

❺ After going through the serious _____ conditions in the airplane last year, Mrs. Spencer claimed to avoid taking any airplanes because of the strong fear of flights.

Violent is in the closest meaning to this word.

A. flexible   C. obscure

B. elementary   D. turbulent

❻ Eco-minded car drivers are encouraged to purchase cars equipped with lower _____ of CO_2 and hybrid engines so as to support global green revolution.

Discharge is in the closest meaning to this word.

A. emissions   C. resources

B. priorities   D. masterpieces

❼ According to medical researches, second-hand smoking is closely _____ with lung cancer.

Connected is in the closest meaning to this word.

A. endangered   C. overtaken

B. undergone   D. associated

❽ Sean's family and friends shared the joy and honor with him because through constant diligence and _____, his dream of entering an ideal college eventually came true.

Perseverance is in the closest meaning to this word.

A. allergy   C. declaration

B. persistence   D. sentiment

❺ 去年在飛機上經歷過嚴重猛烈氣流的狀況後，史班塞太太因為對於飛行強烈的恐懼而聲稱將避免搭乘飛機。

Violent 的意思最接近於這個字。

A. 有彈性的　　　　　　C. 不清楚的

B. 基礎的　　　　　　　D. 猛烈的

❻ 具有環保觀念的駕駛被鼓勵去購買配備有二氧化碳低排放量以及油電混合引擎的汽車以支持地球的綠色革命。

Discharge 的意思最接近於這個字。

A. 排放　　　　　　　　C. 資源

B. 優先　　　　　　　　D. 傑作

❼ 根據醫學研究，二手煙與肺癌有密切的關係。

Connected 的意思最接近於這個字。

A. 危及　　　　　　　　C. 趕上

B. 經歷　　　　　　　　D. 聯想

❽ 尚恩的家人和朋友與他共享喜悅和榮耀，因為經由持續不斷的努力和堅持，他終於實現了進入理想大學的夢想。

Perseverance 的意思最接近於這個字。

A. 過敏　　　　　　　　C. 宣佈

B. 堅持　　　　　　　　D. 感情

1 飲食民生

2 歷史懷舊

3 現代化實用科技

4 資訊與知識傳遞

答案 ❺ D　❻ A　❼ D　❽ B

So at the age of 27, he launched the Iron Foundry and Mechanical Workshop in Mannheim with August Ritter. Business didn't go well though. Benz eventually bought out Ritter's share and started his development to new engines. He created the very first two-stroke engine in 1878, and was granted a patent for it in 1879.

因此，在 27 歲時，他與奧格斯・里特在曼海姆開起了鋼鐵鑄造和機械的工廠。雖然，經營並不順利。賓士最終還是買下了里特的市場份額，並開始了他新的發展引擎。他於 1878 年創建的第一個二段引擎，並在 1879 年獲得了專利。

He then patented the speed regulation system, the ignition using sparks with battery, the gear shift, the water radiator, and many other automobile parts. It was 1885 that Benz finished his creation for the first gasoline powered automobile which he named Motorwagen. It featured wire wheels with a four-stroke engine and a very advanced coil ignition.

他隨後申請了變速系統，利用火花與電池的點火器，排檔，水散熱器，及許多其他汽車零件的專利。1885 年，賓士完成了他創作的第一台汽油動力汽車，他命名 Motorwagen。它擁有鋼絲輪與一個四段引擎和一個非常先進的點火線圈。

It also had the evaporative cooling system. The Motorwagen was patented on January 29, 1886. The following year, Benz created the 2nd generation of the Motorwagen. Benz started to sell the Motorwagen in 1888, which is the first commercially available automobile in history.

它也有蒸氣冷卻系統。Motorwagen 在 1886 年 1 月 29 日獲得了發明專利，賓士並創造了第二代的 Motorwagen。賓士於 1888 年開始銷售 Motorwagen。這是歷史上的第一個商用汽車。

The brand Benz became famous since then. Benz retired from design management in 1903 but remained as director on the Board of Management. He passed away at the age of 84. The Benz home now has been designated as historic and is used as a scientific meeting facility.

自那時以來，該品牌賓士名聲大振。賓士在 1903 年由設計管理職務退休，但仍作為管理委員會的主任。他享年 84 歲。賓士的家目前已被指定為歷史建築，並作為一個科學會議的設施。

1 飲食民生

2 歷史懷舊

3 現代化實用科技

4 資訊與知識傳遞

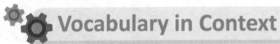 **Vocabulary in Context**

9 After five years of hard-working, Eddie was _____ promoted to the managerial position, and all of his colleagues agreed that he deserved the advancement.
Finally is in the closest meaning to this word.

A. largely   C. eventually

B. systematically   D. simultaneously

10 It is taken for granted that you will be seriously punished if you violate the traffic _____ by driving in the wrong direction.
Rules is in the closest meaning to this word.

A. donations   C. solutions

B. regulations   D. quotations

11 With lots of photos and signatures of movie stars hung on the wall, the famous restaurant was _____ as a dining place frequented by celebrities and movie stars.
Characterized is in the closest meaning to this word.

A. featured   C. prohibited

B. refused   D. allocated

12 Myron was _____ as the leader of the project team and was fully dedicated to the realization of his new ideas.
Appointed is in the closest meaning to this word.

A. analyzed   C. designated

B. ornamented   D. reproached

❾ 經過五年的努力之後，艾迪終於被擢升到經理的職位，他所有的同事都一致認為這份升遷是他應得的。

Finally 的意思最接近於這個字。

A. 主要地   C. 最終地

B. 系統地   D. 同時地

❿ 你因逆向行駛違反交通規則而被嚴厲處罰是件理所當然的事。

Rules 的意思最接近於這個字。

A. 捐贈   C. 解決方案

B. 規則   D. 引語

⓫ 這家著名的餐廳牆上掛著許多電影明星的照片和簽名，它最大的特色在於它是名流和電影明星經常光顧的用餐地點。

Characterized 的意思最接近於這個字。

A. 特色   C. 禁止

B. 拒絕   D. 分配

⓬ 麥倫被指派去擔任專案小組的領導人並努力執行他的新點子。

Appointed 的意思最接近於這個字。

A. 分析   C. 指派

B. 裝飾   D. 責備

答案 ❾ C ❿ B ⓫ A ⓬ C

17-4 同反義詞表

		同反義詞一覽表 Unit 17
contribution	貢獻、捐獻	同義詞 service / donation / endowment
	獲得、得到	反義詞 obtainment / gain / acquirement
depression	蕭條、沮喪	同義詞 recession / frustration / dejection
	繁榮、激勵	反義詞 prosperity / inspiration / encouragement
decline	衰退、婉拒	同義詞 weaken / decrease / refuse
	升高、接受	反義詞 soar / increase / accept
consolidate	鞏固、聯合	同義詞 solidify / secure / unite
	孤立、分散	反義詞 isolate / disconnect / separate
internal	內在的、內部的	同義詞 inner / inside / interior
	外面的、外部的	反義詞 external / outside / exterior
grant	同意、授予	同義詞 consent / allow / award
	分歧、否定	反義詞 disagree / forbid / deny
mature	成熟的、穩重的	同義詞 adult / ripe / developed
	幼稚的、不成熟	反義詞 childish / immature / inexperienced
turbulent	猛烈的、混亂的	同義詞 violent / disorderly / chaotic
	平和的、有秩序	反義詞 peaceful / stable / orderly
emission	排出、發出	同義詞 discharge / release / spread
	吸收、消化	反義詞 absorption / assimilation / digestion

associate	聯想、聯繫	同義詞 combine / connect / link
	中斷、分離	反義詞 disconnect / separate / divide
persistence	堅持、持續	同義詞 insistence / perseverance / sustainment
	放棄、中止	反義詞 abandonment / desertion / cease
requirement	要求、需要	同義詞 demand / need / want
	答覆、拒絕	反義詞 response / reply / refusal
prodigious	巨大的、非凡的	同義詞 enormous / miraculous / extraordinary
	微小的、平常的	反義詞 diminutive / average / common
eventually	最後、終於	同義詞 finally / lastly / ultimately
	開始、最初	反義詞 first / initially / originally
regulation	規定、命令	同義詞 rule / stipulation / order
	遵守、順從	反義詞 conformity / compliance / submission
feature	以…為特色	同義詞 characterize / mark / highlight
	使…一般化	反義詞 generalize / universalize
designate	指派、任命	同義詞 assign / appoint / nominate
	接受、同意	反義詞 accept / consent / approve
advanced	先進的、前衛的	同義詞 progressive / developed / modern
	落伍的、退步的	反義詞 outdated / obsolete / regressive

1 飲食民生

2 歷史懷舊

3 現代化實用科技

4 資訊與知識傳遞

Stethoscope 聽診器

18-1 聽診器的沿革

MP3 52

What if doctors still check Patients' heart sounds by putting their ears on patients' chests? I bet it wouldn't be comfortable for either doctors or patients.

如果醫生需要將自己的耳朵放在患者的胸前才能檢查患者心臟的聲音會怎麼樣？我敢打賭，無論是醫生還是患者都會感到不舒服。

The stethoscope was invented by a French doctor, Rene Laennec in 1816 for exactly that reason.

聽診器是在 1816 年由一個法國醫生蕊內‧拉埃內克所發明，而發明的原因正是如此。

Laennec came up with the thought of the stethoscope because he was uncomfortable placing his ear on women's chests to hear heart sounds. The device he created was similar to

拉埃內克有了聽診器的想法，正是因為要他把他的耳朵放在婦女的胸部以聽到心臟聲音是非常痛苦的。

the common ear trumpet. It was made of a wooden tube and was monaural.

他所創造的設備是類似於常見的助聽器。設計是利用一個木管的單聲道。

It was not until 1840 that the stethoscope with a flexible tube was invented. Back then, the stethoscope still had only single earpiece. In 1851, Arthur Leared, a physician from Ireland first came up with a binaural stethoscope.

直到 1840 年才有軟管的單聽筒聽診器。在 1851 年，來自愛爾蘭的醫生，阿瑟·李納德第一次設計了一個雙耳聽診器。

A year later, George Camman improved the design of the instrument and it has become the standard ever since.

一年後，喬治·卡門進化了儀器的設計，使它成為聽診器的標準。

Vocabulary in Context

❶ The doctor advised the _____ to quit smoking and drinking for the sake of his health.

Sufferer is in the closest meaning to this word.

A. patient   C. consultant

B. surgeon   D. archaeologist

❷ After one whole week's work, Gavin made himself _____ and enjoyed the pleasant Friday night by watching TV and eating snacks on the sofa.

Relaxed is in the closest meaning to this word.

A. savage   C. comfortable

B. pious   D. extravagant

❸ Mr. Emerson consulted a _____ and was prescribed some medicine for his high blood pressure.

Doctor is in the closest meaning to this word.

A. executive   C. physician

B. trader   D. dictator

❹ Leo's interpersonal relationships _____ significantly after he became friendly and active in socializing with others.

Bettered is in the closest meaning to this word.

A. summoned   C. postponed

B. improved   D. grieved

❶ 醫生忠告病患為了健康著想，他應該要戒菸以及戒酒。

Sufferer 的意思最接近於這個字。

A. 病患   C. 顧問

B. 外科醫生   D. 考古學家

❷ 經過一整個禮拜辛苦的工作，蓋文坐在沙發上看電視以及吃點心，很舒適地享受愉快的周五夜晚。

Relaxed 的意思最接近於這個字。

A. 野蠻的   C. 舒服的

B. 虔誠的   D. 浪費的

❸ 愛默生先生看內科醫生，醫生為他開了治療高血壓的處方。

Doctor 的意思最接近於這個字。

A. 執行長   C. 內科醫生

B. 貿易商   D. 獨裁者

❹ 李奧在變得友善以及主動地與別人來往後，他的人際關係有極大的改善。

Bettered 的意思最接近於這個字。

A. 召喚   C. 延遲

B. 改善   D. 哀傷

 答案 ❶ A ❷ C ❸ C ❹ B

1 飲食民生

2 歷史懷舊

3 現代化實用科技

4 資訊與知識傳遞

In the early 1960s, a Harvard Medical School professor, David Littmann, created a new lighter and improved acoustic.

在 1960 年初期,哈佛大學醫學院教授,大衛・利特曼,創造了一個新的、更輕的聽筒,並改進了聲學。

And almost 40 years later, the first external noise reducing stethoscope was patented by Richard Deslauriers.

而近爾後 40 年,第一個外部噪聲降低聽診器的專利申由理查・達斯蘿莉所申請。

The medical technology keeps improving. And it was just recently an open-source 3D-printed stethoscope which was based on the Littmann Cardiology 3 stethoscope was invented by Dr. Tarek Loubani.

由於醫療技術不斷提高。就在最近,利用立得慢心臟 3 聽診器的基礎而發明的 3D 列印聽診器也由塔里克魯邦尼博士所發明。

Rene Laennec was born on February 17th, 1781 at Quimper, France. He grew

蕊內・拉埃內克生於 1781 年 2 月 17 日的

up living with his uncle Guillaime Laennec who worked as a faculty of medicine at the University of Nantes. Influenced by his uncle, that's when Rene first started his study in medicine.

法國，坎佩爾。他與他在南特大學擔任教師的伯父古拉梅拉埃內克一起生活。由於他伯父的影響，拉埃內克開始了他在醫學的研究。

In 1799, he happened to have the privilege of studying under some of the most famous surgeon and expert in cardiology.

1799 年，他在偶然的機會下與某些最有名的外科醫生和專家學習心臟病學研究。

It was when he was 19 that he moved to Paris and studied dissection in Guillaume Duputren's laboratory.

當他 19 歲時，他移居巴黎，並在紀堯姆・都普特的實驗室研究解剖。

1 飲食民生

2 歷史懷舊

3 現代化實用科技

4 資訊與知識傳遞

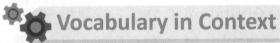

Vocabulary in Context

5 Penicillin, a substance used as a drug to treat or prevent bacteria-caused infections, is undoubtedly the greatest ____ ____ discovery of the 20th century.

Therapeutic is in the closest meaning to this word.

A. medical   C. commercial

B. restless   D. protective

6 The Oscar-winning director Ang Lee adopted advanced movie _____ in his latest film about American soldiers returning home from Iraq, *Billy Lynn.*

Skills is in the closest meaning to this word.

A. fiction   C. penetration

B. regime   D. technology

7 Deeply _____ by his parents' unhappy marriage and divorce, Derrick was afraid to make any commitment and stayed single till he met Nora.

Affected is in the closest meaning to this word.

A. moved   C. influenced

B. tolerated   D. extinguished

8 To Todd, it was such a great _____ to have the chance to interview the contemporary Japanese master of animation.

Honor is in the closest meaning to this word.

A. utility   C. sequence

B. privilege   D. modesty

❺ 盤尼西林是一種用來治療或預防細菌感染的藥物，它無疑地是二十世紀最偉大的醫學發現。

Therapeutic 的意思最接近於這個字。

A. 醫學的　　　　　　　　C. 廣告的

B. 焦躁不安的　　　　　　D. 保護的

❻ 奧斯卡得獎導演李安在他最新描述有關於美國士兵從伊拉克返鄉的電影《比利・林恩》中採用了先進的電影拍攝技術。

Skills 的意思最接近於這個字。

A. 杜撰小說　　　　　　　C. 貫穿

B. 政權　　　　　　　　　D. 技術

❼ 深受父母親不愉快的婚姻以及離婚的影響，戴瑞克在遇見諾拉之前一直畏懼於做出承諾並且保持單身。

Affected 的意思最接近於這個字。

A. 感動　　　　　　　　　C. 影響

B. 忍受　　　　　　　　　D. 熄滅

❽ 對陶德來說，能夠有機會去訪問當代日本動畫大師是一項極大的殊榮。

Honor 的意思最接近於這個字。

A. 效用　　　　　　　　　C. 順序

B. 殊榮　　　　　　　　　D. 謙虛

1 飲食民生

2 歷史懷舊

3 現代化實用科技

4 資訊與知識傳遞

  A D C B

Graduating in medicine in 1804, Laennec became an associate at the Societe de IEcole de Medicine. He then found that tubercle lesions could be present in all organs of the body and not just the lungs.

1804 年畢業於醫藥，拉埃內克成為 Societe de IEcole de Medicine 的一員。之後他發現了結節性病變可能存在於身體的所有器官，而不僅僅是肺部。

By 1816, at the age of 35, he was offered the position of a physician at the Necker Hospital in Paris.

到了 1816 年，在他 35 歲的時候，他得到了巴黎內克爾醫院醫生的位子。

Laennec is considered to be one of the greatest doctors of all time. It was him that introduced auscultation. This method involves listening and identifying various sounds made by different body organs.

拉埃內克被認為是所有時代內最偉大的醫生之一。他引進了聽診技術。這種方法涉及聽力，並確定由不同的身體器官製成各種聲音。

Before the invention of this method, doctors needed to put their ears on patients' chests to diagnose patients' problems. He felt uncomfortable especially while he was diagnosing young women. This led to the innovation of a new device called the stethoscope which he initially termed as "chest examiner".

With stethoscope, nowadays all doctors are able to study different sounds of heart and understand patients' condition in a much more precise way. Laennec's works were way ahead of his times and had a great impact on medical science.

這種方法發明之前，醫生需要把耳朵放在患者的胸前以診斷病人的問題。由其當他診斷年輕女性時，這個方法令他不舒服這促使了一個新的設備的發明，稱為聽診器。他最初稱這個儀器為「胸部測試器」。

因為聽診器，現在所有的醫生都能夠學習心臟的不同的聲音，並以一個更精確的方式了解患者的病情。拉埃內克的作品於是遙遙領先了他所處的時代並對醫學有很大的影響。

1 飲食民生

2 歷史懷舊

3 現代化實用科技

4 資訊與知識傳遞

Vocabulary in Context

9 The witness positively _____ the young suspect as the person who robbed the old lady of her bag the other night.
Distinguished is in the closest meaning to this word.

A. identified   C. modified

B. recruited   D. assaulted

10 Modern people are encouraged to take regular physical check-ups, as the earlier certain illnesses are _____, the sooner they can be treated and cured.
Analyzed is in the closest meaning to this word.

A. speculated   C. compressed

B. ascended   D. diagnosed

11 In the era of _____, what everyone should do is to develop creativity and originality so as to remain competitive.
Creation is in the closest meaning to this word.

A. dignity   C. warranty

B. souvenir   D. innovation

12 For quite a long time, overdevelopment in industry has had a strong _____ on earth, which illustrates the importance of strengthening common people's environmental awareness.
Influence is in the closest meaning to this word.

A. mercy   C. impact

B. switch   D. description

❾ 目擊證人很有把握地指認這名年輕嫌疑犯是前一晚搶奪老婦人皮包的搶匪。

Distinguished 的意思最接近於這個字。

A. 辨認   C. 改良

B. 招募   D. 突襲

❿ 現代人被鼓勵要定期做健康檢查，因為特定疾病的病情越早被診斷出來就可以越快接受治療並痊癒。

Analyzed 的意思最接近於這個字。

A. 推測   C. 壓縮

B. 升高   D. 診斷

⓫ 在這個創新的時代中，人人所應該要做的是發展創意和獨創性以保持競爭力。

Creation 的意思最接近於這個字。

A. 尊嚴   C. 擔保

B. 紀念品   D. 創新

⓬ 長時間以來，工業的過度發展對於地球造成嚴重的衝擊，因此突顯出加強一般民眾環保意識的重要。

Influence 的意思最接近於這個字。

A. 慈悲   C. 衝擊

B. 轉換   D. 描述

答案 ❾ A   ❿ D   ⓫ D   ⓬ C

1 飲食民生

2 歷史懷舊

3 現代化實用科技

4 資訊與知識傳遞

18-4 同反義詞表

同反義詞一覽表 Unit 18		
patient	病人、受害者	同義詞 sufferer / case / victim
	醫生、醫師	反義詞 doctor / physician / surgeon
comfortable	舒服的、自在的	同義詞 cheerful / contented / relaxed
	擔心的、焦慮的	反義詞 uncomfortable / worried / anxious
physician	醫生、治療者	同義詞 doctor / medic / healer
	患者、病人	反義詞 patient / case / sufferer
improve	改善、改進	同義詞 better / advance / progress
	惡化、衰敗	反義詞 worsen / deteriorate / degenerate
exact	準確的、嚴密的	同義詞 precise / accurate / careful
	不準確、鬆散的	反義詞 inexact / obscure / loose
similar	相像的、類似的	同義詞 alike / resemblant / akin
	不同的、相異的	反義詞 dissimilar / different / distinct
medical	醫學的、治療的	同義詞 therapeutic / remedial / healing
	致命的、傷害的	反義詞 fatal / menacing / hazardous
technology	技術、技術機械	同義詞 technique / skill / machinery
	理論、手工製作	反義詞 theory / conception / handiwork
influence	作用、影響	同義詞 affect / sway / impact
	不變、中立	反義詞 fix / stabilize / neutralize

privilege	特權、殊榮	同義詞 advantage / favor / honor
	平等、羞辱	反義詞 equality / disfavor / disgrace
external	外部的、外在的	同義詞 exterior / outside / surface
	內部的、內在的	反義詞 internal / interior / inner
faculty	教員、職員	同義詞 teacher / instructor / staff
	學生、學員	反義詞 student / scholar / pupil
identify	確認、識別	同義詞 recognize / confirm / distinguish
	否認、疑惑	反義詞 deny / doubt / perplex
diagnose	診斷、分析	同義詞 interpret / deduce / analyze
	症狀、病症	反義詞 symptom / case / ailment
innovation	創新、改革	同義詞 creation / transformation / reform
	模仿、守舊	反義詞 imitation / mimicking / conservativeness
impact	衝擊、影響	同義詞 strike / influence / effect
	平和、原因	反義詞 moderation / reason / cause
involve	包含、捲入	同義詞 include / concern / tangle
	除外、排除	反義詞 exclude / except / expel
precise	準確的、確切的	同義詞 clear / accurate / exact
	模糊的、不明確	反義詞 vague / inexact / indefinite

1 飲食民生

2 歷史懷舊

3 現代化實用科技

4 資訊與知識傳遞

Unit 19 Helicopter 直升機

19-1 直升機的發展

MP3 55

Different from an airplane, a helicopter relies on rotors to take off and land vertically, to hover, and to fly forward backward and laterally. Because of its flexibility, it allows taking off and landing at limited areas. Therefore, helicopters are often used for rescues or ironically wars.

與飛機不同,直升機依靠螺旋槳起飛,垂直降落,懸停,前進後退和橫向飛行。由於它的靈活性,它允許在有限的區域內起飛和降落。因此,直升機常常被用於救援或很諷刺的被用在戰爭裡。

The earliest reference of vertical flight originated from a bamboo copter developed in 400 B. C. The theory of the bamboo copter is to spin the stick attached to a rotor. The spinning creates lift, and the toy flies when released. This is the origin of the helicopter development which scientists all over the world spent hundreds of years developing so that

這是在公元 400 年前就開發出來,我們都玩過的玩具。竹蜻蜓的理論是旋轉黏在螺旋槳上的竹籤。因為旋轉造成懸浮力,因此玩具在被釋放時會飛起。這是直升機開發的起源,科學家在世界各地花了幾百年

we can have the helicopter today.

About a thousand years later, Leonardo da Vinci created a design that was made towards vertical flight called "aerial screw". Another 300 years later, Russian scientist Mikhail Lomonosov developed a small coaxial modeled and demonstrated it to the Russian Academy.

It was another 100 years later, in 1861, the word "helicopter" was named by a French inventor, Gustave de Ponton dAmecourt, who made a small, steam powered helicopter made with aluminum. Although, this model never lifted off the ground.

開發，以至於我們能擁有今天的直升機。

大約一千年以後，達芬奇創造了一個垂直飛行的設計，稱為空中螺絲。300 年後，俄羅斯科學家米哈伊爾·羅蒙諾索夫開發了一個小型的同軸建模並在俄羅斯科學院展示。

再 100 年後，於 1861 年，法國發明家，古斯塔夫·德龐頓做了一個小型蒸汽動力的鋁製直升機，他也是第一個命名「直升機」的人。雖然如此，這個模型卻永遠無法離開地面。

1 飲食民生

2 歷史懷舊

3 現代化實用科技

4 資訊與知識傳遞

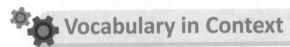 **Vocabulary in Context**

❶ The firefighters tried their best to come to the _____ of the old couple from the burning apartment, but in vain.

Saving is in the closest meaning to this word.

A. rescue   C. fulfillment

B. brood   D. optimism

❷ In high school days, Adam used to boast about becoming a manager and making a lot of money. _____, he works only as a janitor in a mall now.

Sarcastically is in the closest meaning to this word.

A. Personally   C. Generously

B. Temporarily   D. Ironically

❸ In _____, you could take all the work assigned to you. However, in practice, is it possible for you to finish it all by yourself?

Supposition is in the closest meaning to this word.

A. fact   C. analysis

B. theory   D. melody

❹ After being _____ from the prison for only a few months, the ex-convict was put in jail again for lacking money and committing crimes again.

Freed is in the closest meaning to this word.

A. traced   C. released

B. amplified   D. deceived

❶ 消防人員盡最大的力量試圖從燃燒的公寓中將老夫婦救出，但卻徒勞無功。

Saving 的意思最接近於這個字。

A. 拯救　　　　　　　C. 實現

B. 沉思　　　　　　　D. 樂觀

❷ 高中時期，亞當時常自誇要成為公司經理並且賺大錢。諷刺的是，現在他只是一名大賣場裡的清潔人員。

Sarcastically 的意思最接近於這個字。

A. 個人地　　　　　　C. 慷慨地

B. 暫時地　　　　　　D. 諷刺地

❸ 理論上來說，你可以接受所有指派給你的工作。但是，實際上，你有辦法獨自完成所有的工作嗎？。

Supposition 的意思最接近於這個字。

A. 事實　　　　　　　C. 分析

B. 理論　　　　　　　D. 旋律

❹ 這名前科犯出獄不過幾個月，因缺錢花用而犯案，於是又再度入獄了。

Freed 的意思最接近於這個字。

A. 跟蹤　　　　　　　C. 釋放

B. 放大　　　　　　　D. 欺騙

答案　❶ A　❷ D　❸ B　❹ C

Since then, the helicopter development was going on all over the world, from the United States, to England, France, Denmark and even Russia.

此後，直升機在世界各地不停的發展，有來自美國、英國、法國、丹麥，甚至俄羅斯。

But it was not until 1942 that a helicopter designed by Igor Sikorsky reached a full-scale production. The most common helicopter configuration had a single main rotor with anti-torque tail rotor, unlike the earlier designs that had multiple rotors.

直到 1942 年由伊戈爾・西科斯基設計的直升機才達到全面性的生產。最常見的直升機配置有具有抗扭矩尾槳和單一主螺旋槳。不同於早期的設計，有多個螺旋槳。

Centuries of development later, the invention of helicopter improves the transportation of people and cargo, uses for military, construction, firefighting, research, rescue, medical transport, and many others. The contributions of the helicopter are uncountable.

幾個世紀的發展之後，直升機的發明提高了人員和貨物的運輸，使用於軍事、建築、消防、科研、救護，醫療轉運，和許多其他地方。直升機的貢獻是不可數計的。

Some people might recognize the name of Igor Ivanovich Sikorsky from the public airport in Fairfield County, Connecticut.

有些人可能會從康乃狄克州費爾菲爾德縣的大眾機場那裡認出「伊戈爾‧伊万諾維奇‧西科斯基」這個名字。

No doubt that due to the great contributions from Sikorsky to the aviation industry, the airport of his hometown decided to be named after him.

毫無疑問的，由於西科斯基對航空業的巨大貢獻，家鄉的機場決定以他的名字來命名。

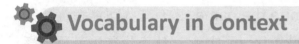

❺ The _____ damage of the disaster was so large that there was no way of making any actual estimation.

Overall is in the closest meaning to this word.

A. high-class

C. close-ranged

B. time-proven

D. full-scale

❻ Among all the public _____ means in the city, the MRT is the most convenient and the most popular one.

Commuting is in the closest meaning to this word.

A. media

C. coordination

B. transportation

D. opposition

❼ The late philanthropist was kind-hearted and generous, whose charity deeds were meaningful and _____.

Countless is in the closest meaning to this word.

A. uncountable

C. numerical

B. climatic

D. redundant

❽ When it comes to _____, the Wright brothers were the greatest and the earliest pioneers.

Flight is in the closest meaning to this word.

A. diplomacy

C. volcano

B. reforestation

D. aviation

❺ 這次災難整體的損害是如此地嚴重以致於無法做確切的評估。

Overall 的意思最接近於這個字。

A. 高級的　　　　　　C. 近距離的

B. 不變的　　　　　　D. 全面的

❻ 所有都市裡的大眾運輸工具中，捷運是最方便，同時也是最受歡迎的。

Commuting 的意思最接近於這個字。

A. 媒體　　　　　　　C. 協調

B. 交通運輸　　　　　D. 反對

❼ 這名已故的慈善家既仁慈又慷慨，他的善行深具意義而且難以計數。

Countless 的意思最接近於這個字。

A. 無法計算的　　　　C. 數字的

B. 氣候的　　　　　　D. 多餘的

❽ 談到飛行，萊特兄弟是最偉大而且是最早期的先驅。

Flight 的意思最接近於這個字。

A. 外交　　　　　　　C. 火山

B. 重新造林　　　　　D. 飛行

答案　❺D　❻B　❼A　❽D

In 1900, he went to Germany with his father who was a physics, and became interested in natural sciences. He began to experiment with flying machines and made a small rubber band powered helicopter at the age of 12.

在 1900 年，他與擔任物理學家的父親一起前往德國，並開始對自然科學產生極大的興趣。在 12 歲時，他便開始試驗飛行器，並做了一個小型的橡皮筋動力直升機。

At the age of 14, he joined the Saint Petersburg Imperial Russian Naval Academy but resigned in a few years because he decided to study in Engineering instead. In 1908, he learned about the Wright brother's Flyer and Ferdinand von Zeppelin's dirigible, he immediately decided to study aviation and concentrate on aviation research for his entire life.

在 14 歲時，他加入了俄羅斯聖彼得海軍學院，但在短短幾年內就休學，因為他決定專攻電機。而在 1908 年時，他得知萊特兄弟和斐迪南・馮・齊柏林的飛船，他立即決定學習航空。專注於航空研究成為了他生活的一切。

A year later, he enrolled in ETACA engineering school in Paris to study

一年後，他就到巴黎專攻航空學，就讀於

aeronautics. At that time, Paris was the center of the aviation world. From 1909 to 1942, Sikorsky designed or helped design at least 11 different kinds of aircraft. Sikorsky immigrated to the United States in 1919 and founded his first company "the Sikorsky Aircraft Corporation" in 1923.

In 1930, he developed the first of Pan American Airways' ocean-conquering flying boats. And in 1939, he designed the first viable helicopter named VS-300. The prototype worked fine but was not suitable for mass production. Therefore, Sikorsky used 3 years to do the modification and created the Sikorsky R-4, which became the world's first mass-produced helicopter.

ETACA 工程學。當時,巴黎是世界的航空中心。1909 年至 1942 年,西科斯基設計或幫忙設計了至少 11 個不同類型的飛機。西科斯基於 1919 年移民美國,並在 1923 年創辦了他的第一家公司「西科斯基飛機公司」。

1930 年,他研製出第一台泛美航空公司的海洋征服飛行船。而在 1939 年,他設計的第一個可用的直升機,命名為 VS-300。原型做得很好,但不適合大規模生產。因此,西科斯基用了 3 年的時間做了修改和創作西科斯基 R-4,從而成為世界上第一個大規模生產的直升機。

1 飲食民生

2 歷史懷舊

3 現代化實用科技

4 資訊與知識傳遞

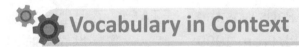

Vocabulary in Context

⑨ Detesting being bossed around, Terry decided to _____ from the low-ranked position and started his own company.
Quit is in the closest meaning to this word.

A. deliver   C. originate

B. resign   D. anticipate

⑩ The enterprise has set up plans to _____ its operations only on merchandise of easy sale so as to maximize profits.
Focus is in the closest meaning to this word.

A. oppress   C. concentrate

B. fascinate   D. restrain

⑪ In the airport, hundreds of baseball fans welcomed the _____ heroes, who had just won the world championship.
Triumphant is in the closest meaning to this word.

A. prevalent   C. justifiable

B. conquering   D. pessimistic

⑫ Bruce felt frustrated and stressed when the professor informed him of the fact that his doctoral dissertation needed considerable _____.
Alteration is in the closest meaning to this word.

A. collection   C. vaccination

B. reproduction   D. modification

❾ 泰瑞厭惡被指使，於是決定辭去低階的工作而去開創自己的公司。

Quit 的意思最接近於這個字。

A. 傳遞　　　　　　　C. 起源於

B. 辭職　　　　　　　D. 預期

❿ 這家公司訂定計畫集中銷售容易販賣的商品以增加到最大的利潤。

Focus 的意思最接近於這個字。

A. 壓迫　　　　　　　C. 專注於

B. 著迷　　　　　　　D. 節制

⓫ 在機場裡，上百名棒球球迷歡迎凱旋而歸的英雄，他們剛剛獲得世界冠軍。

Triumphant 的意思最接近於這個字。

A. 流行的　　　　　　C. 有道理的

B. 戰勝的　　　　　　D. 悲觀的

⓬ 當教授通知他的博士論文需要做大篇幅修改時，布魯斯感受到極大的挫折與壓力。

Alteration 的意思最接近於這個字。

A. 收集　　　　　　　C. 接種疫苗

B. 複製　　　　　　　D. 修改

答案 B　 C　 B　 D

19-4 同反義詞表

		同反義詞一覽表 Unit 19
rescue	救援、解救	同義詞 saving / extrication / release
	俘虜、監禁	反義詞 capture / arrest / imprisonment
ironically	諷刺地、挖苦地	同義詞 satirically / mockingly / sarcastically
	讚賞地、恭維地	反義詞 admiringly/flatteringly/ complementarily
theory	理論、推測	同義詞 conception / supposition / hypothesis
	實踐、實施	反義詞 practice / implementation / execution
release	釋放、鬆開	同義詞 free / liberate / loose
	拘留、束縛	反義詞 capture / arrest / bind
flexibility	彈性、適應性	同義詞 elasticity / plasticity / adaptability
	僵化、固執	反義詞 inflexibility / rigidness / stubbornness
originate	發源、創始	同義詞 emerge / initiate / create
	結束、終止	反義詞 end / conclude / terminate
lift	舉起、升起	同義詞 raise / elevate / hoist
	放下、降級	反義詞 lower / degrade / downgrade
full-scale	全部的、全面的	同義詞 overall / comprehensive / thorough
	狹隘的、有限的	反義詞 narrow / confined / limited

transportation	交通、輸送	同義詞 commuting / conveyance / carrying
	裝載、包裝	反義詞 loading / shipment / packing
uncountable	無數的、不可數	同義詞 countless / innumerable / incalculable
	可數的、可計算	反義詞 countable / calculable / computable
aviation	航空、飛行	同義詞 flying / volitation / flight
	降落、著陸	反義詞 landing / disembarkation / touchdown
military	軍隊、軍方	同義詞 army / troop / soldiers
	民眾、百姓	反義詞 populace / commoner / civilian
public	公眾的、公開的	同義詞 communal / civic / open
	私人的、秘密的	反義詞 private / personal / secret
resign	辭職、順從	同義詞 quit / abandon / comply
	抵抗、反抗	反義詞 resist / oppose / withstand
concentrate	專心、全神貫注	同義詞 focus / absorb / attend
	分心、擾亂	反義詞 distract / interrupt / disturb
conquering	戰勝的、克服的	同義詞 victorious / triumphant / overcoming
	失敗的、不成功	反義詞 defeated / losing / unsuccessful
modification	修改、改變	同義詞 alteration / amendment / change
	維持、保存	反義詞 maintenance / sustenance / preservation
immediately	立刻、馬上	同義詞 instantly / promptly / straightaway
	緩慢地、拖延地	反義詞 slowly / gradually / tardily

1 飲食民生

2 歷史懷舊

3 現代化實用科技

4 資訊與知識傳遞

20-1 火藥的沿革

 MP3 58

Dynamite came from the Greek word "Dynamis" which means "Power". The 18th and the 19th centuries are known as the boom-years of the industrial revolution for the western side of the world.

炸藥來自希臘字「DYNAMIS」，意思是「力量」。第 18 和 19 世紀被稱為西方社會工業革命的景氣年。

The transcontinental railroad across the USA, the gold-rushes in California and Australia, the "Undergroundrailroad" system in London, all of these works required explosives.

橫跨美國橫貫大陸的鐵路正在修建，在澳洲及加州的淘金熱，及在倫敦的「Underground」鐵路系統，正在興建。所有這些工程都需要爆炸物。

However, there were only two main explosives in the mid 19th century which were unstable and hard to

然而在 19 世紀中期只有兩種不穩定且難以控制的主要爆炸

control. The black powder and Nitroglycerine. In 1860, the Swedish industrialist, engineer, and inventor, Alfred Nobel started his invention of dynamite.

Nobel understood that Nitroglycerin is powerful but in its natural liquid state, it is very volatile. Nobel started his research on Nitroglycerin and discovered that by mixing nitroglycerine and silica, it turns into a malleable paste which he called it "dynamite" later on. In 1866, he invented the dynamite successfully.

物：黑火藥和硝化甘油。1860 年，瑞典實業家、工程師和發明家，諾貝爾開始了他的炸藥發明。

諾貝爾了解，硝酸甘油是強大的，但在它的自然液體狀態是非常不穩定的。諾貝爾開始了他對硝酸甘油的研究。他發現通過混合硝酸甘油和二氧化矽，會變化為一個黏土的狀態，他將之命名為「炸藥」。1866 年他成功地發明了炸藥。

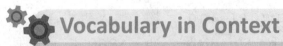 **Vocabulary in Context**

❶ In many _____ countries, lovers celebrate Valentine's Day on February 14. They give each other cards and presents like flowers and chocolate. At night, they enjoy a romantic candlelight dinner together.

Occidental is in the closest meaning to this word.

A. western   C. redundant

B. spatial   D. eligible

❷ The CEO read the files and discussed about the investment projects with his consultants while taking a _____ flight.

Continent-crossing is in the closest meaning to this word.

A. courteous   C. multicultural

B. honorary   D. transcontinental

❸ The _____ city in Turkey has been famous and popular for its structural and historical mystery, which attracts tourists all over the world for sightseeing.

Subterranean is in the closest meaning to this word.

A. compatible   C. underground

B. liberal   D. circular

❹ _____ as Mr. Ford was, his real talent and interest lay in music.

Enterpriser is in the closest meaning to this word.

A. Juvenile   C. Folklore

B. Industrialist   D. Witness

❶ 在許多西方國家裡，情侶在二月十四日慶祝情人節。他們彼此互送卡片及像花以及巧克力的禮物。在夜晚，他們共享浪漫的燭光晚餐。

Occidental 的意思最接近於這個字。

A. 西方的　　　　　　　　C. 多餘的

B. 空間的　　　　　　　　D. 合格的

❷ 在搭乘橫貫大陸的飛行途中，這名總裁閱讀資料並且和顧問討論投資計畫。

Continent-crossing 的意思最接近於這個字。

A. 有禮貌的　　　　　　　C. 多元文化的

B. 名譽的　　　　　　　　D. 橫貫大陸的

❸ 土耳其地下城一向以它結構及歷史的神祕受到注目以及歡迎，而就是這項特點吸引世界各地的觀光客前往一遊。

Subterranean 的意思最接近於這個字。

A. 相容的　　　　　　　　C. 地下的

B. 自由的　　　　　　　　D. 循環的

❹ 雖然福特先生是一名工業家，他真正的天分和興趣是在於音樂。

Enterpriser 的意思最接近於這個字。

A. 青少年　　　　　　　　C. 民俗

B. 工業家　　　　　　　　D. 目擊者

答案　❶ A　❷ D　❸ C　❹ B

飲食民生　1

歷史懷舊　2

現代化實用科技　3

資訊與知識傳遞　4

Dynamite became very popular because construction workers and engineers then had a powerful and safe explosive.

炸藥變得非常流行。因為建築工人和工程師可以有一個強大且安全的爆發物。

Without the dynamite, the industrial revolution might still be successful but would for sure had much more injuries and probably would take a longer time.

沒有炸藥，工業革命依然可能成功，但將肯定有更多的傷患，也可能需要較長的時間。

As we all know, dynamite was not always confined to industrial purposes only. It was also used for murder and assassination plots.

大家都知道，炸藥並不只用於工業用途。它也被用於謀殺和暗殺。

What a shame when you have the right product on the wrong person's hand. Because of publicity like that, Nobel decided to create the famous Nobel prizes that now bear his name.

當正確的東西落在錯誤的人手裡，這是令人惋惜的。由於這樣的負面宣傳，諾貝爾決定創建著名的諾貝爾獎，並以他為名。

Alfred Nobel was the fourth son of Immanuel Nobel and Carolina Andriette Nobel. His father, Immanuel Nobel was an inventor as well; therefore, while growing up, Alfred Nobel was given a lot of freedom to do experiments and eventually became an inventor himself.

阿爾弗雷德‧諾貝爾是伊曼紐爾‧諾貝爾和卡羅來納‧安德烈特‧諾貝爾的第四個兒子。他的父親，伊曼紐爾‧諾貝爾是一位發明家；因此，在成長過程中，諾貝爾被賦予了很多自由做實驗，並最終成為一個發明家。

1　飲食民生

2　歷史懷舊

3　現代化實用科技

4　資訊與知識傳遞

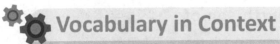

Vocabulary in Context

5 It was disappointing that the whole speech didn't get to the point. The speaker should have _____ himself strictly to the subject.

Restricted is in the closest meaning to this word.

A. confined   C. fostered

B. echoed   D. trespassed

6 The _____ of John F. Kennedy was one of the world's most shocking moments, and the whole nation mourned over the death of the promising young president, who was expected to accomplish great deeds.

Murder is in the closest meaning to this word.

A. efficiency   C. introspection

B. genius   D. assassination

7 Without doubt, the successful _____ and marketing strategies contributed to not only the popularity of Korean culture but the big sales of Korean products.

Propaganda is in the closest meaning to this word.

A. publicity   C. fragment

B. classification   D. misconduct

8 People living in democracy are lucky to enjoy _____ from want and fear, and above all, freedom of speech.

Liberty is in the closest meaning to this word.

A. morality   C. freedom

B. transmission   D. evolution

❺ 令人失望的是整場演講都離題了。演講者應該嚴謹地切合主題做
演説。

Restricted 的意思最接近於這個字。

A. 限制   C. 培養

B. 回聲   D. 擅自進入

❻ 約翰‧甘迺迪總統遇刺是令世人感到最震驚的時刻之一，全國民
眾哀悼這位原先被預期將有偉大成就、前途被看好的年輕總統之
死。

Murder 的意思最接近於這個字。

A. 效率   C. 反省

B. 天份   D. 暗殺

❼ 無疑地，成功的宣傳和行銷策略不僅促成韓國文化的廣受歡迎並
且使得韓國商品大賣。

Propaganda 的意思最接近於這個字。

A. 宣傳   C. 片段

B. 分類   D. 不良行為

❽ 民主政治下的人們很幸運地享受不虞匱乏以及免於恐懼的自由，
尤其是享有言論自由。

Liberty 的意思最接近於這個字。

A. 道德   C. 自由

B. 傳送   D. 演化

答案　❺ A　❻ D　❼ A　❽ C

Nobel was born in Stockholm, Sweden on October 21st, 1833. His family moved to St. Petersburg in Russia in 1842. Nobel was sent to private tutoring, and he excelled in his studies, particularly in chemistry and languages. He achieved fluency in English, French, German and Russian.

諾貝爾於 1833 年 10 月 21 日出生在瑞典斯德哥爾摩。在 1842 年時,他舉家遷往俄羅斯聖彼得堡。諾貝爾被送往私塾,他擅長於學習,特別是在化學和語言。他能精通英語,法語,德語和俄語。

Throughout his life, Nobel only went to school for 18 months. In 1860, Nobel started his invention of dynamite, and it was 1866 when he first invented the dynamite successfully. Nobel never let himself take any rest. He founded Nitroglycerin AB in Stockholm, Sweden in 1864.

終其一生,諾貝爾只去了學校 18 個月。1860 年,諾貝爾開始了炸藥的發明。1866 年,他第一次成功地發明了炸藥。諾貝爾從來沒有讓自己休息。他於 1864 年在瑞典斯德哥爾摩創立硝酸甘油 AB 公司。

A year later, he built the Alfred Nobel & Co. Factory in Hamburg, Germany. In 1866, he established the United States Blasting Oil Company in the U.S.

一年後，他在德國漢堡建立了阿爾弗雷德‧諾貝爾公司的工廠。1866 年，他在美國成立了美國爆破石油公司。

And 4 years later, he established the Société général pour la fabrication de la dynamite in Paris, France.

4 年後，他又在法國巴黎成立了炸藥實驗室。

Nobel was proud to say he is a world citizen. He passed away in 1896. A year before that, he started the Nobel prize which is awarded yearly to people whose work helps humanity. When he died, Alfred Nobel left behind a nine-million-dollar endowment fund.

諾貝爾自豪地說，他是一個世界公民。他在 1896 年過世。在他過世前，他成立諾貝爾獎以鼓勵對人類有幫助的人們 。當他過世時，諾貝爾留下了九百萬美元的捐贈基金。

1 飲食民生

2 歷史懷舊

3 現代化實用科技

4 資訊與知識傳遞

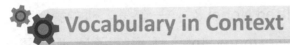

❾ Leonardo da Vinci was a remarkable genius, who _____ in painting, sculpture, architecture, and inventing.

Surpassed is in the closest meaning to this word.

A. hosted
C. substituted

B. excelled
D. undermined

❿ To _____ goals in life, Carl did his utmost to enrich knowledge on one hand and broaden his life experiences on the other.

Accomplish is in the closest meaning to this word.

A. isolate
C. achieve

B. reconcile
D. oppress

⓫ After Max was _____ the Best-Employee of the Year, he worked even harder and eventually got promoted as the store manager.

Given is in the closest meaning to this word.

A. awarded
C. violated

B. represented
D. gratified

⓬ The distinguished alumnus generously left an _____ of three million dollars to the university to show his gratitude and support.

Contribution is in the closest meaning to this word.

A. population
C. unemployment

B. impression
D. endowment

❾ 李奧納多‧達文西是一名精通於繪畫、雕刻、建築，以及發明的曠世奇才。

Surpassed 的意思最接近於這個字。

A. 主持 　　　　C. 替代

B. 優於 　　　　D. 破壞

❿ 為了達成人生的目標，卡爾一方面盡力充實知識，另一方面則拓展人生經驗。

Accomplish 的意思最接近於這個字。

A. 孤立 　　　　C. 達成

B. 和解 　　　　D. 壓迫

⓫ 麥克斯獲頒年度最佳員工獎之後更加努力地工作，最終獲升遷為商店經理。

Given 的意思最接近於這個字。

A. 頒發 　　　　C. 違反

B. 代表 　　　　D. 感激

⓬ 這位傑出校友很慷慨地捐贈三百萬元給大學以表示他的感激和支持。

Contribution的意思最接近於這個字。

A. 人口 　　　　C. 失業

B. 印象 　　　　D. 捐贈

答案　❾ B　❿ C　⓫ A　⓬ D

20-4 同反義詞表

同反義詞一覽表 Unit 20		
western	西方的、向西的	同義詞 occidental / westbound / westward
	東方的、向東的	反義詞 Oriental / Asian / eastern
transcontinental	橫貫大陸的	同義詞 continent-crossing / coast-to-coast
	地方的、區域的	反義詞 local / territorial / regional
underground	地下的、秘密的	同義詞 subterranean / private / secret
	地上的、公佈的	反義詞 over-ground / public / official
industrialist	企業家、商人	同義詞 entrepreneur / enterpriser / businessman
	員工、受雇者	反義詞 staff / worker / employee
mean	意指、打算	同義詞 signify / imply / intend
	實踐、實行	反義詞 practice / implement / execute
control	控制、抑制	同義詞 command / curb / restrain
	依從、順從	反義詞 obey / conform / comply
confine	限制、約束	同義詞 limit / restrict / restrain
	自由、釋放	反義詞 free / liberate / release
assassination	暗殺、殺害	同義詞 murder / kill / homicide
	援救、拯救	反義詞 rescue / save / salvation
publicity	公眾注意、宣傳	同義詞 attention / advertisement / propaganda
	無名氣、不注意	反義詞 obscurity / inattention / indifference

freedom	自由、自主	同義詞 liberty / autonomy / independence
	壓制、約束	反義詞 repression / constraint / confinement
shame	羞恥、羞辱	同義詞 disgrace / dishonor / humiliation
	光榮、榮譽	反義詞 glory / honor / renown
bear	忍受、容忍	同義詞 endure / stand / tolerate
	抱怨、表示不滿	反義詞 complain / grumble / mutter
excel	勝過、優於	同義詞 surpass / exceed / better
	隸屬、低劣	反義詞 subordinate / underlie / lower
achieve	達成、實現	同義詞 accomplish / realize / fulfill
	失敗、放棄	反義詞 fail / abandon / quit
award	授予、獎賞	同義詞 give / grant / reward
	得到、獲得	反義詞 receive / acquire / obtain
endowment	捐贈、賦予才能	同義詞 contribution / bestow / talent
	獲得、平庸	反義詞 gain / obtainment / mediocrity
particularly	特別地、詳盡地	同義詞 especially / thoroughly / specifically
	粗略地、概括地	反義詞 roughly / broadly / generally
fluency	流暢、流利	同義詞 smoothness / flow / eloquence
	猶豫、結巴	反義詞 hesitance / stutter / stammer

1 飲食民生

2 歷史懷舊

3 現代化實用科技

4 資訊與知識傳遞

Unit 21 Plastics 塑膠

 ## 21-1 塑膠的發現

Although different types of pollutions caused by plastic have been public issues for years, it seems hard to get rid of plastic for its relatively low production cost, versatility and imperviousness to water. From grocery bags to toys to even clothes, plastics are used in an enormous and expanding range of products.

雖然因為塑膠所造成的各種污染已是多年來的公共問題,但由於生產成本相對低廉,具通用性及抗滲水性,因此我們似乎無法擺脫這種材料。從食品塑膠袋到玩具,甚至服裝,塑膠產品的範圍不斷擴大。

It is also being widely used in the medical field and construction field. The very first plastic material was discovered by Charles Goodyear during the discovery of vulcanization to thermoset materials derived from natural rubber in the 1800s.

它也被廣泛應用於醫療領域和建築領域。史上第一個塑膠材料是在 1800 年代由查爾斯·固特異在天然橡膠的熱固性材料中發現的硫化物。

After that, many scientists contributed to the discovery of different types of plastics. It was not until 1907, a scientist Leo Baekeland invented "Bakelite" which was the first fully synthetic plastic. He was also the person who coined the term "Plastics".

在此之後，許多科學家促成了不同類型塑膠的發現。直到 1907 年，科學家利奧‧貝克蘭發明了酚醛塑料，這是第一個完全合成的塑膠。他也是命名「塑膠」的人。

The rapid growth in chemical technology led to the invention of many new forms of plastics, such as Polystyrene, Polyvinyl chloride, and polyethylene. Many traditional materials, such as wood, stone, leather, ceramic that we normally used in the past were replaced by plastics.

化學技術的極速成長導致許多形式的塑膠發明，例如聚苯乙烯、聚氯乙烯和聚乙烯。許多傳統材料，例如我們過去常使用的木頭、石頭、皮革和陶瓷都被塑膠取代了。

1 飲食民生

2 歷史懷舊

3 現代化實用科技

4 資訊與知識傳遞

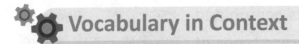 **Vocabulary in Context**

❶ Huge heavy motorcycles in Taiwan not only cause a lot of air _____ but disturb people in quiet neighborhoods, which arouses serious complaints from the general public.

Contamination is in the closest meaning to this word.

A. foundation   C. pollution

B. control   D. survey

❷ _____ speaking, in order to look young and perfect, nowadays, more and more people turn to plastic surgery, though the cost may be amazingly high.

Comparatively is in the closest meaning to this word.

A. Steadily   C. Inconveniently

B. Relatively   D. Medically

❸ Shouldering _____ responsibility to support the family, Roy couldn't but take several part-time jobs besides his regular work.

Huge is in the closest meaning to this word.

A. enormous   C. relevant

B. industrious   D. miraculous

❹ The stressful work and the chronic diseases _____ to Mr. Dewey's serious insomnia at night.

Caused is in the closest meaning to this word.

A. authorized   C. subscribed

B. installed   D. contributed

❶ 台灣的大型重型機車不僅製造大量的空氣汙染，同時也干擾到寧靜住家的住戶們，因此引發一般大眾嚴重的抱怨。

Contamination 的意思最接近於這個字。

A. 基礎　　　　　　　　C. 污染

B. 管制　　　　　　　　D. 調查

❷ 相對而言，雖然花費可能高的驚人，為了要看起來年輕完美，現在越來越多人選擇做整容手術。

Comparatively 的意思最接近於這個字。

A. 穩定地　　　　　　　C. 不方便地

B. 相對地　　　　　　　D. 醫療上地

❸ 羅伊肩負著養家的重大責任，不得不在正規工作之外兼數份差。

Huge 的意思最接近於這個字。

A. 巨大的　　　　　　　C. 相關的

B. 勤勉的　　　　　　　D. 奇蹟的

❹ 極具壓力的工作以及慢性疾病導致杜威先生夜晚嚴重的失眠。

Caused 的意思最接近於這個字。

A. 授權　　　　　　　　C. 訂閱

B. 安裝　　　　　　　　D. 促成

 答案　❶ C　❷ B　❸ A　❹ D

What is plastics exactly? The majority of the polymers are based on chains of carbon atoms alone with oxygen, sulfur, or nitrogen. Most plastics contain other organic or inorganic compounds blended in.

塑膠到底是什麼？大多數聚合物都基於碳原子和氧、硫、或氮的鏈。大多數塑膠混有其他有機或無機化合物。

The amount of additives ranges from zero percentage to more than 50% for certain electronic applications. The invention of plastic was a great success but also brought us a serious environmental concerns regarding its slow decomposition rate after being discarded.

在一些電子應用上，添加劑的量從零至50%以上。塑膠的發明獲得了巨大的成功，但也給我們帶來了關於其被丟棄後緩慢分解所造成嚴重的環境問題。

One way to help with the environment is to practice recycling or use other environmental friendly materials instead.

練習回收或改用其他對環境友好的材料是幫助環境的一種方法。

Another approach is to speed up the development of biodegradable plastic.

另一種方法是，加快生物分解性塑料的開

The father of the Plastics Industry, Leo Baekeland, was born in Belgium on November 14th, 1863.

發。塑膠工業之父，利奧·貝克蘭，於 1863 年 11 月 14 日出生於比利時。

He was best known for his invention of Bakelite which is an inexpensive, nonflammable and versatile plastic.

他最為人知的是酚醛塑的發明，這是一種廉價，不可燃和通用的塑膠。

Because of his invention, the plastic industry started to bloom and became a popular material in many different industries.

由於他的發明，塑料行業開始盛行，在許多不同的行業成為一個受歡迎的材料。

1 飲食民生

2 歷史懷舊

3 現代化實用科技

4 資訊與知識傳遞

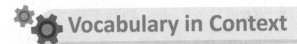

Vocabulary in Context

5 The _____ of the residents were strongly against the construction of a new chemical plant around their neighborhood and planned to stage a protest.

Most is in the closest meaning to this word.

A. grade   C. distribution

B. region   D. majority

6 With the health awareness prevailing, _____ foods, vegetables and fruits have been in high demand these days.

Natural is in the closest meaning to this word.

A. recycling   C. democratic

B. organic   D. alternative

7 As a whole, it's difficult to strike a balance between promoting the global economic growth and lessening the _____ impact of pollution on humans.

Surroundings is in the closest meaning to this word.

A. considerate   C. environmental

B. identical   D. violent

8 The best solution to the issue is to _____ the old prejudice and bad feelings toward each other and cooperate again.

Abandon is in the closest meaning to this word.

A. discard   C. witness

B. complicate   D. participate

❺ 大多數的居民強烈反對在他們的住家附近建造一座新的化工工廠，並且計畫發動抗議活動。

Most 的意思最接近於這個字。

A. 等級　　　　　　　C. 分配

B. 區域　　　　　　　D. 大多數

❻ 隨著健康意識的流行，近日有機食物、蔬菜，以及水果的需求量大增。**Natural** 的意思最接近於這個字。

A. 回收的　　　　　　C. 民主的

B. 有機的　　　　　　D. 替代的

❼ 整體而言，要尋求促進全球經濟成長以及減緩環境污染對於人類的衝擊兩者之間的平衡是困難的。

Surrounding 的意思最接近於這個字。

A. 體貼的　　　　　　C. 環境的

B. 相同的　　　　　　D. 暴力的

❽ 這個問題最佳的解決方法是拋棄原舊有的偏見以及彼此不良的印象而再度齊心合作。

Abandon 的意思最接近於這個字。

A. 拋棄　　　　　　　C. 目睹

B. 使複雜　　　　　　D. 參加

答案　❺ D　❻ B　❼ C　❽ A

Baekeland acquired a Ph D. at chemistry in the University of Ghent and became an associate professor there. He and his wife traveled to New York in 1889 and got a job offer by Richard Anthony who owned a photographic company.

貝克蘭在根特大學攻讀化學並取得化學博士學位，並成為該校特約化學副教授。他和他的妻子在 1889 年前往了紐約，並在理查德・安東尼所擁有的攝影公司裡得到一個工作機會。

Baekeland worked there for 2 years and formed his own business as a consultant. This job didn't last long though. He eventually went back to his old interest of producing a photographic paper that would allow enlargements to be printed by artificial lights.

貝克蘭在那裡工作了 2 年後，組織了自己的顧問公司。但這項工作並沒有持續多久，他最終又回到他舊有的興趣，允許放大到人工燈光打印的相紙開發。

After 2 years of efforts, he invented the first commercial photographic paper "Velox". After inventing Velox, Baekeland set another goal to develop

經過 2 年的努力，他發明了第一個商業相紙「Velox」。發明 Velox 後，貝克蘭訂

something that would bring him fortune the quickest way possible. Baekeland began to investigate the reactions of phenol and formaldehyde.

As always, Baekeland approached the field systematically. He carefully controlled all his work and examed the effects of temperature, pressure and all possible factors.

In 1907, he proudly made his dream plastic-Bakelite. Later, he received many awards and medals, and passed away in 1944.

了另外一個目標，這個目標是要是發明出可以以最快的速度賺取更多的錢的東西。貝克蘭開始調查苯酚和甲醛的反應。

與往常一樣，貝克蘭有系統地小心控管溫度，壓力和所有可能的因素，並測試各種反應。

1907 年，他自豪地做了他的夢想塑膠 - 酚醛塑。之後，他獲得了許多獎章和榮譽並於 1944 年離開人世。

1 飲食民生

2 歷史懷舊

3 現代化實用科技

4 資訊與知識傳遞

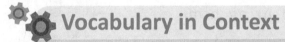

Vocabulary in Context

9 After retirement from the public office, Mr. Costner worked in a private corporation as a _____ on business affairs.

Adviser is in the closest meaning to this word.

A. hitchhiker   C. consultant

B. pharmacist   D. technician

10 Undoubtedly, the rapid progress in the development and outcome of _____ intelligence will take the mankind to a brand-new era.

Man-made is in the closest meaning to this word.

A. visual   C. revolutionary

B. flexible   D. artificial

11 The police intensively _____ possible links between the suspect and the case of suicide, in which telecommunications fraud was allegedly to have cost the victim huge amounts of his pension.

Inspected is in the closest meaning to this word.

A. deterred   C. investigated

B. measured   D. sentenced

12 The researcher _____ collected and analyzed the samples to prove the hypotheses he suggested.

Orderly is in the closest meaning to this word.

A. commercially   C. negatively

B. systematically   D. prehistorically

❾ 從公職退休後，科斯納先生在私人公司擔任商業顧問。

Adviser 的意思最接近於這個字。

A. 搭便車者　　　　　　C. 顧問

B. 藥劑師　　　　　　　D. 技術人員

❿ 無疑地，人工智慧發展及結果的快速進步將會把人類帶入一個全新的紀元。

Man-made 的意思最接近於這個字。

A. 視覺的　　　　　　　C. 革命的

B. 彈性的　　　　　　　D. 人工的

⓫ 警方密切地調查這名嫌疑犯和一椿自殺案件可能存在的關聯性，據説電信詐騙使得受害者損失大筆的退休金。

Inspected 的意思最接近於這個字。

A. 阻止　　　　　　　　C. 調查

B. 測量　　　　　　　　D. 宣判

⓬ 這名研究人員有系統地收集分析樣本以證實他提出的假設。

Orderly 的意思最接近於這個字。

A. 商業地　　　　　　　C. 消極地

B. 有系統地　　　　　　D. 史前地

 答案 ❾ C ❿ D ⓫ C ⓬ B

21-4 同反義詞表

同反義詞一覽表 Unit 21		
pollution	污染、弄髒	同義詞 contamination / taint / defilement
	乾淨、潔淨	反義詞 cleanness / spotlessness / purity
relatively	相對地、相當地	同義詞 correspondently / comparatively / fairly
	絕對地、完全地	反義詞 absolutely / definitely / totally
enormous	巨大的、龐大的	同義詞 large / vast / huge
	微小的、極小的	反義詞 tiny / small / diminutive
contribute	貢獻、促成	同義詞 donate / give / cause
	收到、得到	反義詞 receive / obtain / gain
rapid	快速的、迅速的	同義詞 quick / swift / speedy
	緩慢的、延遲的	反義詞 slow / sluggish / tardy
normally	通常地、慣例地	同義詞 ordinarily / usually / generally
	反常地、例外地	反義詞 abnormally/ uncommonly/ exceptionally
majority	多數、大部份	同義詞 plurality / mass / most
	少數、小量	反義詞 minority / handful / minimum
organic	有機的、天然的	同義詞 natural / untreated / crude
	人造的、合成的	反義詞 artificial / man-made / synthetic

environmental	環境的、周遭的	同義詞 ecological / natural / surrounding
	人類的、都會的	反義詞 human / urban / metropolitan
discard	拋棄、丟棄	同義詞 abandon / desert / forsake
	保留、保存	反義詞 retain / save / preserve
blend	混合、結合	同義詞 mix / mingle / combine
	分類、分離	反義詞 sort / classify / separate
consultant	顧問、指導者	同義詞 adviser / counselor / guide
	學生、病患	反義詞 student / learner / patient
artificial	人工的、假造的	同義詞 man-made / fake / simulated
	自然的、真實的	反義詞 natural / genuine / real
investigate	調查、研究	同義詞 inspect / inquire / research
	證明、證實	反義詞 prove / verify / confirm
systematically	有組織、條理地	同義詞 methodically / orderly / logically
	雜亂地、隨意地	反義詞 disorderly / messily / randomly
enlargement	擴大、擴展	同義詞 magnification/ amplification/ expansion
	減少、削減	反義詞 diminishment / decrease / reduction
goal	目標、終點	同義詞 aim / target / destination
	開始、起源	反義詞 starting / begin / origin
factor	因素、起因	同義詞 element / reason / cause
	結果、後果	反義詞 effect / consequence / outcome

1 飲食民生

2 歷史懷舊

3 現代化實用科技

4 資訊與知識傳遞

Unit 22 Barcode 條碼

22-1 條碼的沿革

Infinity amount of information is being stored by these lines or dots. They limited human errors and sped the transit of information.

無限量的信息被存儲在這些線或點裡。他們將人為錯誤減到最低並加快了訊息的傳訊。

But when we are doing the easy scanning, have we even considered this-What exactly is a barcode? How does it work?

但是，當我們在做這簡單的掃描時，我們是否有想過 - 到底什麼是條碼？它是如何作業的？

A barcode is an optical machine-readable representation of data relating to the object to which it is attached. We see it on almost all products. Originally, barcodes systematically represented data by varying the widths and spacing of parallel lines.

條碼是一個光學儀器可讀取有關連結對象的數據。我們幾乎可以在所有產品上看到它。最初是通過改變寬度和平行線間距的條碼系統來表示數據。

Now we even have the two dimensional barcodes that evolved into rectangles, dots, hexagons and other patterns.

現在，我們甚至有利用矩形、點、六邊形等所演變出的二維條碼。

Also nowadays, we no longer require special optical scanners to read the barcodes. They can be read by smartphones as well.

而且現在，我們不再需要特殊的光學掃描儀讀取條碼。它們可以通過智能電話被讀取。

1 飲食民生

2 歷史懷舊

3 現代化實用科技

4 資訊與知識傳遞

Vocabulary in Context

❶ The Internet brings us a lot of access and conveniences; with only a click of the mouse, we can make collection and _____ of information easily.

Transmission is in the closest meaning to this word.

A. adversity   C. immunity

B. transit   D. reinforcement

❷ Simon was experienced and well-trained in his field and was chosen as an agent to _____ the company.

Delegate is in the closest meaning to this word.

A. harass   C. represent

B. issue   D. anticipate

❸ It was the British naturalist Charles Darwin who established the theory that species _____ through the process of natural selection over long ages.

Develop is in the closest meaning to this word.

A. evolve   C. discriminate

B. thrive   D. navigate

❹ The Nasca Lines in Peru consist of several thousands of geometric _____ and hundreds of distinct animal shapes and have been a great mystery for all time.

Designs is in the closest meaning to this word.

A. effects   C. patterns

B. welfare   D. microscope

❶ 網際網路為我們帶來許多捷徑以及便利；點一下滑鼠，我們就可以輕鬆地收集以及傳送資訊。

Transmission 的意思最接近於這個字。

A. 逆境　　　　　　　C. 免疫

B. 傳送　　　　　　　D. 加強

❷ 賽門在他的領域經驗豐富並且訓練有素，因此被選為代表公司的負責人。

Delegate 的意思最接近於這個字。

A. 騷擾　　　　　　　C. 代表

B. 發行　　　　　　　D. 預期

❸ 英國博物學家查爾斯‧達爾文提出理論認為物種是經由長時間物競天擇的過程演變而成的。

Developed 的意思最接近於這個字。

A. 演化　　　　　　　C. 歧視

B. 興盛　　　　　　　D. 航行

❹ 祕魯的納斯卡線是由數千條幾何圖案及上百個明顯的動物形狀圖案所組成的，長久以來一直是個謎。

Designs 的意思最接近於這個字。

A. 效果

B. 福利

C. 圖案

D. 顯微鏡

答案　❶ B　❷ C　❸ A　❹ C

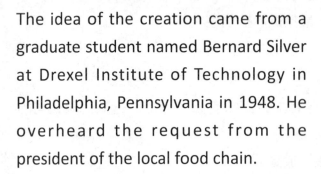

The idea of the creation came from a graduate student named Bernard Silver at Drexel Institute of Technology in Philadelphia, Pennsylvania in 1948. He overheard the request from the president of the local food chain.

這個創作的想法來自一個在賓州費城的 Drexel 技術學院就讀的研究生-伯納德・史維。他當時無意間聽到當地的連鎖食品店老闆的要求。

He immediately saw the demand for the system and then started the development with his friend Norman Joseph Woodland who also went to Drexel. Woodland later on left Drexel and kept his research in Florida.

他立即看到了這個系統的需求，於是他找了也在 Drexel 就讀的朋友-諾曼・伍德蘭一起開發這個系統。後來伍德蘭離開了 Drexel，到了佛羅里達繼續他的開發。

He got the inspiration from Morse code first and then he adapted technology from optical soundtracks in movies in order to read them. The patent for the Barcode was filed as "Classifying Apparatus and Method" on October

他從摩斯密碼得到靈感，爾後再改編電影配樂的技術以便讀取它們。條碼的專利在 1949 年 10 月 20 日被以「分級裝置和方

20th, 1949 by the both of them. Later on, IBM offered to buy the patent but the offer was too low.

法」的方式由兩位共同提出。後來 IBM 提出購買該專利的要求，但報價太低。

Philco later on purchased the patent in 1962 for 15,000 dollars and then sold it to RCA sometime later.

Philco 在 1962 年以 15,000 美元買下專利，並爾後將其賣給了 RCA。

Two students from Drexel Institute of Technology, Bernard Silver and Norman Joseph Woodland jointly developed the barcode technology.

兩名 Drexel 的研究生，伯納德・史維－出生於 1924 年 9 月 21 日和諾曼・喬瑟夫・伍德蘭－出生於 1921 年 9 月 6 日，聯合開發了條碼技術。

Vocabulary in Context

❺ It's a pity that Michael Jackson, who has been an _____ to his pop music fans, died young; otherwise, they could enjoy more of his wonderful works and performances.

Encouragement is in the closest meaning to this word.

A. alienation   C. oppression

B. element   D. inspiration

❻ Though it took Emma several months to _____ to the new working environment, she made it and did a great job.

Adjust is in the closest meaning to this word.

A. adapt   C. diminish

B. resist   D. compliment

❼ As the books in the library are _____ according to their subjects, it's easy to find the books you want.

Categorized is in the closest meaning to this word.

A. reigned   C. classified

B. nominated   D. innovated

❽ The factory decided to modernize the _____ to meet the increasing demand of both domestic and foreign orders.

Equipment is in the closest meaning to this word.

A. utensils   C. apparatus

B. variation   D. ecosystem

❺ 令人惋惜的一件事是對於流行樂迷來說一直是鼓舞力量的麥可·傑克遜英年早逝；否則他們可以享受更多他精彩的作品以及表演。

Encouragement 的意思最接近於這個字。

A. 疏離　　　　　　　C. 壓迫

B. 元素　　　　　　　D. 鼓舞

❻ 雖然艾瑪花了好幾個月的時間去適應新的工作環境，然而她成功了並且表現優異。

Adjust 的意思最接近於這個字。

A. 適應　　　　　　　C. 削減

B. 抗拒　　　　　　　D. 稱讚

❼ 由於圖書館裡的書籍是按照主題分類的，你很容易就可以找到你所要的書籍。

Categorized 的意思最接近於這個字。

A. 統治　　　　　　　C. 分類

B. 提名　　　　　　　D. 革新

❽ 這座工廠決定將設備現代化以符合國內外訂貨量逐漸增加的需求。

Equipment 的意思最接近於這個字。

A. 餐具　　　　　　　C. 設備

B. 變化　　　　　　　D. 生態系統

   答案　❺ D　❻ A　❼ C　❽ C

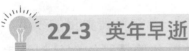

Silver overheard the system request from an owner of a local chain store and started his barcode development with Norman Joseph Woodland. He later on served as a physics instructor at Drexel. Unfortunately, Silver passed away on August 28th, 1963 due to leukemia. He was only 38.

當時，他從當地連鎖店的老闆聽到了系統的要求，於是與諾曼‧伍德蘭開始了條碼的發展。他後來在 Drexel 擔任物理教師。不幸的是，史維在 1963 年 8 月 28 日因白血病過世。當時他只有 38 歲。

Before studying in Mechanical Engineering at Drexel Institute of Technology, Woodland did military service in World War II as a technical assistant in Tennessee. After having earned his Bachelor degree from Drexel, he also worked as a lecturer in mechanical engineer in the same school.

在 Drexel 就讀機械工程系前，伍德蘭在二次世界大戰中服役，在美國田納西州擔任一個技術助理。獲得了他的學士學位後，他還在 Drexel 擔任機械工程師及講師。

Silver and Woodland started the barcode development in 1948.

史維和伍德蘭在 1948 年時開始了條

Woodland then quit his teaching job and moved to Florida to concentrate on his research on the system.

碼的研究，伍德蘭並在 1948 年時辭掉教師工作，搬到佛羅里達州以專注於他的系統研究。

The two of them applied for a patent on October 20, 1949 and received the U.S patent 2 years later.

他們倆在 1949 年 10 月 20 日申請了專利，並在兩年後獲得了美國專利。

The patent covered both linear and circular bulls eye printing designs. In 2011 Silver, alongside Woodland, was inducted into the National Inventors Hall of Fame. A year later, Woodland passed away from the effects of Alzheimer's disease.

該專利涵蓋了直線和圓靶心的印刷設計。2011 年史維與伍德蘭被列入美國國家發明家名人堂。一年後，伍德蘭因阿茲海默症而過世。

1 飲食民生

2 歷史懷舊

3 現代化實用科技

4 資訊與知識傳遞

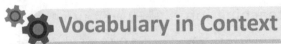

Vocabulary in Context

9 Miss Lopez is a popular foreign _____ in Spanish. She not only makes Spanish interesting and easy to learn but also shows great patience and passion to her students.

Teacher is in the closest meaning to this word.

A. curator   C. ballerina

B. instructor   D. inhabitant

10 _____ innovations in industry have been significant in improving products and raising humans' living standards.

Technological is in the closest meaning to this word.

A. Random   C. Glamorous

B. Abnormal   D. Technical

11 The experience of being a part-time design _____ at night helped Gina a lot in getting official full-time employment as a formal designer after her college graduation.

Helper is in the closest meaning to this word.

A. diplomat   C. pessimist

B. assistant   D. disturber

12 After election, Mr. Major was finally formally _____ into the office of mayor and started fulfilling his campaign promises.

Inaugurated is in the closest meaning to this word.

A. inducted   C. comprehended

B. retrieved   D. disciplined

❾ 羅培茲小姐是一位很受歡迎的西班牙語教師。她不僅使得西班牙語的學習變得有趣輕鬆，並且對學生展現極大的耐心及熱情。

Teacher 的意思最接近於這個字。

A. 館長　　　　　　　C. 女芭蕾舞者

B. 教師　　　　　　　D. 居民

❿ 工業的技術革新在改善產品品質及提升人類生活水準方面具有重大的意義。

Technological 的意思最接近於這個字。

A. 隨機的　　　　　　C. 富有魅力的

B. 反常的　　　　　　D. 技術的

⓫ 夜間擔任兼差設計助理的經驗在吉娜大學畢業後取得擔任全職的正式設計師工作上有極大的幫助。

Helper 的意思最接近於這個字。

A. 外交官　　　　　　C. 悲觀者

B. 助理　　　　　　　D. 干擾者

⓬ 選舉過後，梅傑先生終於正式就任市長的職位，並且開始實踐他的競選承諾。

Inaugurated 的意思最接近於這個字。

A. 就任　　　　　　　C. 理解

B. 收回　　　　　　　D. 訓練

答案　❾ B　❿ D　⓫ B　⓬ A

22-4 同反義詞表

同反義詞一覽表 Unit 22		
transit	運輸、傳送	同義詞 transmission / transfer / transport
	接受、接收	反義詞 accept / get / receive
represent	代表、展現	同義詞 delegate / reveal / demonstrate
	推卻、隱藏	反義詞 refuse / conceal / hide
evolve	進化、發展	同義詞 develop / progress / advance
	退化、衰敗	反義詞 degenerate / deteriorate / decline
pattern	圖案、排列	同義詞 design / configuration / arrangement
	不規則、雜亂	反義詞 irregularity / disorder / disorganization
infinity	無限、無窮	同義詞 limitlessness / endlessness / immensity
	限制、極限	反義詞 limit / restriction / extreme
relating	相關的、有關的	同義詞 connecting / linked / relevant
	不相關、無關的	反義詞 unrelated / irrelevant / disconnected
inspiration	靈感、激勵	同義詞 stimulation / motivation / encouragement
	挫折、氣餒	反義詞 frustration / dejection / discouragement

adapt	修改、適應	同義詞 modify / alter / adjust
	不變、不適應	反義詞 disarrange / unsettle / unfit
classify	分類、整理	同義詞 sort / categorize / organize
	弄亂、混亂	反義詞 mess / clutter / disorganize
apparatus	設備、裝置	同義詞 equipment / gear / device
	組件、零件	反義詞 part / segment / component
local	本地的、局部的	同義詞 native / indigenous / regional
	外國的、整體的	反義詞 foreign / alien / universal
jointly	共同地、聯合地	同義詞 together / collectively / cooperatively
	單獨地、分開地	反義詞 individually / independently / separately
instructor	教師、教練	同義詞 teacher / coach / trainer
	學生、受訓者	反義詞 student / learner / trainee
technical	技術的、專門的	同義詞 technological / professional / specialized
	非技術、一般的	反義詞 unprofessional / ordinary / general
assistant	助理、副手	同義詞 helper / deputy / supporter
	長官、上司	反義詞 chief / superior / leader
induct	就任、引介	同義詞 inaugurate / initiate / introduce
	辭職、辭去	反義詞 resign / leave / quit
lecturer	演講者、講師	同義詞 speaker / presenter / instructor
	聽者、學生	反義詞 listener / auditor / student
quit	放棄、停止	同義詞 resign / stop / forego
	繼續、持續	反義詞 continue / last / persist

1 飲食民生

2 歷史懷舊

3 現代化實用科技

4 資訊與知識傳遞

PART 4

資訊與知識傳遞

單元三大學習法

key 1 主題式記憶
透過主題學習將字彙累績至長期記憶，
而非片段背誦。

key 2 上下文推敲文意
閱讀時不因不熟悉的單字而影響句意理解。

key 3 熟記同反義詞
在雅思各單項中要獲取 7 分以上
需要具備同反義詞轉換的能力。

Unit 23 Google 谷歌

 23-1 谷歌傳奇 MP3 67

Google Inc. is an American multinational technology company. Google is not so much a company that invented one product as a company that invents anything relating to the Internet. Starting from Google's core search engine, it also offers email service-Gmail, a cloud storage service-Google drive, Web browser-Google Chrome, to an even innovative hardware like Google glasses.

谷歌是美國的跨國科技公司。與其說谷歌發明了一種產品,還不如說是谷歌發明所有涉及到互聯網的產品。從谷歌的核心搜索引擎開始,它也提供電子郵件服務 – Gmail、雲存儲服務 – Google Drive、網絡瀏覽器- Google Chrome,甚至創新的硬件,如谷歌眼鏡。

The Google self-driving car is also being invented for years, and they plan to release it to the market in the year 2020. Google was founded as a private

谷歌自動駕駛汽車也被開發多年,他們計劃在 2020 年發布到市場。谷歌是於

company in 1998 by Larry Page and Sergey Brin while they were Ph. D. students at Stanford University. An initial public offering followed on August 19, 2004.

1998 年由拉里・佩奇和謝爾蓋・布林在史丹佛大學攻讀他們博士學位時所創立的私人公司。隨後於 2004 年 8 月 19 日首次上市。

The company's mission was to organize the world's information and made it universally accessible and useful. No doubt, they accomplished their mission and went much further. From the data in 2009, it processes over one billion search requests and about 24 petabytes of user-generated data each day as of 2009. Google.com should have been the most visited website in the world for years.

該公司的使命是整合全球信息，使人人皆可使用並從中受益。毫無疑問，他們完成了他們的使命，且更進一步。根據 2009 年的數據，它的搜索器處理超過十億個搜索請求，用戶每天約 24 PB 的量。Google.com 多年來應該都是世界上訪問量最大的網站。

1 飲食民生

2 歷史懷舊

3 現代化實用科技

4 資訊與知識傳遞

Vocabulary in Context

❶ Though the kidnapper _____ to kill the hostage if he didn't get the ransom, with his location spotted, he was soon nailed and the hostage was saved.

Menaced is in the closest meaning to this word.

A. affected   C. threatened

B. consulted   D. monitored

❷ After Marvin was appointed to _____ the international conference, he devoted himself fully to accomplishing the work.

Arrange is in the closest meaning to this word.

A. organize   C. select

B. arise   D. perceive

❸ With the Internet _____ to us, we can achieve a lot of things; in the meantime, we should be careful not to get addicted or fall victim to net frauds.

Available is in the closest meaning to this word.

A. traditional   C. radiant

B. enormous   D. accessible

❹ The Japanese mountaineer Junko Tabei was the first woman to conquer Mount Everest in 1975. To her, it was the willpower, together with technique and capability, that helped her _____ the impossible task.

Achieve is in the closest meaning to this word.

A. foretell　　　　C. manufacture

B. accomplish　　　D. trigger

❶ 雖然綁匪威脅假使拿不到贖金要殺害人質，但是隨著所在處曝光，他很快地被逮捕，人質因而獲救。

Menaced 的意思最接近於這個字。

A. 影響　　　　　　C. 威脅

B. 諮詢　　　　　　D. 監督

❷ 馬文被指派籌劃國際會議之後，他全心投入於把工作做好。

Arrange 的意思最接近於這個字。

A. 籌備　　　　　　C. 選擇

B. 發生　　　　　　D. 察覺

❸ 有著網際網路供我們便捷地利用，我們可以成就許多事情；在這同時，我們應該要謹慎，不要網路成癮，或是成為網路詐欺的受害者。

Available 的意思最接近於這個字。

A. 傳統的　　　　　C. 容光煥發的

B. 巨大的　　　　　D. 可使用的

❹ 日籍登山家，田部井淳子，在**1975**年成為第一位征服聖母峰的女性。對她而言，意志力，連同技術和能力，幫助她完成不可能的任務。

Achieve 的意思最接近於這個字。

A. 預告　　　　　　C. 製造

B. 完成　　　　　　D. 觸發

 ❶ C　❷ A　❸ D　❹ B

1 飲食民生

2 歷史懷舊

3 現代化實用科技

4 資訊與知識傳遞

The headquarters of Google is located in Mountain View, California. They named it Googleplex. They moved into the facility the same year when the company went IPO in 2004. The company offered 19,605,052 shares at a price of $85 per share. By January 2014, its market capitalization had grown to $397 billion.

谷歌的總部設在加州山景城。他們把它命名為 Googleplex。他們在 2004 年搬進了這棟建築，同時並首次公開發行。該公司以 85 美元美股的金額提供了 19605052 股。到 2014 年 1 月，其市值已增長到 3970 億美元。

Larry Page: Being a child of two computer experts, Larry Page was born in an environment that led him to who he is today. Born in 1973, Page grew up in a standard home that was filled with computers and technical and science magazines in Michigan.

拉里・佩奇：父母皆為電腦專家，拉里・佩奇出生的環境造就了他。出生於 1973 年，佩琪在密西根一個充滿電腦和技術及科學雜誌的標準家庭中長大。

He first played with a computer at the age of six and immediately got

在他六歲的時候，他開始玩他的第一台電

attracted to it. He was the first kid who utilized a word processor to do his homework.

腦，並立即被吸引。他是在他上的小學裡第一個利用文字處理器做功課的小孩。

He was also encouraged by his family to take things apart to see how they work. Maybe that's why he got interested in inventing things.

他的家人也鼓勵他拆解東西來看看是如何運作的。也許這就是為什麼他對發明創造有興趣。

Page earned his Bachelor degree in engineering from the University of Michigan and concentrated on computer engineering at Stanford University where he met his partner Sergey Brin.

佩琪從密歇根大學得到了他的工程學位。之後，他便在史丹佛大學專心於他的資訊工程學位。在那裡他遇到了他的搭檔謝爾蓋・布林。

1 飲食民生

2 歷史懷舊

3 現代化實用科技

4 資訊與知識傳遞

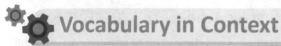

⑤ _____ within the Bermuda Islands, the Bermuda Triangle is an area abounded by Florida, Bermuda, and Puerto Rico, where ships and planes would vanish mysteriously.

Situated is in the closest meaning to this word.

A. Located   C. Deceived

B. Transformed   D. Overestimated

⑥ Robots have been useful in the industry and the househol D. Now in Japan, they also _____ service in the medical field, such as nursing, lifting andtransporting patients, recording and monitoring patients' medical condition.

Provide is in the closest meaning to this word.

A. abolish   C. offer

B. undergo   D. plagiarise

⑦ While scientists _____ nanotechnology to benefit mankind in many fields, both the manipulation and the side-effects of the technology cannot be overemphasized.

Use is in the closest meaning to this word.

A. scan   C. circulate

B. overwhelm   D. utilize

⑧ To cope with the problems of global warming, the public are _____ to recycle and reuse everything, take the mass transportation, and use the electricity economically.

Inspired is in the closest meaning to this word.

A. browsed
B. legislated
C. encouraged
D. rehabilitated

❺ 百慕達三角位於百慕達群島中，它是由佛羅里達、百慕達，和波多黎各所環繞而成的區域，在此處船隻和飛機會神秘地消失。

Situated 的意思最接近於這個字。

A. 位於
B. 轉變
C. 欺騙
D. 高估

❻ 機器人一向實用於工業以及家庭。現今在日本，它們也提供醫療方面的服務，譬如照料、搬移以及護送病患，紀錄並且監督病患的醫療狀況。

Provide 的意思最接近於這個字。

A. 廢除
B. 經歷
C. 提供
D. 剽竊

❼ 科學家利用奈米科技於許多領域以嘉惠人類，然而這項技術的操作以及副作用也應該予以高度地重視。

Use 的意思最接近於這個字。

A. 掃描
B. 壓倒
C. 循環
D. 利用

❽ 為了要對抗全球暖化的問題，大眾被鼓勵要回收並再利用所有的東西，搭乘大眾運輸系統，以及節約用電。

Inspired 的意思最接近於這個字。

A. 瀏覽
B. 立法
C. 鼓勵
D. 康復

 ❺ A　 ❻ C　 ❼ D　 ❽ C

Sergey Brin: A Russian-born American, Sergey Brin immigrated to the United States with his family from the Soviet Union at the age of 6. His father wanted to give Brin an environment where it allowed Brin to get good education and be able to proceed his dream. Brin followed his father's and grandfather's footsteps by studying mathematics and computer science.

謝爾蓋・布林：俄國出生的美國人，謝爾蓋・布林在六歲時與他的家人一起由蘇聯移民到美國。他的父親想給布林一個良好的教育環境，能夠繼續他的夢想的環境。布林跟隨父親和祖父的腳步學習數學和資訊工程。

He earned his bachelor's degree at the University of Maryland. He then moved to Stanford University to acquire a PhD in computer science. The birth of Google: Page and Brin met at an orientation for new students at Stanford. They became close friends after having a disagreement on most subjects.

他在馬里蘭大學獲得了學士學位。爾後，他到史丹佛大學研讀資訊工程博士學位。谷歌的誕生：佩奇和布林在史丹佛大學的一個新生訓練上認識。他們在不同意對方大部分的意見後不久，變成親密的朋友。

The two of them authored a paper titled "The Anatomy of a Large-Scale Hypertextual Web Search Engine" together. They created a search engine that listed results according to the popularity of the pages. It was the basic form of Google Search.

They came up with the name "Google" from the mathematical term "googol". It reflects their mission to organize the humongous amount information on the internet. The program became popular so both of them suspended their PhD studies. Just like HP and Apple, the company started from a garage.

他們倆一同撰寫題為「大規模網絡搜索引擎剖析」的論文。他們當時創立了一個根據網頁的普及率來列出結果的搜索引擎。這是谷歌搜索的基本形式。

他們以數學術語「天文數字」這個詞想出「谷歌」這個名字。這反映了他們的使命，即是組織規劃在互聯網上堆積如山量的訊息。由於這個程式很受歡迎，因此他們都暫停了攻讀博士學位。就像惠普與蘋果電腦，該公司是從一個車庫開始的。

1 飲食民生

2 歷史懷舊

3 現代化實用科技

4 資訊與知識傳遞

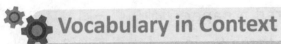

Vocabulary in Context

9 Donna and Scott were in serious _____ over cloning. The former felt that safe cloning to prolong humans' life was OK, while the later was against the idea of playing God.

Argument is in the closest meaning to this word.

A. disagreement   C. revision

B. tourism   D. eruption

10 Knowing the _____ of winning the first prize in the international competition, the coach and all the teammates exclaimed with great joy.

Outcome is in the closest meaning to this word.

A. immunity   C. principle

B. result   D. circumstance

11 Strange and scary dreams often bother people a lot. However, according to researchers, dreams _____ only responses to events in dreamers' personal life and can help us understand ourselves more.

Mirror is in the closest meaning to this word.

A. execute   C. alleviate

B. reflect   D. contaminate

12 William's driving license was _____ for drunk driving, which he later bitterly regretted having done.

Stopped is in the closest meaning to this word.

A. analyzed   C. facilitated

B. congested   D. suspended

❾ 唐娜和史考特對於複製的看法嚴重分歧。前者認為，使用安全的複製方法以延長人類壽命是可行的，然而，後者反對這個扮演上帝的想法。

Argument 的意思最接近於這個字。

A. 意見分歧   C. 校訂

B. 觀光業   D. 爆發

❿ 得知在國際競賽中獲得第一名的結果，教練和所有的隊員高興地歡呼。

Outcome 的意思最接近於這個字。

A. 免疫   C. 原則

B. 結果   D. 情境

⓫ 奇怪且嚇人的夢境經常令大眾感到十分困擾。然而，根據研究學者的說法，夢境只是反映出做夢者日常生活事件的反應，並且可以幫助我們多了解自己。

Mirror 的意思最接近於這個字。

A. 執行   C. 減緩

B. 反映   D. 污染

⓬ 威廉的駕照因酒駕被暫時中止，他事後對於自己的行為感到相當後悔。

Stopped 的意思最接近於這個字。

A. 分析   C. 使便利

B. 擁塞   D. 暫時中止

 答案 ❾ A ❿ B ⓫ B ⓬ D

23-4 同反義詞表

同反義詞一覽表 Unit 23		
threaten	威脅、恐嚇	同義詞 menace / bully / intimidate
	安慰、安撫	反義詞 comfort / ease / soothe
organize	組織、安排	同義詞 systematize / classify / arrange
	弄亂、混亂	反義詞 mess / disorganize / clutter
accessible	可用到、可達到	同義詞 available / reachable / achievable
	得不到、達不到	反義詞 inaccessible / unattainable / unobtainable
accomplish	完成、實現	同義詞 fulfill / achieve / realize
	放棄、失敗	反義詞 abandon / quit / fail
envy	嫉妒、貪圖	同義詞 begrudge / crave / covet
	知足、滿意	反義詞 content / satisfy / gratify
intelligent	聰明的、博學的	同義詞 smart / bright / knowledgeable
	愚笨的、愚蠢的	反義詞 stupid / silly / foolish
mission	工作、任務	同義詞 task / assignment / errand
	分配、指派	反義詞 assignation / designation / appointment
locate	定位於、找出	同義詞 situate / detect / spot
	擾亂、隱藏	反義詞 disrupt / hide / conceal
offer	提供、建議	同義詞 provide / propose / suggest
	得到、接受	反義詞 get / receive / accept

utilize	使用、應用	同義詞 use / employ / apply
	荒廢、棄置	反義詞 waste / disuse / discard
encourage	鼓勵、激發	同義詞 inspire / stimulate / motivate
	挫折、氣餒	反義詞 frustrate / depress / discourage
partner	夥伴、同伴	同義詞 collaborator / mate / companion
	敵人、對手	反義詞 enemy / foe / opponent
disagreement	意見不合、衝突	同義詞 divergence / argument / conflict
	同意、一致	反義詞 agreement / harmony / concord
result	結果、後果	同義詞 effect / outcome / consequence
	原因、起因	反義詞 reason / cause / motive
reflect	反映、反省	同義詞 mirror / meditate / ponder
	掩飾、自滿	反義詞 cover / veil / content
suspend	懸掛、中止	同義詞 hang / stop / halt
	放下、持續	反義詞 lower / last / continue
proceed	繼續、行進	同義詞 continue / progress / advance
	停止、後退	反義詞 cease / halt / recede
search	調查、搜尋	同義詞 investigation / exploration / seeking
	找出、藏匿	反義詞 detection / discovery / hiding

1 飲食民生

2 歷史懷舊

3 現代化實用科技

4 資訊與知識傳遞

Facebook 臉書

 24-1 臉書成立初期 MP3 70

Some people are even addicted to Facebook so much that they could not stop checking it every 2 minutes. Hard to imagine that 10 years ago, this multi-billion business did not even exist.

有些人甚至非常沈迷於臉書，每 2 分鐘就要檢查一次。很難想像 10 年前，這個數十億的產業根本不存在。

Facebook was founded by Mark Zuckerberg and his roommates and friends at Harvard University in 2004.

臉書這個社交網路服務由馬克‧札克伯格和他的室友以及在哈佛大學的朋友在 2004 年時成立臉書。

This social networking service was originally limited to Harvard students, and later on expanded to other colleges in the Boston area, the Ivy Leagues, and gradually most universities in

這個社交網絡服務最初僅限於哈佛學生使用，爾後擴大到波士頓地區的其他學校及常春藤聯盟。逐步的

Canada and the US.

At that time, high school networks required an invitation to join. Facebook later expanded membership eligibility to employees of several companies, including Apple Inc. and Microsoft. It was not available to the public until September 26, 2006.

加入了大部分加拿大和美國的大學。

當時，高中生是需要被邀請才能加入。臉書後來擴大會員資格給幾家大公司，包括蘋果公司和微軟公司的僱員。直到 2006 年 9 月 26 日才開放給社會大眾。

1 飲食民生

2 歷史懷舊

3 現代化實用科技

4 資訊與知識傳遞

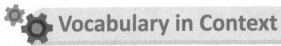

Vocabulary in Context

❶ Arthur was hopelessly _____ to sports betting, and this gambling indulgence in sports lottery has resulted in his losing everything.

Habituated is in the closest meaning to this word.

A. facilitated   C. addicted

B. cynical   D. suspicious

❷ Dinosaurs _____ sixty-five million years ago, but for unknown reasons, either the hit of an asteroid or comet or the sudden freezing cold climate, the once master of the world got wiped out.

Survived is in the closest meaning to this word.

A. absorbed   C. devastated

B. existed   D. fluctuated

❸ With strong _____ conscience in mind, the author wrote novels only about the themes of ecology, human harmony, and universal truths.

Societal is in the closest meaning to this word.

A. social   C. radioactive

B. indigenous   D. explanatory

❹ Melissa was optimistic about her getting the new job, for her qualifications and experience perfectly fit the required _____ for it.

Qualifications is in the closest meaning to this word.

A. fraud

C. vividness

B. prestige

D. eligibility

❶ 亞瑟無可救藥地沉迷於運動賭博，而這種運動彩券的賭癮導致他失去一切。

Habituated 的意思最接近於這個字。

A. 促進

C. 上癮

B. 冷嘲的

D. 懷疑的

❷ 恐龍曾經存在於六千五百萬年前，但是因為不明的原因，也許是小流星或是彗星的撞擊，也或許是氣候的驟降，一度是世界的主宰者就這樣被滅絕了。

Survived 的意思最接近於這個字。

A. 吸收

C. 毀滅

B. 存在

D. 波動

❸ 有著強烈的社會良知，這名作家只寫有關於生態環境、人類和諧，以及普世真理這類主題的小説。

Societal 的意思最接近於這個字。

A. 社會的

C. 輻射的

B. 本土的

D. 説明的

❹ 梅麗莎對於得到新工作感到十分樂觀，因為她的資歷和經驗十分符合這份工作所要求的條件。

Qualifications 的意思最接近於這個字。

A. 詐欺

C. 逼真

B. 聲望

D. 資格

 ❶ C　❷ B　❸ A　❹ D

 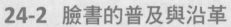

The popularity of Facebook started to generate in 2007. Most of the youngsters back then joined Facebook in 2007. Late in 2007, Facebook had 100,000 business pages which allowed companies to attract potential customers and introduce themselves.

臉書於 2007 年開始普及。當時大部分的年輕人都是在 2007 年加入臉書。2007 年的下半年，臉書開始有企業專頁，使得企業可以介紹自己的企業並吸引潛在客戶。

The business potential for this social network just kept blooming, and on October 2008, Facebook set up its international headquarters in Dublin, Ireland. Statistics from October 2011 showed that over 100 billion photos are shared on Facebook, and over 350 million users accessed Facebook through their mobile phones which is only about 33% of all Facebook traffic.

社會網絡的商業潛力不停地綻放。2008 年 10 月，臉書在愛爾蘭的都柏林設立了國際總部。從 2011 年 10 月的統計顯示，超過一兆的照片在臉書上共享，而超過 350 萬的用戶利用手機查閱臉書，這大概只是 33%的臉書的總流量。

Born in 1984, Mark Zuckerberg was born in White Plains, New York. Zuckerberg began using computers and writing software in middle school. His father taught him Atari BASIC Programming in the 1990s, and later hired software developer David Newman to tutor him privately.

1984 年，馬克‧扎克伯格出生於紐約的懷特普萊恩斯。扎克伯格在中學時期就開始使用電腦和編寫的軟體。他的父親教他寫 90 年代的 Atari BASIC 編程，後來又聘請了軟體開發者大衛‧紐曼私下指導他。

Zuckerberg took a graduate course in the subject at Mercy College near his home while still in high school. He enjoyed developing computer programs, especially communication tools and games.

扎克伯格在高中時便在他家附近的慈悲學院選修研究生的課程。他喜歡開發電腦軟體，特別是通訊工具和遊戲。

1 飲食民生

2 歷史懷舊

3 現代化實用科技

4 資訊與知識傳遞

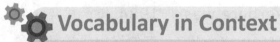

❺ Like all _____, Ken planned to move away and live independently as soon as he entered college, and would still maintain close ties with his family.

Youths is in the closest meaning to this word.

A. linguists   C. hijackers

B. folks   D. youngsters

❻ The real estate business was _____ in the past, but not now. Due to the economic recession and soaring high prices, houses are no more affordable to most people.

Flourishing is in the closest meaning to this word.

A. blooming   C. sponsored

B. thrifty   D. overdue

❼ To attract students to make use of it, the school library provides all kinds of facilities for them to _____ and it also regularly holds activities.

Use is in the closest meaning to this word.

A. preserve   C. access

B. interfere   D. recruit

❽ In modern days, with their multi-functional characteristics, _____ phones have become a must-have kind of equipment to most people.

Movable is in the closest meaning to this word.

A. visual   C. magnetic

B. mobile　　　　　　D. artificial

❺ 如同所有的年輕人，肯恩計畫一上大學就離家獨自生活，而仍舊
會和家人保持密切聯繫。

Youths 的意思最接近於這個字。

A. 語言學家　　　　　C. 劫持者

B. 父母親　　　　　　D. 年輕人

❻ 房地產事業在過去是興盛的行業，但是現在不如以往了。由於經
濟不景氣以及高漲的房價，房子對大多數人來說已經不再負擔得
起。

Flourishing 的意思最接近於這個字。

A. 興旺的　　　　　　C. 贊助的

B. 節儉的　　　　　　D. 逾期的

❼ 為了吸引學生多多利用資源，學校圖書館提供各種供他們使用的
便利設施，並且也定期地舉辦活動。

Use 的意思最接近於這個字。

A. 保存　　　　　　　C. 利用

B. 干涉　　　　　　　D. 招募

❽ 就現代而言，有著多功能的特點，手機對大多數人來說已經成為
一項必備品。

Movable 的意思最接近於這個字。

A. 視覺的　　　　　　C. 磁鐵的

B. 移動的　　　　　　D. 人造的

答案　❺ D　❻ A　❼ C　❽ B

When he studied classes at Harvard, Zuckerberg had already achieved a "reputation as a programming prodigy", notes Vargas. In his sophomore year, he wrote a program he called CourseMatch, which allowed users to make class selection decisions based on the choices of other students and also to help them form study groups.

當他開始在哈佛就讀時，扎克伯格早已經取得了「程式撰寫神童」的美譽 Vargas 提到。在他大二那年，他寫了一個程式叫 CourseMatch，這個程式可以幫助學生選課，也幫助他們組成學習小組。

A short time later, he created a different program he initially called Facemash that lets students select the best looking person from a choice. On February 4, 2004, Zuckerberg launched "The facebook". Zuckerberg dropped out of Harvard on his sophomore year to complete his project.

不久之後，他創造了一個不同的程式，他最初取名為 Facemash 讓學生選擇最好看的人。2004 年 2 月 4 日，扎克伯格推出了「The facebook」。扎克伯格在大二時從哈佛退學，以完成他的計劃。

Once at college, Zuckerberg's Facebook started off as just a "Harvard thing" until Zuckerberg decided to spread it to other schools.

在大學裡時扎克伯格的臉書一開始只是一個「哈佛的事」，直到扎克伯格決定將其傳播到其他學校。

After Zuckerberg moved to Palo Alto, California with Moskovitz and some friends, they leased a small house that served as an office.

扎克伯格和莫斯科維茨以及一些朋友搬到了加利福尼亞州帕洛阿爾托，他們租了一個小房子當辦公室。

They got their first office in mid-2004. In 2007, at the age of 23, Zuckerberg became a billionaire as a result of Facebook's success. The number of Facebook users worldwide reached a total of one billion in 2012.

他們在 2004 年中期成立了第一個辦公室。於 2007，札克伯格 23 歲那年，他因為臉書的成功而成為億萬富翁。臉書在 2012 年的全球用戶數量共達到一十億。

1 飲食民生

2 歷史懷舊

3 現代化實用科技

4 資訊與知識傳遞

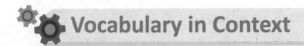 **Vocabulary in Context**

⑨ Mozart was a brilliant and productive composer. He showed his musical talents at three, had his piano concert tour in Europe since six, and was thus praised as the classical music child _____.

Genius is in the closest meaning to this word.

A. architect   C. prodigy

B. workaholic   D. spectator

⑩ In his book, *On the Origin of Species*, Charles Darwin proposed the theory of evolution by natural _____, in which the species best suited to their environments survive and reproduce.

Choice is in the closest meaning to this word.

A. potential   C. breakdown

B. stimulation   D. selection

⑪ After the seminar, all the participants were asked to _____ a questionnaire to offer their opinions for further assessments.

Finish is in the closest meaning to this word.

A. complete   C. publish

B. resemble   D. admonish

⑫ Since 2010, the Sherlock Holmes TV series produced by BBC have successfully reinterpreted the old Holmes as a modern super detective and thus attracted _____ Sherlock fans.

Global is in the closest meaning to this word.

A. magical

C. external

B. worldwide

D. provincial

❾ 莫札特是傑出且多產的作曲家。他在三歲時便展現他的音樂才華，六歲起就在歐洲巡迴演奏鋼琴，因此被世人讚譽為古典音樂神童。

Genius 的意思最接近於這個字。

A. 建築師

C. 天才

B. 工作狂

D. 觀眾

❿ 查爾斯・達爾文在他的書《物種起源》中提出物競天擇的進化論，說明適者生存，不適者淘汰的理論。

Choice 的意思最接近於這個字。

A. 潛力

C. 崩潰

B. 刺激

D. 選擇

⓫ 研討會過後，所有的參加人員被要求填寫一份問卷，提供意見以做日後評估使用。

Finish 的意思最接近於這個字。

A. 完成

C. 出版

B. 相像

D. 告誡

⓬ 自2010年以來，英國廣播公司製作的福爾摩斯電視影集成功地再度詮釋舊式的福爾摩斯為現代超級偵探，因而吸引了世界各地的福爾摩斯迷。

Global 的意思最接近於這個字。

A. 神奇的

C. 外部的

B. 全世界的

D. 偏狹的

 C　D　A　B

24-4 同反義詞表

同反義詞一覽表 Unit 24		
addict	沉迷、上癮	同義詞 indulge / wallow / habituate
	節制、戒除	反義詞 quit / abstain / refrain
exist	存在、生存	同義詞 live / subsist / survive
	死亡、滅亡	反義詞 die / decease / perish
social	社會的、公眾的	同義詞 societal / communal / public
	個人的、個別的	反義詞 personal / individual / private
eligibility	資格、適合	同義詞 qualification / entitlement / suitability
	不合格、不適合	反義詞 disqualification / inadequacy / unfitness
service	服務、幫助	同義詞 assistance / help / aid
	冷淡、妨礙	反義詞 indifference / obstacle / barrier
invitation	邀請、請求	同義詞 asking / imploration / request
	參加、同意	反義詞 participation / assent / consent
including	包含、包括	同義詞 contain / cover / comprise
	排除在外、拒絕	反義詞 exclude / eliminate / reject
youngster	小孩、年輕人	同義詞 child / adolescent / youth
	大人、成年人	反義詞 adult / man / grownup
blooming	興旺的、繁榮的	同義詞 flourishing / thriving / prosperous
	不景氣、蕭條的	反義詞 depressed / declining / recessionary

access	使用、接近	同義詞 use / reach / approach
	迴避、退卻	反義詞 evade / retire / retreat
mobile	可移動、變化的	同義詞 movable / changeable / variable
	不動的、固定的	反義詞 immovable / fixed / stationary
tutor	教導、指導	同義詞 teach / instruct / educate
	學習、汲取	反義詞 learn / absorb / acquire
prodigy	驚奇、奇才	同義詞 marvel / wonder / genius
	平凡、平庸的人	反義詞 normal / ordinary / mediocrity
selection	選擇、挑選	同義詞 choice / option / picking
	被動、順從	反義詞 passiveness / submission / obedience
complete	完成、結束	同義詞 finish / conclude / end
	未完成、繼續	反義詞 incomplete / continue / persist
worldwide	世界、遍及全球	同義詞 universal / global / international
	地方的、地區的	反義詞 local / regional / districtwide
decision	決定、果斷	同義詞 resolution / conclusion / determination
	猶豫、懷疑	反義詞 indecision / hesitation / doubtfulness
lease	出租、租借	同義詞 rent / charter / let
	持有、擁有	反義詞 own / have / possess

1 飲食民生

2 歷史懷舊

3 現代化實用科技

4 資訊與知識傳遞

25-1 電話的發展 MP3 73

The paper cup telephone is a great childhood memory for most of us. Centuries ago, acoustic telephone, the first mechanical telephone was based on the same theory which utilized sound transmission through pipes.

紙杯電話對我們大多數人來説是一個偉大的童年記憶。基於同樣的理論，聲覺電話幾百年前利用管線傳送聲音，是最早的機械電話。

It connects two diaphragms with a string or wire and transmits sound by mechanical vibrations from one side to another. Two hundred years later in 1876, Alexander Graham Bell was awarded the first U.S. patent for the invention of the electrical telephone.

它是英國物理學家羅伯特・胡克於 1667 年利用細繩或金屬絲連接兩個隔膜，由機械振動的原理從一側傳送聲音到另一端。200 年後的 1876 年，亞歷山大・格雷厄姆・貝爾獲得他第一個發明電話的專利。

Although the credit for the invention of the electric telephone is frequently disputed. Many other inventors, such as Charles Bourseul, Antonio Meucci, and others have all been credited with the telephone invention.

雖然這個電話發明的榮譽經常有爭議。許多其他的發明家,如查爾斯・布爾瑟,安東尼奧・穆齊,和其他人都被認為發明了電話。

By 1904 over three million phones were connected by manual switchboard exchanges in the United States.

到 1904 年,美國人工總機總共有超過三百萬個連結。

The US became the world leader in telephone density. The telephone with bell and induction coil which we are familiar with was introduced in the 1930s. Another 30 years later, the touch-tone signaling replaced the rotary dial.

美國的電話密度領先全球。我們所熟悉,有鈴聲和感應線圈的電話在 1930 年代引入。30 年後,按鍵信號取代旋轉撥號。

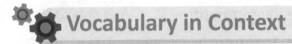

❶ The _____ of dengue fever is mainly through mosquitoes. The symptoms may include a high fever, headache, vomiting, muscle and joint pains, and a skin rash.

Spreading is in the closest meaning to this word.

A. curriculum   C. performance

B. announcement   D. transmission

❷ While the workers were renovating the house, all the neighbors around could feel the _____ from the drilling machines operating inside.

Shaking is in the closest meaning to this word.

A. control   C. phenomenon

B. vibrations   D. moments

❸ Euthanasia, or mercy killing, is a highly controversial issue and has long been _____ from either the medical or the ethical point of view.

Debated is in the closest meaning to this word.

A. disputed   C. flourished

B. constructed   D. provided

❹ Mr. Webb decided to see the cardiologist because recently his chest pains came and went, which could _____ the warning of heart problems.

Indicate is in the closest meaning to this word.

A. rotate   C. signal

B. hazard　　　　　D. overwhelm

❶ 登革熱的傳染主要是經由蚊子。症狀包含高燒、頭疼、嘔吐、肌肉和關節疼痛，以及皮膚紅疹。

Spreading 的意思最接近於這個字。

A. 課程　　　　　C. 表現

B. 宣佈　　　　　D. 傳染

❷ 當工人正在整修房子的時候，所有附近的鄰居都可以感受到屋內鑽孔機操作的震動。

Shaking 的意思最接近於這個字。

A. 控制　　　　　C. 現象

B. 震動　　　　　D. 時刻

❸ 安樂死是一個具高度爭議性的議題，無論是從醫學觀點或是道德觀點來說都一直受到爭論。

Debated 的意思最接近於這個字。

A. 爭論　　　　　C. 興盛

B. 建造　　　　　D. 提供

❹ 韋伯先生決定去看心臟科醫生，因為最近他的胸口不時地隱隱作痛，而這種症狀可能是心臟疾病示警的訊號。

Indicate 的意思最接近於這個字。

A. 旋轉　　　　　C. 示警

B. 危害　　　　　D. 壓倒

答案　D　B　A　C

In 1973, Motorola manager Martin Cooper placed the very first cellular phone call and began the era of the mobile phone. In 2008, over 290 million cell phones were sold worldwide. And after the first debut of smartphone, the boom just never seems to drop. When will the next generation telephone be invented? We are all excited to see.

1973 年，摩托羅拉的經理馬丁‧庫帕撥出第一通移動電話，開始了手機的時代。在 2008 年，全球的手機銷量超過 2.9 億。而智慧型手機第一次亮相後，手機的需求似乎永遠不會下降。下一代的電話又會在什麼時候被發明呢？我們都很期待。

Son of a phonetician, Alexander Graham Bell was born on March 3rd, 1847 in Edinburgh, Scotland. As many other inventors, Bell was a creative brilliant child who had shown curiosity about his world. His first invention was a dehusking machine which automatically dehusked wheat.

一個聲音學家的兒子，亞歷山大‧格雷厄姆‧貝爾於 1847 年 3 月 3 日出生於蘇格蘭的愛丁堡。正如許多其他的發明家，貝爾是一個聰明且具創意的孩子，並對他的世界表現出好奇。他的第一個發明是去麥殼機，可自動脫去小麥的殼。

He was only 12 at that time. At the same year, the hearing loss of Bell's mother led to his study in acoustics. Bell moved to Canada in 1870 with his family. Three years later, Bell became a professor at Boston University specialized in voice physiology. Bell also taught deaf people how to speak, and because of that, he married Mabel Hubbard who was born deaf.

Mabel Hubbard's father Gardiner Greene Hubbard was very wealthy. This gave Bell great help in his invention. In 1874, with his father-in-law and Thomas Sanders' financial support, Bell hired Thomas Watson as his assistant and started his research on the Telephone.

當時他只有 12 歲。同年，他的母親的聽覺喪失促使他研究聲音學。貝爾在 1870 年時與他的家人一起移居加拿大。3 年後，貝爾成為了波士頓大學的教授專門從事語音生理學。貝爾還教聾人怎麼說話，正因為如此，他娶了天生就聽不到的梅布爾–哈伯德。

梅布爾–哈伯德的父親加德納·格林·哈伯德是非常富裕的。這給了貝爾的發明很大的幫助。1874 年，由於他的岳父和托馬斯–桑德斯的資金支持，貝爾僱用了托馬斯·沃森作為他的助手，開始了他對電話的研究。

1 飲食民生

2 歷史懷舊

3 現代化實用科技

4 資訊與知識傳遞

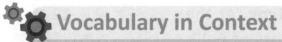

Vocabulary in Context

⑤ The consumers made bitter complaints about the awful food and service the restaurant offere D. After the _____ took an immediate make-up action, the satisfied customers stopped further protests.

Boss is in the closest meaning to this word.

A. heir   C. conqueror

B. manager   D. retailer

⑥ CNBLUE, a South Korean pop rock band, released their _____ Japanese mini-album *Now or Never* in 2009.

First is in the closest meaning to this word.

A. splendor   C. debut

B. advent   D. revenue

❼ In Greek mythology, **Pandora's Box** refers to the story that though warned against opening the box with evils inside, Pandora, out of _____, still opened it, which resulted in serious consequences.

Inquisitiveness is in the closest meaning to this word.

A. formality   C. innovation

B. redemption   D. curiosity

❽ As a _____ CEO, Mark Zuckerberg, the co-founder of Facebook, remains plain, modest, and generous all the time. He never hesitates to help the world, especially children of the following generations.

Rich is in the closest meaning to this word.

A. wealthy   C. rhythmic

B. clumsy   D. indigenous

❺ 這群消費者對於這家餐廳所提供劣質的食物和服務提出強烈的不滿。在經理採取立即的補救後,滿意的顧客才停止進一步的抗議。

Boss 的意思最接近於這個字。

A. 繼承人   C. 征服者

B. 經理   D. 零售商

❻ 南韓搖滾樂團,CNBLUE,在2009年發行他們的首張日文迷你專輯,*Now or Never*。*First* 的意思最接近於這個字。

A. 光輝   C. 初次登場

B. 到臨   D. 總收入

❼ 希臘神話故事中,《潘朵拉的盒子》描述的故事內容是儘管潘朵拉被警告不能打開充滿禍害的盒子,但是由於好奇,她還是打開了盒子,最終導致嚴重的後果。

Inquisitiveness 的意思最接近於這個字。

A. 規範   C. 創新

B. 贖罪   D. 好奇心

❽ 臉書的共同創辦人,馬克·祖克伯,身為富有的總裁,卻一直保持樸實、謙虛,以及慷慨的風範。他毫不猶豫地幫助全世界,尤其是未來世代的孩童。*Rich* 的意思最接近於這個字。

A. 富有的   C. 節奏的

B. 笨拙的   D. 本地的

答案　❺ B　❻ C　❼ D　❽ A

In 1876, Bell filed the patent for the telephone. A year later, Bell, Hubbard, Sanders and Watson formed the Bell Telephone Company. Back then, people still couldn't see the practicality and outlook for telephone.

1876 年，貝爾提出電話的專利。一年後，貝爾‧哈伯德‧桑德斯和沃森組成了貝爾電話公司。那時，人們還無法看到電話的實用性和前景。

Therefore, only hundreds of telephones were sold in the following years. Bell was not interested in doing business so he left the Bell Telephone company in 1879.

因此，只有幾百隻電話於次年銷售出去。貝爾對做生意沒有興趣，於是他於 1879 年離開了貝爾電話公司。

Bell passed away in 1922 at the age of 75. At that time, over 14 million telephones were installed in the United States. Undersea telephone and wireless telephones were also invented. The Bell Telephone company became AT&T which is still the No.1 telephone

貝爾於 1992 年去世，享年 75 歲。當時已有 1400 多萬隻電話被安裝在美國。海底電話和無線電話也已發明了。貝爾電話公司後來成為ＡＴ

company in the United States.

In 1925, the president of AT&T, Walt JiFode acquired the research department of Western Electronics and set up a program called "Bell Telephone Laboratories".

This lab contributed many new inventions with epochal meanings, such as transistors, solar cells LEDs, etc.

＆Ｔ公司，ＡＴ＆Ｔ仍然是美國的第一大電話公司。

1925 年，ＡＴ＆Ｔ公司的總裁沃爾特收購了西方電子公司的研究部門，並成立了一個「貝爾電話實驗室」。

這個實驗室貢獻了許多具有劃時代意義的新發明，例如晶體管、太陽能電池 LED等。

1　飲食民生

2　歷史懷舊

3　現代化實用科技

4　資訊與知識傳遞

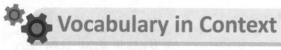

Vocabulary in Context

9 Receiving the full family _____ financially and spiritually, Paul opened a restaurant of his own and achieved prosperous business.

Aid is in the closest meaning to this word.

A. penalty   C. support

B. attitude   D. fabrication

10 Billy was newly appointed head of the market development _____ and was in charge of the research and development of his company's new products.

Division is in the closest meaning to this word.

A. chamber   C. modification

B. sequence   D. department

11 The _____ invention during the 1960s was the Internet, which was originally started by the US government for military purposes. Nowadays, people can use the Net for millions of things everywhere at any time.

Significant is in the closest meaning to this word.

A. perpetual   C. comparative

B. epochal   D. sufficient

12 To reduce the impact of global warming, scientists have been developing alternative energy resources such as _____ or wind power energy.

Sun is in the closest meaning to this word.

A. solar
C. lunar
B. artificial
D. ultraviolet

❾ 得到家人全面經濟和精神上的支援，保羅開了一家自己的餐廳，並且經營地生意興隆。

Aid 的意思最接近於這個字。

A. 處罰
C. 支持
B. 態度
D. 虛構

❿ 比利最近被任命為市場開發部的主任，負責公司新產品的研究及開發的工作。

Division 的意思最接近於這個字。

A. 房間
C. 修改
B. 系列
D. 部門

⓫ 60年代意義最重大的發明就是網際網路，起初是美國政府為了軍事目的而研發的。今日而言，人們可以在任何地方、任何時刻利用網際網路做上百萬件事情。

Significant 的意思最接近於這個字。

A. 永久的
C. 比較的
B. 劃時代的
D. 足夠的

⓬ 為了減緩全球暖化的衝擊，科學家一直在研發像是太陽能或是風力發電的替代能源。

Sun 的意思最接近於這個字。

A. 太陽的
C. 月亮的
B. 人造的
D. 紫外線的

 ❾ C ❿ D ⓫ B   ⓬ A

25-4 同反義詞表

同反義詞一覽表 Unit 25		
transmission	傳送、傳染	同義詞 forwarding / transfer / spread
	扣留、隱藏	反義詞 detention / hiding / concealment
vibration	震動、顫抖	同義詞 shake / quiver / tremble
	平靜、穩定	反義詞 stillness / calm / tranquility
dispute	爭論、爭執	同義詞 argue / debate / quarrel
	同意、贊成	反義詞 agree / assent / consent
signal	打信號、警告	同義詞 gesture / indicate / alert
	制止、靜止	反義詞 stop / prohibit / rest
childhood	幼年期、童年期	同義詞 infancy / babyhood / boyhood
	成年期、成熟	反義詞 adulthood / ripeness / maturity
memory	記憶、回憶	同義詞 remembrance /reminiscence /recollection
	未來、前景	反義詞 future / hereafter / prospect
manual	手動的、人工的	同義詞 hand-operated / hand-made
	機械的、自動的	反義詞 mechanic / machine-operated / automatic
manager	經理、負責人	同義詞 executive / boss / administrator
	職員、員工	反義詞 staff / personnel / employee
debut	首次亮相、就職	同義詞 introduction / first / inauguration
	退休、隱退	反義詞 retirement / withdrawal / retreat

curiosity	好奇心、有興趣	同義詞 inquisitiveness / interest / concern
	沒興趣、不關心	反義詞 indifference / unconcern / apathy
wealthy	富有的、豐富的	同義詞 rich / ample / abundant
	貧困的、欠缺的	反義詞 poor / impoverished / insufficient
excited	興奮的、激動的	同義詞 fevered / agitated / stimulated
	冷靜的、沉著的	反義詞 calm / cool / composed
deaf	聾的、不予理會	同義詞 unheard / unmoved / heedless
	聽得見、清楚的	反義詞 audible / distinct / clear
support	支持、幫助	同義詞 sustenance / maintenance / aid
	放棄、遺棄	反義詞 abandonment / desertion / discard
department	部門、分公司	同義詞 division / section / branch
	企業、總公司	反義詞 enterprise / company / headquarters
epochal	劃時代、重大的	同義詞 epoch-making / significant / momentous
	不重要、無意義	反義詞 unimportant / trivial / meaningless
solar	太陽的、日照的	同義詞 sun / sunny / shiny
	月亮的、微弱的	反義詞 lunar / dim / faint
program	計劃、節目表	同義詞 project / plan / playbill
	實行、演出	反義詞 execution / presentation / performance

1 飲食民生

2 歷史懷舊

3 現代化實用科技

4 資訊與知識傳遞

26-1 銀行的演變

In today's highly technical world, banks are no longer a brick-and-mortar financial institution. From remittance to investment, people nowadays only need to go thru online banking to finish all these works.

在當今高科技的世界裡，銀行不再是實體的金融機構。從匯款到投資，人們現在只需要上網路銀行就可以完成所有的工作。

The concept of online banking has been simultaneously evolving with the development of the World Wide Web, and has actually been accessible around since the early 1980s.

網路銀行這一概念與全球資訊網一同發展演變，自 1980 年代初期就已經出現。

In 1981, the four biggest banks in New York City Citibank, Chase Manhattan, Chemical and Manufacturers Hanover, made the home banking access available to their customers. However, customers didn't really take to the

在 1981 年，紐約的四大銀行，花旗銀行、大通曼哈頓銀行、化工銀行和製造漢諾威銀行提供了家庭銀行給他們的客

initiative. The innovative way of doing business was too advanced and failed to gain momentum until the mid 1990s.

戶。但客戶並沒有真正採取行動。這個生意方式的創新太過先進，直到 1990 年代中期都沒能獲得新的動力。

In October, 1994, Stanford Federal Credit Union offered online banking to all its customers, and about a year later, Presidential Bank offered its customers online account accesses. These were the start of online banking, and soon other banks followed.

1994 年 10 月，史丹佛的聯邦信貸聯盟提供了所有的客戶網上銀行，大約一年後，總統銀行提供客戶網銀的服務。這就是網路銀行的開始。不久後其他銀行隨即跟進。

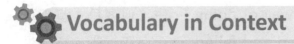 **Vocabulary in Context**

❶ The Internet enables customers to log on the online banking websites and achieve all the financial operations without going to banking _____ in person.

Organizations is in the closest meaning to this word.

A. landmarks　　　　　C. institutions

B. museums　　　　　D. workshops

❷ Daniel made great fortunes from his overseas _____ and was able to fulfill his wishes of helping stray animals as much as possible.

Speculation is in the closest meaning to this word.

A. investments　　　　C. assignments

B. editorials　　　　　D. trademarks

❸ It was quite a coincidence that Madeline and Chester arrived at the award ceremony _____.

Meantime is in the closest meaning to this word.

A. legally　　　　　　C. essentially

B. awkwardly　　　　　D. simultaneously

❹ Austin was clever enough to take the _____; he made self-recommendation and finally got the contract of one year's work.

Lead is in the closest meaning to this word.

A. security　　　　　　C. transformation

B. initiative　　　　　D. metabolism

374

❶ 網際網路讓顧客可以不用親自前往銀行機構而是登入銀行的網站就可以完成所有的金融作業。

Organizations 的意思最接近於這個字。

A. 陸標　　　　　　　C. 機構

B. 博物館　　　　　　D. 工作坊

❷ 丹尼爾從海外投資賺得不少錢，因此有能力實現盡力幫助流浪動物的心願。

Speculation 的意思最接近於這個字。

A. 投資　　　　　　　C. 任務

B. 社論　　　　　　　D. 商標

❸ 梅德琳和切斯特兩人很湊巧地同時抵達頒獎典禮的現場。

Meantime 的意思最接近於這個字。

A. 合法地　　　　　　C. 實質上

B. 尷尬地　　　　　　D. 同時地

❹ 奧斯丁很聰明地採取主動；他自我推薦並因此最終得到一整年的工作合約。

Lead 的意思最接近於這個字。

A. 安全　　　　　　　C. 轉變

B. 主動　　　　　　　D. 新陳代謝

答案 ❶ C　❷ A　❸ D　❹ B

Though customers were hesitant to use online banking at first. Many people didn't trust its security feature. Up until today, some people still have the same concern. It was after the e-commerce started to popularize did the idea of online banking slowly began to catch on. By the year 2000, an overwhelmingly 80% of banks in the U.S. offered online banking services.

不過，顧客們一開始對於使用網路銀行感到遲疑。許多人並不相信它的安全功能。直到今天，有些人仍然有同樣的擔憂。這是自從電子商務開始流行後，網路銀行的想法才開始慢慢流行起來。直到 2000 年，在美國有壓倒性有 80% 的銀行都提供網路銀行的服務。

In 2001, Bank of America gained more than 3 million online banking customers, about 20% of its customer base. Online banking effectively decreases overhead costs to offer more competitive rates and enjoys higher profit margins. It now becomes so widespread all over the world and allows many investors to operate their

在 2001 年，美國銀行擁有了 300 多萬網路銀行客戶。這是約 20%的客戶群。網上銀行有效地降低管理成本，提供更具競爭力的價格，並享受更高的利潤。它現在在世界各地已經非常普

assets around the world with no time difference issues.

及也讓許多投資者可以避免時差問題，在世界各地運營資產。

Stanford Federal Credit Union is a federally chartered credit union located in Palo Alto, California which provides banking services to the Stanford community. Stanford Federal Credit Union was created by a group of Stanford University employees.

史丹佛聯邦信用合作社是一家位於加州帕洛阿爾托，給史丹佛社區提供金融服務的聯邦特許儲蓄合作社。

The credit union eventually expanded its field membership to student and employee members and members of the library.

信用合作社最終擴展了會員許可給學生及員工成員以及圖書館會員。

1 飲食民生

2 歷史懷舊

3 現代化實用科技

4 資訊與知識傳遞

Vocabulary in Context

❺ To maintain health, a balanced diet, regular exercise, and yearly physical check-up are essential. Above all, don't feel _____ to consult the doctor whenever there're unhealthy symptoms or health concerns.

Uncertain is in the closest meaning to this word.

A. hesitant   C. precious

B. risky   D. hospitable

❻ Through excellent teamwork, Ian's group finally won the world championship by defeating all other international competitors _____.

Overpoweringly is in the closest meaning to this word.

A. confidentially   C. overwhelmingly

B. originally   D. vertically

❼ The game software market has become more and more _____, and all the game programmers in the company are exerting their utmost to come up with the best designing works.

Rivaling is in the closest meaning to this word.

A. abnormal   C. surplus

B. inhabitable   D. competitive

❽ As travel addicts, Ernie and Ray had the same craziness for traveling abroad, but they would travel to Western and Eastern countries _____.

Separately is in the closest meaning to this word.

A. misleadingly   C. snobbishly

B. respectively   D. profitably

❺ 要保持健康，均衡的飲食、規律的運動，以及年度健康檢查是必要的。尤其 是任何刻察覺到有不健康的症狀或有健康上的疑慮時，不要遲疑於看醫生。

Uncertain 的意思最接近於這個字。

A. 猶豫的   C. 珍貴的

B. 冒險的   D. 好客的

❻ 藉由絕佳的團隊合作，依恩的團隊壓倒性地打敗所有其他的國際參賽者，終於獲得世界冠軍。

Overpoweringly 的意思最接近於這個字。

A. 機密地   C. 壓倒性地

B. 原來地   D. 垂直地

❼ 遊戲軟體市場變得越來越競爭了，所有公司裡的遊戲程式設計師目前都盡力提出最優質的設計作品。

Rivaling 的意思最接近於這個字。

A. 反常的   C. 過剩的

B. 適於居住的   D. 競爭的

❽ 身為旅遊愛好者，爾尼和雷伊對於國外旅遊具有相同的熱愛，但是他們會分別前往不同的西方和東方國家旅遊。

Separately 的意思最接近於這個字。

A. 誤導地   C. 勢利地

B. 分別地   D. 盈利地

答案 ❺ A   ❻ C   ❼ D   ❽ B

Even though the credit union is relatively small, it is famous for its advance services over the years. In the late 1970s, Stanford Federal Credit Union offered one of the first checking accounts and credit cards. In the early 1980s, it introduced ATMs and banking by telephone.

雖然信用合作社的規模相對比較小，它多年來的先進服務卻很出名。在 1970 年代尾，史丹佛聯邦信用合作社提供了第一個支票賬戶和第一張信用卡之一。在 1980 年代初期，它推出了自動提款機和電話銀行。

In November 1993, it conducted its first four internet transactions; and in 1994, it became the first financial institution to offer online banking when it launched its website. Three years later, it offered online BillPay to its members, and in 2002, it added account aggregation and mobile banking.

1993 年 11 月，它進行了前四個網上交易，並於 1994 年，成為第一個提供網上銀行的金融機構。3 年後，它提供了他的成員網上的 BillPay，並在 2002 年，增加了帳戶的聚集和移動銀行。

The amazing work didn't stop there. In 2005, it became one of the first institutions to implement the Passmark authentication system, and 2 years later, it joined the CO-OP network to provide its members with over 30,000 surcharge-free ATMs worldwide.

令人驚奇的作品並沒有就此停止。它在2005年成為Passmark 認證系統中的第一機構之一。2 年後，它加入了 CO-OP 網絡，為會員提供全球超過 30,000 座免費自動提款機。

Located at the Silicon Valley and gathered the most intelligent engineers, Stanford Federal Credit Union always arouses the most innovative banking systems. We look forward to the next crazy idea it might come up with.

位於矽谷並聚集了最聰明的工程師，史丹佛聯邦信用合作社始終能激發出最具創新性的銀行體系。我們期待著它可能會想出的下一個瘋狂想法。

1 飲食民生

2 歷史懷舊

3 現代化實用科技

4 資訊與知識傳遞

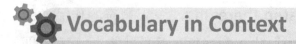

Vocabulary in Context

9 While in Peru, the tourguide _____ us around the ancient Machu Picchu. Though a UNESCO World Heritage Site, due to over-tourism, it is now facing potential dangers and threats.

Led is in the closest meaning to this word.

A. conducted   C. supervised

B. oppressed   D. accumulated

10 One possible way to protect the valuable antiques of ancient times in poor countries from black-market _____ is to lease the artifacts to museums.

Deals is in the closest meaning to this word.

A. schedules   C. transactions

B. monuments   D. characteristics

11 The manager had trouble _____ the marketing reforms in the beginning, but he still held an optimistic attitude toward the prospects of success.

Executing is in the closest meaning to this word.

A. drifting   C. conflicting

B. purifying   D. implementing

12 What _____ Linda's interest in learning oil painting was her constant visiting the art museum and appreciating lots of artistic works.

Stimulated is in the closest meaning to this word.

A. opposed   C. communicated

B. aroused   D. acknowledged

❾ 在祕魯時，導遊引導我們在馬丘比丘古城旅遊。雖然是一個聯合國教科文組織世界文化遺跡所在地，由於過度觀光，它目前正面臨潛在的危險和威脅。

Led 的意思最接近於這個字。

A. 引導   C. 監督

B. 壓迫   D. 累積

❿ 一個保護貧窮國家古代珍貴的古董免於黑市買賣的可能方法是把這些手工藝品租借給博物館。

Deals的意思最接近於這個字。

A. 預定行程   C. 交易

B. 紀念碑   D. 特徵

⓫ 這名經理在剛開始實施行銷改革上遭逢困難，但他對於成功的願景仍舊抱持著樂觀的態度。

Executing 的意思最接近於這個字。

A. 漂流   C. 衝突

B. 淨化   D. 實施

⓬ 激發琳達學習畫油畫的興趣是因為她經常參觀美術館並且欣賞許多藝術畫作。

Stimulated 的意思最接近於這個字。

A. 反對   C. 溝通

B. 激發   D. 承認

 答案 ❾ A ❿ C ⓫ D ⓬ B

26-4 同反義詞表

同反義詞一覽表 Unit 26		
institution	機構、建立	同義詞 organization / establishment / foundation
	破壞、毀壞	反義詞 destruction / demolition / ruin
investment	投資、投入	同義詞 venture / speculation / dedication
	退出、撤退	反義詞 quit / stop / retreat
simultaneously	同時地、同步地	同義詞 concurrently / synchronically /meantime
	分別地、個別地	反義詞 separately / discretely / individually
initiative	主動、開始	同義詞 aggressiveness / lead / start
	怠惰、結束	反義詞 inaction / passiveness / termination
highly	非常、高價地	同義詞 extremely / quite / expensively
	便宜地、節約地	反義詞 cheaply / inexpensively / economically
finish	結束、完成	同義詞 end / conclude / complete
	開始、著手	反義詞 start / begin / commence
hesitant	猶豫的、遲疑的	同義詞 tentative / doubtful / uncertain
	確信的、堅決的	反義詞 certain / firm / determined
overwhelmingly	壓倒地、戰勝地	同義詞 overpoweringly/ awesomely/triumphantly
	無力地、失敗地	反義詞 powerlessly /disastrously / unsuccessfully

competitive	競爭的、對立的	同義詞 rival / conflicting / opposing
	友好的、合作的	反義詞 friendly / familiar / intimate
respectively	分別地、各自地	同義詞 separately / individually / independently
	共同地、一起地	反義詞 corporately / collectively / together
security	安全、保護	同義詞 safety / defense / protection
	危險、威脅	反義詞 danger / jeopardy / threat
widespread	全面的、廣泛的	同義詞 comprehensive / extensive / broad
	狹窄的、限制的	反義詞 narrow / confined / restricted
conduct	引導、實施	同義詞 lead / guide / implement
	誤導、困惑	反義詞 misguide / misdirect / perplex
transaction	交易、處理	同義詞 deal / trade / handling
	蕭條、停頓	反義詞 recession / stagnancy / inactiveness
implement	執行、履行	同義詞 execute / perform / accomplish
	取消、放棄	反義詞 cancel / forgo / abandon
arouse	刺激、喚起	同義詞 stimulate / provoke / awaken
	鎮定、平靜	反義詞 tranquilize / calm / pacify
authentication	證明、證實	同義詞 proof / verification / confirmation
	造假、欺詐	反義詞 fake / forgery / fraud
provide	提供、供給	同義詞 supply / give / furnish
	得到、獲得	反義詞 obtain / get / acquire

1 飲食民生

2 歷史懷舊

3 現代化實用科技

4 資訊與知識傳遞

Unit 27 Printing Press 印刷機

 27-1 機械化製程促成大規模發展 MP3 79

Printing technology was developed during the 1300s to 1400s. People cut letter or images on blocks of wood, dipped in ink and then stamped onto paper.

印刷技術是在 1300 年代到 1400 年代間被發明出來的。人們在木頭塊上刻印字母或圖像，沾墨，然後印在紙上。

Around 1440, Inventor Johannes Gutenberg had the thought of using cut blocks within a machine to make the printing process faster.

大約在 1440 年左右，發明家約翰·古騰堡有了將切割塊放在機器中，使打印過程加快的想法。

Since he worked at a mint before, he created metal blocks instead of wood, and was able to move the metal blocks to create new words and sentences with the movable type machine.

由於他之前在造幣廠工作過，於是他利用金屬塊代替木材，並利用移動式的機器，使金屬塊可以移動，創造出單字或句子。

Therefore, the first printed book was created – the Gutenberg Bible.

因此，第一本印刷書籍古騰堡聖經就這樣被創造出來。

The mechanization of bookmaking led to the first mass production of books in Europe. It could produce 3,600 pages per day which is much more productive than the typographic block type.

造書的機械化帶領了歐洲書籍的大規模生產。它可以每天生產 3,600 頁，它比印刷塊的類型有更高的生產力。

1 飲食民生

2 歷史懷舊

3 現代化實用科技

4 資訊與知識傳遞

Vocabulary in Context

❶ Though eccentric, the future king actually has deep passions. He maintains his royal _____ successfully by his devotion to the royal family and warm care about his dear nation.
Symbol is in the closest meaning to this word.

  A. authority   C. comprehension

  B. image   D. sympathy

❷ The custom-made computer desk is not only functional in usage but easy to handle because of its _____ wheels.
Shiftable is in the closest meaning to this word.

  A. fierce   C. movable

  B. vulnerable   D. complacent

❸ The increasing _____ of operating processes in the factory achieved high productivity and considerable profits at low costs.
Automation is in the closest meaning to this word.

  A. obedience   C. nourishment

  B. precaution   D. mechanization

❹ Using the power of music, painting the ideas that come easily, and taking down notes of the original ideas are what kept the _____ artist creative.
Prolific is in the closest meaning to this word.

  A. urgent   C. productive

  B. excessive   D. transparent

1 飲食民生

2 歷史懷舊

3 現代化實用科技

4 資訊與知識傳遞

❶ 雖然脾氣古怪，這位未來的國王事實上有著強烈的熱情。他透過對於皇室家族的奉獻以及對他摯愛國家溫馨的關切得以成功地維護他的皇室形象。

Symbol 的意思最接近於這個字。

A. 權威　　　　　　　C. 理解

B. 形象　　　　　　　D. 同情

❷ 這張客製化的電腦桌不僅在使用上具多重功能，可移動的輪子也使得它易於操作。

Shiftable 的意思最接近於這個字。

A. 兇猛的　　　　　　C. 活動的

B. 脆弱的　　　　　　D. 自滿的

❸ 工廠裡操作過程逐漸增加的機械化程度得以低成本達到高生產力以及大量的利潤。

Automation 的意思最接近於這個字。

A. 服從　　　　　　　C. 營養

B. 預防措施　　　　　D. 機械化

❹ 利用音樂的力量、繪出油然而生的靈感，並且記載下原創的思維是促使這位多產藝術家保有創意的方法。

Prolific 的意思最接近於這個字。

A. 緊急的　　　　　　C. 多產的

B. 過度的　　　　　　D. 透明的

 答案 ❶B　❷C　❸D　❹C

The demand of printing presses kept expanding through out Europe. By 1500, more than twenty million volumes were produced. And the number kept doubling every year.

印刷機的需求在整個歐洲不斷增加。到 1500 年代，超過兩千萬本書被製作出來。而數字每年保持翻倍成長。

The operation of a printing press became synonymous with the enterprise of printing and lent its name to a new branch of media, the press.

印刷機更與印刷企業劃上等號，因此新媒體的分支新聞界也分用同一個名詞「The Press」。

In the 19th century, steam-powered rotary presses replaced the hand operated presses. It allowed high volume industrial scale printing. Because of the invention of the printing press, the entire classical canon was reprinted and promulgated throughout Europe.

在 19 世紀時，蒸汽動力輪轉印刷機取代了手工操作的印刷機。它實現了大批量的工業規模印刷。由於印刷術的發明，整個古典經文已被重印並廣傳整個歐洲。

It was a very important step towards the democratization of knowledge. Also because of the invention of printing press, it helped unify and standardize the spelling and syntax of vernaculars. Johannes Gutenberg was born in an upper-class family in Mainz Germany, most likely in 1398.

He had been a blacksmith, a goldsmith, and printer, and even a publisher. Gutenberg's understanding of the trade of goldsmithing and possessing of the knowledge and technical skills in metal working originated from his father's working at ecclesiastic mint.

這也是對知識民主化來說非常重要的一步。印刷術發明的同時，它也幫助統一和規範俗語的拼寫和語法。約翰·古騰堡出生於德國美因茨的一個上流家庭。

他當過鐵匠、金匠和印刷商，甚至出版商。因為他的父親在傳教士的造幣廠工作過，因此古騰堡在長大過程中就了解金匠的行業，並擁有金屬加工的知識和技術技能。

1 飲食民生

2 歷史懷舊

3 現代化實用科技

4 資訊與知識傳遞

Vocabulary in Context

❺ When it comes to happiness, wealth alone is not necessarily _____ with it. In fact, health, knowledge, and family should also be included.

Equivalent is in the closest meaning to this word.

A. audible   C. bewildering

B. synonymous   D. miserable

❻ The CEO is a successful businessman with a breadth of vision; both his domestic and foreign _____ have been increasing and prosperous.

Ventures is in the closest meaning to this word.

A. reforms   C. approaches

B. lectures   D. enterprises

❼ The Emperor Qin Shi Huang was an important historical figure in China, for during the third century BC, he _____ the warring China, the Chinese written language, and the systems of laws and weights.

Uniformed is in the closest meaning to this word.

A. unified   C. deprived

B. abused   D. prosecuted

❽ To achieve fairness, the teacher _____ her grades of evaluating students' performances in both the overall behavior and their academic works.

Unified is in the closest meaning to this word.

A. conflicted C. standardized

B. abandoned D. estimated

❺ 論到快樂，單有財富未必等同於幸福。事實上，健康、知識，以及家庭也應該包括在內。

Equivalent 的意思最接近於這個字。

A. 可聽見的 C. 困惑的

B. 同義的 D. 悲慘的

❻ 這名總裁是一位眼光廣闊，事業有成的企業家；他國內以及國外的企業一直在擴張並且蒸蒸日上。

Ventures 的意思最接近於這個字。

A. 改革 C. 方法

B. 講課 D. 企業

❼ 秦始皇在中國是一位重要的歷史人物，因為在西元前三世紀期間，他統一了戰亂的中國、中國文字，以及法律和度量衡的制度。

Uniformed 的意思最接近於這個字。

A. 統一 C. 剝奪

B. 濫用 D. 起訴

❽ 為了達到公平，這名老師訂定統一標準，以學生整體的行為表現以及他們的學術成績作為評分的標準。

Unified 的意思最接近於這個字。

A. 衝突 C. 標準化

B. 放棄 D. 預測

 答案 ❺ B ❻ D ❼ A ❽ C

In 1411, there was an uprising in Mainz against the patricians. Unfortunately, Gutenberg was one of the family that was forced to leave. As a result, Gutenberg might have moved to Eltiville am Rhein, where his mother had an inherited estate there.

1411 年，美因茨發動了對貴族的起義。不幸的，古騰堡就是其中一個被迫離開的家庭。因此，古騰堡可能已經搬離到萊茵河畔的艾莉菲爾，在那裡有他的母親所繼承的遺產。

Evidence had shown that he was instructing a wealthy tradesman on polishing gems in 1437.

有證據表明，在 1437 年，他正在指導一個富商拋光寶石的技能。

A couple of years later, he started his career in making polished metal mirrors. It was the same year that Gutenberg made his first movable printing press and introduce this technology to Europe.

幾年後，他表示他以做拋光金屬鏡子為職業。同一年，古騰堡開發出第一個活動印刷機並將這種技術引入歐洲。

His epochal inventions including movable printing press, oil-based ink for book printing, adjustable molds, etc., allowed the economical mass production of printed books.

他劃時代的發明，包括活動印刷機、印刷書所用的油性油墨、可調節模具等，皆使印刷書籍能大批量的經濟生產。

Gutenberg's printing technology spread rapidly throughout Europe and later the world. Gutenberg died in 1468 and was buried in his hometown Mainz. Unfortunately, the church he was buried got destroyed and his grave is now lost.

古騰堡印刷技術在整個歐洲及爾後的世界迅速蔓延。古騰堡在 1468 去世，並被安葬在他的家鄉美因茨。不幸的是，他下葬的教堂被破壞，他的墳墓現在已經消失。

1 飲食民生

2 歷史懷舊

3 現代化實用科技

4 資訊與知識傳遞

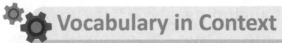 **Vocabulary in Context**

❾ Ever since Robin _____ great fortunes from his parents, he quit his job and pursued material joyfulness, such as buying fancy sports cars and living in luxurious mansions.

Received is in the closest meaning to this word.

A. inherited   C. subsided

B. penalized   D. assembled

❿ Lacking convincing witnesses and concrete _____, the police could not but release the probable murderer, who provided an airtight alibi for the time of the crime.

Proof is in the closest meaning to this word.

A. budget   C. observation

B. evidence   D. transmission

⓫ With their _____ characteristics, the products of this company have been very popular both in the mall and on the Internet.

Adaptable is in the closest meaning to this word.

A. panic   C. ventilating

B. subsequent   D. adjustable

⓬ The high living costs and the low pay forced Tom to live an __ _____ life, which brought about lots of complaints from his wife and children.

Thrifty is in the closest meaning to this word.

A. ignorant   C. economical

B. persuasive   D. uneventful

❾ 自從羅賓繼承雙親龐大的遺產後，他辭職去追求物質的享受，譬如購買豪華跑車以及住奢華的房子。

Received 的意思最接近於這個字。

A. 繼承   C. 消退

B. 處罰   D. 組裝

❿ 由於缺乏可信的目擊證人以及具體的證據，警方不得不釋放涉案成份高的謀殺犯，因為他提出案發當時完美的不在場證明。。

Proof 的意思最接近於這個字。

A. 預算   C. 觀察

B. 證據   D. 輸送

⓫ 這家公司的產品由於具有可調整的特色，在大賣場以及網路上一向頗受歡迎。

Adaptable 的意思最接近於這個字。

A. 恐慌的   C. 通風的

B. 後續的   D. 可調整的

⓬ 高額的生活費用以及低廉的薪資迫使湯姆過著節儉的生活，卻因此導致妻子和孩子許多的抱怨。

Thrifty 的意思最接近於這個字。

A. 無知的   C. 節約的

B. 說服的   D. 平靜無事的

答案 ❾ A ❿ B ⓫ D ⓬ C

同反義詞一覽表 Unit 27		
image	形象、肖像	同義詞 symbol / icon / representation
	內在、精神	反義詞 inner / spirit / mind
movable	可動的、活動的	同義詞 shiftable / mobile / removable
	固定的、不動的	反義詞 fixed / stationary / immovable
mechanization	機械化、呆板	同義詞 automation / stiffness / inflexibility
	人性化、彈性	反義詞 humanization / flexibility / elasticity
productive	生產的、豐富的	同義詞 prolific / creative / plentiful
	貧瘠的、缺乏的	反義詞 barren / unfruitful / deficient
stamp	標記、踐踏	同義詞 mark / label / trample
	維護、保護	反義詞 maintain / preserve / protect
sentence	審判、刑罰	同義詞 condemnation / judgment / punishment
	無罪、釋放	反義詞 guiltlessness / innocence / release
synonymous	同義的、同等的	同義詞 identical / equal / equivalent
	反義的、不同的	反義詞 antonymous / different / varied
enterprise	企業、事業	同義詞 industry / business / venture
	加盟、零售業	反義詞 franchise / retail / grocery

unify	統一、聯合	同義詞 unite / uniform / consolidate
	分離、分裂	反義詞 disunite / divide / split
standardize	標準化、一致	同義詞 normalize / unify / consist
	分類、不同	反義詞 sort / classify / vary
branch	分公司、部門	同義詞 division / subdivision / sector
	總公司、總部	反義詞 company / headquarters / base
classical	古典的、正統的	同義詞 traditional / orthodox / standard
	現代的、當前的	反義詞 modern / contemporary / present
inherit	繼承、得到	同義詞 succeed / receive / obtain
	剝奪、喪失	反義詞 deprive / forfeit / lose
evidence	證據、線索	同義詞 proof / indication / clue
	傳言、謠言	反義詞 hearsay / gossip / rumor
adjustable	調節的、適應的	同義詞 changeable / modifiable / adaptable
	不變的、不適應	反義詞 fixed / unalterable / unadaptable
economical	節儉的、節約的	同義詞 thrifty / saving / frugal
	奢侈的、浪費的	反義詞 luxurious / extravagant / wasteful
uprising	反叛、叛亂	同義詞 rebellion / revolt / mutiny
	效忠、擁護	反義詞 loyalty / allegiance / support
destroy	破壞、毀壞	同義詞 devastate / damage / ruin
	建立、創辦	反義詞 build / establish / found

1 飲食民生

2 歷史懷舊

3 現代化實用科技

4 資訊與知識傳遞

28-1 電視的發展

 MP3 82

From the number of TV audiences in each American household, televisions not only provide entertainments and all kinds of information, but also have become a daily necessity. The word television comes from the Greek prefix "tele" and the Latin word "vision". It converts images into electrical impulses along cables, or by radio waves or satellite to a receiver, and then they are changed back into a picture. As most inventions, more than one individuals contributed to the development of television. The earliest development was recorded in the late 1800s. A German student, Paul Gottlieb Nipkow, developed the first mechanical module of television.

從每個美國家庭電視收看觀眾的數量來看,電視不只提供娛樂和各種訊息,而且成了每日必需品。電視這個字源自於希臘語字首的「遠程」和拉丁字「願景」的組合。它將圖像轉換成電脈衝沿著電纜,或通過無線電波或衛星到接收器,然後將它們再變回為圖像。如同大部分的發明,許多人都對電視的發展有所貢獻。最早的發展記錄是在 19 世紀末期。一位德國學生,保羅・戈特利布–尼普可夫研製了第一台電視的機械模塊。

He sent images through wires with the help of a rotating metal disk. It only had 18 lines of resolution. In 1926, a Scottish amateur scientist, John Logie Baird, transmitted the first moving pictures through the mechanical disk system. In 1934, all television systems had converted into the electronic system, which is what is being used even today.

他透過電線與旋轉金屬盤發送圖像。它只有 18 線的分辨率。1926 年，蘇格蘭業餘科學家，約翰‧勞基‧貝瑞德透過機械磁盤系統發送出第一個動畫。 1934 年，所有的電視系統已轉換成電子系統，這即是今天被使用的系統。

An American inventor, Philo Taylor Farnsworth first had the idea of electronic television at the age of 14. By the time he was 21, he created the first electronic television system which is the basis of all TV we have today. Until the 1900s, all TVs were monochrome. In 1925, color television was just conceptualized, but had never been built. It was not until 1953 that color television become available to the public.

美國發明家，菲洛−泰勒−法恩斯沃思在 14 歲時便有了電子電視的想法。在 21 歲時，他創造了第一個電子電視系統，這是所有我們今天所擁有的所有電視的基礎。直到 1900 年代，所有的電視都還是黑白的。 1925 年時彩色電視都還只是概念，從來沒有被製造過。直到 1953 年，彩色電視才被提供給一般消費者。

Vocabulary in Context

❶ When the Nobel Peace Prize-Winner, Dr. King, delivered his famous speech, *I Have a Dream*, to tell of his dream land of equality, a large _____ of whites and blacks were attracted to share and support his ideals.

Spectators is in the closest meaning to this word.

A. choir   C. audience

B. staff   D. pantheon

❷ With the release of his new single album, the reggae singer and songwriter believed that he was on his way to becoming a _____ name.

Family is in the closest meaning to this word.

A. household   C. prelude

B. resource   D. fulfillment

❸ To Natalie, it has been her lifelong ambition to enter the _____ business, become a celebrity, and make huge amounts of money.

Show is in the closest meaning to this word.

A. egoism   C. transportation

B. judgment   D. entertainment

❹ Starting as an _____ writer, Ryan set up high standards and goals, took an active attitude, and worked non-stop to become professional in his field.

Inexperienced is in the closest meaning to this word.

A. external　　　　　C. uncultured

B. amateur　　　　　D. institutional

❶ 當諾貝爾和平獎得主，金恩博士，發表他著名的演說，《我有一個夢想》，描述他平等的夢想國度時，大群受到吸引的白人及黑人聽眾前來分享並支持他的理念。

Spectators 的意思最接近於這個字。

A. 合唱隊　　　　　C. 觀眾

B. 職員　　　　　　D. 眾神

❷ 隨著他最新單曲的發行，這名雷鬼歌手兼作曲家相信他即將成為家喻戶曉的名歌手。

Family 的意思最接近於這個字。

A. 家庭　　　　　　C. 前奏曲

B. 資源　　　　　　D. 實現

❸ 對娜塔莉來說，她終生的抱負就是要進入演藝圈、成為名流，並且賺大錢。

Show 的意思最接近於這個字。

A. 自我主義　　　　C. 交通運輸

B. 判斷　　　　　　D. 娛樂

❹ 以一名業餘的作家起家，雷恩訂定崇高的標準和目標、採取主動的態度，並且不斷地工作，目標是要成為他領域中的專業人士。

Inexperienced 的意思最接近於這個字。

A. 外部的　　　　　C. 未受教育的

B. 業餘的　　　　　D. 制度的

 ❶ C　 ❷ A　 ❸ D　 ❹ B

During the late 1990s, the bulky, high-voltage CRT screen was replaced by energy efficient, flat-panel screens, such as plasma screens, LCDs, and OLEDs.

在 1990 年代後期，高效節能的平板螢幕，如離子顯示器、液晶顯示器，和 OLED 被發明出來。這種進化發展取代了笨重、高電壓的 CRT 電視。

In the mid-2010s, major manufacturers announced the discontinuation of CRT TVs.

在 2010 年代中期，各大廠商宣布停止 CRT 電視的製造。

Now manufactures again brainstormed and built in the smart TV system so televisions now not only provide TV problems, but also can be used as computers. What will come next? We shall wait and see.

現在電視生產大廠再次的發想，並建立了智能電視系統，電視不只提供電視而已，而且還可以作為電腦。接下來會有什麼樣的發展呢？我們拭目以待。

A talented inventor that came up with the television system idea at the age of 14, Philo Taylor Farnsworth was born on August 19th, 1906, in Beaver, Utah. When he was in high school, he won a national contest with his original invention of a tamper-proof lock.

一個才華橫溢的發明家，在 14 歲時便有了電視系統的想法，菲洛‧泰勒‧法恩斯沃斯在 1906 年 8 月 19 號出生於猶他州的比佛。當他在高中時，他防篡改鎖的發明使他贏得了全國比賽。

He sketched out the television idea from a vacuum tube in his chemistry class during high school but none of his teachers grasped the implications of his concept.

他從化學課的真空管中勾勒出電視的想法，但沒有一位老師抓到他概念的含義。

1 飲食民生

2 歷史懷舊

3 現代化實用科技

4 資訊與知識傳遞

Vocabulary in Context

⑤ Most modern consumers are environmental-minded enough to choose highly energy- _____ and healthful products to purchase.

Economical is in the closest meaning to this word.

A. efficient   C. sensational

B. contagious   D. fundamental

⑥ It was insensible and irresponsible of Mr. Watt's family to _____ the treatment of his cancer and took him home from the hospital.

Stop is in the closest meaning to this word.

A. propel   C. discontinue

B. ascertain   D. compensate

⑦ Steven's family and friends were truly unable to _____why he should have given up the chance of entering a more prestigious university.

Understand is in the closest meaning to this word.

A. despise   C. withdraw

B. grasp   D. enlighten

⑧ The senior supervisor commented that there was still much room left to be desired, which showed the _____ that he wasn't satisfied with the results and we'd better work harder.

Hint is in the closest meaning to this word.

A. outlet
C. measurement

B. elevation
D. implication

5 大多數現代的消費者具有足夠的環保意識去選擇購買高效節能以及健康的產品。

Economical 的意思最接近於這個字。

A. 有效率的
C. 轟動的

B. 傳染性的
D. 基礎的

6 瓦特先生的家人十分不明智並且不負責任地終止他癌症的治療，並將他從醫院帶回家。

Stop 的意思最接近於這個字。

A. 推進
C. 中斷

B. 查明
D. 賠償

7 史蒂芬的家人和朋友真的無法理解為何他竟然放棄了可以進入更具卓越聲譽大學的機會。

Understand 的意思最接近於這個字。

A. 鄙視
C. 撤回

B. 理解
D. 啟發

8 高層主管評論說仍有極大的改善空間，這暗示著他對於結果並不滿意，我們最好更加努力些。

Hint 的意思最接近於這個字。

A. 銷路
C. 測量

B. 提高
D. 暗示

    答案　**5** A　**6** C　**7** B　**8** D

Farnsworth then entered the Brigham Young University in 1922 but due to his father's death, he dropped out 2 years later.

法恩斯沃思隨後在 1922 年進入楊百翰大學，但由於他父親的過世，他 2 年後放棄了學業。

In 1926, he moved to San Francisco to continue his scientific work, and a year later, he unveiled his electronic television prototype made by a "Image dissector", which he had sketched in his chemistry class in high school.

1926 年，他移居舊金山，繼續他的科學工作，而一年之後，他利用他在高中時所勾勒出的「析像儀」，他推出了自己的電子電視。

Throughout the late 1920s and the early 1930s, Farnsworth fought legal charges that his inventions were in violation of a patent by the inventor Vloadimir Zoworkyin a patent that was later on owned by RCA.

在 1920 年末期和 1930 年代初期，法恩斯沃思被指控侵犯發明人 Vloadimir Zoworkyin 的專利，這個專利後來由 RCA 所擁有。

Farnsworth later on moved to Philadelphia for a position at Philco and left Philco company in 1933 to pursue his own avenues of research. He eventually won the lawsuit and received a million dollars from RCA.

He ran a fusion lab at Utah 29 years later and operated under the name of Philo T. Farnsworth Association in Salty Lake City the following year. Unfortunately, he suffered from depression and became an alcoholic in his late years due to his serious debt.

法恩斯沃思後來在1933年實為了追求自己的研究，離開了菲戈公司。他最終贏得了官司，並從RCA獲得一百萬美元。

二十九年後他於猶他州管理一個融合實驗室且於次年以裴洛T.法恩斯沃斯協會之名在鹽城湖運作。不幸地是，他晚年因龐大的債務而受憂鬱症的折磨，並成了酒鬼。

Vocabulary in Context

9 The reports of the investigation _____ the fact that the mayor was behind all these illegal public property deals.

Disclosed is in the closest meaning to this word.

A. refunded   C. embarked

B. unveiled   D. preached

10 Due to drunk driving and breaking the speed limit, the driver was brought to the police station for serious traffic _____.

Law-breaking is in the closest meaning to this word.

A. twist   C. violation

B. rehearsal   D. collaboration

11 After exploring every possible _____, the team finally came up with a good solution and succeeded in achieving the mission.

Means is in the closest meaning to this word.

A. avenue   C. network

B. diversion   D. recollection

12 Depressed with huge debts and bad health, Mr. Haydn ended up being a chronic _____ and had to be sent to a rehabilitation clinic for cure.

Drunkard is in the closest meaning to this word.

A. rival   C. proponent

B. specialist   D. alcoholic

❾ 調查報告揭露的事實顯示是市長主導所有這些非法的公有房地產交易。

Disclosed 的意思最接近於這個字。

A. 退款　　　　　　　C. 裝載

B. 揭露　　　　　　　D. 佈道

❿ 由於酒駕以及超速，這名駕駛因嚴重的交通違規被帶至警局。

Low-breaking 的意思最接近於這個字。

A. 扭曲　　　　　　　C. 違規

B. 排練　　　　　　　D. 合作

⓫ 在探索所有可能的方法後，這個團隊終於提出絕佳的解決方案並且成功地完成任務。

Means 的意思最接近於這個字。

A. 方法　　　　　　　C. 網路

B. 轉向　　　　　　　D. 回憶

⓬ 海頓先生由於高額的債務以及不良的健康狀況深受打擊，最終結果是成為一名慢性酒精中毒者，並且必須送到戒酒康復診所尋求治療。

Drunkard 的意思最接近於這個字。

A. 對手　　　　　　　C. 擁護者

B. 專家　　　　　　　D. 嗜酒者

1 飲食民生

2 歷史懷舊

3 現代化實用科技

4 資訊與知識傳遞

答案 ❾ B ❿ C ⓫ A ⓬ D

28-4 同反義詞表

同反義詞一覽表 Unit 28		
audience	觀眾、聽眾	同義詞 spectator / viewer / listener
	主持人、主席	反義詞 host / president / chairperson
household	家庭、家人	同義詞 family / relative / folks
	外人、陌生人	反義詞 outsider / unknown / stranger
entertainment	演藝、娛樂	同義詞 show / amusement / recreation
	工作、任務	反義詞 work / task / assignment
amateur	業餘的、不熟練	同義詞 inexperienced / inexpert / unskillful
	專業的、精通的	反義詞 professional / veteran / proficient
necessity	需要、必要	同義詞 requirement / inevitability / imperative
	不必要、多餘	反義詞 needlessness / unessential / redundancy
impulse	衝動、刺激	同義詞 impetuosity / compulsion / stimulus
	冷靜、穩定	反義詞 calm / serenity / tranquility
efficient	有效能、勝任的	同義詞 economical / effective / competent
	無效率、效能差	反義詞 inefficient / useless / incapable
discontinue	停止、中止	同義詞 stop / cease / terminate
	繼續、持續	反義詞 continue / last / persist
grasp	抓住、理解	同義詞 seize / comprehend / understand
	鬆開、誤解	反義詞 loosen / misapprehend / misinterpret

implication	牽涉、暗示	同義詞 involvement / hint / suggestion
	排除、告知	反義詞 exclusion / announcement / notification
bulky	龐大的、笨重的 微小的、輕便的	同義詞 massive / vast / weighty 反義詞 tiny / compact / light
contest	競爭、爭論	同義詞 competition / rivalry / debate
	同盟、聯盟	反義詞 alliance / association / union
unveil	揭露、顯示 遮蓋、掩飾	同義詞 expose / uncover / disclose 反義詞 veil / conceal / disguise
violation	違反、違背	同義詞 breaking / infringement / defiance
	遵守、服從	反義詞 observance / submission / obedience
avenue	大街、方法	同義詞 boulevard / approach / means
	小徑、目的	反義詞 path / end / purpose
alcoholic	嗜酒者、醉漢	同義詞 tippler / drunkard / inebriate
	戒酒者、節制者	反義詞 abstainer / nondrinker / refrainer
legal	合法的、正當的	同義詞 lawful / legitimate / authorized
	非法的、犯罪的	反義詞 illegal / illegitimate / criminal
fusion	融合、混合	同義詞 mixture / combination / blending
	分開、分割	反義詞 division / separation / split

1 飲食民生

2 歷史懷舊

3 現代化實用科技

4 資訊與知識傳遞

用最瑣碎的時間，建立學習自信，
輕鬆打下英語學習基礎！

- 用圖「解」複雜又難吸收的文法觀念
- 30天學習進度規劃，不出國也能變身ABC！
- 收錄英文文法三大重點項目：20個必備文法觀念
  ＋30個必學文法句型＋40個必閃文法陷阱。

定 價：NT$ 369元
規 格：386頁/18K/雙色印刷/平裝

應考、備考、教學解說和解題均適用
兼顧「即效性」和「多元學習」！

每題均附三種學習法，依照個人需求選擇：
目光鎖定：以最短時間完成題目
靈活思維：換個方式也不影響答題
組織考點：了解考題設計、問題癥結

定 價：NT$ 429元
規 格：384頁/18K/雙色印刷/平裝

用圖解 輕鬆學寫作！ 附便利貼光碟，
立即完成需要呈現的書寫內容！

- 以圖像搭配相關例句、延伸句型，透析英文句子組成
  元素，加深對句型文法的印象。
- 透過階層圖應用於自傳、報告講稿、短文、商用書信
  四大常用作文主題，立即書寫重點內容，提升效率！

定 價：NT$ 379元
規 格：288頁/18K/雙色印刷/平裝附光碟

沒有冗長的文法解釋，降低學習負擔！用最簡單、濃縮的敘述引用耳熟能詳、的流行英文歌曲，串起學習連結！

◎ 引用歌曲中的共鳴/感動句強化大腦記憶，連結文法重點。

◎「富創意+趣味」的口訣和諧音激起學習文法的動力。

◎ 只給重點精闢解析，輕鬆找出文法脈絡、透徹理解文法核心概念。

定　價：NT$ 399元

規　格：352頁/18K/雙色印刷/平裝

獨家公開考官必問話題！用母語人士的思維，說出與眾不同的高分回答！

◎ 聽力講解篇：先說明概念，再由關鍵句＆小提點，
　做「聽力」+「跟讀」練習，奠定紮實的基礎。

◎ 每單元均有字彙輔助，特別規劃慣用語補充，
　擴充個人字彙庫，面對考試更無往不利。

◎ 跟著講解、演練、實戰篇的順序學習並且多做練習，
　一舉獲取理想成績。

定　價：NT$ 380元

規　格：288頁/18K/雙色印刷/平裝

運用中西諺語，搭配獨家規劃三大類議題，一次就考到雅思寫作6.5up！

◎ 濃縮式提點協助考生擬定作文大綱，**立即掌握**
　作文中的起、承、轉、合。

◎ 收錄必學作文範例，寫出具說服力、論點清楚
　、語句**通順且連貫**的句子或文章！

定　價：NT$ 380元

規　格：288頁/18K/雙色印刷/平裝

國家圖書館出版品預行編目(CIP)資料

一次就考到雅思單字6.5+ / 倍斯特編輯部
著. -- 初版. -- 臺北市 : 倍斯特, 2017.12
面； 公分. -- （考用英語系列 ; 5）
ISBN 978-986-95288-7-0（平裝）
1.國際英語語文測試系統　2.詞彙

805.189　　　　　　　　　　106021427

考用英語系列　005

一次就考到雅思單字6.5＋（附英式發音MP3）

初　　版　　2017年12月
定　　價　　新台幣399元

作　　者　　倍斯特編輯部
出　　版　　倍斯特出版事業有限公司
發 行 人　　周瑞德
電　　話　　886-2-2351-2007
傳　　真　　886-2-2351-0887
地　　址　　100 台北市中正區福州街1號10樓之2
E - m a i l　　best.books.service@gmail.com
官　　網　　www.bestbookstw.com
執行總監　　齊心瑀
行銷經理　　楊景輝
企劃編輯　　陳韋佑
特約編輯　　孟瑞秋
封面構成　　高鍾琪
內頁構成　　菩薩蠻數位文化有限公司
印　　製　　大亞彩色印刷製版股份有限公司

港澳地區總經銷　　泛華發行代理有限公司
地　　址　　香港新界將軍澳工業邨駿昌街7號2樓
電　　話　　852-2798-2323
傳　　真　　852-2796-5471